Stories
into Film

Stories into Film

Edited by

William Kittredge &
Steven M. Krauzer

HARPER COLOPHON BOOKS

Harper & Row, Publishers
New York, Hagerstown,
San Francisco, London

Copyright acknowledgments appear on page 287.

FIRST EDITION

Designed by Janice Stern

Library of Congress Cataloging in Publication Data
Main entry under title:

Stories into film.

    (Harper colophon books)
    Bibliography: p.
    Filmography: p.
    CONTENTS: Robbins, T. Spurs (Freaks)—
Adams, S. H. Night bus (It happened one night)—
Haycox, E. Stage to Lordsburg (Stagecoach) [etc.]
    1. Short stories. 2. Film adaptations.
I. Kittredge, William, 1933– II. Krauzer,
Steven M.
PZ1.S887 [PN6014]   813'.01   78–73542
ISBN 0–06–090638–3 pbk.

For Roberta Olson and Patrick Kittredge,
and for Earl and Bernice Krauzer

Contents

Stories
into Film

Introduction

You see, the nearest art form to the motion picture is, I think, the short story. It's the only form when you ask the audience to sit down and read it in one sitting.

—Alfred Hitchcock

Film has nothing to do with literature; the character and substance of the two art forms are usually in conflict.

—Ingmar Bergman

If art has a purpose, it is something like this: art helps us recognize the patterns around us, and so helps us remodel our world. If we can simply *see* the old models, new ones are assured, and our lives are enlivened.

In this sense, art is the primary thing we do: we make up worlds, and daily reinvent our lives. We come awake in the morning and formulate a plan for our day, but however structured or aimless, the plan never works. The world in its plotless way intrudes, and so we spend most of our time modifying our plan, bringing ourselves into sensible alignment with what is actual. It is the purpose of artists to help us with this process by showing us possibility, by jolting or delighting or beguiling us. When William Carlos Williams reveals the luminosity and specific density of rain gleaming off a red wheelbarrow, we are again awakened to the idea that we are part of a whole that is translucent with significance.

The more truly we see, the more apt we are to survive. This is true in our most mundane and our most grand transactions, not only in dealing with the shopkeeper to get the most for our money

1

but in dealing with our concepts of God and society. Think of Europe in 1939, or American failure in Vietnam. Here are examples of great national and international models of conduct gone wrong because people and nations did not clearly perceive the patterns before them.

Consider these statements, set side by side in George Bluestone's theoretical introduction to his text *Novels into Film* (1957):

My task which I am trying to achieve is, by the power of the written work, to make you hear, to make you feel—it is, before all, to make you see.
    —Joseph Conrad, *preface to* The Nigger of the Narcissus

The task I'm trying to achieve above all, is to make you see.
                                                    —D. W. Griffith

A great novelist and a great filmmaker both affirm the same goal: each wants to make us see consciously and humanely instead of through a haze of sociological and psychological clichés; each wants us to perceive what is real and true, what has substance. It is the difference between pity and compassion: pity is condescending and distancing; compassion requires us to become involved, to understand. If we can see the world compassionately, however fragile that vision, we have hope of living compassionate lives.

There are two kinds of seeing: we see through the real eye, and we see through the mind's eye. The real eye transmits patterns of light to form images on the retina, which are imagined by the mind's eye into forms; the mind's eye creates whatever we are capable of imagining, based largely on what the real eye has seen previously. When we learn to read, we learn to translate marks on a page into images in the mind. The process holds in it the possibility of creating the most fantastic concoctions. If we are asked to imagine an ice-cream sundae the size of the Milky Way, with a cherry on top that burns with the brightness of a thousand suns, we can do so quite readily. In film, however, the images are created for us, to be perceived through the real eye. Film is distinguished from literature by its sensory reality.

This sensory presence is the reason a primarily fictive device such as exposition is so difficult to accomplish gracefully in film.

Things must be rendered to the viewer directly, not discussed obliquely. There are artificial ways around the problem: expository dialogue, voice-over, the close-up of the newspaper headline that tells us war has been declared, the flipping of calendar pages to indicate the passing of time. None is entirely satisfactory. Film should communicate visually and aurally; its meaning should be embedded in sensual experience.

That this can be done with great art was demonstrated by the best of those filmmakers who worked during the twenty-five years when film was without sound altogether. When Chaplin in *The Gold Rush* (1924) carefully boils his shoe and then dines on it with the grace and relish of an epicure, our insight into the dignity of his character and the pathos of his situation is complete. The panoramic shots of the mile-long wagon train snaking across the prairie in the first of the great Western epics, James Cruze's *The Covered Wagon* (1923), vividly evoke the grandeur and daring of those early assaults on the American frontier. In the hands of the better sound-film directors, dialogue becomes a complement to the visual images; used even more imaginatively, it may work against these images in ironic juxtaposition, to create a totality of meaning greater than either the images or the spoken words alone. When film is most advanced, most daring, the vision itself, apart from dialogue, character, or even movement, becomes the controlling messenger of meaning. The resolution of Stanley Kubrick's *2001: A Space Odyssey* (1968) depends entirely on a single visual image: the Starchild, floating luminous above a fragile Earth, curled in fetal position in the womb of space, staring with wide, innocent eyes. Kubrick's concept of rebirth, of transcendence, of *reinvention,* is as clear as if he had printed it as a subtitle across the bottom of the screen.

Literature, then, is indistinguishable from thought, while film exists as an aural and visual phenomenon. The filmmaker must orchestrate these devices to an emotional rhythm, generating meaning much as a lyric poet generates meaning by eliciting image through the written word. In each case, the art lies in the craft of the leaps from image to image, and in the interweaving of those images. Bergman has said that no art has as much in common with film as music.

Film is further distinguished from literature by its immediacy, and because of this, film is denied the flexibility of tense. Fiction is essentially a reflective conversation between the reader and an implied author about what happened—or did not happen. It may provide distance by traditional use of the past tense; it may aspire to a filmlike immediacy through use of the present tense; or it may even attempt a deliberate dislocation by use of the future tense. But film shows us what is happening now, up there on the screen before our eyes, and always in the present.

This is why the literary device of flashback is difficult to bring off in film. We see the slow dissolve, a convention telling us that what comes next will exist in past time, but then we see images on the screen again, and they remain actual before us. We must make a conscious effort to retain the idea that what we are seeing is supposed to have happened in the past if the episode is to have impact as a flashback. If the film keeps us in the flashback too long, we will begin to experience it as present time. As a narrative medium, film must be more linear than fiction. In viewing a movie, we cannot page back to clarify a point, nor jump ahead for a peek at the ending.

But what film can do that fiction cannot is assault our mind's eye and our real eye at the same time. The relationship between the film literally seen and the film in the viewer's imagination is like that between reality and daydream. One supports and complements the other, sometimes in exact ways, sometimes in highly distorted ways. Film's capacity to incite us to imagine is innate; even in the hands of the less-skilled filmmaker, it can be rather easily exploited. For example, we see two pretty girls tied to fence posts, and a maniac with a whirring chain saw approaching them. The maniac reaches one of the girls; the film cuts to the terror on the other's face, while the sound track mixes the first girl's screams with the changing pitch of the chain saw's whine. Then the film cuts again to reveal the maniac with the chain saw, now dripping with pseudo-gore. A still of the scene would show only a man with a red-smeared chain saw. But when this image is embedded in the expectations created by the film's narrative pull, the result is quite satisfyingly horrific. The mind supplies the carnage.

As another example of film's successful adaptation of the expectation that narrative creates in a viewer, consider Alfred Hitchcock's discussion of the difference between surprise and suspense in film:

Let us suppose that there is a bomb underneath this table between us. Nothing happens, and then all of a sudden, "Boom!" There is an explosion. The public is surprised, but prior to this surprise, it has seen an absolutely ordinary scene, of no special consequence. Now, let us take a suspense situation. The bomb is underneath the table and the public knows it, probably because they have seen the anarchist place it there. The public is aware that the bomb is going to explode at one o'clock and there is a clock in the decor. The public can see that it is quarter to one. In these conditions this same innocuous conversation becomes fascinating because the public is participating in the scene. The audience is longing to warn the characters on the screen: "You shouldn't be talking about such trivial matters. There's a bomb beneath you and it's about to explode!"

—*in* Hitchcock, *by François Truffaut (1967)*

When a skilled filmmaker is in control, the medium's ability to inflame our mind's eye is virtually unlimited. The vocabulary of film is visual and aural, but within these categories is an almost infinitely complex blending of such varied elements as color quality, grain, speed of cutting, sound montage, background textures, set and scene, and on and on. The individual filmmaker's use of film's language can be likened to the literary notion of voice. Think of the differing voices of Proust and Hemingway, De Mille and Goddard. Behind any work of art there is an implied personality that projects to us a way of seeing, a vision of the world that cannot help being more or less unique. It is that vision which we experience when we place ourselves under the influence of any work of art, whether a van Gogh or a *Playboy* cartoon, an Updike novel or a comic book, a *Citizen Kane* or an "I Love Lucy."

Film is essentially a narrative art, and from the time film first became a medium of popular entertainment, it recognized the appeal of animations, or visual renderings, of pieces of popular fiction. As early as 1903, when the American Mutoscope Company released a vignette entitled *Sherlock Holmes Baffled,* film was based on fiction. A major appeal of the film adaptation is that it allows us the satisfaction of comparing our mind's-eye image of a story or a novel with the actual image realized in a movie. Frequently, the movie's vision replaces our own. For many readers, Sherlock Holmes bears a striking resemblance to Basil Rathbone. Having seen the film, it is difficult to read Hammett's *The Maltese Falcon* without visualizing Humphrey Bogart as Sam Spade. Even today, we will go to a movie simply because we enjoyed the book. The process has come full circle, with the novelization of original screenplays for the paperback racks. The relationship between fiction and film can become rather bizarrely distorted in some cases. For example, the film version of *The Spy Who Loved Me* (1977) had nothing in common with Ian Fleming's novel except the title and the character of James Bond. To rectify the anomaly, an entirely new novel under the same title appeared simultaneously with the film's release!

When basing his work on fiction, a filmmaker works from the written story, adapting specific episodes and characters to fit the visual medium more appropriately. In addition, the skilled filmmaker usually grafts his own particular vision onto the original material. We see this in *Stagecoach* (1939), where John Ford's concern with innocence and malevolence is conveyed through a highly visual concentration on the dichotomy between wilderness and civilization. When he shows us the stage heading out of Tonto across Arizona's Monument Valley on a wagon-track road that heads directly toward one of those great rock spires lifting toward the sky, he is speaking in unforgettable visual terms. Our first sight of John Wayne as the Ringo Kid is projected against that same majestic background; as the stage ride progresses, Wayne is continually framed against a side window of the coach, and always there is Monument Valley beyond. By emphasizing the relationships between the vulnerability of the human voyage and the grandeur of the natural world, in showing the enormous innocent figure of Ringo, first juxtaposed against the epic wilderness and then enclosed and cramped in the stagecoach with that overwhelming landscape passing by outside, Ford is affirming the unity of his moral vision. The story is Ernest Haycox's, but the language is John Ford's.

But when film develops a complete voice of its own, its relationship to the literature on which it is based becomes more complex, and its ability to suggest new ways of perception becomes that much greater. In *Blow-Up* (1966), Michelangelo Antonioni deals with exactly the philosophical question that the fiction-film relationship implies: the varieties of image and perception, the innate desire to see truly, to make sense of a vision and its meaning. The issue is derived from an experimental short story by Julio Cortazar, but the film gains its events from Antonioni's own interpretation of what the story's theme implies. In creating this filmic interpretation, Antonioni seems to affirm Bergman's statement that the form and substance of film and literature are usually in conflict. Antonioni's film says that only by radical transformation can a story as difficult and disjunct as Cortazar's be transferred from the page to the screen; film and fiction become wholly different worlds of art. The business of adapting literature into film becomes a process of translation from one kind of language into another; as René Clair has pointed out, the faithful translation is often a betrayal of the original.

The narrative voice in Cortazar's story says: "I raised the camera, pretended to study a focus which did not include them, and waited, and watched closely, sure that I would finally catch the revealing expression, one that would sum it all up, life that is rhythmed by movement but which a single stiff image destroys, taking time in cross section, if we do not choose the essential imperceptible fraction of it." Cortazar is talking about freezing time on a photograph so that the life pictured is not lost, or untruly represented. There is perhaps a kind of still moment that contains the past and implies the future. Cortazar's narrator is talking about his possibly futile attempt to capture such a moment and preserve it in a photograph.

When he does take his picture and enlarges it to discover its essence, he thinks he has found a truth—in the film, a man with a gun; in the story, the expression on a man's face and all that it implies—but that truth becomes increasingly elusive and finally vanishes. In the story, the photograph comes to life in Roberto Michel's imagination, and its inhabitants go about living a life that is not at all the one that their still moment seems to reveal. In Antonioni's film, the photograph reveals a man with a gun, the key to a dead body, things that exist and then vanish: filmic terms for

Cortazar's verbal images. Both the film and the story, one through elaborate verbal means, the other with imaginative visual gestures, are speaking to us of the same things, the difficulties inherent in any attempt to see the truth of only a single moment. Thomas's handling of the imaginary tennis ball at the film's end is a visual statement of Roberto Michel's resolution of his internal conflict with his photograph. It affirms what Thomas has learned of the world: that it is mostly what we make it up to be, and we can either make do with the world we perceive or have no world at all. There is no such thing as that single still moment of revelation.

Haycox and Ford respond to the moral problem of how to live properly in the world with others; Cortazar and Antonioni respond to the epistemological problem of discovering what is true about what we experience in that same world. The answers come from the writers' and filmmakers' personal visions, but in the end we are also offered what Mallarmé said poetry gives to the reader's mind: "the delicious joy of believing it is creating." This, then, is the value of the stories in this collection, and the films that derive from them: they help us confront the most fundamental problems we encounter in our world, and allow us to deal with them in the playgrounds of our minds. In a very real sense, they provide practice for living. They fulfill the most fundamental purpose of art, awakening us to sight, vision, perception; helping us to create the sense and meaning and moral insight that allow us to survive and live humanely.

The intent of this collection is to present good short stories that became good movies, and it is our good fortune that all of the films represented are significant examples of motion picture art. The stories and films run the gamut of genre, including horror, suspense, the Western, comedy, science fiction, and both the mainstream and the experimental. The nine films won a total of nine Academy Awards and sixteen nominations. They represent the work of such influential directors as Tod Browning, Frank Capra, John Ford, Alfred Hitchcock, Michelangelo Antonioni, and Stanley Kubrick; and of such enduring performers as Clark Gable, Claudette Colbert, John Wayne, Marlon Brando, James Stewart, Grace Kelly, Paul Newman, Jackie Gleason, George C. Scott,

Edmond O'Brien, David Hemmings, and Vanessa Redgrave. Although this anthology was originally conceived as primarily a short-story collection, the nine films can stand as a fairly comprehensive survey of the changing face of American cinema.

Stories into Film is a source book, a book to work with. Its purpose is to suggest some ideas about the relationship of film to literature, and to encourage the reader to pursue the topic further. To this end, it includes bibliographical and filmographical material. Finally, we hope the reader will find pleasure, as we did, in discovering the short stories behind some important and enjoyable films.

No book of this scope is solely the work of its editors, and we would like to acknowledge the contributions of the people whose suggestions and criticism provoked and encouraged us.

The original concept of *Stories into Film* developed through a valuable discussion with our colleague Earl Ganz. Terry Milne, Peter Blau, Ed Hoch, Garry Quast, and Angelo Panagos offered suggestions that helped us compile the original list of stories from which we made our final selections.

Several critical texts, reference books, and source books aided us in developing the Introduction, the headnotes, and the appendices. We learned a great deal through conversation with George Bluestone, and from his text *Novels into Film. Film and/as Literature,* edited by John Harrington, provided an invaluable compendium of critical articles. We also derived useful reference and anecdotal material from *The American Film Institute Catalog,* Volume F6, 1961–1970, Richard P. Krafsur, executive editor; *The American Movies Reference Book: The Sound Era,* Paul Michael, editor-in-chief; *The Oxford Companion to Film,* edited by Liz-Anne Bawden; *Dictionary of Films* and *Dictionary of Film Makers,* both by Georges Sadoul; *Hitchcock,* by François Truffaut, with Helen G. Scott; *The Art of Alfred Hitchcock,* by Donald Spoto; and *The Name Above the Title,* by Frank Capra.

Norman DeMarco and Harris Ross, of the University of Arkansas at Fayetteville, graciously allowed us to reprint their extensive bibliographies of critical texts and articles on fiction and film; thanks also to Jim Crumley for bringing this material to our attention.

For their headnotes and for their thoughts on the film versions of their short stories, our thanks to Walter Tevis and Dorothy M. Johnson.

Bill Bevis gave us the benefit of his usual perceptive reading of our Introduction. Annick Smith, both in conversation and in her editing of our headnotes, allowed us to draw on her considerable experience both as filmmaker and as editor. Kathleen Royland's research assistance and critical suggestions were of particular help.

For technical and filmographical research we are indebted to Jim Tarlow in Boston, and Ed Landler in Los Angeles.

Angelo L. Scalpello of Select Film Library, Inc., was kind enough to lend us a print of *The Wild One* for review.

June Ching of the University of Montana's Instructional Material Service made her film catalogs available to us, and assisted in researching the availability of sixteen-millimeter rental films.

Finally, our grateful thanks to Jan Schultz for both her secretarial help and her patience; and to Virginia Barber, our literary agent, who provided the support and encouragement that helped us see this book through to completion.

Spurs (Freaks)

Tod Robbins

A Horde of Caricatures of Creation! WARNING! Children will not be permitted to see this picture! Adults not in normal health are urged not to!

—Display advertisement for *Freaks*
in *The New York Times,* July 9, 1932

Tod Browning's Freaks *(1932) opened in New York on July 8, 1932, and was dutifully reviewed in the next day's* New York Times, *alongside the advertisement quoted above, with its blurb worthy of the contemporary horror film. The review is complimentary, particularly in regard to Browning's direction. Although the reviewer calls the film "out of the ordinary," he hesitates to pass judgment: "whether it deserves the title abnormal is a matter of personal opinion."*

Public reaction was another matter; it was mostly shock and disgust. Distributors and theater owners, particularly in rural areas, refused to handle the film. One critic piously insisted that the film's "unwholesome shockery creates morbid audience reactions." In Great Britain, the film was banned outright, and remained on the banned list until 1963.

The reason for the public outrage is apparent: Browning rudely violated the audience's preconceptions. By 1932, filmgoers had become sophisticated; the day of The Great Train Robbery *(1903), whose final shot of a man firing a pistol at the camera made women scream and men faint, was thirty years in the past. Viewers were still willing to surrender themselves to film's ability to fire the imagination, but only with the secure knowledge that* movies, with their fights, pratfalls, and killings, their comedy, drama, and pathos, were only fantasy, make-believe. But Freaks denies artifice, and it is this that makes it so threatening; for all of the film's sixty-four minutes, the audience is compelled to gaze at real, living, and painfully deformed human beings.

Browning's departures from Tod Robbins's short story "Spurs" are deliberately designed to heighten the horror. Despite its brief-ness, it is a complex and effective moral tale. Robbins's skill is particularly apparent in the key wedding banquet segment, where he interweaves humor, horror, egomania, and treachery; Brown-ing's version is one of the film's more striking scenes. But for purposes of adaptation to the screen, the character of Jacques Courbé presents two problems. First, the nuances of his character are presented primarily through the nonvisual literary devices of soliloquy, internal monologue, and variations in point of view. Sec-ondly, Courbé is a paranoid egomaniac as well as a physical freak. For a visual presentation, particularly within the moral and techni-cal bounds that limited Browning in 1932, the character required simplification and a more sympathetic bias.

In Browning's version, the "freaks" and the "normal people" are clearly distinguished, and then set at odds; the audience's controlled expectation that there will be good guys and bad guys is fulfilled. The inhabitants of the sideshow—the midgets Hans and Frieda, the Siamese twins, the bearded lady, the boy with half a torso, the pinheads, the bird girl, the armless won-der—are depicted as innocent, childlike, and even heartwarm-ing in their optimistic and ingenious adjustments to their hand-icaps. The normal people, represented by the strongman Hercules and the trapeze artist Cleopatra, are intolerant, venal, and violent. The viewer is lulled into a false sense of control, into feeling that the conflict, if presented in somewhat bizarre terms, is at least of a form with which he or she is familiar. The unspoken notion with which the viewer begins the film— that grotesque people are somehow malevolent—is assuaged. Thus, the pure horror of the ending is intensified. The viewer learns that his or her hidden fears were correct all along, as the freaks, with ruthless efficiency, kill Hercules and turn Cleopatra into "one of us."

Even Browning felt it necessary to soften this horrific ending; in one early version of the scenario, Hercules is gelded rather than killed. Browning also appends an anticlimactic romantic coda: after the violence, Hans marries Frieda, one of his own "kind." This sugary ending mars the film, although even it has a bizarre aspect: Hans and Frieda are played by Harry and Daisy Earles, brother and sister in real life.

Browning began his career as a circus performer, a background that surely had a great deal to do with the formation of his artistic vision. Freaks was not the first film in which he treated the deformed. The title characters of *The Unholy Three (1925)* are a ventriloquist, a giant, and a dwarf (also played by Harry Earles); *in* The Road to Mandalay *(1926), Lon Chaney plays a man so ugly he is afraid to reveal himself to his own daughter; and in* The Unknown *(1927), Chaney is a criminal who pretends to be armless, and later actually amputates both arms in an attempt to win the love of a girl whose father he has strangled. The relationship between physical and psychological deformity, particularly sexual, and between the grotesque and the innocent, between beauty and the satanic, is central to the dialectic of Browning's moral universe. It is not surprising that a film that may be thought of as a semidocumentary, such as* Freaks, *followed by only a year Browning's best-known film, the first sound version of* Dracula *(1931). It is as though Browning is trying to establish his vision as actual rather than imaginary.*

Browning was the most influential of early American horror movie directors, and is credited with establishing the careers of both Chaney and Bela Lugosi. He directed his last film in 1939 and retired into obscurity, dying in Santa Monica in 1962. His obituary in The New York Times *erroneously identifies him as the director of* The Hunchback of Notre Dame *and does not mention* Freaks *at all, an ironic ending that might have suited Browning's imagination.*

SPURS

1

Jacques Courbé was a romanticist. He measured only twenty-eight inches from the soles of his diminutive feet to the crown of his head; but there were times, as he rode into the arena on his gallant charger, St. Eustache, when he felt himself a doughty knight of old about to do battle for his lady.

What matter that St. Eustache was not a gallant charger except in his master's imagination—not even a pony, indeed, but a large dog of a nondescript breed, with the long snout and upstanding ears of a wolf? What matter that Monsieur Courbé's entrance was invariably greeted with shouts of derisive laughter and bombardments of banana skins and orange peel? What matter that he had no lady and that his daring deeds were severely curtailed to a mimicry of the bareback riders who preceded him? What mattered all these things to the tiny man who lived in dreams and who resolutely closed his shoe-button eyes to the drab realities of life?

The dwarf had no friends among the other freaks in Copo's Circus. They considered him ill-tempered and egotistical, and he loathed them for their acceptance of things as they were. Imagination was the armour that protected him from the curious glances of a cruel, gaping world, from the stinging lash of ridicule, from the bombardments of banana skins and orange peel. Without it, he must have shrivelled up and died. But these others? Ah, they had no armour except their own thick hides! The door that opened on the kingdom of imagination was closed and locked to them; and although they did not wish to open this door, although they did not miss what lay beyond it, they resented and mistrusted anyone who possessed the key.

Now it came about, after many humiliating performances in the arena, made palatable only by dreams, that love entered the circus tent and beckoned commandingly to Monsieur Jacques Courbé. In an instant the dwarf was engulfed in a sea of wild, tumultuous passion.

Mademoiselle Jeanne Marie was a daring bareback rider. It

made Monsieur Jacques Courbé's tiny heart stand still to see her that first night of her appearance in the arena, performing brilliantly on the broad back of her aged mare, Sappho. A tall, blonde woman of the amazon type, she had round eyes of baby blue which held no spark of her avaricious peasant's soul, carmine lips and cheeks, large white teeth which flashed continually in a smile, and hands which, when doubled up, were nearly the size of the dwarf's head.

Her partner in the act was Simon Lafleur, the Romeo of the circus tent—a swarthy, Herculean young man with bold black eyes and hair that glistened with grease like the back of Solon, the trained seal.

From the first performance Monsieur Jacques Courbé loved Mademoiselle Jeanne Marie. All his tiny body was shaken with longing for her. Her buxom charms, so generously revealed in tights and spangles, made him flush and cast down his eyes. The familiarities allowed to Simon Lafleur, the bodily acrobatic contacts of the two performers, made the dwarf's blood boil. Mounted on St. Eustache, awaiting his turn at the entrance, he would grind his teeth in impotent rage to see Simon circling round and round the ring, standing proudly on the back of Sappho and holding Mademoiselle Jeanne Marie in an ecstatic embrace, while she kicked one shapely bespangled leg skyward.

"Ah, the dog!" Monsieur Jacques Courbé would mutter. "Some day I shall teach this hulking stable-boy his place! *Ma foi,* I will clip his ears for him!"

St. Eustache did not share his master's admiration for Mademoiselle Jeanne Marie. From the first he evinced his hearty detestation for her by low growls and a ferocious display of long, sharp fangs. It was little consolation for the dwarf to know that St. Eustache showed still more marked signs of rage when Simon Lafleur approached him. It pained Monsieur Jacques Courbé to think that his gallant charger, his sole companion, his bedfellow, should not also love and admire the splendid giantess who each night risked life and limb before the awed populace. Often, when they were alone together, he would chide St. Eustache on his churlishness.

"Ah, you devil of a dog!" the dwarf would cry. "Why must you always growl and show your ugly teeth when the lovely Jeanne

Marie condescends to notice you? Have you no feelings under your tough hide? Cur, she is an angel and you snarl at her! Do you not remember how I found you, a starving puppy in a Paris gutter? And now you must threaten the hand of my princess! So this is your gratitude, great hairy pig!"

Monsieur Jacques Courbé had one living relative—not a dwarf, like himself, but a fine figure of a man, a prosperous farmer living just outside the town of Roubaix. The elder Courbé had never married and so one day, when he was found dead from heart failure, his tiny nephew—for whom, it must be confessed, the farmer had always felt an instinctive aversion—fell heir to a comfortable property. When the tidings were brought to him, the dwarf threw both arms about the shaggy neck of St. Eustache and cried out:

"Ah, now we can retire, marry and settle down, old friend! I am worth many times my weight in gold!"

That evening, as Mademoiselle Jeanne Marie was changing her gaudy costume after the performance, a light tap sounded on the door.

"Enter!" she called, believing it to be Simon Lafleur, who had promised to take her that evening to the Sign of the Wild Boar for a glass of wine to wash the sawdust out of her throat. "Enter, *mon chéri!*"

The door swung slowly open and in stepped Monsieur Jacques Courbé, very proud and upright, in the silks and laces of a courtier, with a tiny gold-hilted sword swinging at his hip. Up he came, his shoe-button eyes all a-glitter to see the more than partially revealed charms of his robust lady. Up he came to within a yard of where she sat, and down on one knee he went and pressed his lips to her red-slippered foot.

"Oh, most beautiful and daring lady," he cried, in a voice as shrill as a pin scratching on a window-pane, "will you not take mercy on the unfortunate Jacques Courbé? He is hungry for your smiles, he is starving for your lips! All night long he tosses on his couch and dreams of Jeanne Marie!"

"What play-acting is this, my brave little fellow?" she asked, bending down with the smile of an ogress. "Has Simon Lafleur sent you to tease me?"

"May the black plague have Simon!" the dwarf cried, his eyes seeming to flash blue sparks. "I am not play-acting. It is only too true that I love you, mademoiselle, that I wish to make you my lady. And now that I have a fortune, now that—" He broke off suddenly and his face resembled a withered apple. "What is this, mademoiselle?" he said, in the low, droning tone of a hornet about to sting. "Do you laugh at my love? I warn you, mademoiselle—do not laugh at Jacques Courbé!"

Mademoiselle Jeanne Marie's large, florid face had turned purple from suppressed merriment. Her lips twitched at the corners. It was all she could do not to burst out into a roar of laughter.

Why, the ridiculous little manikin was serious in his love-making! This pocket-sized edition of a courtier was proposing marriage to her! He, this splinter of a fellow, wished to make her his wife! Why, she could carry him about on her shoulder like a trained marmoset!

What a joke this was—what a colossal, corset-creaking joke! Wait till she told Simon Lafleur! She could fairly see him throw back his sleek head, open his mouth to its widest dimensions and shake with silent laughter. But *she* must not laugh—not now. First she must listen to everything the dwarf had to say, draw all the sweetness out of this bonbon of humour before she crushed it under the heel of ridicule.

"I am not laughing," she managed to say. "You have taken me by surprise. I never thought, I never even guessed—"

"That is well, mademoiselle," the dwarf broke in. "I do not tolerate laughter. In the arena I am paid to make laughter, but these others pay to laugh at *me.* I always make people pay to laugh at me!"

"But do I understand you aright, Monsieur Courbé? Are you proposing an honourable marriage?"

The dwarf rested his hand on his heart and bowed. "Yes, mademoiselle, an honourable marriage, and the wherewithal to keep the wolf from the door. A week ago my uncle died and left me a large estate. We shall have a servant to wait on our wants, a horse and carriage, food and wine of the best, and leisure to amuse ourselves. And you? Why, you will be a fine lady! I will clothe that beautiful big body of yours with silks and laces! You will be as happy, mademoiselle, as a cherry tree in June!"

The dark blood slowly receded from Mademoiselle Jeanne Marie's full cheeks, her lips no longer twitched at the corners, her eyes had narrowed slightly. She had been a bareback rider for years and she was weary of it. The life of the circus tent had lost its tinsel. She loved the dashing Simon Lafleur, but she knew well enough that this Romeo in tights would never espouse a dowerless girl.

The dwarf's words had woven themselves into a rich mental tapestry. She saw herself a proud lady, ruling over a country estate, and later welcoming Simon Lafleur with all the luxuries that were so near his heart. Simon would be overjoyed to marry into a country estate. These pygmies were a puny lot. They died young! She would do nothing to hasten the end of Jacques Courbé. No, she would be kindness itself to the poor little fellow, but, on the other hand, she would not lose her beauty mourning for him.

"Nothing that you wish shall be withheld from you as long as you love me, mademoiselle," the dwarf continued. "Your answer?"

Mademoiselle Jeanne Marie bent forward and, with a single movement of her powerful arms, raised Monsieur Jacques Courbé and placed him on her knee. For an ecstatic instant she held him thus, as if he were a large French doll, with his tiny sword cocked coquettishly out behind. Then she planted on his cheek a huge kiss that covered his entire face from chin to brow.

"I am yours!" she murmured, pressing him to her ample bosom. "From the first I loved you, Monsieur Jacques Courbé!"

2

The wedding of Mademoiselle Jeanne Marie was celebrated in the town of Roubaix, where Copo's Circus had taken up its temporary quarters. Following the ceremony, a feast was served in one of the tents, which was attended by a whole galaxy of celebrities.

The bridegroom, his dark little face flushed with happiness and wine, sat at the head of the board. His chin was just above the tablecloth, so that his head looked like a large orange that had rolled off the fruit-dish. Immediately beneath his dangling feet, St. Eustache, who had more than once evinced by deep growls his disapproval of the proceedings, now worried a bone with quick, sly glances from time to time at the plump legs of his new mistress. Papa Copo was on the dwarf's right, his large round face as red and benevolent as a harvest moon. Next him sat Griffo, the giraffe boy, who was covered with spots, and whose neck was so long that he looked down on all the rest, including Monsieur Hercule Hippo, the giant. The rest of the company included Mademoiselle Lupa, who had sharp white teeth of an incredible length, and who growled when she tried to talk; the tiresome Monsieur Jejongle, who insisted on juggling fruit, plates and knives, although the whole company was heartily sick of his tricks; Madame Samson, with her trained baby boa constrictors coiled about her neck and peeping out timidly, one above each ear; Simon Lafleur and a score of others.

The bareback rider had laughed silently and almost continually ever since Jeanne Marie had told him of her engagement. Now he sat next to her in his crimson tights. His black hair was brushed back from his forehead and so glistened with grease that it reflected the lights overhead, like a burnished helmet. From time to time he tossed off a brimming goblet of Burgundy, nudged the bride in the ribs with his elbow and threw back his sleek head in another silent outburst of laughter.

"And you are sure that you will not forget me, Simon?" she whispered. "It may be some time before I can get the little ape's money."

"Forget you, Jeanne?" he muttered. "By all the dancing devils in champagne, never! I will wait as patiently as Job till you have fed that mouse some poisoned cheese. But what will you do with him in the meantime, Jeanne? You must allow him no liberties. I grind my teeth to think of you in his arms!"

The bride smiled and regarded her diminutive husband with an appraising glance. What an atom of a man! And yet life might linger in his bones for a long time to come. Monsieur Jacques Courbé had allowed himself only one glass of wine and yet he was far gone in intoxication. His tiny face was suffused with blood and he stared at Simon Lafleur belligerently. Did he suspect the truth?

"Your husband is flushed with wine!" the bareback rider whispered. *"Ma foi, madame,* later he may knock you about! Possibly he is a dangerous fellow in his cups. Should he maltreat you, Jeanne, do not forget that you have a protector in Simon Lafleur."

"You clown!" Jeanne Marie rolled her large eyes roguishly and laid her hand for an instant on the bareback rider's knee. "Simon, I could crack his skull between my finger and thumb, like this hickory nut!" She paused to illustrate her example, and then added reflectively: "And, perhaps, I shall do that very thing, if he attempts any familiarities. Ugh! The little ape turns my stomach!"

By now the wedding guests were beginning to show the effects of their potations. This was especially marked in the case of Monsieur Jacque's associates in the side-show.

Griffo, the giraffe boy, had closed his large brown eyes and was swaying his small head languidly above the assembly, while a slightly supercilious expression drew his lips down at the corners. Monsieur Hercule Hippo, swollen out by his libations to even more colossal proportions, was repeating over and over: "I tell you I am not like other men. When I walk, the earth trembles!" Mademoiselle Lupa, her hairy upper lip lifted above her long white teeth, was gnawing at a bone, growling unintelligible phrases to herself and shooting savage, suspicious glances at her companions. Monsieur Jejongle's hands had grown unsteady and, as he insisted on juggling the knives and plates of each new course, broken bits of crockery littered the floor. Madame Samson, uncoiling her necklace of baby boa constrictors, was feeding them lumps of sugar soaked in rum. Monsieur Jacques Courbé had finished his second glass of wine and was surveying the whispering Simon Lafleur through narrowed eyes.

There can be no genial companionship among great egotists who have drunk too much. Each one of these human oddities thought that he or she alone was responsible for the crowds that daily gathered at Copo's Circus; so now, heated with the good Burgundy, they were not slow in asserting themselves. Their separate egos rattled angrily together, like so many pebbles in a bag. Here was gunpowder which needed only a spark.

"I am a big—a very big man!" Monsieur Hercule Hippo said sleepily. "Women love me. The pretty little creatures leave their pygmy husbands, so that they may come and stare at Hercule Hippo of Copo's Circus. Ha, and when they return home, they laugh at other men always! 'You may kiss me again when you grow up,' they tell their sweethearts.''

"Fat bullock, here is one woman who has no love for you!" cried Mademoiselle Lupa, glaring sidewise at the giant over her bone. "That great carcass of yours is only so much food gone to waste. You have cheated the butcher, my friend. Fool, women do not come to see *you!* As well might they stare at the cattle being led through the street. Ah, no, they come from far and near to see one of their own sex who is not a cat!"

"Quite right," cried Papa Copo in a conciliatory tone, smiling and rubbing his hands together. "Not a cat, mademoiselle, but a wolf. Ah, you have a sense of humour! How droll!"

"I *have* a sense of humour," Mademoiselle Lupa agreed, returning to her bone, "and also sharp teeth. Let the erring hand not stray too near!"

"You, Monsieur Hippo and Mademoiselle Lupa, are both wrong," said a voice which seemed to come from the roof. "Surely it is none other than me whom the people come to stare at!"

All raised their eyes to the supercilious face of Griffo, the giraffe boy, which swayed slowly from side to side on its long, pipe-stem neck. It was he who had spoken, although his eyes were still closed.

"Of all the colossal impudence!" cried the matronly Madame Samson. "As if my little dears had nothing to say on the subject!" She picked up the two baby boa constrictors, which lay in drunken slumber on her lap, and shook them like whips at the wedding guests. "Papa Copo knows only too well that it is on account of these little charmers, Mark Antony and Cleopatra, that the side-show is so well attended!"

The circus owner, thus directly appealed to, frowned in perplexity. He felt himself in a quandary. These freaks of his were difficult to handle. Why had he been fool enough to come to Monsieur Jacques Courbé's wedding feast? Whatever he said would be used against him.

As Papa Copo hesitated, his round face wreathed in ingratiating smiles, the long deferred spark suddenly alighted in the powder.

It all came about on account of the carelessness of Monsieur Jejongle, who had become engrossed in the conversation and wished to put in a word for himself. Absent-mindedly juggling two heavy plates and a spoon, he said in a petulant tone: "You all appear to forget *me!*"

Scarcely were the words out of his mouth when one of the heavy plates descended with a crash on the thick skull of Monsieur Hippo, and Monsieur Jejongle was instantly remembered. Indeed, he was more than remembered, for the giant, already irritated to the boiling-point by Mademoiselle Lupa's insults, at this new affront struck out savagely past her and knocked the juggler head-over-heels under the table.

Mademoiselle Lupa, always quick-tempered and especially so when her attention was focused on a juicy chicken bone, evidently considered her dinner companion's conduct far from decorous and promptly inserted her sharp teeth in the offending hand that had administered the blow. Monsieur Hippo, squealing from rage and pain like a wounded elephant, bounded to his feet, overturning the table.

Pandemonium followed. Every freak's hands, teeth, feet, were turned against the others. Above the shouts, screams, growls and hisses of the combat, Papa Copo's voice could be heard bellowing for peace:

"Ah, my children, my children! This is no way to behave! Calm yourselves, I pray you! Mademoiselle Lupa, remember that you are a lady as well as a wolf!"

There is no doubt that Monsieur Jacques Courbé would have suffered most in this undignified fracas had it not been for St. Eustache, who had stationed himself over his tiny master and who now drove off all would-be assailants. As it was, Griffo, the unfortunate giraffe boy, was the most defenceless and therefore became the victim. His small, round head swayed back and forth to blows like a punching bag. He was bitten by Mademoiselle Lupa, buffeted by Monsieur Hippo, kicked by Monsieur Jejongle, clawed by Madame Samson, and nearly strangled by both the baby boa constrictors, which had wound themselves about his neck like hangmen's nooses. Undoubtedly he would have fallen a victim to circumstances had it not been for Simon Lafleur, the bride and half a dozen of her acrobatic friends, whom Papa Copo had implored to restore peace. Roaring with laughter, they sprang forward and tore the combatants apart.

Monsieur Jacques Courbé was found sitting grimly under a fold of the tablecloth. He held a broken bottle of wine in one hand. The dwarf was very drunk and in a towering rage. As Simon Lafleur approached with one of his silent laughs, Monsieur Jacques Courbé hurled the bottle at his head.

"Ah, the little wasp!" the bareback rider cried, picking up the dwarf by his waistband. "Here is your fine husband, Jeanne! Take him away before he does me some mischief. *Parbleu,* he is a bloodthirsty fellow in his cups!"

The bride approached, her blonde face crimson from wine and laughter. Now that she was safely married to a country estate she took no more pains to conceal her true feelings.

"Oh, *la, la!"* she cried, seizing the struggling dwarf and holding him forcibly on her shoulder. "What a temper the little ape has! Well, we shall spank it out of him before long!"

"Let me down!" Monsieur Jacques Courbé screamed in a paroxysm of fury. "You will regret this, madame! Let me down, I say!"

But the stalwart bride shook her head. "No, no, my little one!" she laughed. "You cannot escape your wife so easily! What, you would fly from my arms before the honeymoon!"

"Let me down!" he cried again. "Can't you see that they are laughing at me?"

"And why should they not laugh, my little ape? Let them laugh, if they will, but I will not put you down. No, I will carry you thus, perched on my shoulder, to the farm. It will set a precedent which brides of the future may find a certain difficulty in following!"

"But the farm is quite a distance from here, my Jeanne," said Simon Lafleur. "You are as strong as an ox and he is only a marmoset, still, I will wager a bottle of Burgundy that you set him down by the roadside."

"Done, Simon!" the bride cried, with a flash of her strong white teeth. "You shall lose your wager, for I swear that I could carry my little ape from one end of France to the other!"

Monsieur Jacques Courbé no longer struggled. He now sat bolt upright on his bride's broad shoulder. From the flaming peaks of blind passion he had fallen into an abyss of cold fury. His love was dead but some quite alien emotion was rearing an evil head from its ashes.

"So, madame, you could carry me from one end of France to the other!" he droned in a monotonous undertone. "From one end of France to the other! I will remember that always, madame!"

"Come!" cried the bride suddenly. "I am off. Do you and the others, Simon, follow to see me win my wager."

They all trooped out of the tent. A full moon rode the heavens and showed the road, lying as white and straight through the meadows as the parting in Simon Lafleur's black, oily hair. The bride, still holding the diminutive bridegroom on her shoulder, burst out into song as she strode forward. The wedding guests followed. Some walked none too steadily. Griffo, the giraffe boy, staggered pitifully on his long, thin legs. Papa Copo alone remained behind.

"What a strange world!" he muttered, standing in the tent door and following them with his round blue eyes. "Ah, these children of mine are difficult at times—very difficult!"

3

A year had rolled by since the marriage of Mademoiselle Jeanne Marie and Monsieur Jacques Courbé. Copo's Circus had once more taken up its quarters in the town of Roubaix. For more than a week the country people for miles around had flocked to the side-show to get a peep at Griffo, the giraffe boy; Monsieur Hercule Hippo, the giant; Mademoiselle Lupa, the wolf lady; Madame Samson, with her baby boa constrictors; and Monsieur Jejongle, the famous juggler. Each was still firmly convinced that he or she alone was responsible for the popularity of the circus.

Simon Lafleur sat in his lodgings at the Sign of the Wild Boar. He wore nothing but red tights. His powerful torso, stripped to the waist, glistened with oil. He was kneading his biceps tenderly with some strong-smelling fluid.

Suddenly there came the sound of heavy, laborious footsteps

on the stairs. Simon Lafleur looked up. His rather gloomy expression lifted, giving place to the brilliant smile that had won for him the hearts of so many lady acrobats.

"Ah, this is Marcelle!" he told himself. "Or perhaps it is Rose, the English girl; or, yet again, little Francesca, although she walks more lightly. Well, no matter—whoever it is, I will welcome her!"

But now the lagging, heavy footfalls were in the hall and, a moment later, they came to a halt outside the door. There was a timid knock.

Simon Lafleur's brilliant smile broadened. "Perhaps some new admirer who needs encouragement," he told himself. But aloud he said: "Enter, mademoiselle!"

The door swung slowly open and revealed the visitor. She was a tall, gaunt woman dressed like a peasant. The wind had blown her hair into her eyes. Now she raised a large, toil-worn hand, brushed it back across her forehead and looked long and attentively at the bareback rider.

"You do not remember me?" she said at length.

Two lines of perplexity appeared above Simon Lafleur's Roman nose; he slowly shook his head. He, who had known so many women in his time, was now at a loss. Was it a fair question to ask a man who was no longer a boy and who had lived? Women change so in a brief time! Now this bag of bones might at one time have appeared desirable to him.

Parbleu! Fate was a conjurer! She waved her wand and beautiful women were transformed into hags, jewels into pebbles, silks and laces into hempen cords. The brave fellow who danced to-night at the prince's ball might tomorrow dance more lightly on the gallows tree. The thing was to live and die with a full belly. To digest all that one could—that was life!

"You do not remember me?" she said again.

Simon Lafleur once more shook his sleek, black head. "I have a poor memory for faces, madame," he said politely. "It is my misfortune, when there are such beautiful faces."

"Ah, but you should have remembered, Simon!" the woman cried, a sob rising up in her throat. "We were very close together, you and I. Do you not remember Jeanne Marie?"

"Jeanne Marie!" the bareback rider cried. "Jeanne Marie, who married a marmoset and a country estate? Don't tell me, madame, that you—"

He broke off and stared at her, open-mouthed. His sharp black eyes wandered from the wisps of wet, straggling hair down her gaunt person till they rested at last on her thick cowhide boots, encrusted with layer on layer of mud from the countryside.

"It is impossible!" he said at last.

"It is indeed Jeanne Marie," the woman answered, "or what is left of her. Ah, Simon, what a life he has led me! I have been merely a beast of burden! There are no ignominies which he has not made me suffer!"

"To whom do you refer?" Simon Lafleur demanded. "Surely you cannot mean that pocket edition husband of yours—that dwarf, Jacques Courbé?"

"Ah, but I do, Simon! Alas, he has broken me!"

"He—that toothpick of a man?" the bareback rider cried, with one of his silent laughs. "Why, it is impossible! As you once said yourself, Jeanne, you could crack his skull between finger and thumb like a hickory nut!"

"So I thought once. Ah, but I did not know him then, Simon! Because he was small, I thought I could do with him as I liked. It seemed to me that I was marrying a manikin. 'I will play Punch and Judy with this little fellow,' I said to myself. Simon, you may imagine my surprise when he began playing Punch and Judy with me!"

"But I do not understand, Jeanne. Surely at any time you could have slapped him into obedience!"

"Perhaps," she assented wearily, "had it not been for St. Eustache. From the first that wolf dog of his hated me. If I so much as answered his master back, he would show his teeth. Once, at the beginning, when I raised my hand to cuff Jacques Courbé, he sprang at my throat and would have torn me limb from limb had not the dwarf called him off. I was a strong woman, but even then I was no match for a wolf!"

"There was poison, was there not?" Simon Lafleur suggested.

"Ah, yes, I, too, thought of poison, but it was of no avail. St. Eustache would eat nothing that I gave him and the dwarf forced me to taste first of all food that was placed before him and his dog.

Unless I myself wished to die, there was no way of poisoning either of them."

"My poor girl!" the bareback rider said, pityingly. "I begin to understand, but sit down and tell me everything. This is a revelation to me, after seeing you stalking homeward so triumphantly with your bridegroom on your shoulder. You must begin at the beginning."

"It was just because I carried him thus on my shoulder that I have had to suffer so cruelly," she said, seating herself on the only other chair the room afforded. "He has never forgiven me the insult which he says I put upon him. Do you remember how I boasted that I could carry him from one end of France to the other?"

"I remember. Well, Jeanne?"

"Well, Simon, the little demon has figured out the exact distance in leagues. Each morning, rain or shine, we sally out of the house—he on my back, the wolf dog at my heels—and I tramp along the dusty roads till my bones tremble beneath me from fatigue. If I so much as slacken my pace, if I falter, he goads me with his cruel little golden spurs, while, at the same time, St. Eustache nips my ankles. When we return home, he strikes so many leagues off a score which he says is the number of leagues from one end of France to the other. Not half that distance has been covered and I am no longer a strong woman, Simon. Look at these shoes!"

She held up one of her feet for his inspection. The sole of the cowhide boot had been worn through; Simon Lafleur caught a glimpse of bruised flesh caked with the mire of the highway.

"This is the third pair that I have had," she continued hoarsely. "Now he tells me that the price of shoe leather is too high, that I shall have to finish my pilgrimage barefooted."

"But why do you put up with all this, Jeanne?" Simon Lafleur asked angrily. "You, who have a carriage and a servant, should not walk at all!"

"At first there was a carriage and a servant," she said, wiping the tears from her eyes with the back of her hand, "but they did not last a week. He sent the servant about his business and sold the carriage at a near-by fair. Now there is no one but me to wait on him and his dog."

"But the neighbours?" Simon Lafleur persisted. "Surely you could appeal to them?"

"We have no near neighbours, the farm is quite isolated. I would have run away many months ago if I could have escaped unnoticed, but they keep a continual watch on me. Once I tried, but I hadn't travelled more than a league before the wolf dog was snapping at my ankles. He drove me back to the farm and the following day I was compelled to carry the little fiend till I fell from sheer exhaustion."

"But tonight you got away?"

"Yes," she said, with a quick, frightened glance at the door. "Tonight I slipped out while they were both sleeping and came here to you. I knew that you would protect me, Simon, because of what we have been to each other. Get Papa Copo to take me back in the circus and I will work my fingers to the bone! Save me, Simon!"

Jeanne Marie could no longer suppress her sobs. They rose in her throat, choking her, making her incapable of further speech.

"Calm yourself, Jeanne," Simon Lafleur said soothingly. "I will do what I can for you. I shall have a talk with Papa Copo tomorrow. Of course, you are no longer the same woman that you were a year ago. You have aged since then, but perhaps our good Papa Copo could find you something to do."

He broke off and eyed her intently. She had stiffened in the chair, her face, even under its coat of grime, had gone a sickly white.

"What troubles you, Jeanne?" he asked a trifle breathlessly.

"Hush!" she said, with a finger to her lips. "Listen!"

Simon Lafleur could hear nothing but the tapping of the rain on the roof and the sighing of the wind through the trees. An unusual silence seemed to pervade the Sign of the Wild Boar.

"Now don't you hear it?" she cried with an inarticulate gasp. "Simon, it is in the house—it is on the stairs!"

At last the bareback rider's less sensitive ears caught the sound his companion had heard a full minute before. It was a steady *pit-pat, pit-pat,* on the stairs, hard to dissociate from the drip of the rain from the eaves, but each instant it came nearer, grew more distinct.

"Oh, save me, Simon, save me!" Jeanne Marie cried, throwing herself at his feet and clasping him about the knees. "Save me! It is St. Eustache!"

"Nonsense, woman!" the bareback rider said angrily, but nevertheless he rose. "There are other dogs in the world. On the second landing there is a blind fellow who owns a dog. Perhaps it is he you hear."

"No, no—it is St. Eustache's step! My God, if you had lived with him a year, you would know it, too! Close the door and lock it!"

"That I will not," Simon Lafleur said contemptuously. "Do you think I am frightened so easily? If it is the wolf dog, so much the worse for him. He will not be the first cur I have choked to death with these two hands!"

Pit-pat, pit-pat—it was on the second landing. *Pit-pat, pit-pat*—now it was in the corridor, and coming fast. *Pit-pat*—all at once it stopped.

There was a moment's breathless silence and then into the room trotted St. Eustache. Monsieur Jacques Courbé sat astride the dog's broad back, as he had so often done in the circus ring. He held a tiny drawn sword, his shoe-button eyes seemed to reflect its steely glitter.

The dwarf brought the dog to a halt in the middle of the room and took in, at a single glance, the prostrate figure of Jeanne Marie. St. Eustache, too, seemed to take silent note of it. The stiff hair on his back rose up, he showed his long white fangs hungrily and his eyes glowed like two live coals.

"So I find you *thus,* madame!" Monsieur Jacques Courbé said at last. "It is fortunate that I have a charger here who can scent out my enemies as well as hunt them down in the open. Without him, I might have had some difficulty in discovering you. Well, the little game is up. I find you with your lover!"

"Simon Lafleur is not my lover!" she sobbed. "I have not seen him once since I married you until tonight! I swear it!"

"Once is enough," the dwarf said grimly. "The impudent stableboy must be chastised!"

"Oh, spare him!" Jeanne Marie implored. "Do not harm him, I beg of you! It is not his fault that I came! I—"

But at this point Simon Lafleur drowned her out in a roar of laughter.

"Ho, ho!" he roared, putting his hands on his hips. "You would chastise me, eh? *Nom d'un chien!* Don't try your circus tricks on *me!* Why, hop-o-my-thumb, you who ride on a dog's back like a flea, out of this room before I squash you! Begone, melt, fade away!" He paused, expanded his barrel-like chest, puffed out his cheeks and blew a great breath at the dwarf. "Blow away, insect," he bellowed, "lest I put my heel on you!"

Monsieur Jacques Courbé was unmoved by this torrent of abuse. He sat very upright on St. Eustache's back, his tiny sword resting on his tiny shoulder.

"Are you done?" he said at last, when the bareback rider had run dry of invectives. "Very well, monsieur! Prepare to receive cavalry!" He paused for an instant, then added in a high, clear voice: "Get him, St. Eustache!"

The dog crouched and, at almost the same moment, sprang at Simon Lafleur. The bareback rider had no time to avoid him and his tiny rider. Almost instantaneously the three of them had come to death grips. It was a gory business.

Simon Lafleur, strong man as he was, was bowled over by the wolf dog's unexpected leap. St. Eustache's clashing jaws closed on his right arm and crushed it to the bone. A moment later the dwarf, still clinging to his dog's back, thrust the point of his tiny sword into the body of the prostrate bareback rider.

Simon Lafleur struggled valiantly, but to no purpose. Now he felt the fetid breath of the dog fanning his neck and the wasp-like sting of the dwarf's blade, which this time found a mortal spot. A convulsive tremor shook him and he rolled over on his back. The circus Romeo was dead.

Monsieur Jacques Courbé cleansed his sword on a kerchief of lace, dismounted and approached Jeanne Marie. She was still crouching on the floor, her eyes closed, her head held tightly between both hands. The dwarf touched her imperiously on the broad shoulder which had so often carried him.

"Madame," he said, "we now can return home. You must be

more careful hereafter. *Ma foi,* it is an ungentlemanly business cutting the throats of stable-boys!"

She rose to her feet, like a large trained animal at the word of command.

"You wish to be carried?" she said between livid lips.

"Ah, that is true, madame," he murmured. "I was forgetting our little wager. Ah, yes! Well, you are to be congratulated, madame —you have covered nearly half the distance."

"Nearly half the distance," she repeated in a lifeless voice.

"Yes, madame," Monsieur Jacques Courbé continued. "I fancy that you will be quite a docile wife by the time you have done." He paused and then added reflectively: "It is truly remarkable how speedily one can ride the devil out of a woman—with spurs!"

Papa Copo had been spending a convivial evening at the Sign of the Wild Boar. As he stepped out into the street he saw three familiar figures preceding him—a tall woman, a tiny man and a large dog with upstanding ears. The woman carried the man on her shoulder, the dog trotted at her heels.

The circus owner came to a halt and stared after them. His round eyes were full of childish astonishment.

"Can it be?" he murmured. "Yes, it is! Three old friends! And so Jeanne Marie still carries him! Ah, but she should not poke fun at Monsieur Jacques Courbé! He is so sensitive; but, alas, they are the kind that are always henpecked!"

Night Bus
(It Happened One Night)

Samuel Hopkins Adams

Frank Capra's It Happened One Night *(1934) was the biggest "sleeper" in the history of American cinema. The film was conceived as no more than a standard light comedy, and was almost not made at all. Two other bus-trip films, the justly forgotten* Fugitive Lovers *and* Cross-Country Cruise, *had been released the previous year, and Columbia's Harry Cohn feared a glut on the market. Casting was a major obstacle. Myrna Loy, Margaret Sullavan, Miriam Hopkins, and Constance Bennett all turned down the female lead before Claudette Colbert accepted the role under the strict condition that she be released within four weeks, to allow her to spend the 1933 Christmas holiday in Sun Valley. On her arrival at the resort, she is reported to have said: "Am I glad to get here. I just finished the worst picture in the world." Her costar, Clark Gable, was on loan to Columbia from MGM, and he was decidedly sullen about what he considered exile to an inferior studio. And yet, a year after its release, on February 27, 1935,* It Happened One Night *won all five of the major Academy Awards: Best Picture, Best Director, Best Actress, Best Actor, and Best Writer (Robert Riskin), and it remains the only film ever to accomplish this coup.*

The film lacks most of the trappings of a major Hollywood production. Production values are only average, there is no use of spectacle or lavish setting, and its pacing and impact are low-key. But Gable and Colbert are ideal in their roles; their teamwork is marvelous as they take their characters from tense strangers to affectionate lovers. Capra's direction takes no chances, risks no experiments, but makes no errors. The script is literate, witty, and well-paced, and if the ending is predictable, it also satisfies. The film is fantasy, but it is fantasy cloaked in a finely wrought created reality, peopled by strong personalities, centering on incidents made plausible. Otis C. Ferguson, writing in The New Republic *in 1934, grudgingly calls the film "better than it has any right to be" and pinpoints the reason. "What the picture as a whole shows is that by changing such types as the usual pooh-bah father and city editor into people with some wit and feeling . . . and by casting actors who are thoroughly up to the work of acting, you can make some rather comely and greenish grasses grow where there was only alkali dust before."*

A second reason for the film's appeal on first release was its perceptive response to contemporary audience mood. Made when the nation was deep in the Great Depression, It Happened One Night *offered the relief of fantasy without resorting to characters and incidents wholly alien to the moviegoer's experience. It is a film about escape, but the getaway vehicle is not a plane or a glamorous yacht but a night bus moving through a world of rainstorms, rural depots, and tourist cabins. The film infuses these mundane settings with the glow of honest romance. The principals persevere and finally triumph, despite being broke.*

It Happened One Night *is the most literal film adaptation represented in this collection. Samuel Hopkins Adams's "Night Bus" (the film's title was changed to remove the word* bus *in deference to Harry Cohn's prejudice) amounts almost to a scenario, a detailed treatment ready for scripting. Films of the thirties obviously influenced Adams's prose. As in film, his story has no consistent point of view, allowing an even balance between the two man figures. The primary purpose of Adams's sparingly used exposition is to move the characters along toward New York; as in the film, the bus trip is a backdrop against which the two principals develop. Characterization depends in large part on stylized dialogue: snappy, flippant, and hard-boiled, yet sounding realistic.*

Robert Riskin's script sharpens the dialogue with an ear toward making it more spoken, less written, and adapts Adams's already visual scenes to exploit the film medium. But every important aspect of the film, from characterization through plot to resolution, including the famous "walls of Jericho" scene, is either directly stated or strongly suggested by the story. The greatest change is in the character of Peter Warne, a sort of high-class gadabout in the story. In an early version of the screenplay, Warne becomes a Bohemian Greenwich Village painter, but this characterization was rightly rejected as too outré *to evoke the audience's sympathy. A far better choice is his incarnation as a reporter, a working-man clearly distinct from Colbert's disgruntled heiress. This aspect of the film, the working stiff wooing and winning the beautiful rich woman, makes* It Happened One Night *a strong affirmation of the American myth of egalitarian democracy, a theme closer to the surface in Capra films such as* Mr. Deeds Goes to Town *(1936),* You Can't Take It with You *(1938),* Mr. Smith Goes to Washington *(1939), and* Meet John Doe *(1941).*

Whether It Happened One Night *is the archetype of screwball comedy, as some critics have suggested, is arguable. It is a bit too sedate, too easygoing, to be considered in the same category as such classics of the form as Howard Hawks's* Bringing Up Baby *(1938) and* His Girl Friday. *(1940). But it certainly provided a platform for the ascension of a new kind of sophisticated light romance, typified in the William Powell–Myrna Loy "Thin Man" series, and the musicals of Fred Astaire and Ginger Rogers.* It Happened One Night *is at bottom a version of the "boy meets, loses, wins girl" formula, but one that lends new spark to this oldest of storytelling ideas. The success of the film depends as much as anything on its ability, even today, to delight, transport, and enchant audiences.*

NIGHT BUS

Through the resonant cave of the terminal, a perfunctory voice boomed out something about Jacksonville, points north, and New York. The crowd at the rail seethed. At the rear, Mr. Peter Warne hoisted the battered weight of his carryall, resolutely declining a porter's aid. Too bad he hadn't come earlier; he'd have drawn a better seat. Asperities of travel, however, meant little to his seasoned endurance.

Moreover, he was inwardly fortified by what the advertisement vaunted as "The Best Fifteen-cent Dinner in Miami; Wholesome,

Clean and Plentiful." The sign knew. Appetite sated, ticket paid for, a safe if small surplus in a secure pocket; on the whole, he was content with life.

Behind him stood and, if truth must be told, shoved a restive girl. Like him she carried her own luggage, a dressing case, small and costly. Like him she had paid for her ticket to New York. Her surplus, however, was a fat roll of high-caste bills. Her dinner at the ornate Seafoam Club had cost somebody not less than ten dollars. But care sat upon her somber brow, and her expression was a warning to all and sundry to keep their distance. She was far from being content with life.

All chairs had been filled when Peter Warne threaded the aisle, having previously tossed his burden into an overhead bracket. Only the rear bench, stretching the full width of the car, offered any space. Three passengers had already settled into it; there was accommodation for two more, but the space was piled full of baled newspapers.

"Hi!" said the late arrival cheerfully to the uniformed driver, who stood below on the pavement looking bored. "I'd like one of these seats."

The driver turned a vacant gaze upon him and turned away again.

"Have this stuff moved, won't you?" requested the passenger, with unimpaired good humor.

The official offered a fair and impartial view of a gray-clad back.

Mr. Warne reflected. "If you want a thing well done, do it yourself," he decided. Still amiable, he opened the window and tossed out four bundles in brisk succession.

Upon this, the occupant of the uniform evinced interest. "Hey! What d'you think you're doin'?" He approached, only to stagger back under the impact of another bale which bounded from his shoulder. With a grunt of rage, he ran around to the rear door, yanked it open and pushed his way in, his face red and threatening.

Having, meantime, disposed of the remainder of the papers, Mr. Warne turned, thrust his hand into his rear pocket, and waited. The driver also waited, lowering but uncertain. Out popped the hand, grasping nothing more deadly than a notebook.

"Well, come ahead," said its owner.

"Come ahead with what?"

"You were figuring to bust me in the jaw, weren't you?"

"Yes; and maybe I *am* goin' to bust you in the jor."

"Good!" He made an entry in the book. "I need the money."

The other goggled. "What money?"

"Well, say ten thousand dollars damages. Brutal and un-provoked assault upon helpless passenger. It ought to be worth that. Eh?"

The official wavered, torn between caution and vindictiveness. A supercilious young voice in the aisle behind Peter Warne said: "Do you mind moving aside?"

Peter Warne moved. The girl glided into the corner he had so laboriously cleared for himself. Peter raised his cap.

"Take my seat, madam," he invited, with empressement. She bestowed upon him a faintly speculative glance, indicating that he was of a species unknown to her, and turned to the window. He sat down in the sole remaining place.

The bus started.

Adjustment to the motion of ten tons on wheels is largely a matter of technique and experience. Toughened traveler as he was, Peter Warne sat upright, swaying from the hips as if on well-oiled hinges. Not so the girl at his side. She undertook to relax into her corner with a view to forgetting her troubles in sleep. This was a major error. She was shuttled back and forth between the wall and her neighbor until her exasperation reached the point of protest.

"Tell that man to drive slower," she directed Peter.

"It may surprise you, but I doubt if he'd do it for me."

"Oh, of course! You're afraid of him. I could see that." Leaning wearily away, she said something not so completely under her breath but that Peter caught the purport of it.

"I suspect," he observed unctuously and with intent to annoy, "that you are out of tune with the Infinite."

Unwitherable though his blithe spirit was, it felt the scorch of her glare. Only too obviously he was, at that moment, the focal point for a hatred which included the whole universe. Something must have seriously upset a disposition which, he judged, was hardly inured to accepting gracefully the contrarieties of a maladjusted world.

She looked like that. Her eyes were dark and wide beneath brows that indicated an imperious temper. The long, bold sweep of the cheek was deeply tanned and ended in a chin which obviously expected to have its own way. But the mouth was broad, soft and generous. Peter wondered what it would look like when, as, and if it smiled. He didn't think it likely that he would find out.

Beyond Fort Lauderdale the bus was resuming speed when the feminine driver of a sports roadster, disdaining the formality of a signal, took a quick turn and ran the heavier vehicle off the road. There was a bump, a light crash, a squealing of brakes, the bus lurched to a stop with a tire ripped loose. After a profane inspection, the driver announced a fifteen-minute wait.

They were opposite that sign manual of Florida's departed boom days, a pair of stone pillars leading into a sidewalked wilderness and flanked by two highly ornamental lamp-posts without glass or wiring. The girl got out for a breath of air, set her dressing case at her feet and leaned against one of the monuments to perishable optimism. As she disembarked, her neighbor, in a spirit of unappreciated helpfulness, had advised her to walk up and down; it would save her from cramps later on.

Just for that she wouldn't do it. He was too officious, that young man. Anyway, the fewer human associations she suffered, the better she would like it. She had a hate on the whole race. Especially men. With a total lack of interest, she observed the parade of her fellow wayfarers up and down the road, before shutting them out from her bored vision.

A shout startled her. The interfering stranger on the opposite side of the road had bounded into the air as if treacherously stabbed from behind, and was now racing toward her like a bull at full charge. At the same time she was aware of a shadow moving away from her elbow and dissolving into the darkness beyond the gates. Close to her, the sprinter swerved, heading down the deserted avenue. Beyond him she heard a crash of brush. His foot caught in a projecting root and he went headlong, rising to limp forward a few yards and give it up with a ruefully shaken head.

"Lost him," he said, coming opposite her.

"I don't know why that should interest me." She hoped that she sounded as disagreeable as she felt. And she did.

"All right," he replied shortly, and made as if to go on, but changed his mind. "He got your bag," he explained.

"Oh!" she ejaculated, realizing that that important equipment was indeed missing. "Who?" she added feebly.

"I don't know his name and address. The thin-faced bird who sat in front of you."

"Why didn't you catch him?" she wailed. "What'll I do now?"

"Did it have much in it?"

"All my things."

"Your money and ticket?"

"Not my ticket; I've got that."

"You can wire for money from Jacksonville, you know."

"Thank you. I can get to New York all right," she returned, with deceptive calm, making a rapid calculation based on the six or eight dollars which she figured (by a considerable overestimate) were still left her.

"Shall I report your loss at the next stop?"

"Please don't." She was unnecessarily vehement. One might almost suppose the suggestion had alarmed her.

Joining the others, she climbed aboard. The departed robber had left a chair vacant next the window. One bit of luck, anyway; now she could get away from that rear seat and her friendly neighbor. She transferred herself, only to regret the change bitterly before ten miles had been covered. For she now had the chair above the curve of the wheel, which is the least comfortable of bus seats. In that rigorously enforced distortion of the body she found her feet asleep, her legs cramped. Oh, for the lesser torments of the place she had so rashly abandoned!

Twisting her stiffening neck, she looked back. The seat was still vacant. The chatty young man seemed asleep.

Lapsing into the corner, she prepared for a night of heroism. The bus fled fast through the dark and wind. Exigencies of travel she had known before; once she had actually slept in the lower berth of a section, all the drawing-rooms and compartments being sold out. But that was less cramped than her present seat. Just the same, she would have stood worse rather than stay at home after what had happened!

If only she had brought something to read. She surveyed her fellow passengers, draped in widely diverse postures. Then the miracle began to work within her. She grew drowsy. It was not so much sleep as the reflex anaesthetic of exhaustion. Consciousness passed from her.

Sun rays struck through the window upon her blinking lids. White villas slid by. A milk cart rattled past. Stiff and dazed, she felt as if her legs had been chilled into paralysis, but all the upper part of her was swathed in mysterious warmth. What were these brown, woolly folds?

The tanned, quick-fingered hands explored, lifted a sleeve which flopped loose, discovered a neatly darned spot; another; a third. It had seen hard service, that garment which wrapped her. She thought, with a vague pleasure of the senses, that it had taken on a sturdy personality of its own connected with tobacco and wood smoke and strong soap; the brisk, faintly troubling smell of clean masculinity. She liked it, that sweater.

From it, her heavy eyes moved to her neighbor who was still asleep. By no stretch of charity could he be called an ornament to the human species. His physiognomy was blunt, rough and smudgy with bristles; his hair reddish and uncompromisingly straight.

Nevertheless, a guarded approval might be granted to the setting of the eyes under a freckled forehead, and the trend of the mouth suggested strong, even teeth within. Nose and chin betokened a careless good humor. As for the capable hands, there was no blinking the stains upon them.

His clothing was rough and baggy, but neat enough except for a gaping rent along one trouser leg which he had come by in chasing her thief. For the first time in her life, she wished that she knew how to sew. This surprised her when she came to consider it later.

For the moment she only smiled. It was a pity that Peter Warne could not have waked up at the brief, warm interval before her lips drooped back to weariness.

Nearly an hour later he roused himself at the entrance to Jacksonville where a change of lines was due, and his first look rested upon a wan and haggard face.

"Breakfast!" said he, with energy and anticipation.

The face brightened. "The Windsor is a good place," stated its owner.

"I wouldn't doubt it for a minute. So is Hungry Joe's."

"Do you expect me to eat at some horrid beanery?"

"Beans have their virtue. But oatmeal and coffee give you the most for your money."

"Oh, money! I'd forgotten about money."

"If you want to change your mind and wire for it—"

"I don't. I want to eat."

"With me?"

She speculated as to whether this might be an invitation; decided that it probably wasn't. "If the place is clean."

"It's cleaner than either of us at the present moment of speaking," he grinned.

Thus recalled to considerations of femininity, she said: "I'll bet I look simply *terrible!*"

"Well, I wouldn't go as far as that," was the cautious reply.

"Anyhow, there's one thing I've got to have right away."

"What's that?"

"If you must know, it's a bath."

"Nothing doing. Bus leaves in fifty minutes."

"We can tell the driver to wait."

"Certainly, we can tell him. But there's just a possibility that he might not do it."

This was lost upon her. "Of course he'll do it. People always wait for me," she added with sweet self-confidence. "If they didn't, I'd never get anywhere."

"This is a hard-boiled line," he explained patiently. "The man would lose his job if he held the bus, like as not."

She yawned. "He could get another, couldn't he?"

"Oh, of course! Just like that. You haven't happened to hear of a thing called unemployment, have you?"

"Oh, that's just socialistic talk. There are plenty of jobs for people who really want to work."

"Yes? Where did you get that line of wisdom?"

She was bored and showed it in her intonation. "Why, everybody knows that. Bill was saying the other day that most of these people are idle because they're just waiting for the dole or something."

"Who's Bill?"

"My oldest brother."

"Oh! And I suppose Bill works?"

"We-ell, he plays polo. Almost every day."

Mr. Warne made a noise like a trained seal.

"What did you say?"

"I said, 'here's the eatery.' Or words to that effect."

The place was speckless. Having a healthy young appetite, the girl disdained to follow the meager example of her escort, and ordered high, wide and handsome. Directing that his fifteen-cent selection be held for five minutes, Peter excused himself with a view to cleaning up. He returned to find his companion gone.

"At the Windsor, having my bath," a scrawl across the bill of fare enlightened him. "Back in half an hour."

That, he figured after consultation of his watch, would leave her just four minutes and twenty seconds to consume an extensive breakfast and get around the corner to the terminal, assuming that she lived up to her note, which struck him as, at the least, doubtful. Well, let the little fool get out of it as best she could. Why bother?

Peter ate slowly, while reading the paper provided free for patrons. At the end of twenty-five minutes, he was craning his neck out of the window. A slight figure turned the corner. Relief was in the voice which bade the waiter rush the order. The figure approached—and passed. Wrong girl. Peter cursed.

Time began to race. Less than five minutes to go now. Half of that was the minimum allowance for getting to the starting place. Peter bore his grip to the door, ready for a flying take-off, in case she appeared. In case she didn't. . . . People always waited for her, did they? Well, he'd be damned if he would! In one short minute he would be leaving. Thirty seconds; twenty; fifteen; five. Sister Ann, do you see anything moving? *Malbrouck s'en va-t'en guerre.* No dust along the road? We're off!

Such was the intention. But something interfered; an intangible something connected with the remembrance of soft contours on a young, sleeping face, of wondering eyes slowly opened. Peter dashed his valise upon the floor, kicked it, cast himself into a chair and sulked. His disposition was distinctly tainted when the truant made triumphal entrance. She was freshened and groomed and radiant, a festal apparition. Up rose then Mr. Warne, uncertain where to begin. She forestalled him.

"Why, how nice you look!" By virtue of his five minutes, the freedom of the washroom, and a pocket kit, he had contrived to shave, brush up, and make the best of a countenance which, if by strict standards unbeautiful, did not wholly lack points. "How much time have I for breakfast?"

"Plenty," barked Peter.

"Swell! I'm starving. I *did* hurry."

"Did you?" he inquired, between his teeth.

"Of course I did. Didn't you just say I had plenty of time?"

"You certainly have. All day."

She set down her coffee cup. "Why, I thought our bus—"

"Our bus is on its way to New York. The next one leaves at eight tonight."

"I do think you might have telephoned them to wait," she protested. A thought struck her impressionable mind. "Why, you missed it, too!"

"So I did. Isn't that extraordinary!"

"Because you were waiting for me?"

"Something of the sort."

"It was awfully nice of you. But why?"

"Because the poor damfool just didn't have the heart to leave a helpless little hick like you alone," he explained.

"I believe you're sore at me."

"Oh, not in the least! Only at myself for getting involved in such a mix-up."

"Nobody asked you to miss the old bus," she stated warmly. "Why did you?"

"Because you remind me of my long-lost angel mother, of course. Don't you ever go to the movies? Now, do you still want to go to New York?"

"We-ell; I've got my ticket. I suppose that's still good."

"Up to ten days. At this rate, it'll take us all of that to get there. The thing is to figure out what to do now."

"Let's go to the races," said she.

"On what?" he inquired.

"I've got some money left."

"How much?"

She examined her purse. "Why, there's only a little over four dollars," she revealed in disappointed accents.

"How far d'you think that'll take you?"

"I could bet it on the first race. Maybe I'd win."

"Maybe you'd lose, too."

"I thought you had that kind of disposition the minute I set eyes on you," she complained. "Pessimist!"

"Economist," he corrected.

"Just as bad. Anyway, we've got a whole day to kill. What's your dashing idea of the best way to do it?"

"A park bench."

"What do you do on a park bench?"

"Sit."

"It sounds dumb."

"It's cheap."

"I hate cheap things, but just to prove I'm reasonable I'll try it for a while."

He led her a block or so to the area of palms and flowers facing the Windsor where they found a bench vacant and sat down. Peter slouched restfully. His companion fidgeted.

"Maybe the band will play by and by," said he encouragingly.

"Wouldn't that be nah-ice!" murmured the girl, and Peter wondered whether a hard slap would break her beyond repair.

"How old are you, anyway?" he demanded. "Fifteen?"

"I'm twenty-one, if you want to know."

"And I suppose it cost your family a bunch of money to bring you to your present fine flower of accomplished womanhood."

"You shouldn't try to be poetic. It doesn't, somehow, go with your face."

"Never mind my face. If I take you to the station and buy you a ticket to Miami—day coach, of course," he interpolated, "will you go back, like a sensible girl?"

"No, I won't. Think how silly I'd look, sneaking back after having—"

"You'd look sillier trying to get to New York at your present rate of expenditure," he warned, as she failed to complete her objection.

"If you can put up the price of a ticket to Miami," said she, with a luminous thought, "you might better lend me the money. I'll pay you back—twice over."

"Tha-anks."

"Meaning you won't?"

"Your powers of interpretation are positively uncanny."

"I might have known you wouldn't." She turned upon him an offended back.

"My name," he said to the back, "is Peter Warne."

A shrug indicated her total indifference to this bit of information. Then she rose and walked away.

He called after her: "I'll be here at six-thirty. Try not to keep me waiting *more* than half an hour."

Just for that—thought the girl—I'll be an hour late.

But she was not. It annoyed her to find how a day could drag in a town where she knew nobody. She went to a movie. She lunched. She went to another movie. She took a walk. Still, it was not yet six o'clock.

At six-thirty-one she started for the park. At six-thirty-four she was at the spot, or what she had believed to be the spot, but which she decided couldn't be, since no Peter Warne was visible. Several other benches were in sight of the vacant band stand. She made the rounds of all. None was occupied by the object of her search. Returning to the first one, she sat down in some perturbation. Perhaps something had happened to Peter Warne. Nothing short of an accident could explain his absence.

There she sat for what seemed like the better part of an hour, until an ugly suspicion seeped into her humiliated mind that she had been left in the lurch. And by a man. A clock struck seven. She rose uncertainly.

"Oh!" she said, in a long exhalation.

Peter Warne was strolling around the corner of the stand.

"Where have you been?" she demanded, like an outraged empress.

He remained unstricken. "You were late," he observed.

"I wasn't. What if I was? Only a minute."

"Nearer five."

"How do you know? You must have been watching. You were here all the time. And you let me think you'd gone away. Oh! Oh! *Oh!*"

"You're pretty casual about keeping other people waiting, you know."

"That's different." She spoke with a profound conviction of privilege.

"I'm not going to argue that with you. Have you any money left?"

"A dollar and four cents," she announced, after counting and recounting.

Coolly he took her purse, transferred the coins to his pocket, and handed it back. "Confiscated for the common necessity," he stated, and she refrained from protest. "Come along."

She fell into step with him. "Could I please have something to eat?"

"Such is the idea. We'll try Hungry Joe's again."

This time he did the ordering for both of them: soup, hash, thick, pulpy griddle cakes and coffee. Total, sixty-five cents. Fortified by this unfamiliar but filling diet, she decided to give Mr. Peter Warne a more fitting sense of their relative status. Some degree of respect was what her soul demanded to bolster her tottering self-confidence. She had heard that a married woman was in a better position to assert herself than a girl. On that basis she would impress Peter.

"You've been treating me like a child," she complained. "You may as well understand right now that I'm not. I'm a married woman. I'm Mrs. Corcoran Andrews." She had selected this name because Corcoran, who was her third or fourth cousin, had been pestering her to marry him for a year. So he wouldn't mind. The effect was immediate.

"Huh?" jerked out the recipient of the information. "I thought Corker Andrews married a pink chorine."

"They're divorced. Do you *know* Corker?"

"Sure I know Corker."

"You're not a *friend* of his?" The implication of her surprise was unflattering.

"I didn't say that." He grinned. "The fact is, I blacked his boots once for three months."

"What did you do that for?"

"What does a man black boots for? Because I had to. So you're Cor—Mr. Andrews' wife." His regard rested upon her small, strong, deeply browned left hand. She hastily pulled it away.

"My ring's in the bag that was stolen."

"Of course," he remarked. (What did he mean by that?) "Time to be moving."

They emerged into a droning pour of rain. "Can't you get a taxi?" she asked.

"We walk," was the uncompromising reply, as he tucked his hand beneath her arm. They caught the bus with little to spare, and again drew the rear seat.

Outside, someone was saying: "Since Thursday. Yep; a hundred miles up the road. There'll be bridges out."

Feeling sleepy and indifferent, she paid no heed. She lapsed into a doze which, beginning bumpily against the wall, subsided into the unrealized comfort of his shoulder.

Water splashing on the floor boards awakened her; it was followed by the whir of the wheels, spinning in reverse.

"Got out by the skin of our teeth," said Peter Warne's lips close to her ear.

"What is it?"

"Some creek or other on the rampage. We'll not make Charleston this night."

He went forward, returning with dreary news. "We're going to stay in the nearest village. It looks like a night in the bus for us."

"Oh, no! I can't stand this bus any longer. I want to go to bed," she wailed.

He fetched out his small notebook and fell to figuring. "It'll be close reckoning," he said, scowling at the estimate. "But if you feel that way about it—" To the driver he shouted: "Let us off at Dake's place."

"What's that?"

"Tourist camp."

"Aren't they awful places? They look it."

"The Dake's chain are clean and decent enough for anybody,"

he answered in a tone so decisive that she followed him meekly out into the night.

Leading her to a sort of waiting room, he vanished into an office, where she could hear his voice in colloquy with an unseen man. The latter emerged with a flash light and indicated that they were to follow. Her escort said to her, quick and low: "What's your name?"

"I told you," she returned, astonished. "I'm Mrs. Cor—"

"Your first name."

"Oh. Elspeth. Why? What's the matter?" She regarded him curiously.

"I had to register as Mr. and Mrs.," he explained nervously. "It's usual for a husband to know his wife's first name."

She asked coldly: "What is the idea?"

"Do you mind," he urged, "talking it over after we get inside?"

Their guide opened the door of a snug cabin, lighted a light and gave Elspeth a shock by saying: "Good night, Mrs. Warne. Good night, Mr. Warne. I hope you find everything comfortable."

Elspeth looked around upon the bare but neat night's lodging: two bunks separated by a scant yard of space, a chair, four clothes hooks, a shelf with a mirror above it. Peter set down his carryall and sat at the head of a bunk.

"Now," said he, "you're free to come or go."

"Go where?" she asked blankly.

"Nowhere, I hope. But it's up to you. You're a lot safer here with me," he added, "than you would be by yourself."

"But why did you have to register that way? To save appearances?"

"To save two dollars," was his grim correction, "which is more to the point. That's the price of a cabin."

"But *you're* not going to stay *here.*"

"Now, let me explain this to you in words of one syllable. We've got darn little money at best. The family purse simply won't stand separate establishments. Get that into your head. And I'm not spending the night outside in this storm!"

"But I—I don't know anything about you."

"All right. Take a look." He held the lamp up in front of what developed into a wholly trustworthy grin.

"I'm looking." Her eyes were wide, exploring, steady, and—there was no doubt about it in his mind—innocent.

"Well; do I look like the villain of the third act?"

"No; you don't." She began to giggle. "You look like a plumber. A nice, honest, intelligent, high-principled plumber."

"The washroom," he stated in the manner of a guidebook, "will be found at the end of this row of shacks."

While she was gone, he extracted a utility kit from his bag, tacked two nails to the end walls, fastened a cord to them and hung a spare blanket, curtain-wise, upon it.

"The walls of Jericho," was his explanation, as she came in. "Solid porphyry and marble. Proof against any assault."

"Grand! What's this?" She recoiled a little from a gaudy splotch ornamenting the foot of her bed.

"Pajamas. My spare set. Hope you can sleep in them."

"I could sleep," she averred with conviction, "in a straitjacket." She had an impulse of irrepressible mischief. "About those walls of Jericho, Peter. You haven't got a trumpet in that big valise of yours, have you?"

"Not even a mouth organ."

"I was just going to tell you not to blow it before eight o'clock."

"Oh, shut up and go to sleep."

So they both went to sleep.

Something light and small, falling upon her blanket, woke Elspeth.

"Wha'za'?" she murmured sleepily.

"Little present for you," answered Peter.

"Oh-h-h-h-h-h!" It was a rapturous yawn. "I never slept so hard in my *whole* life. What time is it?"

"Eight o'clock, and all's well before the walls of Jericho."

She ripped the small package open, disclosing a toothbrush. "What a snappy present! Where did it come from?"

"Village drug store. I'm just back."

"How nice of you! But can we afford it?" she asked austerely.

"Certainly not. It's a wild extravagance. But I'm afraid to cut you off from all luxuries too suddenly. Now, can you get bathed and dressed in twenty minutes?"

"Don't be silly! I'm not even up yet."

"One—two—three—four—"

"What's the count about?"

"On the stroke of ten I'm going to break down the wall, drag you out and dress you myself if neces—"

"Why, you big bum! I believe you wou—"

"—five—six—seven—"

"Wait a *minute!*"

"—eight—ni-i-i-i—"

A blanket-wrapped figure dashed past him and down to the showers. After a record bath she sprinted back to find him squatted above a tiny double grill which he had evidently extracted from that wonder-box of a valise.

"What we waste on luxuries we save on necessities," he pointed out. "Two eggs, one nickel. Two rolls, three cents. Tea from the Warne storehouse. Accelerate yourself, my child."

Odors, wafted from the cookery to her appreciative nostrils, stimulated her to speed. Her reward was a nod of approval from her companion and the best egg that had ever caressed her palate.

"Now you wash up the dishes while I pack. The bus is due in ten minutes."

"But they're greasy," she shuddered.

"That's the point. Get 'em clean. Give 'em a good scraping first."

He vanished within. Well, she would try. Setting her teeth, she scraped and scrubbed and wiped and, at the end, invited his inspection, confident of praise. When, with a pitying glance, he silently did over two plates and a cup before stacking and packing them, she was justifiably hurt. "There's no suiting some people," she reflected aloud and bitterly.

Flood news from the northward, they learned on boarding the bus, compelled a re-routing far inland. Schedules were abandoned. If they made Charleston by nightfall they'd do pretty well, the driver said. Elspeth, refreshed by her long sleep, didn't much care. Peter would bring them through, she felt. . . .

Yellow against the murk of the night sky shone the lights of

Charleston. While Peter was at the terminal office making inquiries, Elspeth, on the platform, heard her name pronounced in astonishment. From a group of company chauffeurs a figure was coming toward her.

"Andy Brinkerhoff! What are you doing in that uniform?"

"Working. Hello, Elspie! How's things?"

"Working? For the bus company?"

"Right," he chirped. "This being the only job in sight and the family having gone bust, I grabbed it. What-ho!"

"How awful!"

"Oh, I dunno. I'd rather be the driver than a passenger. What brought you so low, Elspie?"

"Sh! I've beat it from home."

"Gee! Alone?"

"Yes. That is—yes. Oh, Andy! I never dreamed how awful this kind of travel could be."

"Why don't you quit it, then?"

"No money."

The lad's cherubic face became serious. "I'll raise some dough from the bunch. You could catch the night plane back."

For a moment she wavered. In the distance she sighted Peter Warne scanning the place. There was a kind of expectant brightness on his face. She couldn't quite picture him going on alone in the bus with that look still there. She flattered herself that she had something to do with its presence.

"I'll stick," she decided to herself, but aloud: "Andy, did you ever hear of a man named Peter Warne?"

"Warne? No. What about him?"

"Nothing. What's a telegram to Miami cost?"

"How much of a telegram?"

"Oh, I don't know. Give me a dollar." And then she wrote out a message:

Mr. Corcoran D. Andrews, Bayside Place, Miami Beach, Fla.
Who what and why is Peter Warne Stop Important I should know Stop On my way somewhere and hope to get there some time Stop This is strictly confidential so say nothing to nobody Stop Having a helluva-ruff time and liking it Stop Wire Bessie Smith, Western Union, Raleigh, N.C.

El

"Oh, here you are," said Peter, barely giving her time to smuggle the paper into Brinkerhoff's hand. "We're going on. Think you can stand it?"

"I s'pose I've got to," replied Elspeth.

Incertitude had discouraged about half the passengers. Consequently, the pair secured a window chair apiece. At the moment of starting there entered a spindly young male all aglow with self-satisfaction which glossed him over from his cocky green hat to his vivid spats.

By the essential law of his being it was inevitable that, after a survey of the interior, he should drop easily into a seat affording an advantageous view of the snappy-looking girl who seemed to be traveling alone. He exhumed a magazine from his grip and leaned across.

"Pardon *me.* But would you care to look at this?"

Elspeth wouldn't but she looked at Mr. Horace Shapley with attention which he mistook for interest. He transferred himself with suitable preliminaries to the vacant chair at her side and fell into confidential discourse.

His line, so Elspeth learned, was typewriter supplies and he hailed from Paterson, New Jersey. Business was punk but if you knew how to make yourself solid with the girl behind the machine (and that was his specialty, believe *him*), you could make expenses and a little bit on the side.

Elspeth glanced across at Peter to see how he regarded this development. Peter was asleep. All right, then; if he wanted to leave her unprotected against the advances of casual strangers. Unfamiliar with this particular species, she was mildly curious about its hopeful antics.

She smiled politely, asked a question or two, and Mr. Shapley proceeded to unfold romantic adventures and tales of life among the typewriters. The incidents exhibited a similarity of climax: "And did *she* fall for me! Hot momma!"

"It must be a fascinating business," commented his listener.

"And how! I'll bet," said Mr. Shapley, with arch insinuation, "you could be a naughty little girl yourself, if nobody was lookin'." He offered her a cigaret. She took it with a nod and tossed it across the aisle, catching the somnolent Peter neatly in the neck. He woke up.

"Hi!"

"Come over here, Peter." He staggered up. "I want you to know" (with a slight emphasis on the word) "Mr. Shapley."

"Pleezetomeetcha," mumbled that gentleman in self-refuting accents.

"He thinks," pursued Elspeth, "that I'm probably a naughty little girl. Am I?"

"You can't prove it by me," said Peter.

"Say, what's the idea?" protested the puzzled Mr. Shapley.

"I don't like him; he nestles," stated Elspeth.

"Aw, now, sister! I was just nicin' you along and—"

"Nicing me along!" Elspeth repeated the phrase with icy disfavor. "Peter; what are you going to do about this?"

Peter ruminated. "Change seats with you," he said brightly.

"Oh!" she choked as she rose. As she stepped across her neighbor to gain the aisle, he gave a yelp and glared savagely, though it was presumably an accident that her sharp, high heel had landed upon the most susceptible angle of his shin. After a moment's consideration, Peter followed her to her new position.

So entered discord into that peaceful community. Mr. Shapley sulked in his chair. Elspeth gloomed in hers. Discomfort invaded Peter's amiable soul. He perceived that he had fallen short in some manner.

"What did you expect me to do about that bird?" he queried.

"Nothing."

"Well, that's what I did."

"I should say you did. If it had been me, I'd have punched his nose."

"And got into a fight. I never could see any sense in fighting unless you have to," he argued. "What happens? You both get arrested. If I got arrested and fined here, how do we eat? If they jug me, what becomes of you? Be sensible."

"Oh, you're sensible enough for both of us." It was plain, however, to the recipient of this encomium, that it was not intended as a compliment. "Never mind. What are we stopping for?"

The halt was occasioned by evil reports of the road ahead, and the chauffeur's unwillingness to risk it in darkness.

"I'll do a look-see," said Peter, and came back, pleased, to announce that there was a cheap camp around the turn. Without formality, the improvised Warne family settled in for the night.

Silence had fallen upon the little community when an appealing voice floated across the wall of their seventy-five-cent Jericho. "Peter. Pe-*ter!*"

"Mmpff."

"You're not a very inquisitive person, Peter. You haven't asked me a single question about myself."

"I did. I asked you your name."

"Because you had to. In self-protection."

"Do you want me to think up some more questions?"

She sniffed. "You might show a *little* human interest. You know, I don't like you much, Peter. But I could talk to you, if you'd let me, as freely as if you were—well, I don't know how to put it."

"Another species of animal."

"No-o-o-o. You musn't belittle yourself," said she kindly.

"I wasn't. And I didn't say an inferior species."

It took her a moment to figure this out, and then she thought she must have got it wrong. For how could his meaning possibly be that her species was the inferior? . . . Better pass that and come to her story. She began with emphasis:

"If there's one thing I can't stand, it's unfairness."

"I thought so."

"You thought *what?*"

"Somebody's been interfering with your having your own sweet way, and so you walked out on the show. What was the nature of this infringement upon the rights of American womanhood?"

"Who's making this stump speech; you or me?" she retorted. "It was about King Westley, if you want to know."

"The headline aviator?"

"Yes. He and I have been playing around together."

"How does friend husband like that?"

"Huh? Oh! Why, he's away, you see. Cruising. I'm staying with Dad."

"Then he's the one to object?"

"Yes. Dad doesn't understand me."

"Likely enough. Go ahead."

"I'll bet you're going to be dumb about this, too. Anyway, it was all right till King got the idea of finding the lost scientific expedition in South America. Venezuela, or somewhere. You know."

"Professor Schatze's? South of the Orinoco. I've read about it."

"King wants to fly down there and locate them."

"'S all right by me. But where does he figure he'll land?"

"Why, on the prairie or the pampas."

"Pampas, my glass eye! There isn't any pampas within a thousand miles of the Orinoco."

"What do you know about it?"

"I was there myself, five years ago."

"You were! What doing?"

"Oh, just snooping around."

"Maybe it wasn't the same kind of country we were going to."

"We?" She could hear a rustle and judged that he was sitting upright. She had him interested at last.

"Of course. I was going with him. Why, if we'd found the expedition I'd be another Amelia Earhart."

Again the cot opposite creaked. Its occupant had relaxed. "I guess your family needn't have lost any sleep."

"Why not?" she challenged.

"Because it's all a bluff," he returned. "Westley never took a chance in his life outside of newspaper headlines."

"I think you're positively septic. The family worried, all right. They tried to keep me from seeing him. So he took to nosing down across our place and dropping notes in the swimming pool, and my father had him arrested and grounded for reckless flying. Did you ever hear anything like that?"

"Not so bad," approved Peter.

"Oh-h-h-h! I might know you'd side against me. I suppose you'd have had me sit there and let Dad get away with it."

"Mmmmm. I can't exactly see you doing it. But why take a bus?"

"All the cars were locked up. I had to sneak out. I knew they'd watch the airports and the railroad stations, but they wouldn't think of the bus. Now you've got the whole story, do you blame me?"

"Yes."

"I do think you're unbearable. You'd probably expect me to go back."

"Certainly."

"Maybe you'd like to send me back."

"You wouldn't go. I did try, you know."

"Not alive, I wouldn't! Of *course* you wouldn't think of doing anything so improper as helping me any more."

"Sure, I will," was the cheerful response. "If you've got your mind set on getting to New York, I'll do my best to deliver you there intact. And may God have mercy on your family's soul! By the way, I suppose you left some word at home so they won't worry too much."

"I did not! I hope they worry themselves into convulsions."

"You don't seem to care much about your family," he remarked.

"Oh, Dad isn't so bad. But he always wants to boss everything. I—I expect I didn't think about his worrying. D'you think he will—much?" The query terminated in a perceptible quaver.

"Hm. I wonder if you're really such a hard-boiled little egg as you make out to be. Could you manage with a bag of pecans for dinner tomorrow?"

"Ouch! Do I have to?"

"To wire your father would come to about the price of two dinners."

"Wire him? And have him waiting in New York for me when we get there? If you do, I'll jump through the bus window and you'll never see me again."

"I see. Westley is meeting you. You don't want any interference. Is that it?"

"I left him a note," she admitted.

"Uh-huh. Now that you've got everything movable off your mind, what about a little sleep?"

"I'm for it."

Silence settled down upon the Warne menage.

Sunup brought Peter out of his bunk. From beyond the gently undulant blanket he could hear the rhythm of soft breathing. Stealthily he dressed. As he opened the door, a gust of wind twitched down the swaying screen. The girl half turned in her sleep. She smiled. Peter stood, bound in enchantment.

In something like panic he bade himself listen to sense and reason. That's a spoiled child, Peter. Bad medicine. Willful, self-centered—and sweet. (How had that slipped in?) Impractical, too.

Heaven pity the bird that takes her on! Too big a job for you, Peter, my lad, even if you could get the contract. So don't go fooling with ideas, you poor boob.

Breakfast necessities took him far afield before he acquired at a bargainer's price what he needed. Elspeth had already fished the cooking kit out of the bag and made ready in the shelter of the shack. Not a word did she say about the fallen blanket. This made Peter self-conscious. They breakfasted in some restraint.

A wild sky threatened renewal of the storm. Below the hill a shallow torrent supplanted the road for a space. Nevertheless, the bus was going on. Elspeth washed the dishes—clean, this time.

"You get out and stretch your legs while I pack," advised Peter.

As she stepped from the shack, the facile Mr. Shapley confronted her.

"The cream off the milk to you, sister," said he, with a smile which indicated that he was not one to bear a grudge. "I just want to square myself with you. If I'd known you was a married lady—"

"I'm not," returned Elspeth absently.

Mr. Shapley's eyes shifted from her to the shack. Peter's voice was raised within: "Where are your pajamas, Elspeth?"

"Airing out. I forgot 'em." She plucked them from a bush and tossed them in at the door.

"Oh-oh!" lilted Mr. Shapley, with the tonality of cynical and amused enlightenment. He went away, cocking his hat.

Warning from the bus horn brought out Peter with his bag. They took their seats and were off.

The bus' busy morning was spent mainly in dodging stray watercourses. They made Cheraw toward the middle of the afternoon. There Peter bought two pounds of pecans; a worthy nut and one which satisfies without cloying. They were to be held in reserve, in case. In case of what? Elspeth wished to be informed. Peter shook his head and said, darkly, that you never could tell.

North of Cheraw, the habits of the bus became definitely amphibian. The main route was flowing in a northeasterly direction, and every side road was a contributory stream. A forested rise of land in the distance held out hope of better things, but when they reached it they found cars parked all over the place, waiting for a road-gang to strengthen a doubtful bridge across the swollen river.

"Let's have a look at this neck of the woods," Peter suggested to Elspeth.

To determine their geographical circumstances was not difficult. Rising waters had cut off from the rest of the world a ridge, thinly oval in shape, of approximately a mile in length, and hardly a quarter of a mile across. On this were herded thirty or forty travelers, including the bus passengers.

There was no settlement of any sort within reach; only a ramshackle farmhouse surrounded by a discouraged garden. Peter, however, negotiated successfully for a small box of potatoes, remarking to his companion that there was likely to be a rise in commodity prices before the show was over.

A sound of hammering and clinking, interspersed with rugged profanity, led them to a side path. There they found a well-equipped housekeeping van, the engine of which was undergoing an operation by its owner while his motherly wife sat on the steps watching.

"Cussin' never done you any good with that machine, Abner," said she. "It ain't like a mule."

"It is like a mule. Only meaner." Abner sighted Peter. "Young man, know anything about this kind of critter?"

"Ran one once," answered Peter. He took off his coat, rolled up his sleeves, and set to prodding and poking in a professional manner. Presently the engine lifted up its voice and roared.

Elspeth, perched on a log, reflected that Peter seemed to be a useful sort of person to other people. Why hadn't he done better for himself in life? Maybe that was the reason. This was a new thought and gave her something to mull over while he worked. From the van she borrowed a basin of water, a bar of soap and a towel, and was standing by when he finished the job.

"What do I owe you, young man?" called Abner Braithe, from the van.

"Noth-*uh!*" Elspeth's well-directed elbow had reached its goal in time.

"Don't be an idiot!" she adjured him.

A conference took place.

"You see," said Peter at its close, "my—uh—wife doesn't sleep well outdoors. If you had an extra cot, now—"

"Why, we can fix that," put in Mrs. Braithe. "We haven't got any cot, but if you can sleep in a three-quarter bed—"

"We can't," said both hastily.

"We're used to twin beds," explained Elspeth.

"My wife's quite nervous," put in Peter, "and—and I snore."

"You don't," contradicted Elspeth indignantly, and got a dirty look from him.

It was finally arranged that, as payment for Peter's services, the Braithes were to divide the night into two watches; up to and after one A.M., Elspeth occupying the van bed for the second spell while Peter roosted in the bus. This being settled, the young pair withdrew to cook a three-course dinner over a fire coaxed by Peter from wet brush and a newspaper; first course, thick potato soup; second course, boiled potatoes with salt; dessert, five pecans each.

"We've been Mr. and Mrs. for pretty near three days now, Peter," remarked the girl suddenly, "and I don't know the first darn thing about you."

"What do you want to know?"

"What have you got in the line of information?"

"Not much that's exciting."

"That's too bad. I hoped you were an escaped con or something, traveling incog."

"Nothing so romantic. Just a poor but virtuous specimen of the half-employed."

"Who employs you?"

"I do. I'm a rotten employer."

"Doing what? Besides blacking boots."

"Oh, I've nothing as steady as that since. If you want to know, I've been making some experiments in the line of vegetable chemistry; pine tar, to be exact. I'm hoping to find some sucker with money to take it up and subsidize me and my process. That's what I'm going to New York to see about. Meantime," he grinned, "I'm traveling light."

"What'll the job be worth if you do get it?"

"Seven or eight thousand a year to start with," said he, with pride.

"Is *that* all?" She was scornful.

"Well, I'll be—Look here, Elspeth, I said per year."

"I heard you. My brother Bill says he can't get along on *ten* thousand. And," she added thoughtfully, "he's single."

"So am I."

"You didn't tell me that before. Not that it matters, of course. Except that your wife might misunderstand if she knew we'd been sl—traveling together."

"I haven't any wife, I tell you."

"All right; all *right!* Don't bark at me about it. It isn't my fault."

"Anything else?" he inquired with careful politeness.

"I think it's going to rain some more."

They transferred themselves to the bus and sat there until one o'clock, when he escorted her to the Braithe van. He returned to join his fellow passengers, leaving her with a sensation of lostness and desertion.

Several small streams, drunk and disorderly on spring's strong liquor, broke out of bounds in the night, came crawling down the hills and carried all before them, including the bridge whereby the marooned cars had hoped to escape.

"I don't care," said Elspeth, when the morning's news was broken to her. She was feeling gayly reckless.

"I do," returned Peter soberly.

"Oh, you're worrying about money again. What's the use of money where there's nothing to buy? We're out of the world, Peter. I like it, for a change. What's that exciting smell?"

"Fish." He pointed with pride to his fire, over which steamed a pot. Dishing up a generous portion he handed it to her on a plate. "Guaranteed fresh this morning. How do you like it?"

She tasted it. "It—it hasn't much personality. What kind of fish is it?"

"They call it mudfish, I believe. It was flopping around in a slough and I nailed it with a stick. I thought there'd be enough for dinner, too," said he, crestfallen by her lack of appreciation.

"Plenty," she agreed. "Peter, could I have four potatoes? Raw ones."

"What for?"

"I'm going marketing."

"Barter and exchange, eh? Look out that these tourists don't gyp you."

"Ma feyther's name is Alexander Bruce MacGregor Andrews," she informed him in a rich Scottish accent. "Tak' that to heart, laddie."

"I get it. You'll do."

Quenching his fire, he walked to the van. A semicircle of men and women had grouped about the door. Circulating among them, Abner Braithe was taking up a collection. Yet, it was not Sunday. The explanation was supplied when the shrewd Yankee addressed his audience.

"The morning program will begin right away. Any of you folks whose money I've missed, please raise the right hand. Other news and musical ee-vents will be on the air at five-thirty this P.M. and eight tonight. A nickel admission each, or a dime for the three performances."

Having no nickel to waste on frivolities, Peter moved on. Elspeth, triumphant, rejoined him with her booty.

Item: a small parcel of salt.

Item: a smaller parcel of pepper.

Item: a half pound of lard.

Item: two strips of fat bacon.

Item: six lumps of sugar.

"What d'ye ken about that?" she demanded. "Am I no the canny Scawtswumman?"

"You're a darn bonny one," returned Peter, admiring the flushed cheeks and brilliant eyes.

"Is this the first time you've noticed that?" she inquired impudently.

"It hadn't struck in before," he confessed.

"And now it has? Hold the thought. I can't hurt you." (He felt by no means so sure about that.) "Now Mr. Shapley"—her eyes shifted to the road up which that gentleman was approaching— "got it right away. I wonder what's his trouble."

Gratification, not trouble, signalized his expression as he sighted them. His bow to Elspeth was gravely ceremonious. He then looked at her companion.

"Could I have a minute's conversation apart with you?"

"Don't mind me," said Elspeth, and the two men withdrew a few paces.

"I dont want to butt into your and the lady's private affairs," began Mr. Shapley, "but this is business. I want to know if that lady is your wife."

"She is. Not that it's any concern of yours."

"She said this morning that she wasn't married."

"She hasn't got used to the idea yet," returned Peter, with great presence of mind. "She's only been that way a few days. Honeymoon trip."

"That's as may be," retorted the other. "Even if it's true, it wouldn't put a crimp in the reward."

"What's this?" demanded Peter, eying him in surprise. "Reward? For what?"

"Come off. You heard the raddio this morning, didn'cha?"

"No."

"Well, is that lady the daughter of Mr. A. B. M. Andrews, the yachting millionaire, or ain't she? 'Cause I know she is."

"Oh! You know that, do you! What of it?"

"Ten grand of it. That's what of it," rejoined Mr. Shapley. "For information leadin' to the dis—"

"Keep your voice down."

"Yeah. I'll keep my voice down till the time comes to let it loose. Then I'll collect on that ten thou'. They think she's kidnaped."

"What makes you so sure of your identification?"

"Full description over the air. When the specifications came across on the raddio I spotted the garments. Used to be in ladies' wear," he explained.

"If you so much as mention this to Mi—to Mrs. Warne, I'll—" began Peter.

"Don't get rough, now, brother," deprecated the reward-hunter. "I ain't lookin' for trouble. And I'm not sayin' anything to the little lady, just so long as you and me understand each other."

"What do you want me to understand?"

"That there's no use your tryin' to slip me after we get out of this place. Of course, you can make it hard or easy for me. So, if you want to play in with me and be nice, anyway—I'm ready to talk about a little cut for you . . . No? Well, suit yourself, pal. See you in the mornin'."

He chuckled himself away. Peter, weighing the situation, discovered in himself a violent distaste at the thought of Mr. Horace Shapley collecting Elspeth's family's money for the delivering up of Elspeth. In fact, it afflicted him with mingled nausea and desire for man-slaughter. Out of this unpromising combination emerged an idea. If he, Peter, could reach a wire before the pestilent Shapley, he could get in his information first and block the reward.

Should he tell Elspeth about the radio? Better not, he concluded.

It was characteristic of her and a big credit mark in his estimate of her, that she put no questions as to the interview with Shapley. She did not like that person; therefore, practically speaking, he did not exist. But the mudfish did. With a captivating furrow of doubt between her eyes, she laid the problem before her partner: could it be trusted to remain edible overnight?

"Never mind the fish. Can you swim?"

She looked out across the brown turbulence of the river, more than two hundred yards now to the northern bank. "Not across that."

"But you're used to water?"

"Oh, yes!"

"I've located an old boat in the slough where I killed the fish. I think I can patch her up enough to make it."

"Okay by me; I wouldn't care to settle here permanently. When do we start?"

"Be ready about ten."

"In the dark?"

"We-ell, I don't exactly want the public in on this. They might try to stop us. You know how people are."

"Come clean, Peter. We're running away from something. Is it that Shapley worm?"

"Yes. He thinks he's got something on me." This explanation which he had been at some pains to devise, he hoped would satisfy her. But she followed it to a conclusion which he had not foreseen.

"Is it because he knows we're not married?"

"He doesn't know ex—"

"I told him we weren't. Before I thought how it would look."

"I told him we were."

"Did he believe you?"

"Probably not."

"Then he thinks you're abducting me. Isn't that priceless!"

"Oh, absolutely. What isn't so funny is that there are laws in some states about people—er—traveling as man and wife if they're not married."

She stared at him, wide-eyed. "But so long as— Oh, Peter! I'd *hate* it if I got you into any trouble."

"All we have to do is slip Shapley. Nobody else is on." He sincerely hoped that was true.

The intervening time he occupied in patching up the boat as best he might. He had studied the course of various flotsam and thought that he discerned a definite set of the current toward the northern bank which was their goal. With bailing they ought to be able to keep the old tub afloat.

Through the curtain of the rushing clouds the moon was contriving to diffuse a dim light when they set out. The opposite bank was visible only as a faint, occasional blur. Smooth with treachery, the stream at their feet sped from darkness into darkness.

Peter thrust an oar into Elspeth's hand, the only one he had been able to find, to be used as a steering paddle. For himself he had fashioned a pole from a sapling. The carryall he disposed aft of amidships. Bending over Elspeth as she took the stern seat, he put a hand on her shoulder.

"You're not afraid?"

"No." Just the same, she would have liked to be within reach of that firm grasp through what might be coming.

"Stout fella! All set? Shove!"

The river snatched at the boat, took it into its secret keeping—and held it strangely motionless. But the faintly visible shore slipped backward and away and was presently visible no more. Peter, a long way distant from her in the dimness, was active with his pole, fending to this side and that. It was her job to keep them on the course with her oar. She concentrated upon it.

The boat was leaking profusely now. "Shall I bail?" she called.

"Yes. But keep your oar by you."

They came abreast of an island. As they neared the lower end, an uprooted swamp maple was snatched outward in the movement of the river. Busy with her pan, Elspeth did not notice it until a mass of leafy branches heaved upward from the surface, hovered, descended, and she was struggling in the grasp of a hundred tentacles.

"Peter!" she shrieked.

They had her, those wet, clogging arms. They were dragging her out into the void, fight them as she would in her terror and desperation. Now another force was aiding her; Peter, his powerful arms tearing, thrusting, fending against this ponderous invasion. The boat careened. The water poured inboard. Then, miraculously, they were released as the tree sideslipped, turning again, freeing their craft. Elspeth fell back, bruised and battered.

"Are you all right?"

"Yes. It t-t-tried to drag me overboard!"

"I know." His voice, too, was unsteadied by that horror.

"Don't go away. Hold me. Just for a minute."

The skiff, slowly revolving like a ceremonious dancer in the performance of a solo waltz, proceeded on its unguided course. The girl sighed.

"Where's my oar?" It was gone.

"It doesn't matter now. There's the shore. We're being carried in."

They scraped and checked as Peter clutched at a small sapling, growing at the edge of a swampy forest. From trunk to trunk he guided the course until there was a solid bump.

"Land ho!" he shouted, and helped his shipmate out upon the bank.

"What do we do now?"

"Walk until we find a road and a roost."

Valise on shoulder, he set out across the miry fields, Elspeth plodding on behind. It was hard going. Her breath labored painfully after the first half-mile, and she was agonizingly sleepy.

Now Peter's arm was around her; he was murmuring some encouraging foolishness to her who was beyond courage, fear, hope, or any other emotion except the brutish lust for rest. . . . Peter's voice, angry and harsh, insisting that she throw more of her weight on him and *keep* moving. How silly! She hadn't any weight. She was a bird on a bough. She was a butterfly, swaying on a blossom. She was nothing. . . .

Broad daylight, spearing through a paneless window, played upon her lids, waking her. Where was the shawl of Jericho? In its place were boards, a raw wall. Beneath her was fragrant hay. She was actually alive and rested. She looked about her.

"Why, it's a barn!" she exclaimed. She got up and went to the door. Outside stood Peter.

"How do you like the quarters?" he greeted her. "Room"—he pointed to the barn—"and bath." He indicated a huge horse trough fed by a trickle of clear water. "I've just had mine."

She regarded him with stupefaction. "And now you're *shaving*. Where's the party?"

"Party?"

"Well, if not, why the elaborate toilet?"

"Did you ever travel on the thumb?"

She looked her incomprehension. He performed a digital gesture which enlightened her.

"The first rule of the thumb," explained Peter, "is to look as neat and decent as you can. It inspires confidence in the passing motorist's breast."

"Is that the way we're going to travel?"

"If we're lucky."

"Without eating?" she said wistfully.

"Tluck-tluck!" interposed a young chicken from a near-by hedge, the most ill-timed observation of its brief life.

A handy stick, flung deftly, checked its retreat. Peter pounced. "Breakfast!" he exulted.

"Where do we go now?" inquired his companion, half an hour later, greatly restored.

"The main highways," set forth Peter, thinking of the radio alarm and the state police, "are not for us. Verdant lanes and bosky glens are more in our line. We'll take what traffic we can."

Hitch-hiking on sandy side roads in the South means slow progress. Peter finally decided that they must risk better-traveled roads, but select their transportation cautiously. It was selected for them. They had not footed it a mile beside Route 1, when a touring car, battered but serviceable, pulled up and a ruddy face emitted welcome words.

"Well, well, well! Boys *and* girls! Bound north?"

"Yes." It was a duet, perfect in accord.

"Meet Thad Banker, the good old fatty. Throw in the old trunk."

"What's the arrangement?" queried Peter, cautious financier that he was.

"Free wheeling," burbled the fat man. "You furnish the gas and I furnish the spark." They climbed in with the valise. "Any special place?" asked the obliging chauffeur.

"Do we go through Raleigh?" asked the girl, and upon receiving an affirmative, added to Peter: "There may be a wire there for me."

Which reminded that gentleman that he had something to attend to. At the next town he got a telegraph blank and a stamped envelope. After some cogitation, he produced this composition, addressed to Mr. A. B. M. Andrews, Miami Beach, Fla.

Daughter taking trip for health and recreation. Advise abandonment of efforts to trace which can have no good results and may cause delay. Sends love and says not to worry. Undersigned guarantees safe arrival in New York in a few days. Pay no reward to any other claimant as this is positively first authentic information.

Peter Warne

To this he pinned a dollar bill and mailed it for transmission to Western Union, New Orleans, Louisiana, by way of giving the pursuit, in case one was instituted, a pleasant place to start from. Five cents more of his thin fortune went for a newspaper. Reports from the southward were worth the money; there was no let-up in the flood. Competition from Mr. Shapley would be delayed at least another day.

Mr. Thad Banker was a card. He kept himself in roars of laughter with his witty sallies. Peter, in the rear seat, fell peacefully asleep. Elspeth had to act as audience for the conversational driver.

At Raleigh she found the expected telegram from Corcoran, which she read and thrust into her purse for future use. Shortly after, a traffic light held them up and the policeman on the corner exhibited an interest in the girl on the front seat quite disturbing to Peter.

The traffic guardian was sauntering toward them when the green flashed on. "Step on it," urged Peter.

Mr. Banker obliged. A whistle shrilled.

"Keep going!" snapped Peter.

Mr. Banker still obliged, slipping into a maze of side streets. It did not occur to Peter that their driver's distaste for police interference was instinctive. Also successful, it began to appear; when a motor cop swung around unexpectedly and headed them to the curb. The license was inspected and found in order.

"Who's the lady?" the officer began.

"My niece," said Mr. Banker, with instant candor.

"Is that right, ma'am?"

"Yes, of course it is." (Peter breathed again.)

"And this man behind?"

"Search me."

"He thumbed us and Uncle Thad stopped for him." (Peter's admiration became almost more than he could bear.)

"Have you got a traveling bag with you, ma'am?" (So the radio must have laid weight on the traveling bag, now probably in some Florida swamp.)

"No. Just my purse."

The cop consulted a notebook. "The dress looks like it," he muttered. "And the description sort of fits. Got anything on you to prove who you are, ma'am?"

"No; I'm afraid—Yes; of course I have." She drew out the yellow envelope. "Is that enough?"

"Miss Bessie Smith," he read. "I reckon that settles it. Keep to your right for Greensboro at Morrisville."

"Greensboro, my foot! Us for points east," announced the fat man, wiping his brow as the motor cycle chugged away. "Phe-e-ew! What's it all about? Been lootin' a bank, you two?"

"Eloping," said Peter. "Keep it under your shirt."

"Gotcha." He eyed the carryall. "All your stuff in there?"

"Yes."

"How about a breath of pure, country air? I'm not so strong for all this public attention."

They kept to side roads until long after dark, bringing up before a restaurant in Tarboro. There the supposed elopers consulted and announced that they didn't care for dinner. "Oh, on me!" cried Mr. Banker. "Mustn't go hungry on your honeymoon."

He ordered profusely. While the steak was cooking, he remarked, he'd just have a look at the car; there was a rattle in the engine that he didn't like. As soon as he had gone, Elspeth said:

"Wonder what the idea is. I never heard a sweeter-running engine for an old car. What's more, he's got two sets of license cards. I saw the other one when that inquiring cop—"

But Peter was halfway to the door, after slamming some money on the table and snapping out directions for her to wait, no matter how long he took. Outside, she heard a shout and the rush of a speeding engine. A car without lights sped up the street.

With nothing else to do, Elspeth settled down to leisurely eating. . . .

At nine-thirty, the waiter announced the closing hour as ten, sharp. Beginning to be terrified for Peter and miserable for herself, she ordered more coffee. The bill and tip left her a dollar and fifteen cents.

At nine-fifty, the wreckage of Peter entered the door. Elspeth arose and made a rush upon him, but recoiled.

"Peter! You've been fighting."

"Couldn't help it."

"You've got a black eye."

"That isn't all I've got," he told her.

"No; it isn't. What an *awful*-looking ear!"

"*That* isn't all I've got, either." His grin was bloody, but unbowed.

"Then it must be internal injuries."

"Wrong. It's a car."

"Whose car?"

"Ours now, I expect. I had to come home in something."

"Where's the fat man?"

The grin widened. "Don't know exactly. Neither does he, I reckon. That big-hearted Samaritan, my child, is a road-pirate. He picks people up, plants 'em, and beats it with their luggage. Probably does a little holdup business on the side."

"Tell me what happened, Peter. Go on and eat first."

Between relishing mouthfuls, he unfolded his narrative. "You didn't put me wise a bit too quick. He was moving when I got out but I landed aboard with a flying tackle. Didn't dare grab him for fear we'd crash. He was stepping on it and telling me that when he got me far enough away he was going to beat me up and tie me to a tree. That was an idea! So when he pulled up on some forsaken wood road in a swamp, I beat him up and tied him to a tree."

"Why, Peter! He's twice as big as you."

"I can't help that. It wasn't any time for half measures. It took me an hour to find my way. But here we are."

"I'm glad," she said with a new note in her voice.

"Jumping Jehoshaphat! Is *that* all we've got left?" Aghast, he stared at the sum she put in his hands. "And it's too cold to sleep out tonight. It's an open car, anyhow. Oh, well; our transportation's going to be cheap from now on. What price one more good night's rest? Torney's Haven for Tourists is three miles up the highway. Let's get going."

Torney's provided a cabin for only a dollar. Before turning in, Peter returned to the car, parked a few roads away against a fence, to make a thorough inspection. His companion was in bed on his return.

"I've changed the plates to another set that I found under the seat. Indiana, to match the other set of licenses. It'll be safer in case our friend decides to report the loss, after he gets loose from his tree. There's a nice robe, too. We've come into property. And by the way, Elspeth; you're Mrs. Thaddeus Banker till further notice."

Elspeth pouted. "I'd rather be Mrs. Peter Warne. I'm getting used to that."

"We've got to live up to our new responsibilities." Seated on his cot, he had taken off his shoes, when he started hastily to resume them.

"Where are you going?" she asked plaintively. "Looking for more trouble?"

"Walls of Jericho. I forgot. I'll get the robe out of the car."

"Oh, darn the robe! Why bother? It's pouring, too. Let it go. I don't mind if you don't." All in a perfectly matter-of-fact tone. She added: "You can undress outside. I'm going to sleep."

As soon as he withdrew she got out Corcoran's reply to "Miss Bessie Smith," and read it over again before tearing it into fragments. It ran as follows:

What's all this about P.W.? Watch out for that bird. Dangerous corner, blind road, and all that sorta thing. At any given moment he might be running a pirate fleet or landing on the throne of the Kingdom of Boopa-doopia. Ask him about the bet I stuck him on in college, and then keep your guard up. I'm off for a week on the Keys so you can't get me again until then. Better come back home and be a nice little girl or papa spank. And how!

Cork

The scraps she thrust beneath her pillow and was asleep almost at once. But Peter lay, wakeful, crushing down thoughts that made him furious with himself. At last peace came, and dreams. . . . One of them so poignant, so incredibly dear, that he fought bitterly against its turning to reality.

Yet reality it was; the sense of warmth and softness close upon him; the progress of creeping fingers across his breast, of seeking lips against his throat. His arms drew her down. His mouth found the lips that, for a dizzying moment, clung to his, then trembled aside to whisper:

"No, Peter. I didn't mean—Listen!"

Outside sounded a light clinking.

"Somebody's stealing the car!"

Elspeth's form, in the lurid pajamas, slid away from Peter like a ghost. He followed to the window. Silent as a shadow the dim bulk of the Banker automobile moved deliberately along under a power not its own. Two other shadows loomed in its rear, propelling it by hand.

"Shall I scream?" whispered the girl.

He put a hand on her mouth. "Wait."

Another of his luminous ideas had fired the brain of Peter Warne. In his role of Thad Banker, he would let the robbers get away, then report the theft to the police and, allowing for reasonable luck, get back his property (né Mr. Banker's) with the full blessing of the authorities.

"I'm going to let 'em get away with it," he murmured. "As soon as they really start, I'll telephone the road patrol."

The dwindling shadow trundled out on the pike, where the engine struck up its song and the car sped southward. Simultaneously Peter made a rush for the camp office. It was all right, he reported, on getting back. He'd been able to get the police at once.

"But suppose they don't catch 'em."

"That'll be just too bad," admitted Peter. He yawned.

"You're sleepy again. You're always sleepy."

"What do you expect at three o'clock in the morning?"

"I'm wide awake," complained Elspeth.

Something had changed within her, made uncertain and uneasy, since she had aroused Peter and found herself for one incendiary moment in his arms. She didn't blame him; he was only half awake at the time. But she had lost confidence in him. Or could it be herself in whom she had lost confidence? In any case, the thought of sharing the same room with him the rest of that night had become too formidable.

"Please go outside again, Peter. I'm going to get dressed. I'm restless."

"Oh, my gosh!" he sighed. "Can't you count some sheep or something?"

"No; I can't." A brilliant idea struck her. "How'd you expect me to sleep when they may be back with the car any minute?"

"And then again, they may not be back till morning."

But Elspeth had a heritage of the immovable Scottish obstinacy. In a voice all prickly little italics she announced that she was *going to get up.* And she was going to walk off her nervousness. It needn't make any difference to Peter. He could go back to bed.

"And let you wander around alone in this blackness? You might not come back."

"What else could I do?"

The forlorn lack of alternative for her struck into his heart. Absolute dependence upon a man of a strange breed in circumstances wholly new. What a situation for a girl like her! And how gallantly, on the whole, she was taking it! How sensible it would be for him to go back to that telephone; call up her father (reverse charges, of course) and tell him the whole thing. *And* get himself thoroughly hated for it.

No; he couldn't throw Elspeth down. Not even for her own good. Carry on. There was nothing else for it, especially now that luck was favoring them. The car, if they got it back, was their safest obtainable method of travel. Her dress was the weak spot and would be more of a danger point after Horace Shapley contributed his evidence to the hunt. Couldn't something be done about that? . . . The dress appeared in the doorway, and Peter went in to array himself for the vigil.

The two state police found the pair waiting at the gate. Apologetically they explained that the thieves had got away into the swamp. Nothing could have suited Peter better, since there would now be no question of his being held as complaining witness. To satisfy the authorities of his ownership was easy. They took his address (fictitious), wished him and his wife good luck, and were off.

"Now we can go back to bed," said Peter.

"Oh, dear! Can't we start on?"

"At this hour? Why, I suppose we could, but—"

"Let's, then." In the turmoil of her spirit she wanted to be quit forever of Torney's Haven for Tourists and its atmosphere of unexpected emotions and disconcerting impulses. Maybe something of this had trickled into Peter's mind, too, for presently he said:

"Don't you know it's dangerous to wake a sound sleeper too suddenly?"

"So I've heard."

"You can't tell what might happen. I mean, a man isn't quite responsible, you know, before he comes quite awake."

So he was apologizing. Very proper.

"Let's forget it."

"Yes," he agreed quietly. "I'll have quite a little to forget."

"So will I," she thought, startled at the realization.

They packed, and chugged out, one cylinder missing. "I hope the old junk-heap holds together till we reach New York," remarked Peter.

"Are we going all the way in this?"

"Unless you can think of a cheaper way."

"But it isn't ours. It's the fat man's."

"I doubt it. Looks to me as if it had been stolen and gypped up with new paint and fake numbers. However, we'll leave it somewhere in Jersey if we get that far, and write to both license numbers to come and get it. How does that set on an empty conscience?"

"Never mind my conscience. That isn't the worst emptiness I'm suffering from. What's in the house for breakfast? It's nearly sunup."

"Potatoes. Pecans." He investigated their scanty store and looked up. "There are only three spuds left."

"Is that all?"

Something careless in her reply made him scan her face sharply. "There ought to be five. There are two missing. You had charge of the larder. Well?"

"I took 'em. You see—"

"Without saying a word about it to me? You must have pinched them out when we were on the island and cooked them for yourself while I was working on the boat," he figured somberly. Part of this was true, but not all of it. The rest she was saving to confound him with. "Do you, by any chance, still think that this is a picnic?"

Now she *wouldn't* tell him! She was indignant and hurt. He'd be sorry! When he came to her with a potato now, she would haughtily decline it—if her rueful stomach didn't get the better of her wrathful fortitude.

In resentment more convincing than her own, he built the wayside fire, boiled the water and inserted one lone potato; the smallest at that. He counted out five pecans, added two more, and handed the lot to her. He then got out his pocketknife, opened it, and prodded the bubbling tuber. Judging it soft enough, he neatly speared it out upon a plate. Elspeth pretended a total lack of interest. She hoped she'd have the resolution to decline her half with hauteur. She didn't get the chance.

Peter split the potato, sprinkled on salt, and ate it all.

With difficulty, Elspeth suppressed a roar of rage. That was the kind of man he was, then! Selfish, greedy, mean, tyrannical, unfair, smug, bad-tempered, uncouth—her stock ran thin. How idiotically she had overestimated him! Rough but noble; that had been her formula for his character. And now look at him, pigging down the last delicious fragments while she was to be content with a handful of nuts. Nuts! She rose in regal resentment, flung her seven pecans into the fire, and stalked back to the car.

Somewhere in the vicinity of Emporia, eighty miles north of their breakfast, he spoke. "No good in sulking, you know."

"I'm *not* sulking." Which closed that opening.

Nevertheless, Elspeth was relieved. An oppressive feeling that maybe his anger would prove more lasting than her own had tainted her satisfaction in being the injured party. One solicitude, too, he exhibited. He kept tucking her up in the robe.

This would have been less reassuring had she understood its genesis. He was afraid her costume might be recognized. He even thought of suggesting that she might effect a trade in some secondhand store. In her present state of childish petulance, however, he judged it useless to suggest this. Some other way must be found.

Some money was still left to them. Elspeth saw her companion shaking his head over it when their gas gave out, happily near a filling station. His worried expression weakened her anger, but she couldn't bring herself to admit she was sorry. Not yet.

"There's a cheap camp seventy miles from here," he said. "But if we sleep there we can't have much of a dinner."

"Potatoes," said the recalcitrant Elspeth. She'd teach him!

They dined at a roadside stand which, in ordinary conditions, she would have considered loathsome. Every odor of it now brought prickly sensations to her palate.

The night presented a problem troubling to her mind. No shared but unpartitioned cabin for her! Last night's experience had been too revelatory. What made things difficult was that she had told him she needed no more walls of Jericho to insure peaceful sleep. Now if she asked him to put up the curtain, what would he think?

Pursuant to his policy of avoiding large cities and the possible interest of traffic cops, Peter had planned their route westward again, giving Richmond a wide berth. They flashed without stop through towns with hospitable restaurants only to pull up at a roadside stand of austere menu, near Sweet Briar.

Never had Elspeth seen the important sum of twenty-five cents laid out so economically as by Peter's method. Baked beans with thick, fat, glorious gollups of pork; a half-loaf of bread, and bitter coffee. To say that her hunger was appeased would be overstatement. But a sense of returned well-being comforted her. She even felt that she could face the morning's potato, if any, with courage. Meantime, there remained the arrangements for the night.

Peter handled that decisively, upon their arrival at the camp. Their cabin was dreary, chill, and stoveless. When he brought in the robe from the car, she hoped for it over her bunk. Not at all; out came his little tool kit; up went the separating cord, and over it was firmly pinned the warm fabric.

With a regrettable though feminine want of logic, Elspeth nursed a grievance; he needn't have been at such pains to raise that wall aga.n without a request from the person most interested. She went to sleep crossly but promptly.

In the morning the robe was tucked snugly about her. How long had that been there? She looked around and made a startling discovery. Her clothes were gone. So was Peter. Also, when she looked out, the car. The wild idea occurred to her that he had stolen her outfit and run away, *à la* Thad Banker. One thing was certain: to rise and wander forth clad in those grotesque pajamas was out of the question. Turning over, she fell asleep again.

Some inner sensation of his nearness awoke her, or perhaps it was, less occultly, his footsteps outside, approaching, pausing. She craned upward to bring her vision level with the window. Peter was standing with his side face toward her, a plump bundle beneath his arm. Her clothes, probably, which he had taken out to clean. How nice of him!

He set down his burden and took off his belt. With a knife he slit the stitches in the leather, carefully prying something from beneath the strips. It was a tight-folded bill.

So he had been holding out on her! Keeping her on a gnat's diet. Letting her go hungry while he gorged himself on boiled potato and salt, and gloated over his reserve fund. Beast! This knowledge, too, she would hold back for his ultimate discomfiture. It was a composed and languid voice which responded to his knock on the door.

"Hello! How are you feeling, Elspeth?"

"Very well, thank you. Where have you been?"

"Act two, scene one of matrimonial crisis," chuckled Peter. "Hubby returns early in the morning. Wife demands explanation. Husband is ready with it: 'You'd be surprised.' " There was a distinct trace of nervousness in his bearing.

"Well, surprise me," returned Elspeth, with hardly concealed hostility. "Where are my clothes?"

"That's the point. They're—uh—I—er—well, the fact is, I pawned 'em. In Charlottesville?"

"You—pawned—my—clothes! Where's the money?" If that was the bill in the belt, she proposed to know it.

"I spent most of it. On other clothes. You said your feet hurt you."

"When we were walking. We don't have to walk any more."

"How do you know? We aren't out of the woods yet. And you don't need such a fancy rig, traveling with me. And we do need the little bit extra I picked up on the trade."

Stern and uncompromising was the glare which she directed upon his bundle. "Let me see."

Her immediate reaction to the dingy, shoddy, nondescript outfit he disclosed was an involuntary yip of distress.

"Don't you like 'em?" he asked.

"They're terrible! They're ghastly!"

"The woman said they were serviceable. Put 'em on. I'll wait outside."

It would have taken a sturdier optimism than Peter's to maintain a sun-kissed countenance in the face of the transformation which he presently witnessed. Hardly could he recognize her in that horrid misfit which she was pinning here, adjusting there.

"Hand me the mirror, please."

"Perhaps you'd better not—"

"Will you be so good as to do as I ask?"

"Oh, all *right!*"

She took one long, comprehensive survey and burst into tears.

"Don't, Elspeth," he protested, appalled. "What's the difference? There's no one to see you."

"There's me," she gulped. "And there's you."

"I don't mind." As if he were bearing up courageously under an affliction.

"I'm a *sight,*" she wailed. "I'm hideous! Go and get my things back."

"It can't be done."

"I won't go out in these frightful things. I won't. I won't. I *won't!*"

"Who's going to pay the rent if you stay?"

Obtaining no reply to this pertinent inquiry, he sighed and went out. Down the breeze, there presently drifted to Elspeth's nostrils the tang of wood smoke. Her face appeared in the window.

"About those missing potatoes," said she. (How mean she was going to make him feel in a minute!) "Are you interested in knowing what became of them?"

"It doesn't matter. They're gone."

"They're gone where they'll do the most good," she returned with slow impressiveness. "I gave them away."

"Without consulting me?"

"Do I have to consult you about everything I do?"

"We-ell, some people might figure that I had an interest in those potatoes."

"Well, I gave them to a poor old woman who needed them. She was hungry."

"Umph! Feeling sure, I suppose, that your generosity would cost you nothing, as I'd share the remainder with you. Error Number One."

"Peter, I wouldn't have thought anyone could be so des-des-despicable!"

This left him unmoved. "Who was the starving beneficiary? I'll bet it was that old creature with the black bonnet and gold teeth in the bus."

"How did you know?"

"She's the sort you would help. In case you'd like to know, that old hoarder had her bag half full of almond chocolates. I saw her buy 'em at Charleston."

"Hoarder, yourself!" Enraged at the failure of her bombshell, she fell back on her last ammunition. "What did you take out of your belt this morning?"

"Oh, you saw that, did you? Watchful little angel!"

"I'm not! I just happened to see it. A bill. A big one, I'll bet. You had it all the time. And you've starved me and bullied me and made me walk miles and sleep in barns, while you could just as well have—"

"Hired a special train. On ten dollars."

"Ten dollars is a lot of money." (Ideas change.)

"Now, I'll tell you about that ten dollars," said he with cold precision. "It's my backlog. It's the last resort. It's the untouchable. It's the dead line of absolute necessity."

"You needn't touch it on my account." (Just like a nasty-tempered little brat, she told herself.) "Of course, starvation isn't absolute necessity."

"Can you do simple arithmetic?"

"Yes. I'm not quite an idiot, even if you do think so, Peter."

"Try this one, then. We've got something over five hundred miles to go. Gas will average us seventeen cents. This old mudcart of Banker's won't do better than twelve miles on a gallon. Now, can any bright little girl in this class tell me how much over that leaves us to eat, sleep and live on, not counting oil, ferry charge and incidentals?"

"I can't. And I don't want to," retorted Elspeth, very dispirited. A long, dull silence enclosed them like a globe. She shattered it. "Peter!"

"What?"

"D'you know why I hate you?"

"I'll bite," said he, wearily. "Why?"

"Because, darn you! you're always right and I'm always wrong. Peter! Peter, dear! A potato, Peter. Please, Peter; one potato. Just one. The littlest. I know I don't deserve it, but—"

"Oh, what's the *use!*" vociferated Peter, throwing up both hands in abject and glad surrender. And that quarrel drifted on the smoke of their fire down to the limbo of things become insignificant, yet never quite to be forgotten.

Two young people, haggard, gaunt, shabby, bluish with the chill of an April storm, drove their battered car aboard the Fort Lee ferry as the boat pulled out. They were sharing a bag of peanuts with the conscientious exactitude of penury: one to you; one to me. Quarter of the way across, both were asleep. At the halfway distance the whistle blared and they woke up.

"We're nearly there," observed the girl without any special enthusiasm.

"Yes," said the man with still less.

A hiatus of some length. "Why didn't you tell me about blacking Corker's boots?"

"What about it?"

"It was on a bet, wasn't it?"

"Yes. In college. I picked the wrong team. If I'd won, the Corker would have typed my theses for the term. What put you on?"

"A telegram from Cork."

"Oh! The one to Bessie Smith that saved our lives in Raleigh?"

She nodded. "Anyway, I knew all the time you weren't a valet," she asserted.

He cocked a mild, derisive eye at her. "You're not building up any rosy picture of me as a perfect gentleman, are you?"

"No-o. I don't know what you are."

"Don't let it worry you. Go back to sleep."

"You're always telling me to go to sleep," she muttered discontentedly. She rubbed her nose on his shoulder. "Peter."

He sighed and kissed her.

"You needn't be so solemn about it."

"I'm not feeling exactly sprightly."

"Because we're almost home? But we'll be seeing each other soon."

"I thought that headliner of the air was waiting to fly you somewhere."

"Who? Oh-h-h-h, King." She began to laugh. "Isn't that funny! I'd absolutely forgotten about King. He doesn't matter. When am I going to see you?" As he made no reply, she became vaguely alarmed. . . . "You're not going right back?"

"No. I've got that possible contract to look after. Down in Jersey."

"But you'll be in town again. And I'll see you then."

"No."

"Peter! Why not?"

"Self-preservation," he proclaimed oracularly, "is the first law of nature."

"You don't want to see me again?"

"Put it any way you like," came the broad-minded permission, "just so the main point gets across."

"But I think that's absolutely lousy!" Another point occurred to her. "There's no reason why you shouldn't if it's because—well, that business about my being married was a good deal exaggerated. If that makes any difference."

"It does. It makes it worse."

"Oh! . . . You don't seem surprised, though."

"Me? I should say not! I've known from the first that was all bunk."

"Have you, Smarty? How?"

"You tried to put it over that you'd been wearing a wedding ring. But there was no band of white on the tan of your finger."

"Deteckative! I haven't had a bit of luck trying to fool you about anything, have I, Peter? Not even putting across the superior-goddess idea. And now you're the one that's being snooty."

"I'm not. I'm being sensible. See here, Elspeth. It may or may not have been called to your attention that you're a not wholly unattractive young person—and that I myself am not yet beyond the age of—"

"Consent," broke in the irrepressible Elspeth.

"—damfoolishness," substituted Peter, with severity. "So," he concluded, with an effect of logic, "we may as well call it a day."

"Not to mention several nights." She turned the brilliance of mirthful eyes upon him. "Wouldn't it be funny if you fell in love with me, Peter?"

"Funny for the spectators. Painful for the bear."

"Then don't mention it, Bear!" Another idea occurred to her. "How much money have you got left?"

"Forty-odd cents."

"Now that you're in New York you can get more, of course."

"Yes? Where?"

"At the bank, I suppose. Where does one get money?"

"That's what I've always wanted to know," he grinned.

"I can get all I want tomorrow. I'll lend you a hundred dollars. Or more if you want it."

"No; thank you."

"But I borrowed yours!" she cried. "At least, you paid for me."

"That's different."

"I don't see how." Of course she did see, and inwardly approved. "But—but I owe you money!" she cried. "I'd forgotten all about that. You'll let me pay that back, of course."

If she expected him to deprecate politely the idea she was swiftly undeceived. "The sooner, the better," said Peter cheerfully.

"I'll bet you've got it all set down in that precious notebook of yours."

"Every cent." He tore out a leaf which he handed to her.

"Where can I send it?"

He gave her an address on a street whose name she had never before heard; Darrow, or Barrow, or some such matter.

In the splendor of the great circular court off Park Avenue, the bedraggled automobile looked impudently out of place. The doorkeeper almost choked with amazement as the luxurious Miss Elspeth Andrews, clad in such garments as had never before affronted those august portals, jumped out, absently responding to his greeting.

"I think your father is expecting you, miss," said he.

"Oh, Lord!" exclaimed Elspeth. "Now, what brought him here?"

Peter could have told her, but didn't. He was looking straight through the windshield. She was looking at him with slightly lifted brows.

"Good-by, Elspeth," said he huskily.

"Good-by, Peter. You've been awfully mean to me. I've loved it."

Why, thought Peter as he went on his way, did she have to use that particular word in that special tone at that unhappy moment?

Between Alexander Bruce MacGregor Andrews and his daughter, Elspeth, there existed a lively and irritable affection of precarious status, based upon a fundamental similarity of character and a prevalent lack of mutual understanding. That she should have willfully run away from home and got herself and him on the front pages of the papers, seemed to him an outrage of the first order.

"But it was your smearing the thing all over the air that got us into the papers," pointed out Elspeth, which didn't help much as a contribution to the *entente cordiale*. Both sulked for forty-eight hours.

Meantime, there arrived by special delivery a decidedly humid shoebox addressed in an uncompromisingly straight-up-and-down hand—just exactly the kind one would expect, thought the girl, knowing whose it was at first sight—full of the freshest, most odorous bunch of arbutus she had ever beheld. Something about it unmistakably defined it as having been picked by the sender.

Elspeth searched minutely for a note; there was none. She carried the box to her room and threw three clusters of orchids and a spray of gardenias into the scrapbasket. After that she went to a five-and-ten-cent store, made a purchase at the toy counter, had it boxed, and herself mailed it to the address given her by Peter Warne. The shipment did not include the money she owed him. That detail had escaped her mind.

"Scotty, dear." She greeted her father in the style of their companionable moods. "Do let's be sensible."

Mr. Andrews grunted suspiciously. "Suppose you begin."

"I'm going to. Drink your cocktail first." She settled down on the arm of his chair.

"Now what devilment are you up to?" demanded the apprehensive parent.

"Not a thing. I've decided to tell you about my trip."

Having her narrative all duly mapped out, she ran through it smoothly enough, hoping that he would not notice a few cleverly glossed passages. Disapproval in the paternal expression presently yielded to amused astonishment.

"Nervy kid!" he chuckled. "I'll bet it did you good."

"It didn't do me any harm. And I certainly found out a few things I'd never known before."

"Broadening effect of travel. Who did you say this young man was that looked after you?"

"I'm coming to that. The question is, what are you going to do for him?"

"What does he want?"

"I don't know that he exactly wants anything. But he's terribly poor, Scotty. Why, just think! He had to reckon up each time how much he could afford to spend on a meal!"

"Yes? I'm told there are quite a few people in this country in the same fix," observed Mr. Andrews dryly. "How much'll I make out the check for?"

"That's the trouble. I don't believe he'd take it. He's one of these inde-be-goshdarn-pendent birds. Wouldn't listen to my lending him some money."

"Humph! That probably means he's fallen for your fair young charms. Be funny if he hadn't."

"I'll tell you what would be funnier."

"What?"

"If I'd fallen for him," was the brazen response.

"Poof! You're always imagining you're in love with the newest hero in sight. Remember that young Danish diplo—"

"Yes; I do. What of it? I always get over it, don't I? And I'll get over this. You'd think he was terrible, Dad. He's sure rough. You ought to have seen Little Daughter being bossed around by him and taking it."

"Is that so?" said her father, spacing his words sardonically. "Bossed you, did he? He and who else?"

"Oh, Peter doesn't need any help."

The grin was wiped off the Andrews face. "Who?"

"Peter. That's his name. Peter Warne."

"What?"

"Gracious! Don't yell so. Do you know him?"

"I haven't that pleasure as yet. Just let me make sure about this." He went into the adjoining room, whence he emerged with a sheaf of papers. "Peter Warne. So he's poor, is he?"

"Desperately."

"Well, he won't be, after tomorrow."

"Oh, Scotty! How do you know? Is he going to get some money? I'm so glad!"

"Some money is correct. Ten thousand dollars, to be exact."

"From his tar-pine or something process? How did *you* know about it?"

"From me. I don't know anything about—"

"From you?" Her lips parted; her eyes were wide and alarmed. "What for?"

"Information leading to the discovery and return of Elspeth, daughter of—"

"The reward? For me? Peter? I don't believe it. Peter wouldn't do such a thing. Take money for—"

"He has done it. Put in his claim for the reward. Do you want to see the proof?"

"I wouldn't believe it anyway."

Alexander Andrews studied her defiant face with a concern that became graver. This looked serious. Selecting a letter and a telegram from his dossier, he put them into her reluctant hand. At sight of the writing her heart sank. It was unmistakably that of the address on the box of arbutus. The note cited the writer's telegram of the fourteenth ("That's the day after we got off the island," thought Elspeth. "He was selling me out then.") and asked for an appointment.

"He's coming to my office at ten-thirty Thursday morning."

"Are you going to give him the money?"

"It looks as if I'd have to."

"He certainly worked hard enough for it," she said bitterly. "And I expect he needs it."

"I might be able to work a compromise," mused the canny Scot. "Though I'm afraid he's got the material for a bothersome lawsuit. If any of the other claimants"—he indicated the sheaf of letters and telegrams—"had a decent case, we could set off one against the other. The most insistent is a person named Shapley."

"Don't let him have it," said the girl hastily. "I'd rather Peter should get it, though I'd never have believed—Sold down the river!" She forced a laugh. "I brought a price, anyway."

"I've a good mind to give him a fight for it. It would mean more publicity, though."

"Oh, no!" breathed Elspeth.

"Enough's enough, eh? Though it couldn't be worse than what we've had."

"It could. Much worse. If you're going to see Pe— Mr. Warne,

I'd better tell you something, Father. I've been traveling as Mrs. Peter Warne."

"Elspeth!"

"It isn't what you think. Purely economy—with the accent on the 'pure.' But it wouldn't look pretty in print. Oh, damn!" Her voice broke treacherously. "I thought Peter was so straight."

Her father walked up and down the room several times. He then went over and put his arm around his daughter's shoulders. "It's all right, dautie. We'll get you out of it. And we'll find a way to keep this fellow's mouth shut. I'm having a detectaphone set up in my office, and if he makes one slip we'll have him by the short hairs for blackmail."

"Peter doesn't make slips," returned his daughter. "It's his specialty not to. Oh, well, let's go in to dinner, Scotty."

Resolutely, she put the arbutus out of her room when she went up to bed that night. But the spicy odor from far springtime woodlands clung about the place like a plea for the absent.

Stern logic of the morning to which she sorrowfully awoke filled in the case against Peter. Nevertheless and notwithstanding, "I don't believe it," said Elspeth's sore heart. "And I won't believe it until—until—"

Severe as were the fittings of Mr. Alexander Bruce MacGregor Andrews' spacious office, they were less so than the glare which apprised Peter Warne, upon his entry, that this spare, square man did not like him and probably never would. That was all right with Peter. He was prepared not to like Mr. Andrews, either. On this propitious basis the two confronted each other.

After a formidable silence which the younger man bore without visible evidence of discomposure, his host barked:

"Sit down."

"Thank you," said Peter. He sat down.

"You have come about the money, I assume."

"Yes."

"Kindly reduce your claim to writing."

"You'll find it there." He handed over a sheet of paper. "Itemized."

"What's this?" Mr. Andrews' surprised eye ran over it.

"Traveling expenses. Elsp—your daughter's."

The father gave the column of figures his analytical attention. "Boat, twenty dollars," he read. "You didn't take my daughter to Cuba, did you?"

"I had to steal a boat to get through the flood. The owner ought to be reimbursed. If you think that's not a fair charge, I'll assume half of it. Everything else is split."

"Humph! My daughter's share of food, lodging and gasoline, excluding the—er—alleged boat, seems to figure up to eighteen dollars and fifty-six cents. Where did you lodge?"

"Wherever we could."

With the paper before him, Mr. Andrews began to hammer his desk. "You have the temerity, the impudence, the effrontery, the —the—anyway, you come here to hold me up for ten thousand dollars and on top of that you try to spring a doctored expense account on me!"

"Doctored!" echoed Peter. "Maybe you think you could do it for less?"

Taken aback, Mr. Andrews ceased his operations on the desk. "We'll pass that for the main point," he grunted. "Upon what do you base your claim for the ten thousand dollars?"

"Nothing," was the placid reply. "I made no claim."

"Your telegram. Your letter—"

"You couldn't have read them. I simply warned you against paying anybody else's claim. You had others, I suppose."

"Others! A couple of hundred!"

"One signed Horace Shapley?"

"I believe so."

"I don't like him," observed Peter, and explained.

"Then your idea," interposed Mr. Andrews, "was to get in first merely to block off this other person. Is that it?"

"Yes."

"And you aren't claiming any part of the reward?"

"No."

"You're crazy," declared the other. "Or maybe I am. What *do* you want?"

Peter gently indicated the expense account. Mr. Andrews went over it again.

"You mean to tell me that you kept my daughter for five days and more on a total of eighteen dollars and fifty-six cents?"

"There are the figures."

Mr. Andrews leaned forward. "Did she kick much?"

Peter's grin was a bit rueful. "There were times when—"

"You'd have liked to sock her. I know. Why didn't you present your bill to her?"

"I did. I reckon she just forgot it."

"She would! . . . Have a cigar." As the young fellow lighted up, his entertainer was writing and entering a check.

"As a matter of correct business, I ought to have Elspeth's O.K. on this bill. However, I'll pass it, including the boat. Receipt here, please." The amount was $1,038.56.

Shaking his head, Peter pushed the check across the desk. "Thank you, but I can't take this, Mr. Andrews."

"Bosh! Elspeth told me you were broke."

"I am . . . No; I'm not, either. I forgot. I've just made a deal on a new process of mine. Anyway, I couldn't take that—that bonus."

"That's funny. If you're no longer broke, I should think you'd be above bringing me a trifling expense account for—er—entertaining my daughter."

"It's a matter of principle," returned Peter firmly.

Mr. Andrews rose and smote his caller on the shoulder. "I begin to see how you made that little spitfire of mine toe the mark. More than I've been able to do for the past ten years. Eighteen dollars and fifty-six cents, huh?" He sank back in his chair and laughed. "See here, my boy; I like you. I like your style. Will you take that money as a present from me?"

"Sorry, sir, but I'd rather not."

The older man stared him down. "Because I'm Elspeth's father, eh? You're in love with her, I suppose."

Peter grew painfully red. "God forbid!" he muttered.

"What do you mean, God forbid?" shouted the magnate. "Better men than you have been in love with her."

"All right, Mr. Andrews," said Peter in desperation. "Then I am, too. I have been from the first. Now, you tell me—you're her father—what's the sense of it with a girl like Elspeth? I'm going back to Florida with a contract for eight thousand a year, to complete my process."

"That's more than I was making at your age."

"It's more than I expect to be making at yours," said Peter with candor. "But how far would that go with her? Look me over, sir. Even if I had a chance with Elspeth, would you advise a fellow like me to try to marry her?"

"No, I wouldn't!" roared the father. "You're too darn good for her."

"Don't talk like a fool," snapped Peter.

"Just for that," reflected Mr. Andrews as his caller withdrew, jamming a substituted check into his pocket, "I'll bet you'll have little enough to say about it when the time comes."

He sent for Elspeth and left her alone with the detectaphone. What that unpoetic cylinder spouted forth rang in her heart like the music of the spheres with the morning and evening stars in the solo parts. So *that* was how Peter felt about it.

Memory obligingly supplied the number on Darrow or Farrow or Barrow or whatever strange street it was. The taxi man whom she hailed earned her admiration by knowing all about it.

Peter said: "Come in," in a spiritless manner. With a totally different vocal effect he added: "What are *you* doing *here?"* and tacked onto that "You oughtn't to be here at all."

"Why not?" Elspeth sat down.

He muttered something wherein the word "proper" seemed to carry the emphasis, and in which the term "landlady" occurred.

"Proper!" jeered his visitor. "You talk to me about propriety after we've been traveling together and sharing the same room for nearly a week!"

"But this is New York," he pointed out.

"And you're packing up to leave it. When?"

"Tonight."

"Without the ten thousand dollar reward?"

"How did you know about that? Your fath—"

"I've just come from his office. You might better have taken the check."

"Don't want it."

"That's silly. What," she inquired reasonably, "have you got to get married on?"

"Eight thousand a ye— I'm not going to get married," he interrupted himself with needless force.

"Not after compromising a young and innocent—"

"I haven't compromised anyone." Sulkily and doggedly.

"Peter! I suppose registering me as your wife all over the map isn't compromising. Did you ever hear of the Mann Act?"

"B-b-b-but—"

"Yes; I know all about that 'but.' It's a great big, important 'but,' but there's another bigger 'but' to be considered. We know what happened and didn't happen on our trip, *but* nobody else would ever believe it in this world. I certainly wouldn't."

"Nor I," he agreed. "Unless," he qualified hastily, "the girl was you."

"Or the man was you."

They laughed with dubious heartiness. When they had done laughing, there seemed to be nothing to follow, logically. Elspeth got up slowly.

"Where are you going?" demanded Peter, in a panic.

"If you don't like me any more"—she put the slightest possible stress on the verb, leaving him to amend it if he chose—"I'm sorry I came."

To this rueful observation, Peter offered no response.

"You did like me once, you know. You as much as admitted it."

Peter swore.

"Did you or did you not tell my father that you would never get over it?"

"It?"

"Well—me."

"Your father," said Peter wrathfully, "is a human sieve."

"No; he isn't. There was a detectaphone listening in on everything you said. I got it all from that."

"In that case," said the now desperate and reckless Peter, "I may as well get it off my chest." And he repeated what he had earlier said about his feelings, with a fervor that wiped the mischief from Elspeth's face.

"Oh-h-h-h!" she murmured, a little dazed. "That's the way you feel."

"No, it isn't. It isn't half of it."

"Where do we go from here?" thought the girl. The atmosphere of sprightly combat and adventure had changed. She was not breathing quite so easily. Her uncertain look fell upon an object at the top of the half-packed carryall. "Oh!" she exclaimed. "You got my present."

"Yes; I got it."

"I hope you liked it." Politely.

"Not particularly."

Her eyes widened. "Why not?"

"Well, I may be oversensitive where you're concerned, but I don't care so much about being called a tinhorn sport, because —well, I don't know, but I suppose it's because I let you pay back the money for our trip. What do I know about the way girls look at those things, anyway?" he concluded morosely.

One girl was looking at him with a mixture of contempt, amusement, pity, and something stronger than any of these. "Oh, you boob!" she breathed. "That isn't a tinhorn. That's a trumpet."

"A *trumpet?*"

"The kind What's-his-name blew before the walls of Jericho, if you have to have a diagram. Oh, *Pee*-ter; you're such a dodo!" sighed Elspeth. "What am I ever going to do about you? Would you like to kiss me, Peter?"

"Yes," said Peter. And he did.

"This means," he informed her presently, and dubiously, "our having to live in a Florida swamp—"

"On eighteen dollars and fifty-six cents?"

"On eight thousand a year. That isn't much more, to you. You'll hate it."

"I'll love it. D'you know where I'd like to land on our wedding trip, Peter?"

"Yes. Dake's Two-dollar Cabins; Clean; Comfortable; Reasonable."

"*And* respectable. You're too clever, Peter, darling."

"Because that's exactly what I'd like. Social note: Mr. and Mrs. Peter Warne are stopping in Jaw-jaw on their return trip South."

"Let's go," said Elspeth joyously.

Mrs. Dake, in the wing off the tourist-camp office, yawned herself awake of an early May morning and addressed her husband. "That's a funny couple in Number Seven, Tim. Do you reckon they're respectable?"

"I should worry. They registered all right, didn't they?"

"Uh-huh. Wouldn't take any other cabin but Seven. And wanted an extra blanket. This hot night."

"Well, we could spare it."

"That isn't the only queer thing about 'em. After you was asleep, I looked out and there was the young fellah mopin' around. By and by he went in, and right soon somebody blew a horn. Just as plain as you ever heard. What do you think about that, Tim?"

Mr. Dake yawned. "What they do after they're registered and paid up is their business, not our'n."

Which is the proper and practical attitude for the management of a well-conducted tourist camp.

Stage to Lordsburg (Stagecoach)

Ernest Haycox

John Ford is known for giving different answers on different occasions to the same question, and in at least one interview he has said that Stagecoach *(1939) is based not on Ernest Haycox's story "Stage to Lordsburg," as the credits indicate, but on "Boule-de-suif" by Guy de Maupassant. In the de Maupassant story, a group of French travelers, fleeing the Germans during the Franco-Prussian War, pressures one of its number, a prostitute, to sleep with an enemy officer and persuade him to let them pass. She finally assents, and the response of the others is contempt rather than gratitude. The relationship of this story to the film is tangential at best, but it does indicate Ford's concern, crucial to the effectiveness of* Stagecoach, *with the primacy of character over event. In Henry James's phrase, and in Ford's vision, action is the result of character. Perhaps Ford saw Haycox's story line as a setting for the theme from* "Boule-de-suif," *the humble saving the arrogant.*

Stagecoach, *like Haycox's story, belongs to a sub genre that might be called the "Grand Hotel" formula, in which a group of individuals emblematic of various social strata are placed in a small, usually isolated setting, and forced by circumstances to interact. This formula survives today in the disaster film. Its appeal is dependent on the evocation of clear emotional response to the diverse characters, and on the viewer's reaction to their various successes and failures.*

In the case of Stagecoach, *the short story on which it is based served strongly as a suggestive outline for Dudley Nichol's script. Haycox was a careful and precise craftsman, particularly adept at using understatement to tell a great deal while stating very little.*

Thus, despite its compactness, "Stage to Lordsburg" provides a framework that presents many possibilities for filmic expansion. It includes two of the classical action confrontations of the Western film: the Indian attack, and the showdown/shoot-out. Yet, like the film, the primary focus is on the passengers. At the story's beginning, they are presented as types, but soon they evolve into full-blown characters. Malpais Bill is at first a hard man who will kill before being dissuaded from his revenge, but he is soon revealed as thoughtful, considerate, and able to respond emotionally to Henriette. The gambler seems self-centered and prone to jump to judgment on the difference between the army girl and the whore, but he later acts almost fatherly toward Henriette before dying in her defense. We come to know the members of the group as we come to know people we encounter in life, first as types, then as individual personalities. It is like the process of making friends: it involves us deeply with the fates of people we have learned to know; they have earned our interest by their human qualities.

In the film, each of the passengers becomes complex enough to support a subplot. The group members are quickly established in the early expository shots. Dallas, the prostitute, is first seen walking down a street, head held high, followed by a posse of darkly dressed, horse-faced women cackling in shocked, hysterical tones. The alcoholic Doc Boone staggers out of his lodging, his landlady hounding him for back rent as he heads for the saloon. Hatfield, the gambler, turns in his chair at the poker table and peers from under his broad-brimmed hat at Mrs. Mallory, the cavalry officer's wife; his prior incarnation as a Southern gentleman is suggested by his dandyish demeanor and the swirling of his cape. Gatewood, the embezzling banker, glowers at the camera in a grimace of venality. Peacock, the whiskey drummer, is constantly mistaken for a preacher. When he first appears afoot on the trail, the Ringo Kid, escaped from prison and out to seek revenge in Lordsburg, is immediately established as a nice young man. As he is being arrested by the sheriff, Ringo asks the coach driver about the man's wife and children.

Subsequent incidents reveal the interrelationships. Doc Boone redeems himself when he delivers Mrs. Mallory's child. We learn that Hatfield served in Mrs. Mallory's father's Confederate regi-

ment, and that he joined the passengers at the last minute to offer his protection to her. The softer side of Dallas emerges during her ministrations to Mrs. Mallory during the childbirth. Ringo proves his essential goodness by forgoing escape in order to stay and help repel the Apaches. As the attack becomes inevitable, the suspense is paralleled by the viewer's increasing involvement with the passengers.

At the same time, Ford fully exploits the action sequences. The Indian attack is a model of this kind of scene, full of running inserts, point-of-view shots from the top of the coach, and spectacular stuntwork. The shoot-out scene is equally masterful. Ford adopts the story's device of leaving this climactic scene to occur offstage, enhancing the suspense by a perfect use of scenes and set. Lordsburg is a dark, malevolent place; it appears to consist only of saloons and whorehouses. The Plummers are drunken, surly louts, and the taut saloon scene in which Doc Boone disarms Luke Plummer sets the mood for the showdown to come. The release of this tension is accomplished by a lovely bit of cinematic craft: shots are heard, and a moment later Luke Plummer pushes through the doors of the saloon. For a moment he seems dazed but unhurt; then he steps forward and pitches to the floor, the camera swooping in on him as he goes down, to end on a close-up of his face, his defeat.

Stagecoach stands as a milestone: the first truly adult sound Western. For the preceding decade, Westerns existed mostly as "B," or budget, films, hurriedly made on shoestring budgets and intended for juvenile audiences. The plot was always the same—good guy conquers bad—and the players were stereotyped rather than characterized. Stagecoach, with its stunning locations in Monument Valley and its focus on believable people reasonably motivated, was an experiment in quality that worked. The film established the career of John Wayne, greatest and most enduring of cowboy heroes, and brought John Ford an Academy Award nomination for his direction. Most important, it restored to major film status the Western, that most uniquely American of film genres.

STAGE TO LORDSBURG

This was one of those years in the Territory when Apache smoke signals spiraled up from the stony mountain summits and many a ranch cabin lay as a square of blackened ashes on the ground and the departure of a stage from Tonto was the beginning of an adventure that had no certain happy ending. . . .

The stage and its six horses waited in front of Weilner's store on the north side of Tonto's square. Happy Stuart was on the box, the ribbons between his fingers and one foot teetering on the brake. John Strang rode shotgun guard and an escort of ten cavalrymen waited behind the coach, half asleep in their saddles.

At four-thirty in the morning this high air was quite cold, though the sun had begun to flush the sky eastward. A small crowd stood in the square, presenting their final messages to the passengers now entering the coach. There was a girl going down to marry an infantry officer, a whisky drummer from St. Louis, an Englishman all length and bony corners and bearing with him an enormous sporting rifle, a gambler, a solid-shouldered cattleman on his way to New Mexico and a blond young man upon whom both Happy Stuart and the shotgun guard placed a narrow-eyed interest.

This seemed all until the blond man drew back from the coach door; and then a girl known commonly throughout the Territory as Henriette came quietly from the crowd. She was small and quiet, with a touch of paleness in her cheeks and her quite dark eyes lifted at the blond man's unexpected courtesy, showing surprise. There was this moment of delay and then the girl caught up her dress and stepped into the coach.

Men in the crowd were smiling but the blond one turned, his motion like the swift cut of a knife, and his attention covered that group until the smiling quit. He was tall, hollow-flanked, and definitely stamped by the guns slung low on his hips. But it wasn't the guns alone; something in his face, so watchful and so smooth, also showed his trade. Afterwards he got into the coach and slammed the door.

Happy Stuart kicked off the brakes and yelled, "Hi!" Tonto's people were calling out their last farewells and the six horses broke into a trot and the stage lunged on its fore and aft springs and rolled from town with dust dripping off its wheels like water, the cavalrymen trotting briskly behind. So they tipped down the long grade, bound on a journey no stage had attempted during the last forty-five days. Out below in the desert's distance stood the relay stations they hoped to reach and pass. Between lay a country swept empty by the quick raids of Geronimo's men.

The Englishman, the gambler and the blond man sat jammed together in the forward seat, riding backward to the course of the stage. The drummer and the cattleman occupied the uncomfortable middle bench; the two women shared the rear seat. The cattleman faced Henriette, his knees almost touching her. He had one arm hooked over the door's window sill to steady himself. A huge gold nugget slid gently back and forth along the watch chain slung across his wide chest and a chunk of black hair lay below his hat. His eyes considered Henriette, reading something in the girl that caused him to show her a deliberate smile. Henriette dropped her glance to the gloved tips of her fingers, cheeks unstirred.

They were all strangers packed closely together, with nothing in common save a destination. Yet the cattleman's smile and the boldness of his glance were something as audible as speech, noted by everyone except the Englishman, who sat bolt upright with his stony indifference. The army girl, tall and calmly pretty, threw a quick side glance at Henriette and afterwards looked away with a touch of color. The gambler saw this interchange of glances and showed the cattleman an irritated attention. The whisky drummer's eyes narrowed a little and some inward cynicism made a faint change on his lips. He removed his hat to show a bald head already beginning to sweat; his cigar smoke turned the coach cloudy and ashes kept dropping on his vest.

The blond man had observed Henriette's glance drop from the cattleman; he tipped his hat well over his face and watched her —not boldly but as though he were puzzled. Once her glance lifted and touched him. But he had been on guard against that and was quick to look away.

The army girl coughed gently behind her hand, whereupon the gambler tapped the whisky drummer on the shoulder. "Get rid of that." The drummer appeared startled. He grumbled, "Beg pardon," and tossed the smoke through the window.

All this while the coach went rushing down the ceaseless turns of the mountain road, rocking on its fore and aft springs, its heavy wheels slamming through the road ruts and whining on the curves. Occasionally the strident yell of Happy Stuart washed back. "Hi, Nellie! By God—!" The whisky drummer braced himself against the door and closed his eyes.

Three hours from Tonto the road, making a last round sweep, let them down upon the flat desert. Here the stage stopped and the men got out to stretch. The gambler spoke to the army girl, gently: "Perhaps you would find my seat more comfortable." The army girl said "Thank you," and changed over. The cavalry sergeant rode up to the stage, speaking to Happy Stuart.

"We'll be goin' back now—and good luck to ye."

The men piled in, the gambler taking the place beside Henriette. The blond man drew his long legs together to give the army girl more room, and watched Henriette's face with a soft, quiet care. A hard sun beat fully on the coach and dust began to whip up like fire smoke. Without escort they rolled across a flat earth broken only by cacti standing against a dazzling light. In the far distance, behind a blue heat haze, lay the faint suggestion of mountains.

The cattleman reached up and tugged at the ends of his mustache and smiled at Henriette. The army girl spoke to the blond man. "How far is it to the noon station?" The blond man said courteously: "Twenty miles." The gambler watched the army girl with the strictness of his face relaxing, as though the run of her voice reminded him of things long forgotten.

The miles fell behind and the smell of alkali dust got thicker. Henriette rested against the corner of the coach, her eyes dropped to the tips of her gloves. She made an enigmatic, disinterested shape there; she seemed past stirring, beyond laughter. She was young, yet she had a knowledge that put the cattleman and the gambler and the drummer and the army girl in their exact places; and she knew why the gambler had offered the army girl his seat. The army girl was in one world and she was in another, as everyone in the coach understood. It had no effect on her for this was a distinction she had learned long ago. Only the blond man broke through her indifference. His name was Malpais Bill and she could see the wildness in the corners of his eyes and in the long crease of his lips; it was a stamp that would never come off. Yet something flowed out of him toward her that was different than the predatory curiosity of other men; something unobtrusively gallant, unexpectedly gentle.

Upon the box Happy Stuart pointed to the hazy outline two miles away. "Injuns ain't burned that anyhow." The sun was directly overhead, turning the light of the world a cruel brass-yellow. The crooked crack of a dry wash opened across the two deep ruts that made this road. Johnny Strang shifted the gun in his lap. "What's Malpais Bill ridin' with us for?"

"I guess I wouldn't ask him," returned Happy Stuart and studied the wash with a troubled eye. The road fell into it roughly and he got a tighter grip on his reins and yelled: "Hang on! Hi, Nellie! God damn you, hi!" The six horses plunged down the rough side of the wash and for a moment the coach stood alone, high and lonely on the break, and then went reeling over the rim. It struck the gravel with a roar, the front wheels bouncing and the back wheels skewing around. The horses faltered but Happy Stuart cursed at his leaders and got them into a run again. The horses lunged up the far side of the wash two and two, their muscles bunching and the soft dirt flying in yellow clouds. The front wheels struck solidly and something cracked like a pistol shot; the stage rose out of the wash, teetered crosswise and then fell ponderously on its side, splintering the coach panels.

Johnny Strang jumped clear. Happy Stuart hung to the handrail with one hand and hauled on the reins with the other; and stood up while the passengers crawled through the upper door. All the men, except the whisky drummer, put their shoulders to the coach and heaved it upright again. The whisky drummer stood strangely in the bright sunlight shaking his head dumbly while the others climbed back in. Happy Stuart said, "All right, brother, git aboard."

The drummer climbed in slowly and the stage ran on. There was a low, gray dobe relay station squatted on the desert dead ahead with a scatter of corrals about it and a flag hanging limp on a crooked pole. Men came out of the dobe's dark interior and stood in the shade of the porch gallery. Happy Stuart rolled up and stopped. He said to a lanky man: "Hi, Mack. Where's the God-damned Injuns?"

The passengers were filing into the dobe's dining room. The lanky one drawled: "You'll see 'em before tomorrow night." Hostlers came up to change horses.

The little dining room was cool after the coach, cool and still. A fat Mexican woman ran in and out with the food platters. Happy Stuart said: "Ten minutes," and brushed the alkali dust from his mouth and fell to eating.

The long-jawed Mack said: "Catlin's ranch burned last night. Was a troop of cavalry around here yesterday. Came and went. You'll git to the Gap tonight all right but I do' know about the mountains beyond. A little trouble?"

"A little," said Happy, briefly, and rose. This was the end of rest. The passengers followed, with the whisky drummer straggling at the rear, reaching deeply for wind. The coach rolled away again, Mack's voice pursuing them. "Hit it a lick, Happy, if you see any dust rollin' out of the east."

Heat had condensed in the coach and the little wind fanned up by the run of the horses was stifling to the lungs; the desert floor projected its white glitter endlessly away until lost in the smoky haze. The cattleman's knees bumped Henriette gently and he kept watching her, a celluloid toothpick drooped between his lips. Happy Stuart's voice ran back, profane and urgent, keeping the speed of the coach constant through the ruts. The whisky drummer's eyes were round and strained and his mouth was open and all the color had gone out of his face. The gambler observed this without expression and without care; and once the cattleman, feeling the sag of the whisky drummer's shoulder, shoved him away. The Englishman sat bolt upright, staring emotionlessly at the passing desert. The army girl spoke to Malpais Bill: "What is the next stop?"

"Gap Creek."

"Will we meet soldiers there?"

He said: "I expect we'll have an escort over the hills into Lordsburg."

And at four o'clock of this furnace-hot afternoon the whisky drummer made a feeble gesture with one hand and fell forward into the gambler's lap.

The cattleman shrugged his shoulders and put a head through the window, calling up to Happy Stuart: "Wait a minute." When the stage stopped everybody climbed out and the blond man helped the gambler lay the whisky drummer in the sweltering patch of shade created by the coach. Neither Happy Stuart nor the shotgun guard bothered to get down. The whisky drummer's lips moved a little but nobody said anything and nobody knew what to do—until Henriette stepped forward.

She dropped to the ground, lifting the whisky drummer's shoulders and head against her breasts. He opened his eyes and there was something in them that they could all see, like relief and ease, like gratefulness. She murmured: "You are all right," and her smile was soft and pleasant, turning her lips maternal. There was this wisdom in her, this knowledge of the fears that men concealed behind their manners, the deep hungers that rode them so savagely, and the loneliness that drove them to women of her kind. She repeated, "You are all right," and watched this whisky drummer's eyes lose the wildness of what he knew.

The army girl's face showed shock. The gambler and the cattleman looked down at the whisky drummer quite impersonally. The blond man watched Henriette through lids half closed, but the flare of a powerful interest broke the severe lines of his cheeks. He held a cigarette between his fingers; he had forgotten it.

Happy Stuart said: "We can't stay here."

The gambler bent down to catch the whisky drummer under the arms. Henriette rose and said, "Bring him to me," and got into the coach. The blond man and the gambler lifted the drummer through the door so that he was lying along the back seat, cushioned on Henriette's lap. They all got in and the coach rolled on. The drummer groaned a little, whispering: "Thanks—thanks," and the blond man, searching Henriette's face for every shred of expression, drew a gusty breath.

They went on like this, the big wheels pounding the ruts of the road while a lowering sun blazed through the coach windows. The mountain bulwarks began to march nearer, more definite in the blue fog. The cattleman's eyes were small and brilliant and touched Henriette personally, but the gambler bent toward Henriette to say: "If you are tired—"

"No," she said. "No. He's dead."

The army girl stifled a small cry. The gambler bent nearer the whisky drummer, and then they were all looking at Henriette; even the Englishman stared at her for a moment, faint curiosity in his eyes. She was remotely smiling, her lips broad and soft. She held the drummer's head with both her hands and continued to hold him like that until, at the swift fall of dusk, they rolled across the last of the desert floor and drew up before Gap Station.

The cattleman kicked open the door and stepped out, grunting as his stiff legs touched the ground. The gambler pulled the drummer up so that Henriette could leave. They all came out, their bones tired from the shaking. Happy Stuart climbed from the box, his face a gray mask of alkali and his eyes bloodshot. He said: "Who's dead?" and looked into the coach. People sauntered from the station yard, walking with the indolence of twilight. Happy Stuart said, "Well, he won't worry about tomorrow," and turned away.

A short man with a tremendous stomach shuffled through the dusk. He said: "Wasn't sure you'd try to git through yet, Happy."

"Where's the soldiers for tomorrow?"

"Other side of the mountains. Everybody's chased out. What ain't forted up here was sent into Lordsburg. You men will bunk in the barn. I'll make out for the ladies somehow." He looked at the army girl and he appraised Henriette instantly. His eyes slid on to Malpais Bill standing in the background and recognition stirred him then and made his voice careful. "Hello, Bill. What brings you this way?"

Malpais Bill's cigarette glowed in the gathering dusk and Henriette caught the brief image of his face, serene and watchful. Malpais Bill's tone was easy, it was soft. "Just the trip."

They were moving on toward the frame house whose corners seemed to extend indefinitely into a series of attached sheds. Lights glimmered in the windows and men moved around the place, idly talking. The unhitched horses went away at a trot. The tall girl walked into the station's big room, to face a soldier in a disheveled uniform.

He said: "Miss Robertson? Lieutenant Hauser was to have met you here. He is at Lordsburg. He was wounded in a brush with the Apaches last night."

The tall army girl stood very still. She said: "Badly?"

"Well," said the soldier, "yes."

The fat man came in, drawing deeply for wind. "Too bad—too bad. Ladies, I'll show you the rooms, such as I got."

Henriette's dove-colored dress blended with the background shadows. She was watching the tall army girl's face whiten. But there was a strength in the army girl, a fortitude that made her think of the soldier. For she said quietly, "You must have had a bad trip."

"Nothing—nothing at all," said the soldier and left the room. The gambler was here, his thin face turning to the army girl with a strained expression, as though he were remembering painful things. Malpais Bill had halted in the doorway, studying the softness and the humility of Henriette's cheeks. Afterwards both women followed the fat host of Gap Station along a narrow hall to their quarters.

Malpais Bill wheeled out and stood indolently against the wall of this desert station, his glance quick and watchful in the way it touched all the men loitering along the yard, his ears weighing all the night-softened voices. Heat died from the earth and a definite chill rolled down the mountain hulking so high behind the house. The soldier was in his saddle, murmuring drowsily to Happy Stuart.

"Well, Lordsburg is a long ways off and the damn' mountains are squirmin' with Apaches. You won't have any cavalry escort tomorrow. The troops are all in the field."

Malpais Bill listened to the hoofbeats of the soldier's horse fade out, remembering the loneliness of a man in those dark mountain passes, and went back to the saloon at the end of the station. This was a low-ceilinged shed with a dirt floor and whitewashed walls that once had been part of a stable. Three men stood under a lantern in the middle of this little place, the light of the lantern palely shining in the rounds of their eyes as they watched him. At the far end of the bar the cattleman and the gambler drank in taciturn silence. Malpais Bill took his whisky when the bottle came, and noted the barkeep's obscure glance. Gap's host put in his head and wheezed, "Second table," and the other men in here began to move out. The barkeep's words rubbed together, one tone above a whisper. "Better not ride into Lordsburg. Plummer and Shanley are there."

Malpais Bill's lips were stretched to the long edge of laughter and there was a shine like wildness in his eyes. He said, "Thanks, friend," and went into the dining room.

When he came back to the yard night lay wild and deep across the desert and the moonlight was a frozen silver that touched but could not dissolve the world's incredible blackness. The girl Henriette walked along the Tonto road, swaying gently in the vague shadows. He went that way, the click of his heels on the hard earth bringing her around.

Her face was clear and strange and incurious in the night, as though she waited for something to come, and knew what it would be. But he said: "You're too far from the house. Apaches like to crawl down next to a settlement and wait for strays."

She was indifferent, unafraid. Her voice was cool and he could hear the faint loneliness in it, the fatalism that made her words so even. "There's a wind coming up, so soft and good."

He took off his hat, long legs braced, and his eyes were both attentive and puzzled. His blond hair glowed in the fugitive light.

She said in a deep breath: "Why do you do that?"

His lips were restless and the sing and rush of strong feeling was like a current of quick wind around him. "You have folks in Lordsburg?"

She spoke in a direct, patient way as though explaining something he should have known without asking. "I run a house in Lordsburg."

"No," he said, "it wasn't what I asked."

"My folks are dead—I think. There was a massacre in the Superstition Mountains when I was young."

He stood with his head bowed, his mind reaching back to fill in that gap of her life. There was a hardness and a rawness to this land and little sympathy for the weak. She had survived and had paid for her survival, and looked at him now in a silent way that offered no explanations or apologies for whatever had been; she was still a pretty girl with the dead patience of all the past years in her eyes, in the expressiveness of her lips.

He said: "Over in the Tonto Basin is a pretty land. I've got a piece of a ranch there—with a house half built."

"If that's your country why are you here?"

His lips laughed and the rashness in him glowed hot again and he seemed to grow taller in the moonlight. "A debt to collect."

"That's why you're going to Lordsburg? You will never get through collecting those kind of debts. Everybody in the Territory knows you. Once you were just a rancher. Then you tried to wipe out a grudge and then there was a bigger one to wipe out—and the debt kept growing and more men are waiting to kill you. Someday a man will. You'd better run away from the debts."

His bright smile kept constant, and presently she lifted her shoulders with resignation. "No," she murmured, "you won't run." He could see the sweetness of her lips and the way her eyes were sad for him; he could see in them the patience he had never learned.

He said, "We'd better go back," and turned her with his arm. They went across the yard in silence, hearing the undertone of men's drawling talk roll out of the shadows, seeing the glow of men's pipes in the dark corners. Malpais Bill stopped and watched her go through the station door; she turned to look at him once more, her eyes all dark and her lips softly sober, and then passed down the narrow corridor to her own quarters. Beyond her window, in the yard, a man was murmuring to another man: "Plummer and Shanley are in Lordsburg. Malpais Bill knows it." Through the thin partition of the adjoining room she heard the army girl crying with a suppressed, uncontrollable regularity. Henriette stared at the dark wall, her shoulders and head bowed; and afterwards returned to the hall and knocked on the army girl's door and went in.

Six fresh horses fiddled in front of the coach and the fat host of Gap Station came across the yard swinging a lantern against the dead, bitter black. All the passengers filed sleep-dulled and miserable from the house. Johnny Strang slammed the express box in the boot and Happy Stuart gruffly said: "All right, folks."

The passengers climbed in. The cattleman came up and Malpais Bill drawled: "Take the corner spot, mister," and got in, closing the door. The Gap host grumbled: "If they don't jump you on the long grade you'll be all right. You're safe when you get to Al

Schrieber's ranch." Happy's bronze voice shocked the black stillness and the coach lurched forward, its leather springs squealing.

They rode for an hour in this complete darkness, chilled and
uncomfortable and half asleep, feeling the coach drag on a heavy-
climbing grade. Gray dawn cracked through, followed by a sunless
light rushing all across the flat desert now far below. The road
looped from one barren shoulder to another and at sunup they had
reached the first bench and were slamming full speed along a
boulder-strewn flat. The cattleman sat in the forward corner, the
left corner of his mouth swollen and crushed, and when Henriette
saw that her glance slid to Malpais Bill's knuckles. The army girl
had her eyes closed, her shoulders pressing against the Englishman, who remained bolt upright with the sporting gun between his
knees. Beside Henriette the gambler seemed to sleep, and on the
middle bench Malpais Bill watched the land go by with a thin
vigilance.

At ten they were rising again, with juniper and scrub pine showing on the slopes and the desert below them filling with the pow-
dered haze of another hot day. By noon they reached the summit
of the range and swung to follow its narrow rock-ribbed meadows.
The gambler, long motionless, shifted his feet and caught the
army girl's eyes.

"Schrieber's is directly ahead. We are past the worst of it."

The blond man looked around at the gambler, making no comment; and it was then that Henriette caught the smell of smoke
in the windless air. Happy Stuart was cursing once more and the
brake blocks began to cry. Looking through the angled vista of the
window panel Henriette saw a clay and rock chimney standing up
like a gaunt skeleton against the day's light. The house that had
been there was a black patch on the ground, smoke still rising
from pieces that had not been completely burnt.

The stage stopped and all the men were instantly out. An iron
stove squatted on the earth, with one section of pipe stuck upright
to it. Fire licked lazily along the collapsed fragments of what had
been a trunk. Beyond the location of the house, at the foot of a
corral, lay two nude figures grotesquely bald, with deliberate knife
slashes marking their bodies. Happy Stuart went over there and
had his look; and came back.

"Schriebers. Well—"

Malpais Bill said: "This morning about daylight." He looked at the gambler, at the cattleman, at the Englishman who showed no emotion. "Get back in the coach." He climbed to the coach's top, flattening himself full length there. Happy Stuart and Strang took their places again. The horses broke into a run.

The gambler said to the army girl: "You're pretty safe between those two fellows," and hauled a .44 from a back pocket and laid it over his lap. He considered Henriette more carefully than before, his taciturnity breaking. He said: "How old are you?"

Her shoulders rose and fell, which was the only answer. But the gambler said gently, "Young enough to be my daughter. It is a rotten world. When I call to you, lie down on the floor."

The Englishman had pulled the rifle from between his knees and laid it across the sill of the window on his side. The cattleman swept back the skirt of his coat to clear the holster of his gun.

The little flinty summit meadows grew narrower, with shoulders of gray rock closing in upon the road. The coach wheels slammed against the stony ruts and bounced high and fell again with a jar the springs could not soften. Happy Stuart's howl ran steadily above this rattle and rush. Fine dust turned all things gray.

Henriette sat with her eyes pinned to the gloved tips of her fingers, remembering the tall shape of Malpais Bill cut against the moonlight of Gap Station. He had smiled at her as a man might smile at any desirable woman, with the sweep and swing of laughter in his voice; and his eyes had been gentle. The gambler spoke very quietly and she didn't hear him until his fingers gripped her arm. He said again, not raising his voice: "Get down."

Henriette dropped to her knees, hearing gunfire blast through the rush and run of the coach. Happy Stuart ceased to yell and the army girl's eyes were round and dark. The walls of the canyon had tapered off. Looking upward through the window on the gambler's side, Henriette saw the weaving figure of an Apache warrior reel nakedly on a calico pony and rush by with a rifle raised and pointed in his bony elbows. The gambler took a cool aim; the stockman fired and aimed again. The Englishman's sporting rifle blasted heavy echoes through the coach, hurting her ears, and the smell of powder got rank and bitter. The blond man's boots scraped the coach top and round small holes began to dimple the paneling as the Apache bullets struck. An Indian came boldly abreast the coach and made a target that couldn't be missed. The cattleman dropped him with one shot. The wheels screamed as they slowed around the sharp ruts and the whole heavy superstructure of the coach bounced high into the air. Then they were rushing downgrade.

The gambler said quietly, "You had better take this," handing Henriette his gun. He leaned against the door with his small hands gripping the sill. Pallor loosened his cheeks. He said to the army girl: "Be sure and keep between those gentlemen," and looked at her with a way that was desperate and forlorn and dropped his head to the window's sill.

Henriette saw the bluff rise up and close in like a yellow wall. They were rolling down the mountain without brake. Gunfire fell off and the crying of the Indians faded back. Coming up from her knees then she saw the desert's flat surface far below, with the angular pattern of Lordsburg vaguely on the far borders of the heat fog. There was no more firing and Happy Stuart's voice lifted again and the brakes were screaming on the wheels, and going off, and screaming again. The Englishman stared out of the window sullenly; the army girl seemed in a deep desperate dream; the cattleman's face was shining with a strange sweat. Henriette reached over to pull the gambler up, but he had an unnatural weight to him and slid into the far corner. She saw that he was dead.

At five o'clock that long afternoon the stage threaded Lordsburg's narrow streets of dobe and frame houses, came upon the center square and stopped before a crowd of people gathered in the smoky heat. The passengers crawled out stiffly. A Mexican boy ran up to see the dead gambler and began to yell his news in shrill Mexican. Malpais Bill climbed off the top, but Happy Stuart sat back on his seat and stared taciturnly at the crowd. Henriette noticed then that the shotgun messenger was gone.

A gray man in a sleazy white suit called up to Happy. "Well, you got through."

Happy Stuart said: "Yeah. We got through."

An officer stepped through the crowd, smiling at the army girl.

He took her arm and said, "Miss Robertson, I believe. Lieutenant Hauser is quite all right. I will get your luggage—"

The army girl was crying then, definitely. They were all standing around, bone-weary and shaken. Malpais Bill remained by the wheel of the coach, his cheeks hard against the sunlight and his eyes riveted on a pair of men standing under the board awning of an adjoining store. Henriette observed the manner of their waiting and knew why they were here. The blond man's eyes, she noticed, were very blue and flame burned brilliantly in them. The army girl turned to Henriette, tears in her eyes. She murmured: "If there is anything I can ever do for you—"

But Henriette stepped back, shaking her head. This was Lordsburg and everybody knew her place except the army girl. Henriette said formally, "Good-by," noting how still and expectant the two men under the awning remained. She swung toward the blond man and said, "Would you carry my valise?"

Malpais Bill looked at her, laughter remote in his eyes, and reached into the luggage pile and got her battered valise. He was still smiling as he went beside her, through the crowd and past the two waiting men. But when they turned into an anonymous and dusty little side street of the town, where the houses all sat shoulder to shoulder without grace or dignity, he had turned sober. He said: "I am obliged to you. But I'll have to go back there."

They were in front of a house no different from its neighbors; they had stopped at its door. She could see his eyes travel this street and comprehend its meaning and the kind of traffic it bore. But he was saying in that gentle, melody-making tone:

"I have watched you for two days." He stopped, searching his mind to find the thing he wanted to say. It came out swiftly. "God made you a woman. The Tonto is a pretty country."

Her answer was quite barren of feeling. "No. I am known all through the Territory. But I can remember that you asked me."

He said: "No other reason?" She didn't answer but something in her eyes pulled his face together. He took off his hat and it seemed to her he was looking through this hot day to that far-off country and seeing it fresh and desirable. He murmured: "A man can escape nothing. I have got to do this. But I will be back."

He went along the narrow street, made a quick turn at the end of it, and disappeared. Heat rolled like a heavy wave over Lordsburg's housetops and the smell of dust was very sharp. She lifted her valise, and dropped it and stood like that, mute and grave before the door of her dismal house. She was remembering how tall he had been against the moonlight at Gap Station.

There were four swift shots beating furiously along the sultry quiet, and a shout, and afterwards a longer and longer silence. She put one hand against the door to steady herself, and knew that those shots marked the end of a man, and the end of a hope. He would never come back; he would never stand over her in the moonlight with the long gentle smile on his lips and with the swing of life in his casual tone. She was thinking of all that humbly and with the patience life had beaten into her. . . .

She was thinking of all that when she heard the strike of boots on the street's packed earth; and turned to see him, high and square in the muddy sunlight, coming toward her with his smile.

Cyclists' Raid (The Wild One)

Frank Rooney

On page thirty-one of the July 21, 1947, issue of Life *magazine there appears a full-page photograph of a young man on a motorcycle. The bike is propped on its kickstand, and the man is lounging back and sipping from a bottle of beer, his insolent gaze on the camera. There is a litter of empties on the ground. Under the headline* CYCLIST'S HOLIDAY *and the subhead "He and friends terrorize a town," the copy reads:*

On the Fourth of July weekend 4,000 members of a motorcycle club roared into Hollister, Calif. for a three-day convention. They quickly tired of ordinary motorcycle thrills and turned to more exciting stunts. Racing their vehicles down the main street and through traffic lights, they rammed into restaurants and bars, breaking furniture and mirrors. . . . Police arrested many for drunkenness and indecent exposure but could not restore order. Finally, after two days, the cyclists left with a brazen explanation. "We like to show off. It's just a lot of fun." But Hollister's police chief took a different view. Wailed he, "It's just one hell of a mess."

The incident in general, and this particular photograph, were the inspirations for Frank Rooney's "Cyclists' Raid." The story in turn was the basis for Laslo Benedek's The Wild One *(1954). But in the progress from actual incident to short story to film, some significant and to some critics disturbing changes took place.*

Rooney's story is told from the point of view of townsman Joel Bleeker, a former professional soldier who desperately attempts to retain his self-control as the outlaw weekend progresses. The siege of the town, senseless and unresolved, becomes meaningful because it is also, in a significant parallel, warfare against Bleeker's ability to cope as a man of society with antisocietal forces, a conflict resolved in his personal tragedy. But the story has no hero; Bleeker's vision is as flawed as that of the biker outlaws.

To Rooney, the gang members are absolutely lacking in individuality. Only two have personality: Gar Simpson, the cold-blooded paramilitaristic leader; and the young misfit, who is not given a name. The gang becomes a naturalistic force, a tide against which the town or any one of its citizens is impotent.

Rooney's prose is almost calculatedly cinematographic. Background noise runs through the story, from the first alien roar announcing the cyclists' arrival to the constant rising din as their rampage goes out of control. Visual images are as detailed as photographs: we see "the sudden, shocking exposure of [Cathy's] flesh, the robe and the gown torn away from the leg as if pushed aside by the blood welling from her thigh." Rooney even evokes slow-motion:

> The motorcycle on the sidewalk speeded up and skidded obliquely into a plate-glass window, the front wheel bucking and climbing the brick base beneath the window. A single large section of glass slipped edge-down to the sidewalk and fell slowly toward the cyclist who, with his feet spread and kicking at the cement, backed clumsily away from it. Bleeker could feel the crash in his teeth.

The film version of the story grafts a hero, or antihero, to Rooney's action. The Wild One is a vehicle for the young Marlon Brando, who had scored a major success three years earlier playing another alienated young man, Stanley Kowalski, in A Streetcar Named Desire (1951). Johnny is a combination of Gar Simpson and the misfit youth; he remains an outlaw, but he also reveals self-doubts and sensitivities that make him a more sympathetic focus for the viewer's response to the mayhem. His cool superiority holds him apart from the evident immaturity of the other gang members. He is further isolated by his distance from the rival gang leader, Chico (Lee Marvin), who is much more traditionally an outlaw: he is a lousy drunk, dresses shabbily, needs a shave, smokes cigars, and is likely to throw a sucker punch when Johnny is off guard.

The film is heavy with overtones of homosexuality, going well

*beyond the subtle suggestion inherent in the gang's leather out-
fits. On two occasions, gang members dress in women's clothing.
Chico declares several times, with drunken semi-irony, "I love you,
Johnny." Even Johnny's manhood is called into question: his
romantic interlude with Kathy (Mary Murphy) makes it painfully
evident that he has no notion of how to behave with a woman.*

*The film begins with a superimposed prologue: "This is a shock-
ing story. It could never take place in most American towns. But
it did in this one. It is a public challenge not to let it happen again."
But as the story develops, it becomes unclear whether the statement refers to the gang's outlaw actions or to the vigilante reaction of the townsfolk, which is directly responsible for the only
death. This ambiguity seriously mars the ending, when Johnny is
released by the police and leaves town, only to return to signify
his repentance and emerging maturity by flashing his only smile
of the film.*

*This implies that the gang's behavior is excused, which leaves
the vigilante townspeople as unredeemed villains. Both public and
critics were upset. Hollis Alpert of* The Saturday Review *placed
himself in the minority when he called the film "something in the
way of a public service." Time deplored the film's violence as
gratuitous, saying: "The script . . . says that the community is as
much to blame as the young delinquents are, but it is hard to
believe such talk. The effect of the movie is not to throw light on
a public problem, but to shoot adrenaline through the moviegoer's
veins." Newsweek agreed that the film "lacks both the social significance and dramatic resolution to justify the heavy going." In
England the reaction was more severe: the movie was banned
completely by the board of censors, and was not released to
general exhibition for fifteen years.*

CYCLISTS' RAID

Joel Bleeker, owner and operator of the Pendleton Hotel, was
adjusting the old redwood clock in the lobby when he heard the
sound of the motors. At first he thought it might be one of those
four-engine planes on the flights from Los Angeles to San Fran-

cisco which occasionally got far enough off course to be heard in the valley. And for a moment, braced against the steadily approaching vibrations of the sound, he had the fantastic notion that the plane was going to strike the hotel. He even glanced at his daughter, Cathy, standing a few feet to his right and staring curiously at the street.

Then, with his fingers still on the hour hand of the clock, he realized that the sound was not something coming down from the air but the high, sputtering racket of many vehicles moving along the ground. Cathy, and Bert Timmons, who owned one of the two drugstores in the town, went out onto the veranda, but Bleeker stayed by the clock, consulting the railroad watch he pulled from his vest pocket and moving the hour hand on the clock forward a minute and a half. He stepped back deliberately, shut the glass case, and looked at the huge brass numbers and the two ornate brass pointers. It was eight minutes after seven, approximately twenty-two minutes until sundown. He put the railroad watch back in his pocket and walked slowly and incuriously through the open doors of the lobby. He was methodical and orderly, and the small things he did every day—like setting the clock—were important to him. He was not to be hurried—especially by something as elusively irritating as a sound, however unusual.

There were only three people on the veranda when Bleeker came out of the lobby—his daughter Cathy, Timmons, and Francis LaSalle, co-owner of LaSalle and Fleet, Hardware. They stood together quietly, looking, without appearing to stare, at a long stern column of red motorcycles coming from the south, filling the single main street of the town with the noise of a multitude of pistons and the crackling of exhaust pipes. They could see now that the column was led by a single white motorcycle which, when it came abreast of the hotel, turned abruptly right and stopped. They saw, too, that the column, without seeming to slow down or to execute any elaborate movement, had divided itself into two single files. At the approximate second, having received a signal from their leader, they also turned right and stopped.

The whole flanking action, singularly neat and quite like the various vehicular formations he remembered in the army, was distasteful to Bleeker. It recalled a little too readily his tenure as a lieutenant colonel overseas in England, France, and finally Germany.

"Mr. Bleeker?"

Bleeker realized the whole troop—no one in the town either then or after that night was ever agreed on the exact number of men in the troop—had dismounted and that the leader was addressing him.

"I'm Bleeker." Although he hadn't intended to, he stepped forward when he spoke, much as he had stepped forward in the years when he commanded a battalion.

"I'm Gar Simpson and this is Troop B of the Angeleno Motorcycle Club," the leader said. He was a tall, spare man, and his voice was coldly courteous to the point of mockery. "We expect to bivouac outside your town tonight and we wondered if we might use the facilities of your hotel. Of course, sir, we'll pay."

"There's a washroom downstairs. If you can put up with that—"

"That will be fine, sir. Is the dining room still open?"

"It is."

"Could you take care of twenty men?"

"What about the others?"

"They can be accommodated elsewhere, sir."

Simpson saluted casually and, turning to the men assembled stiffly in front of the hotel, issued a few quiet orders. Quickly and efficiently, the men in the troop parked their motorcycles at the curb. About a third of the group detached itself and came deferentially but steadily up the hotel steps. They passed Bleeker who found himself maneuvered aside and went into the lobby. As they passed him, Bleeker could see the slight converted movement of their faces—though not their eyes, which were covered by large green goggles—toward his daughter Cathy. Bleeker frowned after them but before he could think of anything to say, Simpson, standing at his left, touched his arm.

"I've divided the others into two groups," he said quietly. "One group will eat at the diner and the other at the Desert Hotel."

"Very good," Bleeker said. "You evidently know the town like a book. The people, too. Have you ever been here before?"

"We have a map of all the towns in this part of California, sir. And of course we know the names of all the principal hotels and their proprietors. Personally, I could use a drink. Would you join me?"

"After you," Bleeker said.

He stood watching Simpson stride into the lobby and without any hesitation go directly to the bar. Then he turned to Cathy, seeing Timmons and LaSalle lounging on the railing behind her, their faces already indistinct in the plummeting California twilight.

"You go help in the kitchen, Cathy," Bleeker said. "I think it'd be better if you didn't wait on tables."

"I wonder what they look like behind those goggles," Cathy said.

"Like anybody else," Timmons said. He was about thirty, somewhat coarse and intolerant and a little embarrassed at being in love with a girl as young as Cathy. "Where did you think they came from? Mars?"

"What did they say the name of their club was?" Cathy said.

"Angeleno," LaSalle said.

"They must be from Los Angeles. Heigh-ho. Shall I wear my very best gingham, citizen colonel?"

"Remember now—you stay in the kitchen," Bleeker said.

He watched her walk into the lobby, a tall slender girl of seventeen, pretty and enigmatic, with something of the brittle independence of her mother. Bleeker remembered suddenly, although he tried not to, the way her mother had walked away from him that frosty January morning two years ago saying, "I'm going for a ride." And then the two-day search in the mountains after the horse had come back alone and the finding of her body—the neck broken—in the stream at the foot of the cliff. During the war he had never really believed that he would live to get back to Cathy's mother, and after the war he hadn't really believed he would be separated from her—not again—not twice in so short a time.

Shaking his head—as if by that motion he could shed his memories as easily as a dog sheds water—Bleeker went in to join Gar Simpson who was sitting at a table in the barroom. Simpson stood politely when Bleeker took the opposite chair.

"How long do you fellows plan to stay?" Bleeker asked. He took the first sip of his drink, looked up, and stared at Simpson.

"Tonight and tomorrow morning," Simpson said.

Like all the others, he was dressed in a brown windbreaker, khaki shirt, khaki pants, and, as Bleeker had previously observed, wore dark calf-length boots. A cloth and leather helmet lay on the table beside Simpson's drink, but he hadn't removed his flat green goggles, an accouterment giving him and the men in his troop the appearance of some tropical tribe with enormous semiprecious eyes, lidless and immovable. That was Bleeker's first impression and, absurd as it was, it didn't seem an exaggeration of fancy but of truth.

"Where do you go after this?"

"North." Simpson took a rolled map from a binocular case slung over his shoulder and spread it on the table. "Roughly we're following the arc of an ellipse with its southern tip based on Los Angeles and its northern end touching Fresno."

"Pretty ambitious for a motorcycle club."

"We have a month," Simpson said. "This is our first week, but we're in no hurry and we're out to see plenty of country."

"What are you interested in mainly?"

"Roads. Naturally, being a motorcycle club—you'd be surprised at the rate we're expanding—we'd like to have as much of California as possible opened up to us."

"I see."

"Keeps the boys fit, too. The youth of America. Our hope for the future." Simpson pulled sternly at his drink, and Bleeker had the impression that Simpson was repressing, openly, and with pride, a vast sparkling ecstasy.

Bleeker sat and watched the young men in the troop file upstairs from the public washroom and stroll casually but nevertheless with discipline into the dining room. They had removed their helmets and strapped them to their belts, each helmet in a prescribed position to the left of the belt-buckle, but—like Simpson—they had retained their goggles. Bleeker wondered if they ever removed the goggles long enough to wash under them and, if they did, what the flesh under them looked like.

"I think I'd better help out at the tables," Bleeker said. He stood up, and Simpson stood with him. "You say you're from Troop B? Is that right?"

"Correct. We're forming Troop G now. Someday—"

"You'll be up to Z," Bleeker said.

"And not only in California."

"Where else for instance?"

"Nevada—Arizona—Colorado—Wyoming."

Simpson smiled, and Bleeker, turning away from him abruptly, went into the dining room where he began to help the two waitresses at the tables. He filled water glasses, set out extra forks, and brought steins of beer from the bar. As he served the troop, their polite thank you's, ornate and insincere, irritated him. It reminded him of tricks taught to animals, the animals only being allowed to perform under certain obvious conditions of security. And he didn't like the cool way they stared at the two waitresses, both older women and fixtures in the town, and then leaned their heads together as if every individual thought had to be pooled and divided equally among them. He admitted, after some covert study, that the twenty men were really only variations of one, the variations, with few exceptions, being too subtle for him to recognize and differentiate. It was the goggles, he decided, covering that part of the face which is most noteworthy and most needful for identification—the eyes and the mask around the eyes.

Bleeker went into the kitchen, pretending to help but really to be near Cathy. The protective father, he thought ironically, watching his daughter cut pie and lay the various colored wedges on the white blue-bordered plates.

"Well, Daddy, what's the verdict?" Cathy looked extremely grave, but he could see that she was amused.

"They're a fine body of men."

"Uh-huh. Have you called the police yet?"

He laughed. "It's a good thing you don't play poker."

"Child's play." She slid the last piece of blueberry pie on a plate. "I saw you through the door. You looked like you were ready to crack the Siegfried line—singlehanded."

"That man Simpson."

"What about him?"

"Why don't you go upstairs and read a book or something?"

"Now, Daddy—you're the only professional here. They're just acting like little tin soldiers out on a spree."

"I wish to God they were made of tin."

"All right. I'll keep away from them. I promise." She made a gesture of crossing her throat with the thin edge of a knife. He leaned over and kissed her forehead, his hand feeling awkward and stern on her back.

After dinner the troop went into the bar, moving with a strange co-ordinated fluency that was both casual and military, and sat jealously together in one corner of the room. Bleeker served them pitchers of beer, and for the most part they talked quietly together, Simpson at their center, their voices guarded and urgent as if they possessed information which couldn't be disseminated safely among the public.

Bleeker left them after a while and went upstairs to his daughter's room. He wasn't used to being severe with Cathy and he was a little embarrassed by what he had said to her in the kitchen. She was turning the collars of some of his old shirts, using a portable sewing machine he had bought her as a present on her last birthday. As he came in, she held one of the shirts comically to the floor lamp, and he could see how thin and transparent the material was. Her mother's economy in small things, almost absurd when compared to her limitless generosity in matters of importance, had been one of the family jokes. It gave him an extraordinary sense of pleasure, so pure it was like a sudden inhalation of oxygen, to see that his daughter had not only inherited this tradition but had considered it meaningful enough to carry on. He went down the hall to his own room without saying anything further to her. Cathy was what he himself was in terms which could mean absolutely nothing to anyone else.

He had been in his room for perhaps an hour, working on the hotel accounts and thinking obliquely of the man Simpson, when he heard, faintly and apparently coming from no one direction, the sound of singing. He got up and walked to the windows overlooking the street. Standing there, he thought he could fix the sound farther up the block toward Cunningham's bar. Except for something harsh and mature in the voices, it was the kind of singing that might be heard around a Boy Scout campfire, more rhythmic than melodic and more stirring than tuneful. And then he could hear it almost under his feet, coming out of the hotel lobby and making three or four people on the street turn and smile foolishly toward the doors of the veranda.

Oppressed by something sternly joyous in the voices, Bleeker went downstairs to the bar, hearing, as he approached, the singing become louder and fuller. Outside of Simpson and the twenty men in the troop there were only three townsmen—including La-Salle—in the bar. Simpson, seeing Bleeker in the door, got up and walked over to him, moving him out into the lobby where they could talk.

"I hope the boys aren't disturbing you," he said.

"It's early," Bleeker said.

"In an organization as large and selective as ours it's absolutely necessary to insist on a measure of discipline. And it's equally necessary to allow a certain amount of relaxation."

"The key word is selective, I suppose."

"We have our standards," Simpson said primly.

"May I ask you what the hell your standards are?"

Simpson smiled. "I don't quite understand your irritation, Mr. Bleeker."

"This is an all-year-round thing, isn't it? This club of yours?"

"Yes."

"And you have an all-year-round job with the club?"

"Of course."

"That's my objection, Simpson. Briefly and simply stated, what you're running is a private army." Bleeker tapped the case slung over Simpson's shoulder. "Complete with maps, all sorts of local information, and of course a lobby in Sacramento."

"For a man who has traveled as widely as you have, Mr. Bleeker, you display an uncommon talent for exaggeration."

"As long as you behave yourselves I don't care what you do. This is a small town and we don't have many means of entertainment. We go to bed at a decent hour and I suggest you take that into consideration. However, have your fun. Nobody here has any objections to that."

"And of course we spend our money."

"Yes," Bleeker said. "You spend your money."

He walked away from Simpson and went out onto the veranda. The singing was now both in front and in back of him. Bleeker stood for a moment on the top steps of the veranda looking at the moon, hung like a slightly soiled but luminous pennant in the sky. He was embarrassed by his outburst to Simpson and he couldn't think why he had said such things. Private army. Perhaps, as Simpson had said, he was exaggerating. He was a small-town man and he had always hated the way men surrendered their individuality to attain perfection as a unit. It had been necessary during the war but it wasn't necessary now. Kid stuff—with an element of growing pains.

He walked down the steps and went up the sidewalk toward Cunningham's bar. They were singing there, too, and he stood outside the big plate-glass window peering in at them and listening to the harsh, pounding voices colored here and there with the sentimentalism of strong beer. Without thinking further he went into the bar. It was dim and cool and alien to his eyes, and at first he didn't notice the boy sitting by himself in a booth near the front. When he did, he was surprised—more than surprised, shocked—to see that the boy wasn't wearing his goggles but had placed them on the table by a bottle of Coca-Cola. Impulsively, he walked over to the booth and sat across from the boy.

"This seat taken?"

He had to shout over the noise of the singing. The boy leaned forward over the table and smiled.

"Hope we're not disturbing you."

Bleeker caught the word "disturbing" and shook his head negatively. He pointed to his mouth, then to the boy and to the rest of the group. The boy, too, shook his head. Bleeker could see that he was young, possibly twenty-five, and that he had dark straight hair cut short and parted neatly at the side. The face was square but delicate, the nose short, the mouth wide. The best thing about the boy, Bleeker decided, were his eyes, brown, perhaps, or dark gray, set in two distorted ovals of white flesh which contrasted sharply with the heavily tanned skin on the cheeks, forehead and jaws. With his goggles on he would have looked like the rest. Without them he was a pleasant young man, altogether human and approachable.

Bleeker pointed to the Coca-Cola bottle. "You're not drinking."

"Beer makes me sick."

Bleeker got the word "beer" and the humorous ulping motion the boy made. They sat exchanging words and sometimes phrases, illustrated always with a series of clumsy, groping gestures until the singing became less coherent and spirited and ended finally in a few isolated coughs. The men in the troop were moving about individually now, some leaning over the bar and talking in hoarse whispers to the bartender, others walking unsteadily from group to group and detaching themselves immediately to go over to another group, the groups, usually two or three men, constantly edging away from themselves and colliding with and being held briefly by others. Some simply stood in the center of the room and brayed dolorously at the ceiling.

Several of the troop walked out of the bar, and Bleeker could see them standing on the wide sidewalk looking up and down the street—as contemptuous of one another's company as they had been glad of it earlier. Or not so much contemptuous as unwilling to be coerced too easily by any authority outside themselves. Bleeker smiled as he thought of Simpson and the man's talk of discipline.

"They're looking for women," the boy said.

Bleeker had forgotten the boy temporarily, and the sudden words spoken in a normal voice startled and confused him. He thought quickly of Cathy—but then Cathy was safe in her room— probably in bed. He took the watch from his vest pocket and looked at it carefully.

"Five minutes after ten," he said.

"Why do they do that?" the boy demanded. "Why do they have to be so damned indecent about things like that? They haven't got the nerve to do anything but stare at waitresses. And then they get a few beers in them and go around pinching and slapping— they——"

Bleeker shivered with embarrassment. He was looking directly into the boy's eyes and seeing the color run under the tears and the jerky pinching movement of the lids as against something injurious and baleful. It was an emotion too rawly infantile to be seen without being hurt by it, and he felt both pity and contempt for a man who would allow himself to display such a feeling— without any provocation—so nakedly to a stranger.

"Sorry," the boy said.

He picked up the green goggles and fitted them awkwardly over his eyes. Bleeker stood up and looked toward the center of the room. Several of the men turned their eyes and then moved their heads away without seeming to notice the boy in the booth. Bleeker understood them. This was the one who could be approached. The reason for that was clear, too. He didn't belong. Why and wherefore he would probably never know.

He walked out of the bar and started down the street toward the hotel. The night was clear and cool and smelled faintly of the desert, of sand, of heated rock, of the sweetly-sour plants growing without water and even of the sun which burned itself into the earth and never completely withdrew. There were only a few townsmen on the sidewalk wandering up and down, lured by the presence of something unusual in the town and masking, Bleeker thought, a ruthless and menacing curiosity behind a tolerant grin. He shrugged his shoulders distastefully. He was like a cat staring into a shadow the shape of its fears.

He was no more than a hundred feet from the hotel when he heard—or thought he heard—the sound of automatic firing. It was a well-remembered sound but always new and frightening.

Then he saw the motorcycle moving down the middle of the street, the exhaust sputtering loudly against the human resonance of laughter, catcalls, and epithets. He exhaled gently, the pain in his lungs subsiding with his breath. Another motorcycle speeded after the first, and he could see four or five machines being wheeled out and the figures of their riders leaping into the air and bringing their weight down on the starting pedals. He was aware, too, that the lead motorcycles, having traversed the length of the street, had turned and were speeding back to the hotel. He had the sensation of moving—even when he stood still—in relation to the objects heading toward each other. He heard the high unendurable sound of metal squeezing metal and saw the front wheel of a motorcycle twist and wobble and its rider roll along the asphalt toward the gutter where he sat up finally and moved his goggled head feebly from side to side.

As Bleeker looked around him, he saw the third group of men which had divided earlier from the other two coming out of the bar across the street from Cunningham's, waving their arms in recognizable motions of cheering. The boy who had been thrown from the motorcycle vomited quietly into the gutter. Bleeker walked very fast toward the hotel. When he reached the top step of the veranda, he was caught and jostled by some five or six cyclists running out of the lobby, one of whom fell and was kicked rudely down the steps. Bleeker staggered against one of the pillars and broke a fingernail catching it. He stood there for a moment, fighting his temper, and then went into the lobby.

A table had been overthrown and lay on its top, and wooden legs stiffly and foolishly exposed, its magazines scattered around it, some with their pages spread face down so that the bindings rose along the back. He stepped on glass and realized one of the panels in the lobby door had been smashed. One of the troop walked stupidly out of the bar, his body sagging against the impetus propelling him forward until without actually falling he lay stretched on the floor, beer gushing from his mouth and nose and making a green and yellow pool before it sank into the carpet.

As Bleeker walked toward the bar, thinking of Simpson and of what he could say to him, he saw two men going up the stairs toward the second floor. He ran over to intercept them. Recognizing the authority in his voice, they came obediently down the stairs and walked across the lobby to the veranda, one of them saying over his shoulder, "Okay, Pop, okay—keep your lid on." The smiles they exchanged enraged him. After they were out of sight, he ran swiftly up the stairs, panting a little, and along the hall to his daughter's room.

It was quiet and there was no strip of light beneath the door. He stood listening for a moment with his ear to the panels and then turned back toward the stairs.

A man or boy, any of twenty or forty or sixty identical figures, goggled and in khaki, came around the corner of the second-floor corridor and put his hand on the knob of the door nearest the stairs. He squeezed the knob gently and then moved on to the next door, apparently unaware of Bleeker. Bleeker, remembering not to run or shout or knock the man down, walked over to him, took his arm and led him down the stairs, the arm unresisting, even flaccid, in his grip.

Bleeker stood indecisively at the foot of the stairs, watching the man walk automatically away from him. He thought he should go back upstairs and search the hall. And he thought, too, he had to reach Simpson. Over the noise of the motorcycles moving rapidly up and down the street, he heard a crash in the bar, a series of drunken elongated curses, ending abruptly in a small sound like a man's hand laid flatly and sharply on a table.

His head was beginning to ache badly and his stomach to sour under the impact of a slow and steady anger. He walked into the bar and stood staring at Francis LaSalle—LaSalle and Fleet, Hardware—who lay sprawled on the floor, his shoulders touching the brass rail under the bar and his head turned so that his cheek rubbed the black polished wood above the rail. The bartender had his hands below the top of the bar and he was watching Simpson and a half a dozen men arranged in a loose semicircle above and beyond LaSalle.

Bleeker lifted LaSalle, who was a little dazed but not really hurt, and set him on a chair. After he was sure LaSalle was all right, he walked up to Simpson.

"Get your men together," he said. "And get them out of here."

Simpson took a long yellow wallet folded like a book and laid some money on the bar.

"That should take care of the damages," he said. His tongue was a little thick, and his mouth didn't quite shut after the words were spoken, but Bleeker didn't think he was drunk. Bleeker saw, too—or thought he saw—the little cold eyes behind the glasses as bright and as sterile as a painted floor. Bleeker raised his arm slightly and lifted his heels off the floor, but Simpson turned abruptly and walked away from him, the men in the troop swaying at his heels like a pack of lolling hounds. Bleeker stood looking foolishly after them. He had expected a fight, and his body was still poised for one. He grunted heavily.

"Who hit him?" Bleeker motioned toward LaSalle.

"Damned if I know," the bartender said. "They all look alike to me."

That was true, of course. He went back into the lobby, hearing LaSalle say, weakly and tearfully, "Goddamn them—the bastards." He met Campbell, the deputy sheriff, a tall man with the arms and shoulders of a child beneath a foggy, bloated face.

"Can you do anything?" Bleeker asked. The motorcycles were racing up and down the street, alternately whining and backfiring, and one had jumped the curb and was cruising on the sidewalk.

"What do you want me to do?" Campbell demanded. "Put 'em all in jail?"

The motorcycle on the sidewalk speeded up and skidded obliquely into a plate-glass window, the front wheel bucking and climbing the brick base beneath the window. A single large section of glass slipped edge-down to the sidewalk and fell slowly toward the cyclist who, with his feet spread and kicking at the cement, backed clumsily away from it. Bleeker could feel the crash in his teeth.

Now there were other motorcycles on the sidewalk. One of them hit a parked car at the edge of the walk. The rider standing astride his machine beat the window out of the car with his gloved fists. Campbell started down the steps toward him but was driven back by a motorcycle coming from his left. Bleeker could hear the squeal of the tires against the wooden riser at the base of the steps. Campbell's hand was on his gun when Bleeker reached him.

"That's no good," he yelled. "Get the state police. Ask for a half dozen squad cars."

Campbell, angry but somewhat relieved, went up the steps and into the lobby. Bleeker couldn't know how long he stood on the veranda watching the mounting devastation on the street—the cyclist racing past store windows and hurling, presumably, beer bottles at the glass fronts; the two, working as a team, knocking down weighing machines and the signs in front of the motion-picture theater; the innumerable mounted men running the angry townspeople, alerted and aroused by the awful sounds of damage to their property, back into their suddenly lighted homes again or up the steps of his hotel or into niches along the main street, into doorways, and occasionally into the ledges and bays of glassless windows.

He saw Simpson—or rather a figure on the white motorcycle, helmeted and goggled—stationed calmly in the middle of the street under a hanging lamp. Presumably, he had been there for

some time but Bleeker hadn't seen him, the many rapid movements on the street making any static object unimportant and
even, in a sense, invisible. Bleeker saw him now and he felt again
that spasm of anger which was like another life inside his body.
He could have strangled Simpson then, slowly and with infinite
pride. He knew without any effort of reason that Simpson was
making no attempt to control his men but waiting rather for that
moment when their minds, subdued but never actually helpless,
would again take possession of their bodies.

Bleeker turned suddenly and went back into the lobby as if by
that gesture of moving away he could pin his thoughts to Simpson,
who, hereafter, would be responsible for them. He walked over to
the desk where Timmons and Campbell, the deputy, were talking.

"You've got the authority," Timmons was saying angrily. "Fire
over their heads. And if that doesn't stop them—"

Campbell looked uneasily at Bleeker. "Maybe if we could get
their leader—"

"Did you get the police?" Bleeker asked.

"They're on their way," Campbell said. He avoided looking at
Timmons and continued to stare hopefully and miserably at
Bleeker.

"You've had your say," Timmons said abruptly. "Now I'll have
mine."

He started for the lobby doors, but Campbell, suddenly in-
censed, grabbed his arm.

"You leave this to me," he said. "You start firing a gun——"

Campbell's mouth dropped, and Bleeker, turning his head, saw
the two motorcycles coming through the lobby doors. They circled
leisurely around for a moment and then one of them shot suddenly
toward them, the goggled rider looming enormously above the
wide handlebars. They scattered, Bleeker diving behind a pillar,
and Campbell and Timmons jumping behind the desk. The noise
of the two machines assaulted them with as much effect as the
sight of the speeding metal itself.

Bleeker didn't know why, in course of watching the two riders,
he looked into the hall toward the foot of the stairway. Nor did it
seem at all unreasonable that when he looked he should see
Cathy standing there. Deeply, underneath the outward preoccupa-

tion of his mind, he must have been thinking of her. Now there she was. She wore the familiar green robe, belted and pulled in at the waist, and beneath its hem he could see the white slippers and the pink edge of her nightgown. Her hair was down, and he had the impression her eyes were not quite open, although, obviously, they were. She looked, he thought, as if she had waked, frowned at the clock, and come downstairs to scold him for staying up too late. He had no idea what time it was.

He saw—and of course Cathy saw—the motorcycle speeding toward her. He was aware that he screamed at her, too. She did take a slight backward step and raise her arms in a pathetic warding gesture toward the inhuman figure on the motorcycle, but neither could have changed—in that dwarfed period of time and in that short, unmaneuverable space—the course of their actions.

She lay finally across the lower steps, her body clinging to and equally arching away from the base of the newel post. And there was the sudden, shocking exposure of her flesh, the robe and the gown torn away from the leg as if pushed aside by the blood welling from her thigh. When he reached her, there was blood in her hair, too, and someone—not Cathy—was screaming into his ears.

After a while the doctor came, and Cathy, her head bandaged and her leg in splints, could be carried into his office and laid on the couch. Bleeker sat on the edge of the couch, his hand over Cathy's, watching the still white face whose eyes were closed and would not, he knew, open again. The doctor, after his first examination, had looked up quickly, and since Bleeker, too, had been bent over Cathy, their heads had been very close together for a moment. The doctor had assumed, almost immediately, his expression of professional austerity, but Bleeker had seen him in that moment when he had been thinking as a man, fortified of course by a doctor's knowledge, and Bleeker had known then that Cathy would die but that there would be also this interval of time.

Bleeker turned from watching Cathy and saw Timmons standing across the room. The man was—or had been—crying, but his face wasn't set for it, and the tears, points of colorless, sparkling water on his jaws, were unexpectedly delicate against the coarse texture of his skin. Timmons waved a bandaged hand awkwardly, and

Bleeker remembered, abruptly and jarringly, seeing Timmons diving for the motorcycle which had reversed itself, along with the other, and raced out of the lobby.

There was no sound now either from the street or the lobby. It was incredible, thinking of the racket a moment ago, that there should be this utter quietude, not only the lack of noise but the lack of the vibration of movement. The doctor came and went, coming to bend over Cathy and then going away again. Timmons stayed. Beyond shifting his feet occasionally, he didn't move at all but stood patiently across the room, his face toward Cathy and Bleeker but not, Bleeker thought once when he looked up, actually seeing them.

"The police," Bleeker said sometime later.

"They're gone," Timmons said in a hoarse whisper. And then after a while, "They'll get 'em—don't worry."

Bleeker saw that the man blushed helplessly and looked away from him. The police were no good. They would catch Simpson. Simpson would pay damages. And that would be the end of it. Who could identify Cathy's assailant? Not himself, certainly—not Timmons nor Campbell. They were all alike. They were standardized figurines, seeking in each other a willful loss of identity, dividing themselves equally among one another until there was only a single mythical figure, unspeakably sterile and furnishing the norm for hundreds of others. He could not accuse something which didn't actually exist.

He wasn't sure of the exact moment when Cathy died. It might have been when he heard the motorcycle, unbelievably solitary in the quiet night, approaching the town. He knew only that the doctor came for the last time and that there was now a coarse, heavy blanket laid mercifully over Cathy. He stood looking down at the blanket for a moment, whatever he was feeling repressed and delayed inside him, and then went back to the lobby and out onto the veranda. There were a dozen men standing there looking up the street toward the sound of the motorcycle, steadily but slowly coming nearer. He saw that when they glanced at each other their faces were hard and angry but when they looked at him they were respectful and a little abashed.

Bleeker could see from the veranda a number of people moving

among the smashed store-fronts, moving, stopping, bending over
and then straightening up to move somewhere else, all dressed
somewhat extemporaneously and therefore seeming without purpose. What they picked up they put down. What they put down
they stared at grimly and then picked up again. They were like a
dispossessed minority brutally but lawfully discriminated against.
When the motorcycle appeared at the north end of the street, they
looked at it and then looked away again, dully and seemingly
without resentment.

It was only after some moments that they looked up again, this
time purposefully, and began to move slowly toward the hotel
where the motorcycle had now stopped, the rider standing on the
sidewalk, his face raised to the veranda.

No one on the veranda moved until Bleeker, after a visible effort, walked down the steps and stood facing the rider. It was the
boy Bleeker had talked to in the bar. The goggles and helmet were
hanging at his belt.

"I couldn't stand it any longer," the boy said. "I had to come
back."

He looked at Bleeker as if he didn't dare look anywhere else.
His face was adolescently shiny and damp, the marks, Bleeker
thought, of a proud and articulate fear. He should have been
heroic in his willingness to come back to the town after what had
been done to it, but to Bleeker he was only a dirty little boy
returning to a back fence his friends had defaced with pornographic writing and calling attention to the fact that he was afraid
to erase the writing but was determined nevertheless to do it.
Bleeker was revolted. He hated the boy far more than he could
have hated Simpson for bringing this to his attention when he did
not want to think of anything or anyone but Cathy.

"I wasn't one of them," the boy said. "You remember, Mr.
Bleeker. I wasn't drinking."

This declaration of innocence—this willingness to take blame
for acts which he hadn't committed—enraged Bleeker.

"You were one of them," he said.

"Yes. But after tonight——"

"Why didn't you stop them?" Bleeker demanded loudly. He felt
the murmur of the townspeople at his back and someone

breathed harshly on his neck. "You were one of them. You could have done something. Why in God's name didn't you do it?"

"What could I do?" the boy said. He spread his hands and stepped back as if to appeal to the men beyond Bleeker.

Bleeker couldn't remember, either shortly after or much later, exactly what he did then. If the boy hadn't stepped back like that —if he hadn't raised his hand. . . . Bleeker was in the middle of a group of bodies and he was striking with his fists and being struck. And then he was kneeling on the sidewalk, holding the boy's head in his lap and trying to protect him from the heavy shoes of the men around him. He was crying out, protesting, exhorting, and after a time the men moved away from him and someone helped him carry the boy up the steps and lay him on the veranda. When he looked up finally, only Timmons and the doctor were there. Up and down the street there were now only shadows and the diminishing sounds of invisible bodies. The night was still again as abruptly as it had been confounded with noise.

Some time later Timmons and the doctor carried the boy, alive but terribly hurt, into the hotel. Bleeker sat on the top step of the veranda, staring at the moon which had shifted in the sky and was now nearer the mountains in the west. It was not in any sense romantic or inflamed but coldly clear and sane. And the light it sent was cold and sane and lit in himself what he could have liked to hide.

He could have said that having lost Cathy he was not afraid any longer of losing himself. No one would blame him. Cathy's death was his excuse for striking the boy, hammering him to the sidewalk, and stamping on him as he had never believed he could have stamped on any living thing. No one would say he should have lost Cathy lightly—without anger and without that appalling desire to avenge her. It was utterly natural—as natural as a man drinking a few beers and riding a motorcycle insanely through a town like this. Bleeker shuddered. It might have been all right for a man like Timmons who was and would always be incapable of thinking what he—Joel Bleeker—was thinking. It was not—and would never be—all right for him.

Bleeker got up and stood for a moment on the top step of the veranda. He wanted, abruptly and madly, to scream his agony into the night with no more restraint than that of an animal seeing his guts beneath him on the ground. He wanted to smash something —anything—glass, wood, stone—his own body. He could feel his fists going into the boy's flesh. And there was that bloody but living thing on the sidewalk and himself stooping over to shield it.

After a while, aware that he was leaning against one of the wooden pillars supporting the porch and aware, too, that his flesh was numb from being pressed against it, he straightened up slowly and turned to go back into the hotel.

There would always be time to make his peace with the dead. There was little if any time to make his peace with the living.

Rear Window

Cornell Woolrich

Alfred Hitchcock is the most phenomenal of American motion-picture directors. From almost the beginning of the sound era, he has devoted himself exclusively to suspense, producing a consistently superior product. Aside from Walt Disney, Hitchcock's is perhaps the only filmmaker's name familiar to all segments of the moviegoing public; billboards and marquees display his name as prominently as those of his principal actors. The French director François Truffaut describes Hitchcock as "the world's foremost technician," a director who combines a meticulous grasp of craft with an unerring sense of his audience's expectations. Hitchcock has shown that adherence to a genre does not imply the limitations of a formula, and his work remains unique and innovative: he is master of the experiment that works. At least ten of his forty-four sound films are American classics: The Thirty-Nine Steps (1935), The Lady Vanishes (1938), Rebecca (1940), Shadow of a Doubt (1943), Strangers on a Train (1951), Dial M for Murder (1953), Rear Window (1954), Vertigo (1958), North by Northwest (1959), and Psycho (1960).

Rear Window is an excellent example of Hitchcock's experimentation because much of what makes it fresh and exciting derives from a direct violation of film's normally omniscient point of view. The protagonist, L. B. Jeffries (James Stewart), is confined to his room by a broken leg. He passes time by observing other people's lives through the rear windows of the apartments around the areaway upon which his own apartment looks. Hitchcock confines his camera in the same way, revealing the other rear windows only as Jeffries can see them, drawing the viewer to participate in Jeffries's voyeurism.

This successful adaptation of a primarily literary device depends strongly on Cornell Woolrich's short story, in which first-person narration also takes on a unique character. As normally used, first-person narration identifies the narrator with the implied author, but in "Rear Window," the narrator becomes closely tied to the reader himself. Except in the story's climax, Jeffries is, like the reader, a viewer rather than a participant. He can attempt to manipulate the actors he observes, but he is never entirely successful in getting them to do just what he wants. The result in both story and film is that the reader or viewer becomes so absorbed in watching the unfolding action through the hero's eyes that he is as frightened as Jeffries when danger sneaks up from behind and taps him on the shoulder.

Both the story and the film are about voyeurism and its lethal potential. Jeffries's observation in the story that "it was a little bit like prying, could even have been mistaken for the fevered concentration of a Peeping Tom" is echoed and brought into sharper perspective by Stella, Jeffries's nurse in the film, who protests: "We've become a race of Peeping Toms. What people ought to do is get outside their own houses and look in for a change." This idea is underlined by making the film's protagonist a professional photographer, a paid voyeur who has already been physically injured for insinuating himself into other people's business (Jeffries's broken leg is the result of an accident suffered while photographing an automobile race). Like Thomas in Blow-Up, Jeff is conditioned to see life through a viewfinder: he instinctively reaches for his 400-millimeter lens when he wants to bring the Lars Thorwald apartment into close-up. At first the scenes of apartment life—the lovemaking of the young newlyweds, the playacting of the lonely spinster, the creative struggles of the songwriter, the graceful calisthenics of the attractive ballerina—all are benign, or at worst, bittersweet. But as the plot develops, the life out there in the picture frame becomes increasingly malevolent. What begins for Jeffries as pastime becomes obsession.

Hitchcock films are directly concerned with good and evil, innocence and guilt. In Rear Window he strengthens the dichotomy already inherent in the Woolrich story by setting up a parallel between witness and murderer. Jeffries, like Mrs. Thorwald, is *invalided and confined; Lisa must be the instrument of his action. Mrs. Thorwald is murdered, and Thorwald is brought to bay and evil is confounded; Jeffries survives and realizes his love for Lisa. Those capable of attachment and caring are those who live; alienation suggests death.*

Twenty-six of Hitchcock's films are based on novels or short stories, and Hitchcock demonstrates, both in the films and in his discussions of them, that he is highly fluent in the vocabulary of fiction-film translation. In his interview with Hitchcock, Truffaut mentions the efficiency of the opening shots in Rear Window. *The camera moves from Jeffries's broken leg to his broken camera, then to photographs of crashing race cars. In one brief sequence, the director has established Jeffries's character, his profession, and its relationship to his accident. In a discussion of this scene, Hitchcock reveals the precision and skill with which a perceptive director can manipulate the storytelling potential of the visual medium.*

That's simply using cinematic means to relate a story. It's a great deal more interesting than if we had someone asking Stewart, "How did you happen to break your leg?" and Stewart answering, "As I was taking a picture of a motorcar race, a wheel fell off one of the speeding cars and smashed into me." That would be the average scene. To me, one of the cardinal sins for a scriptwriter, when he runs into some difficulty, is to say, "We can cover that by a line of dialogue." Dialogue should simply be a sound among other sounds, just something that comes out of the mouths of people whose eyes tell the story in visual terms.

REAR WINDOW

I didn't know their names. I'd never heard their voices. I didn't even know them by sight, strictly speaking, for their faces were too small to fill in with identifiable features at that distance. Yet I could have constructed a timetable of their comings and goings, their daily habits and activities. They were the rear-window dwellers around me.

Sure, I suppose it *was* a little bit like prying, could even have been mistaken for the fevered concentration of a Peeping Tom.

That wasn't my fault, that wasn't the idea. The idea was, my movements were strictly limited just around this time. I could get from the window to the bed, and from the bed to the window, and that was all. The bay window was about the best feature my rear bedroom had in the warm weather. It was unscreened, so I had to sit with the light out or I would have had every insect in the vicinity in on me. I couldn't sleep, because I was used to getting plenty of exercise. I'd never acquired the habit of reading books to ward off boredom, so I hadn't that to turn to. Well, what should I do, sit there with my eyes tightly shuttered?

Just to pick a few at random: Straight over, and the windows square, there was a young jitter-couple, kids in their teens, only just married. It would have killed them to stay home one night. They were always in such a hurry to go, wherever it was they went, they never remembered to turn out the lights. I don't think it missed once in all the time I was watching. But they never forgot altogether, either. I was to learn to call this delayed action, as you will see. He'd always come skittering madly back in about five minutes, probably from all the way down in the street, and rush around killing the switches. Then fall over something in the dark on his way out. They gave me an inward chuckle, those two.

The next house down, the windows already narrowed a little with perspective. There was a certain light in that one that always went out each night too. Something about it, it used to make me a little sad. There was a woman living there with her child, a young widow I suppose. I'd see her put the child to bed, and then bend over and kiss her in a wistful sort of way. She'd shade the light off her and sit there painting her eyes and mouth. Then she'd go out. She'd never come back till the night was nearly spent. Once I was still up, and I looked and she was sitting there motionless with her head buried in her arms. Something about it, it used to make me a little sad.

The third one down no longer offered any insight, the windows were just slits like in a medieval battlement, due to foreshortening. That brings us around to the one on the end. In that one, frontal vision came back full-depth again, since it stood at right angles to the rest, my own included, sealing up the inner hollow all these houses backed on. I could see into it, from the rounded projection of my bay window, as freely as into a doll house with its rear wall sliced away. And scaled down to about the same size.

It was a flat building. Unlike all the rest it had been constructed originally as such, not just cut up into furnished rooms. It topped them by two stories and had rear fire escapes, to show for this distinction. But it was old, evidently hadn't shown a profit. It was in the process of being modernized. Instead of clearing the entire building while the work was going on, they were doing it a flat at a time, in order to lose as little rental income as possible. Of the six rearward flats it offered to view, the topmost one had already been completed, but not yet rented. They were working on the fifth-floor one now, disturbing the peace of everyone all up and down the "inside" of the block with their hammering and sawing.

I felt sorry for the couple in the flat below. I used to wonder how they stood it with that bedlam going on above their heads. To make it worse the wife was in chronic poor health, too; I could tell that even at a distance by the listless way she moved about over there, and remained in her bathrobe without dressing. Sometimes I'd see her sitting by the window, holding her head. I used to wonder why he didn't have a doctor in to look her over, but maybe they couldn't afford it. He seemed to be out of work. Often their bedroom light was on late at night behind the drawn shade, as though she were unwell and he was sitting up with her. And one night in particular he must have had to sit up with her all night, it remained on until nearly daybreak. Not that I sat watching all that time. But the light was still burning at three in the morning, when I finally transferred from chair to bed to see if I could get a little sleep myself. And when I failed to, and hopscotched back again around dawn, it was still peering wanly out behind the tan shade.

Moments later, with the first brightening of day, it suddenly dimmed around the edges of the shade, and then shortly afterward, not that one, but a shade in one of the other rooms—for all of them alike had been down—went up, and I saw him standing there looking out.

He was holding a cigarette in his hand. I couldn't see it, but I could tell it was that by the quick, nervous little jerks with which he kept putting his hand to his mouth, and the haze I saw rising around his head. Worried about her, I guess. I didn't blame him for that. Any husband would have been. She must have only just dropped off to sleep, after night-long suffering. And then in another hour or so, at the most, that sawing of wood and clattering of buckets was going to start in over them again. Well, it wasn't any of my business, I said to myself, but he really ought to get her out of there. If I had an ill wife on my hands. . . .

He was leaning slightly out, maybe an inch past the window frame, carefully scanning the back faces of all the houses abutting on the hollow square that lay before him. You can tell, even at a distance, when a person is looking fixedly. There's something about the way the head is held. And yet his scrutiny wasn't held fixedly to any one point, it was a slow, sweeping one, moving along the houses on the opposite side from me first. When it got to the end of them, I knew it would cross over to my side and come back along there. Before it did, I withdrew several yards inside my room, to let it go safely by. I didn't want him to think I was sitting there prying into his affairs. There was still enough blue night-shade in my room to keep my slight withdrawal from catching his eye.

When I returned to my original position a moment or two later, he was gone. He had raised two more of the shades. The bedroom one was still down. I wondered vaguely why he had given that peculiar, comprehensive, semicircular stare at all the rear windows around him. There wasn't anyone at any of them, at such an hour. It wasn't important, of course. It was just a little oddity, it failed to blend in with his being worried or disturbed about his wife. When you're worried or disturbed, that's an internal preoccupation, you stare vacantly at nothing at all. When you stare around you in a great sweeping arc at windows, that betrays external preoccupation, outward interest. One doesn't quite jibe with the other. To call such a discrepancy trifling is to add to its importance. Only someone like me, stewing in a vacuum of total idleness, would have noticed it at all.

The flat remained lifeless after that, as far as could be judged by its windows. He must have either gone out or gone to bed himself. Three of the shades remained at normal height, the one masking the bedroom remained down. Sam, my day houseman, came in not long after with my eggs and morning paper, and I had that to kill time with for awhile. I stopped thinking about other people's windows and staring at them.

The sun slanted down on one side of the hollow oblong all morning long, then it shifted over to the other side for the afternoon. Then it started to slip off both alike, and it was evening again —another day gone.

The lights started to come on around the quadrangle. Here and there a wall played back, like a sounding board, a snatch of radio program that was coming in too loud. If you listened carefully you could hear an occasional clink of dishes mixed in, faint, far off. The chain of little habits that were their lives unreeled themselves. They were all bound in them tighter than the tightest straitjacket any jailer ever devised, though they all thought themselves free. The jitterbugs made their nightly dash for the great open spaces, forgot their lights, he came careening back, thumbed them out, and their place was dark until the early morning hours. The woman put her child to bed, leaned mournfully over its cot, then sat down with heavy despair to redden her mouth.

In the fourth-floor flat at right angles to the long, interior "street" the three shades had remained up, and the fourth shade had remained at full length, all day long. I hadn't been conscious of that because I hadn't particularly been looking at it, or thinking of it, until now. My eyes may have rested on those windows at times, during the day, but my thoughts had been elsewhere. It was only when a light suddenly went up in the end room behind one of the raised shades, which was their kitchen, that I realized that the shades had been untouched like that all day. That also brought something else to my mind that hadn't been in it until now: I hadn't seen the woman all day. I hadn't seen any sign of life within those windows until now.

He'd come in from outside. The entrance was at the opposite side of their kitchen, away from the window. He'd left his hat on, so I knew he'd just come in from the outside.

He didn't remove his hat. As though there was no one there to remove it for any more. Instead, he pushed it farther to the back of his head by pronging a hand to the roots of his hair. That gesture didn't denote removal of perspiration, I knew. To do that a person makes a sidewise sweep—this was up over his forehead.

It indicated some sort of harassment or uncertainty. Besides, if he'd been suffering from excess warmth, the first thing he would have done would be to take off his hat altogether.

She didn't come out to greet him. The first link, of the so-strong chain of habit, of custom, that binds us all, had snapped wide open.

She must be so ill she had remained in bed, in the room behind the lowered shade, all day. I watched. He remained where he was, two rooms away from there. Expectancy became surprise, surprise incomprehension. Funny, I thought, that he doesn't go in to her. Or at least go as far as the doorway, look in to see how she is.

Maybe she was asleep, and he didn't want to disturb her. Then immediately: but how can he know for sure that she's asleep, without at least looking in at her? He just came in himself.

He came forward and stood there by the window, as he had at dawn. Sam had carried out my tray quite some time before, and my lights were out. I held my ground, I knew he couldn't see me within the darkness of the bay window. He stood there motionless for several minutes. And now his attitude was the proper one for inner preoccupation. He stood there looking downward at nothing, lost in thought.

He's worried about her, I said to myself, as any man would be. It's the most natural thing in the world. Funny, though, he should leave her in the dark like that, without going near her. If he's worried, then why didn't he at least look in on her on returning? Here was another of those trivial discrepancies, between inward motivation and outward indication. And just as I was thinking that, the original one, that I had noted at daybreak, repeated itself. His head went up with renewed alertness, and I could see it start to give that slow circular sweep of interrogation around the panorama of rearward windows again. True, the light was behind him this time, but there was enough of it falling on him to show me the microscopic but continuous shift of direction his head made in the process. I remained carefully immobile until the distant glance had passed me safely by. Motion attracts.

Why is he so interested in other people's windows, I wondered detachedly. And of course an effective brake to dwelling on that thought too lingeringly clamped down almost at once: Look who's talking. What about you yourself?

An important difference escaped me. I wasn't worried about anything. He, presumably, was.

Down came the shades again. The lights stayed on behind their beige opaqueness. But behind the one that had remained down all along, the room remained dark.

Time went by. Hard to say how much—a quarter of an hour, twenty minutes. A cricket chirped in one of the back yards. Sam came in to see if I wanted anything before he went home for the night. I told him no, I didn't—it was all right, run along. He stood there for a minute, head down. Then I saw him shake it slightly, as if at something he didn't like. "What's the matter?" I asked.

"You know what that means? My old mammy told it to me, and she never told me a lie in her life. I never once seen it to miss, either."

"What, the cricket?"

"Any time you hear one of them things, that's a sign of death —someplace close around."

I swept the back of my hand at him. "Well, it isn't in here, so don't let it worry you."

He went out, muttering stubbornly: "It's somewhere close by, though. Somewhere not very far off. Got to be."

The door closed after him, and I stayed there alone in the dark.

It was a stifling night, much closer than the one before. I could hardly get a breath of air even by the open window at which I sat. I wondered how he—that unknown over there—could stand it behind those drawn shades.

Then suddenly, just as idle speculation about this whole matter was about to alight on some fixed point in my mind, crystallize into something like suspicion, up came the shades again, and off it flitted, as formless as ever and without having had a chance to come to rest on anything.

He was in the middle windows, the living room. He'd taken off his coat and shirt, was bare-armed in his undershirt. He hadn't been able to stand it himself, I guess—the sultriness.

I couldn't make out what he was doing at first. He seemed to be busy in a perpendicular, up-and-down way rather than lengthwise. He remained in one place, but he kept dipping down out of sight and then straightening up into view again, at irregular intervals. It was almost like some sort of calisthenic exercise, except that the dips and rises weren't evenly timed enough for that. Sometimes he'd stay down a long time, sometimes he'd bob right up again, sometimes he'd go down two or three times in rapid succession. There was some sort of a widespread black V railing him off from the window. Whatever it was, there was just a sliver of it showing above the upward inclination to which the window sill deflected my line of vision. All it did was strike off the bottom of his undershirt, to the extent of a sixteenth of an inch maybe. But I hadn't seen it there at other times, and I couldn't tell what it was.

Suddenly he left it for the first time since the shades had gone up, came out around it to the outside, stooped down into another part of the room, and straightened again with an armful of what looked like varicolored pennants at the distance at which I was. He went back behind the V and allowed them to fall across the top of it for a moment, and stay that way. He made one of his dips down out of sight and stayed that way a good while.

The "pennants" slung across the V kept changing color right in front of my eyes. I have very good sight. One moment they were white, the next red, the next blue.

Then I got it. They were a woman's dresses, and he was pulling them down to him one by one, taking the topmost one each time. Suddenly they were all gone, the V was black and bare again, and his torso had reappeared. I knew what it was now, and what he was doing. The dresses had told me. He confirmed it for me. He spread his arms to the ends of the V, I could see him heave and hitch, as if exerting pressure, and suddenly the V had folded up, become a cubed wedge. Then he made rolling motions with his whole upper body, and the wedge disappeared off to one side.

He'd been packing a trunk, packing his wife's things into a large upright trunk.

He reappeared at the kitchen window presently, stood still for a moment. I saw him draw his arm across his forehead, not once but several times, and then whip the end of it off into space. Sure, it was hot work for such a night. Then he reached up along the wall and took something down. Since it was the kitchen he was in, my imagination had to supply a cabinet and a bottle.

I could see the two or three quick passes his hand made to his mouth after that. I said to myself tolerantly: That's what nine men out of ten would do after packing a trunk—take a good stiff drink. And if the tenth didn't, it would only be because he didn't have any liquor at hand.

Then he came closer to the window again, and standing edgewise to the side of it, so that only a thin paring of his head and shoulder showed, peered watchfully out into the dark quadrilateral, along the line of windows, most of them unlighted by now, once more. He always started on the left-hand side, the side opposite mine, and made his circuit of inspection from there on around.

That was the second time in one evening I'd seen him do that. And once at daybreak, made three times altogether. I smiled mentally. You'd almost think he felt guilty about something. It was probably nothing, just an odd little habit, a quirk, that he didn't know he had himself. I had them myself, everyone does.

He withdrew into the room again, and it blacked out. His figure passed into the one that was still lighted next to it, the living room. That blacked next. It didn't surprise me that the third room, the bedroom with the drawn shade, didn't light up on his entering there. He wouldn't want to disturb her, of course—particularly if she was going away tomorrow for her health, as his packing of her trunk showed. She needed all the rest she could get, before making the trip. Simple enough for him to slip into bed in the dark.

It did surprise me, though, when a match-flare winked some time later, to have it still come from the darkened living room. He must be lying down in there, trying to sleep on a sofa or something for the night. He hadn't gone near the bedroom at all, was staying out of it altogether. That puzzled me, frankly. That was carrying solicitude almost too far.

Ten minutes or so later, there was another match-wink, still from that same living room window. He couldn't sleep.

The night brooded down on both of us alike, the curiosity-monger in the bay window, the chain-smoker in the fourth-floor flat, without giving any answer. The only sound was that interminable cricket.

I was back at the window again with the first sun of morning. Not because of him. My mattress was like a bed of hot coals. Sam found me there when he came in to get things ready for me. "You're going to be a wreck, Mr. Jeff," was all he said.

First, for awhile, there was no sign of life over there. Then suddenly I saw his head bob up from somewhere down out of sight in the living room, so I knew I'd been right; he'd spent the night on a sofa or easy chair in there. Now, of course, he'd look in at her, to see how she was, find out if she felt any better. That was only common ordinary humanity. He hadn't been near her, so far as I could make out, since two nights before.

He didn't. He dressed, and he went in the opposite direction, into the kitchen, and wolfed something in there, standing up and using both hands. Then he suddenly turned and moved off side, in the direction in which I knew the flat-entrance to be, as if he had just heard some summons, like the doorbell.

Sure enough, in a moment he came back, and there were two men with him in leather aprons. Expressmen. I saw him standing by while they laboriously maneuvered that cubed black wedge out between them, in the direction they'd just come from. He did more than just stand by. He practically hovered over them, kept shifting from side to side, he was so anxious to see that it was done right.

Then he came back alone, and I saw him swipe his arm across his head, as though it was he, not they, who was all heated up from the effort.

So he was forwarding her trunk, to wherever it was she was going. That was all.

He reached up along the wall again and took something down. He was taking another drink. Two. Three. I said to myself, a little at a loss: Yes, but he hasn't just packed a trunk this time. That trunk has been standing packed and ready since last night. Where does the hard work come in? The sweat and the need for a bracer?

Now, at last, after all those hours, he finally did go in to her. I saw his form pass through the living room and go beyond, into the bedroom. Up went the shade, that had been down all this time. Then he turned his head and looked around behind him. In a certain way, a way that was unmistakable, even from where I was.

Not in one certain direction, as one looks at a person. But from side to side, and up and down, and all around, as one looks at— *an empty room.*

He stepped back, bent a little, gave a fling of his arms, and an unoccupied mattress and bedding upended over the foot of a bed, stayed that way, emptily curved. A second one followed a moment later.

She wasn't in there.

They use the expression "delayed action." I found out then what it meant. For two days a sort of formless uneasiness, a disembodied suspicion, I don't know what to call it, had been flitting and volplaning around in my mind, like an insect looking for a landing place. More than once, just as it had been ready to settle, some slight thing, some slight reassuring thing, such as the raising of the shades after they had been down unnaturally long, had been enough to keep it winging aimlessly, prevent it from staying still long enough for me to recognize it. The point of contact had been there all along, waiting to receive it. Now, for some reason, within a split second after he tossed over the empty mattresses, it landed—*zoom!* And the point of contact expanded—or exploded, whatever you care to call it—into a certainty of murder.

In other words, the rational part of my mind was far behind the instinctive, subconscious part. Delayed action. Now the one had caught up to the other. The thought-message that sparked from the synchronization was: He's done something to her!

I looked down and my hand was bunching the goods over my kneecap, it was knotted so tight. I forced it to open. I said to myself, steadyingly: Now wait a minute, be careful, go slow. You've seen nothing. You know nothing. You only have the negative proof that you don't see her any more.

Sam was standing there looking over at me from the pantry way. He said accusingly: "You ain't touched a thing. And your face looks like a sheet."

It felt like one. It had that needling feeling, when the blood has left it involuntarily. It was more to get him out of the way and give myself some elbow room for undisturbed thinking, than anything else, that I said: "Sam, what's the street address of that building down there? Don't stick your head too far out and gape at it."

"Somep'n or other Benedict Avenue." He scratched his neck helpfully.

"I know that. Chase around the corner a minute and get me the exact number on it, will you?"

"Why you want to know that for?" he asked as he turned to go.

"None of your business," I said with the good-natured firmness that was all that was necessary to take care of that once and for all. I called after him just as he was closing the door: "And while you're about it, step into the entrance and see if you can tell from the mailboxes who has the fourth-floor rear. Don't get me the wrong one now. And try not to let anyone catch you at it."

He went out mumbling something that sounded like, "When a man ain't got nothing to do but just sit all day, he sure can think up the blamest things——" The door closed and I settled down to some good constructive thinking.

I said to myself: What are you really building up this monstrous supposition on? Let's see what you've got. Only that there were several little things wrong with the mechanism, the chain-belt, of their recurrent daily habits over there. 1. The lights were on all night the first night. 2. He came in later than usual the second night. 3. He left his hat on. 4. She didn't come out to greet him— she hasn't appeared since the evening before the lights were on all night. 5. He took a drink after he finished packing her trunk. But he took three stiff drinks the next morning, immediately after her trunk went out. 6. He was inwardly disturbed and worried, yet superimposed upon this was an unnatural external concern about the surrounding rear windows that was off-key. 7. He slept in the living room, didn't go near the bedroom, during the night before the departure of the trunk.

Very well. If she had been ill that first night, and he had sent her away for her health, that automatically canceled out points 1, 2, 3, 4. It left points 5 and 6 totally unimportant and unincriminating. But when it came up against 7, it hit a stumbling block.

If she went away immediately after being ill that first night, why didn't he want to sleep in their bedroom *last night?* Sentiment? Hardly. Two perfectly good beds in one room, only a sofa or uncomfortable easy chair in the other. Why should he stay out of there if she was already gone? Just because he missed her, was lonely? A grown man doesn't act that way. All right, then she was still in there.

Sam came back parenthetically at this point and said: "That house is Number 525 Benedict Avenue. The fourth-floor rear, it got the name of Mr. and Mrs. Lars Thorwald up."

"Sh-h," I silenced, and motioned him backhand out of my ken.

"First he want it, then he don't," he grumbled philosophically, and retired to his duties.

I went ahead digging at it. But if she was still in there, in that bedroom last night, then she couldn't have gone away to the country, because I never saw her leave today. She could have left without my seeing her in the early hours of yesterday morning. I'd missed a few hours, been asleep. But this morning I had been up before he was himself, I only saw his head rear up from that sofa after I'd been at the window for some time.

To go at all she would have had to go yesterday morning. Then why had he left the bedroom shade down, left the mattresses undisturbed, until today? Above all, why had he stayed out of that room last night? That was evidence that she hadn't gone, was still in there. Then today, immediately after the trunk had been dispatched, he went in, pulled up the shade, tossed over the mattresses, and showed that she hadn't been in there. The thing was like a crazy spiral.

No, it wasn't either. *Immediately after the trunk had been dispatched——*

The trunk.

That did it.

I looked around to make sure the door was safely closed between Sam and me. My hand hovered uncertainly over the telephone dial a minute. Boyne, he'd be the one to tell about it. He was on Homicide. He had been, anyway, when I'd last seen him. I didn't want to get a flock of strange dicks and cops into my hair. I didn't want to be involved any more than I had to. Or at all, if possible.

They switched my call to the right place after a couple of wrong tries, and I got him finally.

"Look, Boyne? This is Hal Jeffries——"

"Well, where've you been the last sixty-two years?" he started to enthuse.

"We can take that up later. What I want you to do now is take down a name and address. Ready? Lars Thorwald. Five twenty-five Benedict Avenue. Fourth-floor rear. Got it?"

"Fourth-floor rear. Got it. What's it for?"

"Investigation. I've got a firm belief you'll uncover a murder there if you start digging at it. Don't call on me for anything more than that—just a conviction. There's been a man and wife living there until now. Now there's just the man. Her trunk went out early this morning. If you can find someone who saw *her* leave herself——"

Marshaled aloud like that and conveyed to somebody else, a lieutenant of detectives above all, it did sound flimsy, even to me. He said hesitantly, "Well, but——" Then he accepted it as was. Because I was the source. I even left my window out of it completely. I could do that with him and get away with it because he'd known me years, he didn't question my reliability. I didn't want my room all cluttered up with dicks and cops taking turns nosing out of the window in this hot weather. Let them tackle it from the front.

"Well, we'll see what we see," he said. "I'll keep you posted."

I hung up and sat back to watch and wait events. I had a grandstand seat. Or rather a grandstand seat in reverse. I could only see from behind the scenes, but not from the front. I couldn't watch Boyne go to work. I could only see the results, when and if there were any.

Nothing happened for the next few hours. The police work that I knew must be going on was as invisible as police work should be. The figure in the fourth-floor windows over there remained in sight, alone and undisturbed. He didn't go out. He was restless, roamed from room to room without staying in one place very long, but he stayed in. Once I saw him eating again—sitting down this time—and once he shaved, and once he even tried to read the paper, but he didn't stay with it long.

Little unseen wheels were in motion around him. Small and harmless as yet, preliminaries. If he knew, I wondered to myself, would he remain there quiescent like that, or would he try to bolt out and flee? That mightn't depend so much upon his guilt as upon his sense of immunity, his feeling that he could outwit them. Of his guilt I myself was already convinced, or I wouldn't have taken the step I had.

At three my phone rang. Boyne calling back. "Jeffries? Well, I don't know. Can't you give me a little more than just a bald statement like that?"

"Why?" I fenced. "Why do I have to?"

"I've had a man over there making inquiries. I've just had his report. The building superintendent and several of the neighbors all agree she left for the country, to try and regain her health, early yesterday morning."

"Wait a minute. Did any of them *see* her leave, according to your man?"

"No."

"Then all you've gotten is a second-hand version of an unsupported statement by him. Not an eyewitness account."

"He was met returning from the depot, after he'd bought her ticket and seen her off on the train."

"That's still an unsupported statement, once removed."

"I've sent a man down there to the station to try and check with the ticket agent if possible. After all, he should have been fairly conspicuous at that early hour. And we're keeping him under observation, of course, in the meantime, watching all his movements. The first chance we get we're going to jump in and search the place."

I had a feeling that they wouldn't find anything, even if they did.

"Don't expect anything more from me. I've dropped it in your lap. I've given you all I have to give. A name, an address, and an opinion."

"Yes, and I've always valued your opinion highly before now, Jeff——"

"But now you don't, that it?"

"Not at all. The thing is, we haven't turned up anything that seems to bear out your impression so far."

"You haven't gotten very far along, so far."

He went back to his previous cliché. "Well, we'll see what we see. Let you know later."

Another hour or so went by, and sunset came on. I saw him start to get ready to go out, over there. He put on his hat, put his hand in his pocket and stood still looking at it for a minute. Counting change, I guess. It gave me a peculiar sennse of suppressed excitement, knowing they were going to come in the minute he left. I thought grimly, as I saw him take a last look around: If you've got anything to hide, brother, now's the time to hide it.

He left. A breath-holding interval of misleading emptiness descended on the flat. A three-alarm fire couldn't have pulled my eyes off those windows. Suddenly the door by which he had just left parted slightly and two men insinuated themselves, one behind the other. There they were now. They closed it behind them, separated at once, and got busy. One took the bedroom, one the kitchen, and they started to work their way toward one another again from those extremes of the flat. They were thorough. I could see them going over everything from top to bottom. They took the living room together. One cased one side, the other man the other.

They'd already finished before the warning caught them. I could tell that by the way they straightened up and stood facing one another frustratedly for a minute. Then both their heads turned sharply, as at a tip-off by doorbell that he was coming back. They got out fast.

I wasn't unduly disheartened, I'd expected that. My own feeling all along had been that they wouldn't find anything incriminating around. The trunk had gone.

He came in with a mountainous brown-paper bag sitting in the curve of one arm. I watched him closely to see if he'd discover that someone had been there in his absence. Apparently he didn't. They'd been adroit about it.

He stayed in the rest of the night. Sat tight, safe and sound. He did some desultory drinking, I could see him sitting there by the window and his hand would hoist every once in a while, but not to excess. Apparently everything was under control, the tension had eased, now that—the trunk was out.

Watching him across the night, I speculated: Why doesn't he get out? If I'm right about him, and I am, why does he stick around —after it? That brought its own answer: Because he doesn't know anyone's on to him yet. He doesn't think there's any hurry. To go too soon, right after she has, would be more dangerous than to stay awhile.

The night wore on. I sat there waiting for Boyne's call. It came later than I thought it would. I picked the phone up in the dark. He was getting ready to go to bed, over there, now. He'd risen from where he'd been sitting drinking in the kitchen, and put the light out. He went into the living room, lit that. He started to pull his shirt-tail up out of his belt. Boyne's voice was in my ear as my eyes were on him, over there. Three-cornered arrangement.

"Hello, Jeff? Listen, absolutely nothing. We searched the place while he was out——"

I nearly said, "I know you did, I saw it," but checked myself in time.

"—and didn't turn up a thing. But——" He stopped as though this was going to be important. I waited impatiently for him to go ahead.

"Downstairs in his letter box we found a post card waiting for him. We fished it up out of the slot with bent pins——"

"And?"

"And it was from his wife, written only yesterday from some farm upcountry. Here's the message we copied: 'Arrived O.K. Already feeling a little better. Love, Anna.' "

I said, faintly but stubbornly: "You say, written only yesterday. Have you proof of that? What was the postmark-date on it?"

He made a disgusted sound down in his tonsils. At me, not it. "The postmark was blurred. A corner of it got wet, and the ink smudged."

"All of it blurred?"

"The year-date," he admitted. "The hour and the month came out O.K. August. And seven thirty P.M., it was mailed at."

This time I made the disgusted sound, in my larynx. "August, seven thirty P.M.—1937 or 1939 or 1942. You have no proof how it got into that mail box, whether it came from a letter carrier's pouch or from the back of some bureau drawer!"

"Give up, Jeff," he said. "There's such a thing as going too far."

I don't know what I would have said. That is, if I hadn't happened to have my eyes on the Thorwald flat living room windows just then. Probably very little. The post card *had* shaken me, whether I admitted it or not. But I was looking over there. The light had gone out as soon as he'd taken his shirt off. But the bedroom didn't light up. A match-flare winked from the living room, low down, as from an easy chair or sofa. With two unused beds in the bedroom, he was *still staying out of there*.

"Boyne," I said in a glassy voice, "I don't care what post cards from the other world you've turned up, I say that man has done away with his wife. Trace that trunk he shipped out. Open it up when you've located it—and I think you'll find her!"

And I hung up without waiting to hear what he was going to do about it. He didn't ring back, so I suspected he was going to give my suggestion a spin after all, in spite of his loudly proclaimed skepticism.

I stayed there by the window all night, keeping a sort of death-watch. There were two more match-flares after the first, at about half-hour intervals. Nothing more after that. So possibly he was asleep over there. Possibly not. I had to sleep some time myself, and I finally succumbed in the flaming light of the early sun. Anything that he was going to do, he would have done under cover of darkness and not waited for broad daylight. There wouldn't be anything much to watch, for a while now. And what was there that he needed to do any more, anyway? Nothing, just sit tight and let a little disarming time slip by.

It seemed like five minutes later that Sam came over and touched me, but it was already high noon. I said irritably: "Didn't you lamp that note I pinned up, for you to let me sleep?"

He said: "Yeah, but it's your old friend Inspector Boyne. I figured you'd sure want to——"

It was a personal visit this time. Boyne came into the room behind him without waiting, and without much cordiality.

I said to get rid of Sam: "Go inside and smack a couple of eggs together."

Boyne began in a galvanized-iron voice: "Jeff, what do you mean by doing anything like this to me? I've made a fool out of myself, thanks to you. Sending my men out right and left on wild-goose chases. Thank God, I didn't put my foot in it any worse than I did, and have this guy picked up and brought in for question-ing."

"Oh, then you don't think that's necessary?" I suggested, drily.

The look he gave me took care of that. "I'm not alone in the department, you know. There are men over me I'm accountable to for my actions. That looks great, don't it, sending one of my fellows one-half-a-day's train ride up into the sticks to some God-forsaken whistle-stop or other at departmental expense——"

"Then you located the trunk?"

"We traced it through the express agency," he said flintily.

"And you opened it?"

"We did better than that. We got in touch with the various farmhouses in the immediate locality, and Mrs. Thorwald came down to the junction in a produce-truck from one of them and opened it for him herself, with her own keys!"

Very few men have ever gotten a look from an old friend such as I got from him. At the door he said, stiff as a rifle barrel: "Just let's forget all about it, shall we? That's about the kindest thing either one of us can do for the other. You're not yourself, and I'm out a little of my own pocket money, time and temper. Let's let it go at that. If you want to telephone me in the future I'll be glad to give you my home number."

The door went *whopp!* behind him.

For about ten minutes after he stormed out my numbed mind was in a sort of straitjacket. Then it started to wriggle its way free. The hell with the police. I can't prove it to them, maybe, but I can prove it to myself, one way or the other, once and for all. Either I'm wrong or I'm right. He's got his armor on against them. But his back is naked and unprotected against me.

I called Sam in. "Whatever became of that spyglass we used to have, when we were bumming around on that cabin-cruiser that season?"

He found it some place downstairs and came in with it, blowing on it and rubbing it along his sleeve. I let it lie idle in my lap first. I took a piece of paper and a pencil and wrote six words on it: *What have you done with her?*

I sealed it in an envelope and left the envelope blank. I said to Sam: "Now here's what I want you to do, and I want you to be slick about it. You take this, go in that building 525, climb the stairs to the fourth-floor rear, and ease it under the door. You're fast, at least you used to be. Let's see if you're fast enough to keep from being caught at it. Then when you get safely down again, give the outside doorbell a little poke, to attract attention."

His mouth started to open.

"And don't ask me any questions, you understand? I'm not fooling."

He went, and I got the spyglass ready.

I got him in the right focus after a minute or two. A face leaped up, and I was really seeing him for the first time. Dark-haired, but unmistakable Scandinavian ancestry. Looked like a sinewy customer, although he didn't run to much bulk.

About five minutes went by. His head turned sharply, profile-wards. That was the bell-poke, right there. The note must be in already.

He gave me the back of his head as he went back toward the flat-door. The lens could follow him all the way to the rear, where my unaided eyes hadn't been able to before.

He opened the door first, missed seeing it, looked out on a level. He closed it. Then he dipped, straightened up. He had it. I could see him turning it this way and that.

He shifted in, away from the door, nearer the window. He thought danger lay near the door, safety away from it. He didn't know it was the other way around, the deeper into his own rooms he retreated the greater the danger.

He'd torn it open, he was reading it. God, how I watched his expression. My eyes clung to it like leeches. There was a sudden widening, a pulling—the whole skin of his face seemed to stretch back behind the ears, narrowing his eyes to Mongoloids. Shock. Panic. His hand pushed out and found the wall, and he braced himself with it. Then he went back toward the door again slowly. I could see him creeping up on it, stalking it as though it were something alive. He opened it so slenderly you couldn't see it at all, peered fearfully through the crack. Then he closed it, and he came back, zigzag, off balance from sheer reflex dismay. He toppled into a chair and snatched up a drink. Out of the bottle neck itself this time. And even while he was holding it to his lips, his head was turned looking over his shoulder at the door that had suddenly thrown his secret in his face.

I put the glass down.

Guilty! Guilty as all hell, and the police be damned!

My hand started toward the phone, came back again. What was

the use? They wouldn't listen now any more than they had before. "You should have seen his face, etc." And I could hear Boyne's answer: "Anyone gets a jolt from an anonymous letter, true or false. You would yourself." They had a real live Mrs. Thorwald to show me—or thought they had. I'd have to show them the dead one, to prove that they both weren't one and the same. I, from my window, had to show them a body.

Well, he'd have to show me first.

It took hours before I got it. I kept pegging away at it, pegging away at it, while the afternoon wore away. Meanwhile he was pacing back and forth there like a caged panther. Two minds with but one thought, turned inside-out in my case. How to keep it hidden, how to see that it wasn't kept hidden.

I was afraid he might try to light out, but if he intended doing that he was going to wait until after dark, apparently, so I had a little time yet. Possibly he didn't want to himself, unless he was driven to it—still felt that it was more dangerous than to stay.

The customary sights and sounds around me went on unnoticed, while the main stream of my thoughts pounded like a torrent against that one obstacle stubbornly damming them up: how to get him to give the location away to me, so that I could give it away in turn to the police.

I was dimly conscious, I remember, of the landlord or somebody bringing in a prospective tenant to look at the sixth-floor apartment, the one that had already been finished. This was two over Thorwald's; they were still at work on the in-between one. At one point an odd little bit of synchronization, completely accidental of course, cropped up. Landlord and tenant both happened to be near the living room windows on the sixth at the same moment that Thorwald was near those on the fourth. Both parties moved onward simultaneously into the kitchen from there, and, passing the blind spot of the wall, appeared next at the kitchen windows. It was uncanny, they were almost like precision-strollers or puppets manipulated on one and the same string. It probably wouldn't have happened again just like that in another fifty years. Immediately afterwards they digressed, never to repeat themselves like that again.

The thing was, something about it had disturbed me. There had been some slight flaw or hitch to mar its smoothness. I tried for a moment or two to figure out what it had been, and couldn't. The landlord and tenant had gone now, and only Thorwald was in sight. My unaided memory wasn't enough to recapture it for me. My eyesight might have if it had been repeated, but it wasn't.

It sank into my subconscious, to ferment there like yeast, while I went back to the main problem at hand.

I got it finally. It was well after dark, but I finally hit on a way. It mightn't work, it was cumbersome and roundabout, but it was the only way I could think of. An alarmed turn of the head, a quick precautionary step in one certain direction, was all I needed. And to get this brief, flickering, transitory give-away, I needed two phone calls and an absence of about half an hour on his part between them.

I leafed a directory by matchlight until I'd found what I wanted: *Thorwald, Lars. 525 Bndct. . . . SWansea 5-2114.*

I blew out the match, picked up the phone in the dark. It was like television. I could see to the other end of my call, only not along the wire but by a direct channel of vision from window to window.

He said "Hullo?" gruffly.

I thought: How strange this is. I've been accusing him of murder for three days straight, and only now I'm hearing his voice for the first time.

I didn't try to disguise my own voice. After all, he'd never see me and I'd never see him. I said: "You got my note?"

He said guardedly: "Who is this?"

"Just somebody who happens to know."

He said craftily: "Know what?"

"Know what you know. You and I, we're the only ones."

He controlled himself well. I didn't hear a sound. But he didn't know he was open another way too. I had the glass balanced there at proper height on two large books on the sill. Through the window I saw him pull open the collar of his shirt as though its stricture was intolerable. Then he backed his hand over his eyes like you do when there's a light blinding you.

His voice came back firmly. "I don't know what you're talking about."

"Business, that's what I'm talking about. It should be worth something to me, shouldn't it? To keep it from going any further." I wanted to keep him from catching on that it was the windows. I still needed them, I needed them now more than ever. "You weren't very careful about your door the other night. Or maybe the draft swung it open a little."

That hit him where he lived. Even the stomach-heave reached me over the wire. "You didn't see anything. There wasn't anything to see."

"That's up to you. Why should I go to the police?" I coughed a little. "If it would pay me not to."

"Oh," he said. And there was relief of a sort in it. "D'you want to—see me? Is that it?"

"That would be the best way, wouldn't it? How much can you bring with you for now?"

"I've only got about seventy dollars around here."

"All right, then we can arrange the rest for later. Do you know where Lakeside Park is? I'm near there now. Suppose we make it there." That was about thirty minutes away. Fifteen there and fifteen back. "There's a little pavilion as you go in."

"How many of you are there?" he asked cautiously.

"Just me. It pays to keep things to yourself. That way you don't have to divvy up."

He seemed to like that too. "I'll take a run out," he said, "just to see what it's all about."

I watched him more closely than ever, after he'd hung up. He flitted straight through to the end room, the bedroom, that he didn't go near any more. He disappeared into a clothes-closet in there, stayed a minute, came out again. He must have taken something out of a hidden cranny or niche in there that even the dicks had missed. I could tell by the piston-like motion of his hand, just before it disappeared inside his coat, what it was. A gun.

It's a good thing, I thought, I'm not out there in Lakeside Park waiting for my seventy dollars.

The place blacked and he was on his way.

I called Sam in. "I want you to do something for me that's a little risky. In fact, damn risky. You might break a leg, or you might get shot, or you might even get pinched. We've been together ten years, and I wouldn't ask you anything like that if I could do it myself. But I can't, and it's got to be done." Then I told him. "Go out the back way, cross the back yard fences, and see if you can get into that fourth-floor flat up the fire escape. He's left one of the windows down a little from the top."

"What do you want me to look for?"

"Nothing." The police had been there already, so what was the good of that? "There are three rooms over there. I want you to disturb everything just a little bit, in all three, to show someone's been in there. Turn up the edge of each rug a little, shift every chair and table around a little, leave the closet doors standing out. Don't pass up a thing. Here, keep your eyes on this." I took off my own wrist watch, strapped it on him. "You've got twenty-five minutes, starting from now. If you stay within those twenty-five minutes, nothing will happen to you. When you see they're up, don't wait any longer, get out and get out fast."

"Climb back down?"

"No." He wouldn't remember, in his excitement, if he'd left the windows up or not. And I didn't want him to connect danger with the back of his place, but with the front. I wanted to keep my own window out of it. "Latch the window down tight, let yourself out the door, and beat it out of the building the front way, for your life!"

"I'm just an easy mark for you," he said ruefully, but he went.

He came out through our own basement door below me, and scrambled over the fences. If anyone had challenged him from one of the surrounding windows, I was going to backstop for him, explain I'd sent him down to look for something. But no one did. He made it pretty good for anyone his age. He isn't so young any more. Even the fire escape backing the flat, which was drawn up short, he managed to contact by standing up on something. He got in, lit the light, looked over at me. I motioned him to go ahead, not weaken.

I watched him at it. There wasn't any way I could protect him, now that he was in there. Even Thorwald would be within his rights in shooting him down—this was break and entry. I had to stay in back behind the scenes, like I had been all along. I couldn't get out in front of him as a lookout and shield him. Even the dicks had had a lookout posted.

He must have been tense, doing it. I was twice as tense, watching him do it. The twenty-five minutes took fifty to go by. Finally he came over to the window, latched it fast. The lights went, and he was out. He'd made it. I blew out a bellyful of breath that was twenty-five minutes old.

I heard him keying the street door, and when he came up I said warningly: "Leave the light out in here. Go and build yourself a great big two-story whisky punch; you're as close to white as you'll ever be."

Thorwald came back twenty-nine minutes after he'd left for Lakeside Park. A pretty slim margin to hang a man's life on. So now for the finale of the long-winded business, and here was hoping. I got my second phone call in before he had time to notice anything amiss. It was tricky timing but I'd been sitting there with the receiver ready in my hand, dialing the number over and over, then killing it each time. He came in on the 2 of 5-2114, and I saved that much time. The ring started before his hand came away from the light switch.

This was the one that was going to tell the story.

"You were supposed to bring money, not a gun; that's why I didn't show up." I saw the jolt that threw into him. The window still had to stay out of it. "I saw you tap the inside of your coat, where you had it, as you came out on the street." Maybe he hadn't, but he wouldn't remember by now whether he had or not. You usually do when you're packing a gun and aren't an habitual carrier.

"Too bad you had your trip out and back for nothing. I didn't waste my time while you were gone, though. I know more now than I knew before." This was the important part. I had the glass up and I was practically fluoroscoping him. "I've found out where —it is. You know what I mean. I know now where you've got—it. I was there while you were out."

Not a word. Just quick breathing.

"Don't you believe me? Look around. Put the receiver down and take a look for yourself. I found it."

He put it down, moved as far as the living room entrance, and touched off the lights. He just looked around him once, in a sweeping, all-embracing stare, that didn't come to a head on any one fixed point, didn't center at all.

He was smiling grimly when he came back to the phone. All he said, softly and with malignant satisfaction, was: "You're a liar."

Then I saw him lay the receiver down and take his hand off it. I hung up at my end.

The test had failed. And yet it hadn't. He hadn't given the location away as I'd hoped he would. And yet that "You're a liar" was a tacit admission that it was there to be found, somewhere around him, somewhere on those premises. In such a good place that he didn't have to worry about it, didn't even have to look to make sure.

So there was a kind of sterile victory in my defeat. But it wasn't worth a damn to me.

He was standing there with his back to me, and I couldn't see what he was doing. I knew the phone was somewhere in front of him, but I thought he was just standing there pensive behind it. His head was slightly lowered, that was all. I'd hung up at my end. I didn't even see his elbow move. And if his index finger did, I couldn't see it.

He stood like that a moment or two, then finally he moved aside. The lights went out over there; I lost him. He was careful not even to strike matches, like he sometimes did in the dark.

My mind no longer distracted by having him to look at, I turned to trying to recapture something else—that troublesome little hitch in synchronization that had occurred this afternoon, when the renting agent and he both moved simultaneously from one window to the next. The closest I could get was this: it was like when you're looking at someone through a pane of imperfect glass, and a flaw in the glass distorts the symmetry of the reflected image for a second, until it has gone on past that point. Yet that wouldn't do, that was not it. The windows had been open and there had been no glass between. And I hadn't been using the lens at the time.

My phone rang. Boyne, I supposed. It wouldn't be anyone else at this hour. Maybe, after reflecting on the way he'd jumped all over me—I said "Hello" unguardedly, in my own normal voice

There wasn't any answer.

I said: "Hello? Hello? Hello?" I kept giving away samples of my voice.

There wasn't a sound from first to last.

I hung up finally. It was still dark over there, I noticed.

Sam looked in to check out. He was a bit thick-tongued from his restorative drink. He said something about "Awri' if I go now?" I half heard him. I was trying to figure out another way of trapping *him* over there into giving away the right spot. I motioned my consent absently.

He went a little unsteadily down the stairs to the ground floor and after a delaying moment or two I heard the street door close after him. Poor Sam, he wasn't much used to liquor.

I was left alone in the house, one chair the limit of my freedom of movement.

Suddenly a light went on over there again, just momentarily, to go right out again afterwards. He must have needed it for something, to locate something that he had already been looking for and found he wasn't able to put his hands on readily without it. He found it, whatever it was, almost immediately, and moved back at once to put the lights out again. As he turned to do so, I saw him give a glance out the window. He didn't come to the window to do it, he just shot it out in passing.

Something about it struck me as different from any of the others I'd seen him give in all the time I'd been watching him. If you can qualify such an elusive thing as a glance, I would have termed it a glance with a purpose. It was certainly anything but vacant or random, it had a bright spark of fixity in it. It wasn't one of those precautionary sweeps I'd seen him give, either. It hadn't started over on the other side and worked its way around to my side, the right. It had hit dead-center at my bay window, for just a split second while it lasted, and then was gone again. And the lights were gone, and he was gone.

Sometimes your senses take things in without your mind translating them into their proper meaning. My eyes saw that look. My mind refused to smelter it properly. "It was meaningless," I thought. "An unintentional bull's-eye, that just happened to hit square over here, as he went toward the lights on his way out."

Delayed action. A wordless ring of the phone. To test a voice? A period of bated darkness following that, in which two could have played at the same game—stalking one another's window-squares, unseen. A last-moment flicker of the lights, that was bad

strategy but unavoidable. A parting glance, radioactive with malignant intention. All these things sank in without fusing. My eyes did
their job, it was my mind that didn't—or at least took its time about
it.

Seconds went by in packages of sixty. It was very still around
the familiar quadrangle formed by the back of the houses. Sort of
a breathless stillness. And then a sound came into it, starting up
from nowhere, nothing. The unmistakable, spaced clicking a
cricket makes in the silence of the night. I thought of Sam's superstition about them, that he claimed had never failed to fulfill itself
yet. If that was the case, it looked bad for somebody in one of
these slumbering houses around here——

Sam had been gone only about ten minutes. And now he was
back again, he must have forgotten something. That drink was
responsible. Maybe his hat, or maybe even the key to his own
quarters uptown. He knew I couldn't come down and let him in,
and he was trying to be quiet about it, thinking perhaps I'd dozed
off. All I could hear was this faint jiggling down at the lock of the
front door. It was one of those old-fashioned stoop houses, with
an outer pair of storm doors that were allowed to swing free all
night, and then a small vestibule, and then the inner door, worked
by a simple iron key. The liquor had made his hand a little unreliable, although he'd had this difficulty once or twice before, even
without it. A match would have helped him find the keyhole
quicker, but then, Sam doesn't smoke. I knew he wasn't likely to
have one on him.

The sound had stopped now. He must have given up, gone
away again, decided to let whatever it was go until tomorrow. He
hadn't gotten in, because I knew his noisy way of letting doors
coast shut by themselves too well, and there hadn't been any
sound of that sort, that loose slap he always made.

Then suddenly it exploded. Why at this particular moment, I
don't know. That was some mystery of the inner workings of my
own mind. It flashed like waiting gunpowder which a spark has finally reached along a slow train. Drove all thoughts of Sam, and
the front door, and this and that completely out of my head. It had
been waiting there since midafternoon today, and only now——
More of that delayed action. Damn that delayed action.

The renting agent and Thorwald had both started even from the living room window. An intervening gap of blind wall, and both had reappeared at the kitchen window, still one above the other. But some sort of a hitch or flaw or jump had taken place, right there, that bothered me. The eye is a reliable surveyor. There wasn't anything the matter with their timing, it was with their parallel-ness, or whatever the word is. The hitch had been vertical, not horizontal. There had been an upward "jump."

Now I had it, now I knew. And it couldn't wait. It was too good. They wanted a body? Now I had one for them.

Sore or not, Boyne would *have* to listen to me now. I didn't waste any time, I dialed his precinct-house then and there in the dark, working the slots in my lap by memory alone. They didn't make much noise going around, just a light click. Not even as distinct as that cricket out there——

"He went home long ago," the desk sergeant said.

This couldn't wait. "All right, give me his home phone number."

He took a minute, came back again. "Trafalgar," he said. Then nothing more.

"Well? Trafalgar what?" Not a sound.

"Hello? Hello?" I tapped it. "Operator, I've been cut off. Give me that party again." I couldn't get her either.

I hadn't been cut off. My wire had been cut. That had been too sudden, right in the middle of—— And to be cut like that it would have to be done somewhere right here inside the house with me. Outside it went underground.

Delayed action. This time final, fatal, altogether too late. A voiceless ring of the phone. A direction-finder of a look from over there. "Sam" seemingly trying to get back in a while ago.

Surely, death was somewhere inside the house here with me. And I couldn't move, I couldn't get up out of this chair. Even if I had gotten through to Boyne just now, that would have been too late. There wasn't time enough now for one of those camera-finishes in this. I could have shouted out the window to that gallery of sleeping rear-window neighbors around me, I supposed. It would have brought them to the windows. It couldn't have brought them over here in time. By the time they had even figured which particular house it was coming from, it would stop again, be over with. I didn't open my mouth. Not because I was brave, but because it was so obviously useless.

He'd be up in a minute. He must be on the stairs now, although I couldn't hear him. Not even a creak. A creak would have been a relief, would have placed him. This was like being shut up in the dark with the silence of a gliding, coiling cobra somewhere around you.

There wasn't a weapon in the place with me. There were books there on the wall, in the dark, within reach. Me, who never read. The former owner's books. There was a bust of Rousseau or Montesquieu, I'd never been able to decide which, one of those gents with flowing manes, topping them. It was a monstrosity, bisque clay, but it too dated from before my occupancy.

I arched my middle upward from the chair seat and clawed desperately up at it. Twice my fingertips slipped off it, then at the third raking I got it to teeter, and the fourth brought it down into my lap, pushing me down into the chair. There was a steamer rug under me. I didn't need it around me in this weather, I'd been using it to soften the seat of the chair. I tugged it out from under and mantled it around me like an Indian brave's blanket. Then I squirmed far down in the chair, let my head and one shoulder dangle out over the arm, on the side next to the wall. I hoisted the bust to my other, upward shoulder, balanced it there precariously for a second head, blanket tucked around its ears. From the back, in the dark, it would look—I hoped——

I proceeded to breathe adenoidally, like someone in heavy upright sleep. It wasn't hard. My own breath was coming nearly that labored anyway, from tension.

He was good with knobs and hinges and things. I never heard the door open, and this one, unlike the one downstairs, was right behind me. A little eddy of air puffed through the dark at me. I could feel it because my scalp, the real one, was all wet at the roots of the hair right then.

If it was going to be a knife or head-blow, the dodge might give me a second chance, that was the most I could hope for, I knew. My arms and shoulders are hefty. I'd bring him down on me in a bear-hug after the first slash or drive, and break his neck or collarbone against me. If it was going to be a gun, he'd get me anyway in the end. A difference of a few seconds. He had a gun, I knew, that he was going to use on me in the open, over at Lakeside Park. I was hoping that here, indoors, in order to make his own escape more practicable——

Time was up.

The flash of the shot lit up the room for a second, it was so dark. Or at least the corners of it, like flickering, weak lightning. The bust bounced on my shoulder and disintegrated into chunks.

I thought he was jumping up and down on the floor for a minute with frustrated rage. Then when I saw him dart by me and lean over the window sill to look for a way out, the sound transferred itself rearwards and downwards, became a pummeling with hoof and hip at the street door. The camera-finish after all. But he still could have killed me five times.

I flung my body down into the narrow crevice between chair arm and wall, but my legs were still up, and so was my head and that one shoulder.

He whirled, fired at me so close that it was like looking a sunrise in the face. I didn't feel it, so—it hadn't hit.

"You——" I heard him grunt to himself. I think it was the last thing he said. The rest of his life was all action, not verbal.

He flung over the sill on one arm and dropped into the yard. Two-story drop. He made it because he missed the cement, landed on the sod-strip in the middle. I jacked myself up over the chair arm and flung myself bodily forward at the window, nearly hitting it chin first.

He went all right. When life depends on it, you go. He took the first fence, rolled over that bellywards. He went over the second like a cat, hands and feet pointed together in a spring. Then he was back in the rear yard of his own building. He got up on something, just about like Sam had—— The rest was all footwork, with quick little corkscrew twists at each landing stage. Sam had latched his windows down when he was over there, but he'd reopened one of them for ventilation on his return. His whole life depended now on that casual, unthinking little act——

Second, third. He was up to his own windows. He'd made it. Something went wrong. He veered out away from them in another pretzel-twist, flashed up toward the fifth, the one above. Something sparked in the darkness of one of his own windows where he'd been just now, and a shot thudded heavily out around the quadrangle-enclosure like a big bass drum.

He passed the fifth, the sixth, got up to the roof. He'd made it a second time. Gee, he loved life! The guys in his own windows couldn't get him, he was over them in a straight line and there was too much fire escape interlacing in the way.

I was too busy watching him to watch what was going on around me. Suddenly Boyne was next to me, sighting. I heard him mutter: "I almost hate to do this, he's got to fall so far."

He was balanced on the roof parapet up there, with a star right over his head. An unlucky star. He stayed a minute too long, trying to kill before he was killed. Or maybe he was killed, and knew it.

A shot cracked, high up against the sky, the window pane flew apart all over the two of us, and one of the books snapped right behind me.

Boyne didn't say anything more about hating to do it. My face was pressing outward against his arm. The recoil of his elbow jarred my teeth. I blew a clearing through the smoke to watch him go.

It was pretty horrible. He took a minute to show anything, standing up there on the parapet. Then he let his gun go, as if to say: "I won't need this any more." Then he went after it. He missed the fire escape entirely, came all the way down on the outside. He landed so far out he hit one of the projecting planks, down there out of sight. It bounced his body up, like a springboard. Then it landed again—for good. And that was all.

I said to Boyne: "I got it. I got it finally. The fifth-floor flat, the one over his, that they're still working on. The cement kitchen floor, raised above the level of the other rooms. They wanted to comply with the fire laws and also obtain a dropped living room effect, as cheaply as possible. Dig it up——"

He went right over then and there, down through the basement and over the fences, to save time. The electricity wasn't turned on yet in that one, they had to use their torches. It didn't take them long at that, once they'd got started. In about half an hour he came to the window and wigwagged over for my benefit. It meant yes.

He didn't come over until nearly eight in the morning; after they'd tidied up and taken them away. Both away, the hot dead and the cold dead. He said: "Jeff, I take it all back. That damn fool that I sent up there about the trunk—well, it wasn't his fault, in a way. I'm to blame. He didn't have orders to check on the woman's description, only on the contents of the trunk. He came back and touched on it in a general way. I go home and I'm in bed already, and suddenly pop! into my brain—one of the tenants I questioned two whole days ago had given us a few details and they didn't tally with his on several important points. Talk about being slow to catch on!"

"I've had that all the way through this damn thing," I admitted ruefully. "I call it delayed action. It nearly killed me."

"I'm a police officer and you're not."

"That how you happened to shine at the right time?"

"Sure. We came over to pick him up for questioning. I left them planted there when we saw he wasn't in, and came on over here by myself to square it up with you while we were waiting. How did you happen to hit on that cement floor?"

I told him about the freak synchronization. "The renting agent showed up taller at the kitchen window in proportion to Thorwald, than he had been a moment before when both were at the living room windows together. It was no secret that they were putting in cement floors, topped by a cork composition, and raising them considerable. But it took on new meaning. Since the top floor one has been finished for some time, it had to be the fifth. Here's the way I have it lined up, just in theory. She's been in ill health for years, and he's been out of work, and he got sick of that and of her both. Met this other——"

"She'll be here later today, they're bringing her down under arrest."

"He probably insured her for all he could get, and then started to poison her slowly, trying not to leave any trace. I imagine—and remember, this is pure conjecture—she caught him at it that night the light was on all night. Caught on in some way, or caught him in the act. He lost his head, and did the very thing he had wanted all along to avoid doing. Killed her by violence—strangulation or a blow. The rest had to be hastily improvised. He got a better break than he deserved at that. He thought of the apartment upstairs, went up and looked around. They'd just finished laying the floor, the cement hadn't hardened yet, and the materials were still around. He gouged a trough out of it just wide enough to take her body, put her in it, mixed fresh cement and recemented over her, possibly raising the general level of the flooring an inch or two so that she'd be safely covered. A permanent, odorless coffin. Next day the workmen came back, laid down the cork surfacing on top of it without noticing anything, I suppose he'd used one of their own trowels to smooth it. Then he sent his accessory upstate fast, near where his wife had been several summers before, but to a different farmhouse where she wouldn't be recognized, along with the trunk keys. Sent the trunk up after her, and dropped himself an already used post card into his mailbox, with the year-date blurred. In a week or two she would have probably committed 'suicide' up there as Mrs. Anna Thorwald. Despondency due to ill health. Written him a farewell note and left her clothes beside some body of deep water. It was risky, but they might have succeeded in collecting the insurance at that."

By nine Boyne and the rest had gone. I was still sitting there in the chair, too keyed up to sleep. Sam came in and said: "Here's Doc Preston."

He showed up rubbing his hands, in that way he has. "Guess we can take that cast off your leg now. You must be tired of sitting there all day doing nothing."

The Hustler

Walter Tevis

A note by the author of *The Hustler*

    I wrote "The Hustler" when I was a young man, still fairly fresh from the poolrooms where I had spent far too much of my time in college. I was in my second year as a high school English teacher at the time, enthusiastic about Hemingway—as some of the story's sentences may show—and already romanticizing the idea of pool-sharking. I had never been more than a B-minus player myself, but I had seen some of the best of them play. That was in the old billiard room—now long gone—of the Phoenix Hotel in Lexington, Kentucky. Professional hustlers of pool and of a good deal more than pool would congregate there during the times when the Keeneland Racetrack was in session a few miles from Lexington. I had the good fortune to see a lot of good pool being played. Just how good that fortune had been only began to be apparent after I left Lexington and became a teacher. In the next five or six years I published a dozen stories and one novel dealing with pool players. And I took the title of the novel from the story in this collection.

    From where I sit now, it seems that I wrote from a glamorized idea of the game and of the excitements of playing it for big money. Certainly I never saw anyone like Big Sam Willis or Louisville Fats. Louisville Fats, expanded in all but girth, became the Minnesota Fats of my book, and later the movie. And not too long after the book came out, there appeared from nowhere a fat pool player calling himself Minnesota Fats. Pool players who do in fact live by the game have written or called me to ask if one of my characters had been modeled on themselves. Apparently they, the people who really know much more about hustling than I ever did as a gawking college boy in a crowd that watched the profes-

168

sionals, were convinced that my stories were modeled on life. Well, they weren't—although the belief that they were is flattering.

Actually, the fatness of Louisville Fats was suggested to my imagination by a gracefully corpulent junior high teacher of social sciences, female, who worked in the same Kentucky school system I did. And I had a student that year who dyed her hair red. . . .

The novel The Hustler is quite different from this story. Its hero, Fast Eddie Felson, is much younger and less experienced. Eddie is, in a way, Sam at a younger age, learning his first lesson in how you can win and lose at the same time. And the two men named Fats are essentially the same. The novel involves itself in a lot of matters, both psychological and sexual, that I wasn't ready to go into when I wrote the story. But without this story I never would have been able to do the book. Of all the pool stories I wrote in those unadventurous years as a high school teacher in rural Kentucky, it is, I think, the one that best served to show me where, in the imagined heroic contests over the charmed rectangle of green cloth, the story lay.

—Walter Tevis

Those matters that Walter Tevis "wasn't ready to go into" in his short story, but which emerge in the novel, provide the essential ingredients of Robert Rossen's The Hustler (1961). Big Sam Willis of the story is a man who wants to win because winning is all that remains to him. His motivations are indicated through primarily fictive devices: his feeling of completeness as he picks up the cue once more and rediscovers his skill; his fear resolving itself into self-control in the game with Fats; his feelings almost akin to relief when the inevitable happens and he faces death. In the film, however, motivation must be demonstrated in a more visual way; the action must be expanded to show, rather than describe, the protagonist on his path to self-destruction.

In Tevis's story, Sam Willis is the champ, and the question is not whether he can beat Fats but whether he can get away with it. Sam understands that whoever actually wins the game, he will remain what he has always been: a loser. The story portrays his unsuccessful attempt to live with this awareness.

In the film, however, Eddie has no such self-awareness. He can obviously shoot pool, and he is a brash and accomplished hustler, but his challenge to Fats, the tough, stoical, almost superhuman champ, is another matter. Fats is Eddie's ideal, everything he believes he wants to be, and Eddie will give up everything to become like him. This even includes the life of Sarah Packard, the woman who has accepted his love, in whose death rests the film's moral center: The Hustler *is about masculine games, and only Sarah is playing no games at all. She becomes Eddie's ritual sacrifice, by dint of which he overcomes Fats in the climactic pool game. But in winning, Eddie discovers the depth of his loss, and by renouncing those who pushed him to win, he is redeemed. The film's ending suggests that Eddie will retain this new insight and that he will not become the man Sam Willis is.*

The strength of the film also derives from its authentic evocations of the seedy, gritty poolhalls that Tevis creates with such authority. The lost souls who populate this milieu are cast with particular care. Of all Paul Newman's portrayals of alienated heroes, in films such as The Left-Handed Gun *(1957),* Hud *(1963),* Hombre *(1967), and* Butch Cassidy and the Sundance Kid *(1969), Eddie Felson is inarguably his best performance. Jackie Gleason's dramatic authority as Minnesota Fats was startling at the time; it surfaced again the next year in* Requiem for a Heavyweight *(1962), another film about the underbelly of professional combat. But perhaps the most powerful performance in the film comes from George C. Scott as Bert Gordon, the gambler and pool hustler pimp. In Bosley Crowther's phrase, Scott plays the role "as though the devil himself had donned dark glasses and taken up residence in a rancid billiard hall."*

THE HUSTLER

They took Sam out of the office, through the long passageway, and up to the big metal doors. The doors opened, slowly, and they stepped out.

The sunlight was exquisite; warm on Sam's face. The air was clear and still. A few birds were circling in the sky. There was a gravel path, a road, and then, grass. Sam drew a long breath. He could see as far as the horizon.

A guard drove up in a gray station wagon. He opened the door and Sam got in, whistling softly to himself. They drove off, down the gravel path. Sam did not turn around to look at the prison walls; he kept his eyes on the grass that stretched ahead of them, and on the road through the grass.

When the guard stopped to let him off in Richmond he said, "A word of advice, Willis."

"Advice?" Sam smiled at the guard.

"That's right. You got a habit of getting in trouble, Willis. That's why they didn't parole you, made you serve full time, because of that habit."

"That's what the man told me," Sam said. "So?"

"So stay out of pool rooms. You're smart. You can earn a living."

Sam started climbing out of the station wagon. "Sure," he said. He got out, slammed the door, and the guard drove away.

It was still early and the town was nearly empty. Sam walked around, up and down different streets, for about an hour, looking at houses and stores, smiling at the people he saw, whistling or humming little tunes to himself.

In his right hand he was carrying his little round tubular leather case, carrying it by the brass handle on the side. It was about 30 inches long, the case, and about as big around as a man's forearm.

At ten o'clock he went to the bank and drew out the 600 dollars he had deposited there under the name of George Graves. Only it was 680; it had gathered that much interest.

Then he went to a clothing store and bought a sporty tan coat, a pair of brown slacks, brown suede shoes and a bright green sport shirt. In the store's dressing room he put the new outfit on, leaving the prison-issued suit and shoes on the floor. Then he bought two extra sets of underwear and socks, paid, and left.

About a block up the street there was a clean-looking beauty parlor. He walked in and told the lady who seemed to be in charge, "I'm an actor. I have to play a part in Chicago tonight that requires red hair." He smiled at her. "Can you fix me up?"

The lady was all efficiency. "Certainly," she said. "If you'll just step back to a booth we'll pick out a shade."

A half hour later he was a redhead. In two hours he was on board a plane for Chicago, with a little less than 600 dollars in his pocket and one piece of luggage. He still had the underwear and socks in a paper sack.

In Chicago he took a 14 dollar a night room in the best hotel he could find. The room was big, and pleasant. It looked and smelled clean.

He sat down on the side of the bed and opened his little leather case at the top. The two-piece billiard cue inside was intact. He took it out and screwed the brass joint together, pleased that it still fit perfectly. Then he checked the butt for tightness. The weight was still firm and solid. The tip was good, its shape had held up; and the cue's balance and stroke seemed easy, familiar; almost as though he still played with it every day.

He checked himself in the mirror. They had done a perfect job on his hair; and its brightness against the green and brown of his new clothes gave him the sporty, racetrack sort of look he had always avoided before. His once ruddy complexion was very pale. Not a pool player in town should be able to recognize him: he could hardly recognize himself.

If all went well he would be out of Chicago for good in a few days; and no one would know for a long time that Big Sam Willis had even played there. Six years on a manslaughter charge could have its advantages.

In the morning he had to walk around town for a while before he found a pool room of the kind he wanted. It was a few blocks off the Loop, small; and from the outside it seemed to be fairly clean and quiet.

Inside, there was a short order and beer counter up front. In back there were four tables; Sam could see them through the door in the partition that separated the lunch room from the pool room proper. There was no one in the place except for the tall, blond boy behind the counter.

Sam asked the boy if he could practice.

"Sure." The boy's voice was friendly. "But it'll cost you a dollar an hour."

"Fair enough." He gave the boy a five dollar bill. "Let me know when this is used up."

The boy raised his eyebrows and took the money.

In the back room Sam selected the best 20-ounce cue he could find in the wall rack, one with an ivory point and a tight butt, chalked the tip, and broke the rack of balls on what seemed to be the best of the four tables.

He tried to break safe, a straight pool break, where you drive the two bottom corner balls to the cushions and back into the stack where they came from, making the cue ball go two rails and return to the top of the table, killing itself on the cushion. The break didn't work, however; the rack of balls spread wide, five of them came out into the table, and the cue ball stopped in the middle. It would have left an opponent wide open for a big run. Sam shuddered.

He pocketed the 15 balls, missing only once—a long shot that had to be cut thin into a far corner—and he felt better, making balls. He had little confidence on the hard ones, he was awkward; but he still knew the game, he knew how to break up little clusters of balls on one shot so that he could pocket them on the next. He knew how to play position with very little English on the cue, by shooting "natural" shots, and letting the speed of the cue ball do the work. He could still figure the spread, plan out his shots in advance from the positions of the balls on the table, and he knew what to shoot at first.

He kept shooting for about three hours. Several times other players came in and played for a while but none of them paid any attention to him, and none of them stayed long.

The place was empty again and Sam was practicing cutting balls down the rail, working on his cue ball and on his speed, when he looked up and saw the boy who ran the place coming back. He was carrying a plate with a hamburger in one hand and two bottles of beer in the other.

"Hungry?" He set the sandwich down on the arm of the chair. "Or thirsty, maybe?"

Sam looked at his watch. It was 1:30. "Come to think of it," he said, "I am." He went to the chair, picked up the hamburger, and sat down.

"Have a beer," the boy said, affably. Sam took it and drank from the bottle. It tasted delicious.

"What do I owe you?" he said, and took a bite out of the hamburger.

"The burger's 30 cents," the boy said. "The beer's on the house."

"Thanks," Sam said, chewing. "How do I rate?"

"You're a good customer," the boy said. "Easy on the equipment, cash in advance, and I don't even have to rack the balls for you."

"Thanks." Sam was silent for a minute, eating.

The boy was drinking the other beer. Abruptly, he set the bottle down. "You on the hustle?" he said.

"Do I look like a hustler?"

"You practice like one."

Sam sipped the beer quietly for a minute, looking over the top of the bottle, once, at the boy. Then he said, "I might be looking around." He set the empty bottle down on the wooden chair arm. "I'll be back tomorrow; we can talk about it then. There might be something in it for you, if you help me out."

"Sure, mister," the boy said. "You pretty good?"

"I think so," Sam said. Then when the boy got up to leave, he added, "Don't try to finger me for anybody. It won't do you any good."

"I won't." The boy went back up front.

Sam practiced, working mainly on his stroke and his position, for three more hours. When he finished his arm was sore and his feet were tired; but he felt better. His stroke was beginning to work for him, he was getting smooth, making balls regularly, playing good position. Once, when he was running balls continuously, racking 14 and 1, he ran 47 without missing.

The next morning, after a long night's rest, he was even better. He ran more than 90 balls one time, missing, finally, on a difficult rail shot.

The boy came back at 1:00 o'clock, bringing a ham sandwich this time and two beers. "Here you go," he said. "Time to make a break."

Sam thanked him, laid his cue stick on the table, and sat down.

"My name's Barney," the boy said.

"George Graves." Sam held out his hand, and the boy shook it. "Just," he smiled inwardly at the thought, "call me Red."

"You *are* good," Barney said. "I watched you a couple of times."

"I know." Sam took a drink from the beer bottle. "I'm looking for a straight pool game."

"I figured that, Mister Graves. You won't find one here, though. Up at Bennington's they play straight pool."

Sam had heard of Bennington's. They said it was a hustler's room, a big money place.

"You know who plays pool there, Barney?" he said.

"Sure. Bill Peyton, he plays there. And Shufala Kid, Louisville Fats, Johnny Vargas, Henry Keller, a little guy they call 'The Policeman' . . ."

Henry Keller was the only familiar name; Sam had played him once, in Atlantic City, maybe 14 years ago. But that had been even before the big days of Sam's reputation, before he had got so good that he had to trick hustlers into playing him. That was a long time ago. And then there was the red hair; he ought to be able to get by.

"Which one's got money," he asked, "and plays straight pool?"

"Well," Barney looked doubtful. "I think Louisville Fats carries a big roll. He's one of the old Prohibition boys; they say he keeps an army of hoods working for him. He plays straights. But he's good. And he doesn't like being hustled."

It looked good; but dangerous. Hustlers didn't take it very well to find out a man was using a phony name so he could get a game. Sam remembered the time someone had told Bernie James whom he had been playing and Bernie had got pretty rough about it. But this time it was different; he had been out of circulation six years, and he had never played in Chicago before.

"This Fats. Does he bet big?"

"Yep, he bets big. Big as you want." Barney smiled. "But I tell you he's mighty good."

"Rack the balls," Sam said, and smiled back. "I'll show you something."

Barney racked. Sam broke them wide open and started running.

He went through the rack, then another, another, and another. Barney was counting the balls, racking them for him each time. When he got to 80 Sam said, "Now I'll bank a few." He banked 7, knocking them off the rails, across, and into the pockets. When he missed the 8 he said, "What do you think?"

"You'll do," Barney said. He laughed. "Fats is good; but you might take him."

"I'll take him," Sam said. "You lead me to him. Tomorrow night you get somebody to work for you. We're going up to Bennington's."

"Fair enough, Mister Graves," Barney said. He was grinning. "We'll have a beer on that."

At Bennington's you took an elevator to the floor you wanted: billiards on the first, pocket pool on the second, snooker and private games on the third. It was an old-fashioned set-up, high ceilings, big, shaded incandescent lights, overstuffed leather chairs.

Sam spent the morning on the second floor, trying to get the feel of the tables. They were different from Barney's, with softer cushions and tighter cloths, and it was a little hard to get used to them; but after about two hours he felt as though he had them pretty well, and he left. No one had paid any attention to him.

After lunch he inspected his hair in the restaurant's bathroom mirror; it was still as red as ever and hadn't yet begun to grow out. He felt good. Just a little nervous, but good.

Barney was waiting for him at the little pool room. They took a cab up to Bennington's.

Louisville Fats must have weighed 300 pounds. His face seemed to be bloated around the eyes like the face of an Eskimo, so that he was always squinting. His arms, hanging from the short sleeves of his white silk shirt, were pink and dough-like. Sam noticed his hands; they were soft looking, white and delicate. He wore three rings, one with a diamond. He had on dark green, wide suspenders.

When Barney introduced him, Fats said, "How are you, George?" but didn't offer his hand. Sam noticed that his eyes, almost buried beneath the face, seemed to shift from side to side, so that he seemed not really to be looking at anything.

"I'm fine," Sam said. Then, after a pause, "I've heard a lot about you."

"I got a reputation?" Fats' voice was flat, disinterested. "Then I must be pretty good maybe?"

"I suppose so," Sam said, trying to watch the eyes.

"You a good pool player, George?" The eyes flickered, scanning Sam's face.

"Fair. I like playing. Straight pool."

"Oh," Fats grinned, abruptly, coldly. "That's my game too, George." He slapped Barney on the back. The boy pulled away, slightly, from him. "You pick good, Barney. He plays my game. You can finger for me, sometime, if you want."

"Sure," Barney said. He looked nervous.

"One thing." Fats was still grinning. "You play for money, George? I mean, you gamble?"

"When the bet's right."

"What you think is a right bet, George?"

"50 dollars."

Fats grinned even more broadly; but his eyes still kept shifting. "Now that's close, George," he said. "You play for a hundred and we play a few."

"Fair enough," Sam said, as calmly as he could.

"Let's go upstairs. It's quieter."

"Fine. I'll take my boy if you don't mind. He can rack the balls."

Fats looked at Barney. "You level with that rack, Barney? I mean, you rack the balls tight for Fats?"

"Sure," Barney said, "I wouldn't try to cross you up."

"You know better than that, Barney. OK."

They walked up the back stairs to the third floor. There was a small, bare-walled room, well lighted, with chairs lined up against the walls. The chairs were high ones, the type used for watching pool games. There was no one else in the room.

They uncovered the table, and Barney racked the balls. Sam lost the toss and broke, making it safe; but not too safe. He undershot, purposely, and left the cue ball almost a foot away from the end rail.

They played around, shooting safe, for a while. Then Fats pulled a hard one off the edge of the rack, ran 35, and played him safe. Sam jockeyed with him, figuring to lose for a while, only wanting the money to hold out until he had the table down pat, until he had the other man's game figured, until he was ready to raise the bet.

He lost three in a row before he won one. He wasn't playing his best game; but that meant little, since Fats was probably pulling his punches too, trying to take him for as much as possible. After he won his first game he let himself go a little and made a few tricky ones. Once he knifed a ball thin into the side pocket and went two cushions for a break up; but Fats didn't even seem to notice.

Neither of them tried to run more than 40 at a turn. It would have looked like a game between only fair players, except that neither of them missed very often. In a tight spot they didn't try anything fancy, just shot a safe and let the other man figure it out. Sam played safe on some shots that he was sure he could make; he didn't want to show his hand. Not yet. They kept playing and, after a while, Sam started winning more often.

After about three hours he was five games ahead and shooting better all the time. Then, when he won still another game, Sam said, "You're losing money, Fats. Maybe we should quit." He looked at Barney and winked. Barney gave him a puzzled, worried look.

"Quit? You think we should quit?" Fats took a big silk handkerchief from his side pocket and wiped his face. "How much money you won, George?" he said.

"That last makes 600." He felt, suddenly, a little tense. It was coming. The big push.

"Suppose we play for 600, George." He put the handkerchief back in his pocket. "Then we see who quits."

"Fine." He felt really nervous now, but he knew he would get over it. Nervousness didn't count. At 600 a game he would be in clover and in San Francisco in two days. If he didn't lose.

Barney racked the balls and Sam broke. He took the break slowly, putting to use his practice of three days, and his experience of 27 years. The balls broke perfectly, reracking the original triangle, and the cue ball skidded to a stop right on the end cushion.

"You shoot pretty good," Fats said, looking at the safe table that Sam had left him. But he played safe, barely tipping the cue ball off one of the balls down at the foot of the table and returning back to the end rail.

Sam tried to return the safe by repeating the same thing; but the cue ball caught the object ball too thick and he brought out a shot, a long one, for Fats. Fats stepped up, shot the ball in, played position, and ran out the rest of the rack. Then he ran out another rack and Sam sat down to watch; there was nothing he could do now. Fats ran 78 points and then, seeing a difficult shot, played him safe.

He had been afraid that something like that might happen. He tried to fight his way out of the game, but couldn't seem to get into the clear long enough for a good run. Fats beat him badly—125 to 30—and he had to give back the 600 dollars from his pocket. It hurt.

What hurt even worse was that he knew he had less than 600 left of his own money.

"Now we see who quits," Fats stuffed the money in his hip pocket. "You want to play for another 600?"

"I'm still holding my stick," Sam said. He tried not to think about that "army of hoods" that Barney had told him about.

He stepped up to the table and broke. His hand shook a little; but the break was a perfect one.

In the middle of the game Fats missed an easy shot, leaving Sam a dead set-up. Sam ran 53 and out. He won. It was as easy as that. He was 600 ahead again, and feeling better.

Then something unlucky happened. Downstairs they must have closed up because six men came up during the next game and sat around the table. Five of them Sam had never seen, but one of them was Henry Keller. Henry was drunk now, evidently, and he didn't seem to be paying much attention to what was going on; but Sam didn't like it. He didn't like Keller, and he didn't like having a man who knew who he was around him. It was too much like that other time. That time in Richmond when Bernie James had come after him with a bottle. That fight had cost him six years. He didn't like it. It was getting time to wind things up here, time to be cutting out. If he could win two more games quick, he would have enough to set him up hustling on the West Coast. And on the West Coast there weren't any Henry Kellers who knew that Big Sam Willis was once the best straight-pool shot in the game.

After Sam had won the game by a close score Fats looked at his fingernails and said, "George, you're a hustler. You shoot better straights than anybody in Chicago shoots. Except me."

This was the time, the time to make it quick and neat, the time to push as hard as he could. He caught his breath, held steady, and said, "You've got it wrong, Fats. I'm better than you are. I'll play you for all of it. The whole 1200."

It was very quiet in the room. Then Fats said, "George, I like that kind of talk." He started chalking his cue. "We play 1200."

Barney racked the balls and Fats broke them. They both played safe, very safe, back and forth, keeping the cue ball on the rail, not leaving a shot for the other man. It was nerve-wracking. Over and over.

Then he missed. Missed the edge of the rack, coming at it from an outside angle. His cue ball bounced off the rail and into the rack of balls, spreading them wide, leaving Fats at least five shots. Sam didn't sit down. He just stood and watched Fats come up and start his run. He ran the balls, broke on the 15th, and ran another rack. 28 points. And he was just getting started. He had his rack break set up perfectly for the next shot.

Then, as Fats began chalking up, preparing to shoot, Henry Keller stood up from his seat and pointed his finger at Sam.

He was drunk; but he spoke clearly, and loudly. "You're Big Sam Willis," he said. "You're the World's Champion." He sat back in his chair, heavily. "You got red hair, but you're Big Sam." He sat silent, half slumped in the big chair, for a moment, his eyes glassy, and red at the corners. Then he closed his eyes and said, "There's nobody beats Big Sam, Fats. Nobody *never.*"

The room was quiet for what seemed to be a very long while. Sam noticed how thick the tobacco smoke had become in the air; motionless. It was like a heavy brown mist, and over the table it was like a cloud. The faces of the men in the chairs were impassive; all of them, except Henry, watching him.

Fats turned to him. For once his eyes were not shifting from side to side. He looked Sam in the face and said, in a voice that was flat and almost a whisper, "You Big Sam Willis, George?"

"That's right, Fats."

"You must be pretty smart, Sam," Fats said, "to play a trick like that. To make a sucker out of me."

"Maybe." His chest and stomach felt very tight. It was like when Bernie James had caught him at the same game, except without the red hair. Bernie hadn't said anything though; he had just picked up a bottle.

But, then, Bernie James was dead now. Sam wondered, momentarily, if Fats had ever heard about that.

Suddenly Fats split the silence, laughing. The sound of his laughing filled the room, he threw his head back and laughed; and the men in the chairs looked at him, astonished, hearing the laughter. "Big Sam," he said, "you're a hustler. You put on a great act; and fool me good. A great act." He slapped Sam on the back. "I think the joke's on me."

It was hard to believe. But Fats could afford the money, and Sam knew that Fats knew who would be the best if it came to muscle. And there was no certainty whose side the other men were on.

Fats shot, ran a few more balls, and then missed.

When Sam stepped up to shoot he said, "Go ahead, Big Sam, and shoot your best. You don't have to act now. I'm quitting you anyway after this one."

The funny thing was that Sam had been shooting his best for the past five or six games—or thought he had—but when he stepped up to the table this time he was different. Maybe it was Fats or Keller, something made him feel as he hadn't felt for a long time. It was like being the old Big Sam, back before he had quit playing the tournaments and exhibitions, the Big Sam who could run 125 when he was hot and the money was up. His stroke was smooth, steady, accurate, like a balanced, precision instrument moving on well-oiled bearings. He shot easily, calmly, clicking the shots off in his mind and then pocketing them on the table, watching everything on the green, forgetting himself, forgetting even the money, just dropping the balls into the pockets, one after another.

He did it. He ran the game. 125 points, 125 shots without missing. When he finished Fats took 1200 from his still-big roll and counted it out, slowly, to him. He said, "You're the best I've ever seen, Big Sam." Then he covered the table with the oilcloth cover.

After Sam had dropped Barney off he had the cab take him by his hotel and let him off at a little all-night lunch room. He ordered bacon and eggs, over light, and talked with the waitress while she fried them. The place seemed strange, gay almost; his nerves felt electric, and there was a pleasant fuzziness in his head, a dim, insistent ringing sound coming from far off. He tried to think for a moment, tried to think whether he should go to the airport now without even going back to the hotel, now that he had made out so well, had made out better, even, than he had planned to be able to do in a week. But there was the waitress and then the food, and when he put a quarter in the jukebox he couldn't hear the ringing in his ears any more. This was no time for plane trips, it was a time for talk and music, time for the sense of triumph, the sense of being alive and having money again, and then time for sleep. He was in a chromium and plastic booth in the lunch room and he leaned back against the padded plastic backrest and felt an abrupt, deep, gratifying sense of fatigue, loosening his muscles and killing, finally, the tension that had ridden him like a fury for the past three days. There would be plane flights enough tomorrow. Now, he needed rest. It was a long way to San Francisco.

The bed at his hotel was impeccably made; the pale blue spread seemed drum-tight, but soft and round at the edges and corners. He didn't even take off his shoes.

When he awoke, he awoke suddenly. The skin at the back of his neck was itching, sticky with sweat from where the collar of his shirt had been pressed, tight, against it. His mouth was dry and his feet felt swollen, stuffed, in his shoes. The room was as quiet as death. Outside the window a car's tires groaned gently, rounding a corner, then were still.

He pulled the chain on the lamp by the bed and the light came on. Squinting, he stood up, and realized that his legs were aching. The room seemed too big, too bright. He stumbled into the bathroom and threw handfuls of cold water on his face and neck. Then he dried off with a towel and looked in the mirror. Startled, he let go the towel momentarily; the red hair had caught him off guard; and with the eyes now swollen, the lips pale, it was not his face at all. He finished drying quickly, ran his comb through his hair, straightened out his shirt and slacks hurriedly. The startling strangeness of his own face had crystallized the dim, half-conscious feeling that had awakened him, the feeling that something was wrong. The hotel room, himself, Chicago; they were all wrong. He should not be here, not now; he should be on the West Coast, in San Francisco.

He looked at his watch. 4:00 o'clock. He had slept three hours. He did not feel tired, not now, although his bones ached and there was sand under his eyelids. He could sleep, if he had to, on the plane. But the important thing, now, was getting on the plane, clearing out, moving West. He had slept with his cue, in its case, on the bed. He took it and left the room.

The lobby, too, seemed too bright and too empty. But when he had paid his bill and gone out to the street the relative darkness seemed worse. He began to walk down the street hastily, looking for a cab stand. His own footsteps echoed around him as he walked. There seemed to be no cabs anywhere on the street. He began walking faster. The back of his neck was sweating again. It was a very hot night; the air felt heavy against his skin. There were no cabs.

And then, when he heard the slow, dense hum of a heavy car moving down the street in his direction, heard it from several blocks away and turned his head to see it and to see that there was no cablight on it, he knew—abruptly and lucidly, as some men at some certain times know these things—what was happening.

He began to run; but he did not know where to run. He turned a corner while he was still two blocks ahead of the car and when he could feel its lights, palpably, on the back of his neck, and tried to hide in a doorway, flattening himself out against the door. Then, when he saw the lights of the car as it began its turn around the corner he realized that the doorway was too shallow, that the lights would pick him out. Something in him wanted to scream. He pushed himself from his place, stumbled down the street, visualizing in his mind a place, some sort of a place between buildings where he could hide completely and where the car could never follow him. But the buildings were all together, with no space at all between them; and when he saw that this was so he also saw at the same instant that the car lights were flooding him. And then he heard the car stop. There was nothing more to do. He turned around and looked at the car, blinking.

Two men had got out of the back seat; there were two more in front. He could see none of their faces; but was relieved that he could not, could not see the one face that would be bloated like an Eskimo's and with eyes like slits.

The men were holding the door open for him.

"Well," he said. "Hello, boys," and climbed into the back seat. His little leather case was still in his right hand. He gripped it tightly. It was all he had.

The Man Who Shot Liberty Valance

Dorothy M. Johnson

A note by the author of *The Man Who Shot Liberty Valance*

I do not understand the motion-picture business and do not need to, because on the occasions (three) when our courses have collided my agent did the navigating and I simply cashed the check—wondering wistfully why other writers get such staggering sums of money. Still, those stories had already appeared in print and I had been paid for them, so what did I have to complain about?

"The Man Who Shot Liberty Valance" was first published in Cosmopolitan. *If you have looked at that magazine lately (I can't bear to), you may find this hard to believe. But it used to be a family magazine.*

When the movie came out, strange things had happened. Bert Barricune had become Tom Doniphon, played by John Wayne. (On his autographed photograph he wrote: "Have you anyone else you want shot?") Ransome Foster was now Ransome Stoddard (James Stewart). Liberty Valance (Lee Marvin) still went by the same name, but I never dreamed up such a dastardly villain.

A whole lot of people I hadn't even thought of had entered the action, and the plot was vastly complicated. That I could understand. My story was short; the screenwriter had to add complications to make it big enough for a feature film.

He almost pinned down the locale geographically by mentioning the "Picketwire"—the Purgatoire River, which is in southeastern Colorado. I never did specify, but the rocks where I visualized Ranse doing his pistol practice are on the Cheyenne Reservation in Montana, not that it matters.

This may not be the place for a public confession, but. . . . The story begins in 1910 with the arrival of Senator Ranse What's-his-

name and wife in the old town for a funeral. It flashes back, way back. It ends with their departure for Washington, D.C., after the funeral. Here is the confession: in Cosmopolitan, *at the end the couple "rode out to the airport."*

I had rewritten that story several times, moved it around in the nineteenth and twentieth centuries, made appropriate changes— but not that one. Cosmopolitan*'s eagle-eyed editors hadn't caught it. Only one reader wrote to inquire, "An airport in 1910?"*

Ballantine Books brought out a collection of my Western stories called Indian Country *in 1953. I hollered and stomped and warned them, after reading the galley proofs, to take out that airport, but nobody listened. So if you have that book with a 1910 airport, it's a first edition. Last time I looked, there had been fifteen U.S. printings, some of them under the title* A Man Called Horse. *The Spanish edition is* Tierra India; *in Italian it's* Tomahawk; *in Indonesian,* Tipi dan Mokasin *(you do read Indonesian, of course?). Royalties on* Tomahawk *are figured in lots of Italian* lire; *converted to British pounds and then to U.S. dollars, minus agents' commissions, this brings me enough to take a friend to dinner twice a year.*

James Warner Bellah was coauthor of the screenplay of The Man Who Shot Liberty Valance. *Later a series of frantic phone calls took place between Hollywood, New York, and Missoula, Montana, where I live. Mr. Bellah had written a "novelization" based on his screenplay and had a publisher for it. But my contract with the producer had that angle covered—he needed my permission. (I'm not smart. My agent was.) So how much money did I want (or how little would I accept) to release the "novelization" rights?*

We argued for a couple of days. A novel by Mr. Bellah based on a script by Mr. Bellah based on a story by Miss Johnson—it seemed strange, but it was legal. I concluded that it wasn't immoral, either. So I told my agent a thousand dollars and got it, minus her 10 percent.

And a dean at the University of Montana remarked, "Dorothy, I always knew what you are. Now I know what your price is."

The contract for that movie is more than forty pages long, and the only provision in it that I understood was that if the author should become "an object of public obloquy and disgrace" she

*wouldn't get any screen credit. My name was still on the credits
(if you look fast) last time it came around on television, so whatever the dean meant, nobody has caught me at it yet.*
                                                  —Dorothy M. Johnson

*The protagonist of a Dorothy M. Johnson short story is often a
man or woman torn by conflict, a person who must either over-
come an emotional disability or turn it into a strength. In "The Man
Who Shot Liberty Valance," Ransome Foster is possessed by
demons he cannot identify. He has deliberately abandoned his
past and come West, and there he is brutalized and driven to seek
revenge according to a code that is alien to him. Triumph over
Liberty Valance is also a triumph over his own conflicts, which the
outlaw has come to symbolize for him. Ranse becomes a more
complete man, drawn into an active role with civilization and politics, but paradoxically, through a course of violence. Yet the hero
of the story is the native son of the West, Bert Barricune.*

In John Ford's The Man Who Shot Liberty Valance *(1962),
Ranse's conflict is broadened and takes on greater meaning. At
first, Ranse's weakness is coded in a traditional way, as dudism;
he simply does not understand the ways of the frontier. When
Liberty demands, "What kind of a man are you?" Ranse declares,
"I am an attorney-at-law." Liberty is singularly unimpressed. When
he recovers from his wounds, Ranse's first thought is to bring
charges against Liberty in a court of law, but Tom Doniphon disa-
buses Ranse of that notion. "You better start packing a handgun,"
Doniphon advises. "Out here a man settles his own problems."
Finally Ranse is forced to pick up the gun and become a reluctant
hero; he faces Liberty Valance because his girl friend Hallie and
Tom Doniphon and the code of the West all demand it of him.*

*In Ford's version, Ranse's conflict becomes metaphor for the
film's primary theme; at its most basic, the film celebrates the
victory of law and order and democracy over the role of the gun,
over violence. Ranse develops from dude into avatar of the new
order. He establishes Shinbone's first school and teaches the
rough cowpokes to read and write; he defends the freedom of the
press against hooliganism; and finally, he becomes the political*

patriarch who leads the territory to statehood. Whether or not he actually is the man who shot Liberty Valance, he demonstrates the strength of his unwavering conviction that the lawbook is mightier than the gun.

At the same time, the film is a bittersweet epitaph for the West that was. When Tom Doniphon burns his house, he is not only mourning the loss of his girl friend, Hallie, but also his own imminent passage from hero to relic. In Miss Johnson's story, the frame-story and flashback device serve to illuminate the character of Ranse, who sees the man he once was, and the man he has become. The film retains the story-within-a-story form of narration, but now the focus is not only on Ranse, but also on nostalgia for a lost world, symbolized by Tom Doniphon. The past has become mythic, but the present continues to depend on what has come before. The truth about Liberty Valance's death is subordinate to what that death has come to epitomize. "When the facts become legend," the new editor of the Shinbone Star *declares, "print the legend."*

Two other short stories by Miss Johnson have been filmed. The Hanging Tree *(1959), directed by Delmar Daves and starring Gary Cooper and Maria Schell, is a skillful and gripping version of Miss Johnson's novella.* A Man Called Horse *(1970), directed by Elliot Silverstein and starring Richard Harris and Dame Judith Anderson, is far less successful, and is most notable for its embarrassingly patronizing treatment of the Indians Miss Johnson ennobles in her original story.*

THE MAN WHO SHOT LIBERTY VALANCE

Bert Barricune died in 1910. Not more than a dozen persons showed up for his funeral. Among them was an earnest young reporter who hoped for a human-interest story; there were legends that the old man had been something of a gunfighter in the early days. A few aging men tiptoed in, singly or in pairs, scowling and edgy, clutching their battered hats—men who had been Bert's companions at drinking or penny ante while the world passed them by. One woman came, wearing a heavy veil that concealed her face. White and yellow streaks showed in her black-dyed hair. The reporter made a mental note: Old friend from the old District. But no story there—can't mention that.

One by one they filed past the casket, looking into the still face of old Bert Barricune, who had been nobody. His stubbly hair was white, and his lined face was as empty in death as his life had been. But death had added dignity.

One great spray of flowers spread behind the casket. The card read, "Senator and Mrs. Ransome Foster." There were no other flowers except, almost unnoticed, a few pale, leafless, pink and yellow blossoms scattered on the carpeted step. The reporter, squinting, finally identified them: son of a gun! Blossoms of the prickly pear. Cactus flowers. Seems suitable for the old man— flowers that grow on prairie wasteland. Well, they're free if you want to pick 'em, and Barricune's friends don't look prosperous. But how come the Senator sends a bouquet?

There was a delay, and the funeral director fidgeted a little, waiting. The reporter sat up straighter when he saw the last two mourners enter.

Senator Foster—sure, there's the crippled arm—and that must be his wife. Congress is still in session; he came all the way from Washington. Why would he bother, for an old wreck like Bert Barricune?

After the funeral was decently over, the reporter asked him. The Senator almost told the truth, but he caught himself in time. He said, "Bert Barricune was my friend for more than thirty years."

He could not give the true answer: He was my enemy; he was my conscience; he made me whatever I am.

Ransome Foster had been in the Territory for seven months when he ran into Liberty Valance. He had been afoot on the prairie for two days when he met Bert Barricune. Up to that time, Ranse Foster had been nobody in particular—a dude from the East, quietly inquisitive, moving from one shack town to another; just another tenderfoot with his own reasons for being there and no aim in life at all.

When Barricune found him on the prairie, Foster was indeed a tenderfoot. In his boots there was a warm, damp squidging where his feet had blistered, and the blisters had broken to bleed. He was bruised, sunburned, and filthy. He had been crawling, but when he saw Barricune riding toward him, he sat up. He had no horse, no saddle and, by that time, no pride.

Barricune looked down at him, not saying anything. Finally Ranse Foster asked, "Water?"

Barricune shook his head. "I don't carry none, but we can go where it is."

He stepped down from the saddle, a casual Samaritan, and with one heave pulled Foster upright.

"Git you in the saddle, can you stay there?" he inquired.

"If I can't," Foster answered through swollen lips, "shoot me."

Bert said amiably, "All right," and pulled the horse around. By twisting its ear, he held the animal quiet long enough to help the anguished stranger to the saddle. Then, on foot—and like any cowboy Bert Barricune hated walking—he led the horse five miles to the river. He let Foster lie where he fell in the cottonwood grove and brought him a hat full of water.

After that, Foster made three attempts to stand up. After the third failure, Barricune asked, grinning, "Want me to shoot you after all?"

"No," Foster answered. "There's something I want to do first."

Barricune looked at the bruises and commented, "Well, I should think so." He got on his horse and rode away. After an hour he returned with bedding and grub and asked, "Ain't you dead yet?"

The bruised and battered man opened his uninjured eye and said, "Not yet, but soon." Bert was amused. He brought a bucket of water and set up camp—a bedroll on a tarp, an armload of wood for a fire. He crouched on his heels while the tenderfoot, with cautious movements that told of pain, got his clothes off and splashed water on his body. No gunshot wounds, Barricune observed, but marks of kicks, and a couple that must have been made with a quirt.

After a while he asked, not inquisitively, but as one who has a right to know how matters stood, "Anybody looking for you?"

Foster rubbed dust from his clothes, being too full of pain to shake them.

"No," he said. "But I'm looking for somebody."

"I ain't going to help you look," Bert informed him. "Town's over that way, two miles, when you get ready to come. Cache the stuff when you leave. I'll pick it up."

Three days later they met in the town marshal's office. They glanced at each other but did not speak. This time it was Bert Barricune who was bruised, though not much. The marshal was just letting him out of the one-cell jail when Foster limped into the office. Nobody said anything until Barricune, blinking and walking not quite steadily, had left. Foster saw him stop in front of the next building to speak to a girl. They walked away together, and it looked as if the young man were being scolded.

The marshal cleared his throat. "You wanted something, Mister?"

Foster answered, "Three men set me afoot on the prairie. Is that an offense against the law around here?"

The marshal eased himself and his stomach into a chair and frowned judiciously. "It ain't customary," he admitted. "Who was they?"

"The boss was a big man with black hair, dark eyes, and two gold teeth in front. The other two—"

"I know. Liberty Valance and a couple of his boys. Just what's your complaint, now?" Foster began to understand that no help was going to come from the marshal.

"They rob you?" the marshal asked.

"They didn't search me."

"Take your gun?"

"I didn't have one."

"Steal your horse?"

"Gave him a crack with a quirt, and he left."

"Saddle on him?"

"No. I left it out there."

The marshal shook his head. "Can't see you got any legal complaint," he said with relief. "Where was this?"

"On a road in the woods, by a creek. Two days' walk from here."

The marshal got to his feet. "You don't even know what jurisdiction it was in. They knocked you around; well, that could happen. Man gets in a fight—could happen to anybody."

Foster said dryly, "Thanks a lot."

The marshal stopped him as he reached the door. "There's a reward for Liberty Valance."

"I still haven't got a gun," Foster said. "Does he come here often?"

"Nope. Nothing he'd want in Twotrees. Hard man to find." The marshal looked Foster up and down. "He won't come after you here." It was as if he had added, *Sonny!* "Beat you up once, he won't come again for that."

And I, Foster realized, am not man enough to go after him.

"Fact is," the marshal added, "I can't think of any bait that would bring him in. Pretty quiet here. Yes sir." He put his thumbs in his galluses and looked out the window, taking credit for the quietness.

Bait, Foster thought. He went out thinking about it. For the first time in a couple of years he had an ambition—not a laudable one, but something to aim at. He was going to be the bait for Liberty Valance and, as far as he could be, the trap as well.

At the Elite Cafe he stood meekly in the doorway, hat in hand, like a man who expects and deserves to be refused anything he might ask for. Clearing his throat, he asked, "Could I work for a meal?"

The girl who was filling sugar bowls looked up and pitied him. "Why, I should think so. Mr. Anderson!" She was the girl who had walked away with Barricune, scolding him.

The proprietor came from the kitchen, and Ranse Foster repeated his question, cringing, but with a suggestion of a sneer.

"Go around back and split some wood," Anderson answered, turning back to the kitchen.

"He could just as well eat first," the waitress suggested. "I'll dish up some stew to begin with."

Ranse ate fast, as if he expected the plate to be snatched away. He knew the girl glanced at him several times, and he hated her for it. He had not counted on anyone's pitying him in his new role of sneering humility, but he knew he might as well get used to it.

When she brought his pie, she said, "If you was looking for a job . . ."

He forced himself to look at her suspiciously. "Yes?"

"You could try the Prairie Belle. I heard they needed a swamper."

Bert Barricune, riding out to the river camp for his bedroll, hardly knew the man he met there. Ranse Foster was haughty, condescending, and cringing all at once. He spoke with a faint sneer, and stood as if he expected to be kicked.

"I assumed you'd be back for your belongings," he said. "I realized that you would change your mind."

Barricune, strapping up his bedroll, looked blank. "Never changed it," he disagreed. "Doing just what I planned. I never give you my bedroll."

"Of course not, of course not," the new Ranse Foster agreed with sneering humility. "It's yours. You have every right to reclaim it."

Barricune looked at him narrowly and hoisted the bedroll to sling it up behind his saddle. "I should have left you for the buzzards," he remarked.

Foster agreed, with a smile that should have got him a fist in the teeth. "Thank you, my friend," he said with no gratitude. "Thank you for all your kindness, which I have done nothing to deserve and shall do nothing to repay."

Barricune rode off, scowling, with the memory of his good deed irritating him like lice. The new Foster followed, far behind, on foot.

Sometimes in later life Ranse Foster thought of the several men he had been through the years. He did not admire any of them very much. He was by no means ashamed of the man he finally became, except that he owed too much to other people. One man he had been when he was young, a serious student, gullible and quick-tempered. Another man had been reckless and without an aim; he went West, with two thousand dollars of his own, after a quarrel with the executor of his father's estate. That man did not last long. Liberty Valance had whipped him with a quirt and kicked him into unconsciousness, for no reason except that Liberty, meeting him and knowing him for a tenderfoot, was able to do so. That man died on the prairie. After that, there was the man who set out to be the bait that would bring Liberty Valance into Two-trees.

Ranse Foster had never hated anyone before he met Liberty

Valance, but Liberty was not the last man he learned to hate. He hated the man he himself had been while he waited to meet Liberty again.

The swamper's job at the Prairie Belle was not disgraceful until Ranse Foster made it so. When he swept floors, he was so obviously contemptuous of the work and of himself for doing it that other men saw him as contemptible. He watched the customers with a curled lip as if they were beneath him. But when a poker player threw a white chip on the floor, the swamper looked at him with half-veiled hatred—and picked up the chip. They talked about him at the Prairie Belle, because he could not be ignored.

At the end of the first month, he bought a Colt .45 from a drunken cowboy who needed money worse than he needed two guns. After that, Ranse went without part of his sleep in order to walk out, seven mornings a week, to where his first camp had been and practice target shooting. And the second time he overslept from exhaustion, Joe Mosten of the Prairie Belle fired him.

"Here's your pay," Joe growled, and dropped the money on the floor.

A week passed before he got another job. He ate his meals frugally in the Elite Cafe and let himself be seen stealing scraps off plates that other diners had left. Lillian, the older of the two waitresses, yelled her disgust, but Hallie, who was young, pitied him.

"Come to the back door when it's dark," she murmured, "and I'll give you a bit. There's plenty to spare."

The second evening he went to the back door, Bert Barricune was there ahead of him. He said gently, "Hallie is my girl."

"No offense intended," Foster answered. "The young lady offered me food, and I have come to get it."

"A dog eats where it can," young Barricune drawled.

Ranse's muscles tensed and rage mounted in his throat, but he caught himself in time and shrugged. Bert said something then that scared him: "If you wanted to get talked about, it's working fine. They're talking clean over in Dunbar."

"What they do or say in Dunbar," Foster answered, "is nothing to me."

"It's where Liberty Valance hangs out," the other man said casually. "In case you care."

Ranse almost confided then, but instead said stiffly, "I do not quite appreciate your strange interest in my affairs."

Barricune pushed back his hat and scratched his head. "I don't understand it myself. But leave my girl alone."

"As charming as Miss Hallie may be," Ranse told him, "I am interested only in keeping my stomach filled."

"Then why don't you work for a living? The clerk at Dowitts' quit this afternoon."

Jake Dowitt hired him as a clerk because nobody else wanted the job.

"Read and write, do you?" Dowitt asked. "Work with figures?"

Foster drew himself up. "Sir, whatever may be said against me, I believe I may lay claim to being a scholar. That much I claim, if nothing more. I have read law."

"Maybe the job ain't good enough for you," Dowitt suggested.

Foster became humble again. "Any job is good enough for me. I will also sweep the floor."

"You will also keep up the fire in the stove," Dowitt told him. "Seven in the morning till nine at night. Got a place to live?"

"I sleep in the livery stable in return for keeping it shoveled out."

Dowitt had intended to house his clerk in a small room over the store, but he changed his mind. "Got a shed out back you can bunk in," he offered. "You'll have to clean it out first. Used to keep chickens there."

"There is one thing," Foster said. "I want two half-days off a week."

Dowitt looked over the top of his spectacles. "Now what would you do with time off? Never mind. You can have it—for less pay. I give you a discount on what you buy in the store."

The only purchase Foster made consisted of four boxes of cartridges a week.

In the store, he weighed salt pork as if it were low stuff but himself still lower, humbly measured lengths of dress goods for the women customers. He added vanity to his other unpleasantnesses and let customers discover him combing his hair admiringly before a small mirror. He let himself be seen reading a small black book, which aroused curiosity.

It was while he worked at the store that he started Twotrees' first school. Hallie was responsible for that. Handing him a plate heaped higher than other customers got at the café, she said gently, "You're a learned man, they say, Mr. Foster."

With Hallie he could no longer sneer or pretend humility, for Hallie was herself humble, as well as gentle and kind. He protected himself from her by not speaking unless he had to.

He answered, "I have had advantages, Miss Hallie, before fate brought me here."

"That book you read," she asked wistfully, "what's it about?"

"It was written by a man named Plato," Ranse told her stiffly. "It was written in Greek."

She brought him a cup of coffee, hesitated for a moment, and then asked, "You can read and write American, too, can't you?"

"English, Miss Hallie," he corrected. "English is our mother tongue. I am quite familiar with English."

She put her red hands on the café counter. "Mr. Foster," she whispered, "will you teach me to read?"

He was too startled to think of an answer she could not defeat.

"Bert wouldn't like it," he said. "You're a grown woman besides. It wouldn't look right for you to be learning to read now."

She shook her head. "I can't learn any younger." She sighed. "I always wanted to know how to read and write." She walked away toward the kitchen, and Ranse Foster was struck with an emotion he knew he could not afford. He was swept with pity. He called her back.

"Miss Hallie. Not you alone—people would talk about you. But if you brought Bert—"

"Bert can already read some. He don't care about it. But there's some kids in town." Her face was so lighted that Ranse looked away.

He still tried to escape. "Won't you be ashamed, learning with children?"

"Why, I'll be proud to learn any way at all," she said.

He had three little girls, two restless little boys, and Hallie in Twotrees' first school sessions—one hour each afternoon, in Dowitt's storeroom. Dowitt did not dock his pay for the time spent, but he puzzled a great deal. So did the children's parents. The children themselves were puzzled at some of the things he read aloud, but they were patient. After all, lessons lasted only an hour.

"When you are older, you will understand this," he promised, not looking at Hallie, and then he read Shakespeare's sonnet that begins:

> *No longer mourn for me when I am dead*
> *Than you shall hear the surly sullen bell*

and ends:

> *Do not so much as my poor name rehearse,*
> *But let your love even with my life decay,*
> *Lest the wise world should look into your moan*
> *And mock you with me after I am gone.*

Hallie understood the warning, he knew. He read another sonnet, too:

> *When in disgrace with Fortune and men's eyes,*
> *I all alone beweep my outcast state,*

and carefully did not look up at her as he finished it:

> *For thy sweet love rememb'red such wealth brings*
> *That then I scorn to change my state with kings.*

Her earnestness in learning was distasteful to him—the anxious way she grasped a pencil and formed letters, the little gasp with which she always began to read aloud. Twice he made her cry, but she never missed a lesson.

He wished he had a teacher for his own learning, but he could not trust anyone, and so he did his lessons alone. Bert Barricune caught him at it on one of those free afternoons when Foster, on a horse from the livery stable, had ridden miles out of town to a secluded spot.

Ranse Foster had an empty gun in his hand when Barricune stepped out from behind a sandstone column and remarked, "I've seen better."

Foster whirled, and Barricune added, "I could have been some-body else—and your gun's empty."

"When I see somebody else, it won't be," Foster promised.

"If you'd asked me," Barricune mused, "I could've helped you. But you didn't want no helping. A man shouldn't be ashamed to ask somebody that knows better than him." His gun was suddenly in his hand, and five shots cracked their echoes around the skull-white sandstone pillars. Half an inch above each of five cards that Ranse had tacked to a dead tree, at the level of a man's waist, a splintered hole appeared in the wood. "Didn't want to spoil your targets," Barricune explained.

"I'm not ashamed to ask you," Foster told him angrily, "since you know so much. I shoot straight but slow. I'm asking you now."

Barricune, reloading his gun, shook his head. "It's kind of late for that. I come out to tell you that Liberty Valance is in town. He's interested in the dude that anybody can kick around—this here tenderfoot that boasts how he can read Greek."

"Well," said Foster softly. "Well, so the time has come."

"Don't figure you're riding into town with me," Bert warned. "You're coming all by yourself."

Ranse rode into town with his gun belt buckled on. Always before, he had carried it wrapped in a slicker. In town, he allowed himself the luxury of one last vanity. He went to the barbershop, neither sneering nor cringing, and said sharply, "Cut my hair. Short."

The barber was nervous, but he worked understandably fast.

"Thought you was partial to that long wavy hair of yourn," he remarked.

"I don't know why you thought so," Foster said coldly.

Out in the street again, he realized that he did not know how to go about the job. He did not know where Liberty Valance was, and he was determined not to be caught like a rat. He intended to look for Liberty.

Joe Mosten's right-hand man was lounging at the door of the Prairie Belle. He moved over to bar the way.

"Not in there, Foster," he said gently. It was the first time in months that Ranse Foster had heard another man address him respectfully. His presence was recognized—as a menace to the fixtures of the Prairie Belle.

When I die, sometime today, he thought, they won't say I was a coward. They may say I was a damn fool, but I won't care by that time.

"Where is he?" Ranse asked.

"I couldn't tell you that," the man said apologetically. "I'm young and healthy, and where he is is none of my business. Joe'd be obliged if you stay out of the bar, that's all."

Ranse looked across toward Dowitt's store. The padlock was on the door. He glanced north, toward the marshal's office.

"That's closed, too," the saloon man told him courteously. "Marshal was called out of town an hour ago."

Ranse threw back his head and laughed. The sound echoed back from the false-fronted buildings across the street. There was nobody walking in the street; there were not even any horses tied to the hitching racks.

"Send Liberty word," he ordered in the tone of one who has a right to command. "Tell him the tenderfoot wants to see him again."

The saloon man cleared his throat. "Guess it won't be necessary. That's him coming down at the end of the street, wouldn't you say?"

Ranse looked, knowing the saloon man was watching him curiously.

"I'd say it is," he agreed. "Yes, I'd say that was Liberty Valance."

"I'll be going inside now," the other man remarked apologetically. "Well, take care of yourself." He was gone without a sound.

This is the classic situation, Ranse realized. Two enemies walking to meet each other along the dusty, waiting street of a western town. What reasons other men have had, I will never know. There are so many things I have never learned! And now there is no time left.

He was an actor who knew the end of the scene but had forgotten the lines and never knew the cue for them. One of us ought to say something, he realized. I should have planned this all out in advance. But all I ever saw was the end of it.

Liberty Valance, burly and broad-shouldered, walked stiff-legged, with his elbows bent.

When he is close enough for me to see whether he is smiling, Ranse Foster thought, somebody's got to speak.

He looked into his own mind and realized, This man is afraid, this Ransome Foster. But nobody else knows it. He walks and is afraid, but he is no coward. Let them remember that. Let Hallie remember that.

Liberty Valance gave the cue. "Looking for me?" he called between his teeth. He was grinning.

Ranse was almost grateful to him; it was as if Liberty had said, The time is now!

"I owe you something," Ranse answered. "I want to pay my debt."

Liberty's hand flashed with his own. The gun in Foster's hand exploded, and so did the whole world.

Two shots to my one, he thought—his last thought for a while.

He looked up at a strange, unsteady ceiling and a face that wavered like a reflection in water. The bed beneath him swung even after he closed his eyes. Far away someone said, "Shove some more cloth in the wound. It slows the bleeding."

He knew with certain agony where the wound was—in his right shoulder. When they touched it, he heard himself cry out.

The face that wavered above him was a new one, Bert Barricune's.

"He's dead," Barricune said.

Foster answered from far away, "I am not."

Barricune said, "I didn't mean you."

Ranse turned his head away from the pain, and the face that had shivered above him before was Hallie's, white and big-eyed. She put a hesitant hand on his, and he was annoyed to see that hers was trembling.

"Are you shaking," he asked, "because there's blood on my hands?"

"No," she answered. "It's because they might have been getting cold."

He was aware then that other people were in the room; they stirred and moved aside as the doctor entered.

"Maybe you're gonna keep that arm," the doctor told him at last. "But it's never gonna be much use to you."

The trial was held three weeks after the shooting, in the hotel room where Ranse lay in bed. The charge was disturbing the peace; he pleaded guilty and was fined ten dollars.

When the others had gone, he told Bert Barricune, "There was a reward, I heard. That would pay the doctor and the hotel."

"You ain't going to collect it," Bert informed him. "It'd make you too big for your britches." Barricune sat looking at him for a moment and then remarked, "You didn't kill Liberty."

Foster frowned. "They buried him."

"Liberty fired once. You fired once and missed. I fired once, and I don't generally miss. I ain't going to collect the reward, neither. Hallie don't hold with violence."

Foster said thoughtfully, "That was all I had to be proud of."

"You faced him," Barricune said. "You went to meet him. If you got to be proud of something, you can remember that. It's a fact you ain't got much else."

Ranse looked at him with narrowed eyes. "Bert, are you a friend of mine?"

Bert smiled without humor. "You know I ain't. I picked you up off the prairie, but I'd do that for the lowest scum that crawls. I wisht I hadn't."

"Then why—"

Bert looked at the toe of his boot. "Hallie likes you. I'm a friend of Hallie's. That's all I ever will be, long as you're around."

Ranse said, "Then I shot Liberty Valance." That was the nearest he ever dared come to saying "Thank you." And that was when Bert Barricune started being his conscience, his Nemesis, his lifelong enemy and the man who made him great.

"Would she be happy living back East?" Foster asked. "There's money waiting for me there if I go back."

Bert answered, "What do you think?" He stood up and stretched. "You got quite a problem, ain't you? You could solve it easy by just going back alone. There ain't much a man can do here with a crippled arm."

He went out and shut the door behind him.

There is always a way out, Foster thought, if a man wants to take it. Bert had been his way out when he met Liberty on the street of Twotrees. To go home was the way out of this.

I learned to live without pride, he told himself. I could learn to forget about Hallie.

When she came, between the dinner dishes and setting the tables for supper at the café, he told her.

She did not cry. Sitting in the chair beside his bed, she winced and jerked one hand in protest when he said, "As soon as I can travel, I'll be going back where I came from."

She did not argue. She said only, "I wish you good luck, Ransome. Bert and me, we'll look after you long as you stay. And remember you after you're gone."

"How will you remember me?" he demanded harshly.

As his student she had been humble, but as a woman she had her pride. "Don't ask that," she said, and got up from the chair.

"Hallie, Hallie," he pleaded, "how can I stay? How can I earn a living?"

She said indignantly, as if someone else had insulted him, "Ranse Foster, I just guess you could do anything you wanted to."

"Hallie," he said gently, "sit down."

He never really wanted to be outstanding. He had two aims in life: to make Hallie happy and to keep Bert Barricune out of trouble. He defended Bert on charges ranging from drunkenness to stealing cattle, and Bert served time twice.

Ranse Foster did not want to run for judge, but Bert remarked, "I think Hallie would kind of like it if you was His Honor." Hallie was pleased but not surprised when he was elected. Ranse was surprised but not pleased.

He was not eager to run for the legislature—that was after the territory became a state—but there was Bert Barricune in the background, never urging, never advising, but watching with half-closed, bloodshot eyes. Bert Barricune, who never amounted to anything, but never intruded, was a living, silent reminder of three debts: a hat full of water under the cottonwoods, gunfire in a dusty street, and Hallie, quietly sewing beside a lamp in the parlor. And the Fosters had four sons.

All the things the opposition said about Ranse Foster when he ran for the state legislature were true, except one. He had been a lowly swamper in a frontier saloon; he had been a dead beat, accepting handouts at the alley entrance of a café; he had been despicable and despised. But the accusation that lost him the election was false. He had not killed Liberty Valance. He never served in the state legislature.

When there was talk of his running for governor, he refused. Handy Strong, who knew politics, tried to persuade him.

"That shooting, we'll get around that. 'The Honorable Ransome Foster walked down a street in broad daylight to meet an enemy of society. He shot him down in a fair fight, of necessity, the way you'd shoot a mad dog—but Liberty Valance could shoot back, and he did. Ranse Foster carries the mark of that encounter today in a crippled right arm. He is still paying the price for protecting law-abiding citizens. And he was the first teacher west of Rosy Buttes. He served without pay.' You've come a long way, Ranse, and you're going further."

"A long way," Foster agreed, "for a man who never wanted to go anywhere. I don't want to be governor."

When Handy had gone, Bert Barricune sagged in, unwashed, unshaven. He sat down stiffly. At the age of fifty, he was an old man, an unwanted relic of the frontier that was gone, a legacy to more civilized times that had no place for him. He filled his pipe deliberately. After a while he remarked, "The other side is gonna say you ain't fitten to be governor. Because your wife ain't fancy enough. They're gonna say Hallie didn't even learn to read till she was growed up."

Ranse was on his feet, white with fury. "Then I'm going to win this election if it kills me."

"I don't reckon it'll kill you," Bert drawled. "Liberty Valance couldn't."

"I could have got rid of the weight of that affair long ago," Ranse reminded him, "by telling the truth."

"You could yet," Bert answered. "Why don't you?"

Ranse said bitterly, "Because I owe you too much. . . . I don't think Hallie wants to be the governor's lady. She's shy."

"Hallie don't never want nothing for herself. She wants things for you. The way I feel, I wouldn't mourn at your funeral. But what Hallie wants, I'm gonna try to see she gets."

"So am I," Ranse promised grimly.

"Then I don't mind telling you," Bert admitted, "that it was me reminded the opposition to dig up that matter of how she couldn't read."

As the Senator and his wife rode home after old Bert Barricune's barren funeral, Hallie sighed. "Bert never had much of anything. I guess he never wanted much."

He wanted you to be happy, Ranse Foster thought, and he did the best he knew how.

"I wonder where those prickly-pear blossoms came from," he mused.

Hallie glanced up at him, smiling. "From me," she said.

Blow-Up

Julio Cortazar

The last two stories in this collection are both concerned with problems of perception, with the changing face of reality and the idea that something first seen clearly and directly can quickly change and become more dense, more complex. Each also explores the consequences of distorted vision. The films based on these stories expand this theme by deliberately violating what viewers have come to accept as the normal method of cinematic narration. As in poetry, the author (or auteur) uses abstract images to develop a unified impression, a meaning.

Julio Cortazar's "Blow-Up" is a dense, rich, difficult short story. Its impact depends on a controlled distorting of the prose writer's traditional tools: language, tense, point of view. Cortazar's Roberto Michel is a romantic, a visionary whose attempt to "choose between looking and the reality looked at, to strip things of all their unnecessary clothing" leads him to a discovery of the visible manifestation of evil. What Michel first observes through the limiting frame of his viewfinder is not what he captures in his picture, which refuses to remain static. He is forced to go beyond his voyeurism and become a participant, an actor in other people's lives; he cannot maintain the detachment of an eye behind a lens. His secure knowledge that he has "only to go without the Contax to recover the keynote of distraction" is shattered; his perception is transformed until he finally sees nothing beyond a drifting field of vaguely threatening clouds.

In Blow-Up (1966), Michelangelo Antonioni sharpens the distinction between what is perceived and what is real. His protagonist Thomas is a professional photographer whose detachment is a tool of his trade. He uses his sexuality to coax poses from a beautiful model, but when the shooting session is over, he turns cold. Ideally, Thomas desires to be one with his camera, the observer unobserved.

During an apparently aimless stroll in a park, Thomas takes the photograph that becomes the film's central image; he appears to have captured the image of two lovers at play. But when he develops the shot, a shadowy figure of a man with a gun appears in the corner of the frame. Thomas is disturbed because the camera has revealed something he himself did not see. In the sanctuary of his darkroom, he repeatedly enlarges sections of the picture; with each new blow-up, his obsession with seeing truly what his camera has discerned becomes more urgent. Yet with each enlargement the picture becomes less distinct.

Thomas is driven to return to the park, where he discovers the body of the man he saw embracing the woman. The body is real; he touches it. Coping with that reality becomes his new obsession. Thomas chooses to evade responsibility; he goes to a party, gets stoned, and when he finally returns, the body is gone. All that he sees is a group of street mummers, playing tennis with an imaginary ball and rackets. Thomas watches for a moment, and when, after a wild swing, the mummers turn to stare at him, he realizes that the imaginary ball has rolled to his feet. He hesitates, bends, and throws it back.

In Antonioni's version the evil becomes more immediate, more tangible, more visible, more real, but no less elusive. Thomas knows the body was there, and then he knows it is gone, and that is all he knows. At the film's end, the body is no more real than the invisible tennis ball, but to Thomas, no less real, either. The evidence of murder continues to exist in the photograph; yet that is not reality, but only a representation of it. Reality is subjective and changeable.

At a superficial level, Blow-Up is a murder mystery, complete with victim, killer, and detective. For the first half of the film, Thomas could be a typical Hitchcock protagonist, the uninvolved bystander drawn inexorably into the apprehension of evil. Yet Antonioni deliberately violates our expectations by refusing to resolve this aspect of the plot. Like Cortazar, Antonioni is not concerned with what happened, or why, but with how we respond

*to what has happened. Film and story deliver the same message:
ultimate insight must depend on our ability to accept new ways of
seeing, and on the degree of moral responsibility with which we
respond to what is seen.*

BLOW-UP

It'll never be known how this has to be told, in the first person or
in the second, using the third person plural or continually inventing
modes that will serve for nothing. If one might say: I will see the
moon rose, or: we hurt me at the back of my eyes, and especially:
you the blond woman was the clouds that race before my your his
our yours their faces. What the hell.

Seated ready to tell it, if one might go to drink a bock over there,
and the typewriter continue by itself (because I use the machine),
that would be perfection. And that's not just a manner of speaking.
Perfection, yes, because here is the aperture which must be
counted also as a machine (of another sort, a Contax 1.1.2) and
it is possible that one machine may know more about another
machine than I, you, she—the blond—and the clouds. But I have
the dumb luck to know that if I go this Remington will sit turned
to stone on top of the table with the air of being twice as quiet that
mobile things have when they are not moving. So, I have to write.
One of us all has to write, if this is going to get told. Better that
it be me who am dead, for I'm less compromised than the rest; I
who see only the clouds and can think without being distracted,
write without being distracted (there goes another, with a grey
edge) and remember without being distracted, I who am dead (and
I'm alive, I'm not trying to fool anybody, you'll see when we get to
the moment, because I have to begin some way and I've begun
with this period, the last one back, the one at the beginning, which
in the end is the best of the periods when you want to tell something).

All of a sudden I wonder why I have to tell this, but if one begins
to wonder why he does all he does do, if one wonders why he
accepts an invitation to lunch (now a pigeon's flying by and it
seems to me a sparrow), or why when someone has told us a

good joke immediately there starts up something like a tickling in the stomach and we are not at peace until we've gone into the office across the hall and told the joke over again; then it feels good immediately, one is fine, happy, and can get back to work. For I imagine that no one has explained this, that really the best thing is to put aside all decorum and tell it, because, after all's done, nobody is ashamed of breathing or of putting on his shoes; they're things that you do, and when something weird happens, when you find a spider in your shoe or if you take a breath and feel like a broken window, then you have to tell what's happening, tell it to the guys at the office or to the doctor. Oh, doctor, every time I take a breath . . . Always tell it, always get rid of that tickle in the stomach that bothers you.

And now that we're finally going to tell it, let's put things a little bit in order, we'd be walking down the staircase in this house as far as Sunday, November 7, just a month back. One goes down five floors and stands then in the Sunday in the sun one would not have suspected of Paris in November, with a large appetite to walk around, to see things, to take photos (because we were photographers, I'm a photographer). I know that the most difficult thing is going to be finding a way to tell it, and I'm not afraid of repeating myself. It's going to be difficult because nobody really knows who it is telling it, if I am I or what actually occurred or what I'm seeing (clouds, and once in a while a pigeon) or if, simply, I'm telling a truth which is only my truth, and then is the truth only for my stomach, for this impulse to go running out and to finish up in some manner with, this, whatever it is.

We're going to tell it slowly, what happens in the middle of what I'm writing is coming already. If they replace me, if, so soon, I don't know what to say, if the clouds stop coming and something else starts (because it's impossible that this keep coming, clouds passing continually and occasionally a pigeon), if something out of all this . . . And after the "if" what am I going to put if I'm going to close the sentence structure correctly? But if I begin to ask questions, I'll never tell anything, maybe to tell would be like an answer, at least for someone who's reading it.

Roberto Michel, French-Chilean, translator and in his spare time an amateur photographer, left number 11, rue Monsieur-le-Prince

Sunday November 7 of the current year (now there're two small
ones passing, with silver linings). He had spent three weeks working on the French version of a treatise on challenges and appeals
by José Norberto Allende, professor at the University of Santiago.
It's rare that there's wind in Paris, and even less seldom a wind
like this that swirled around corners and rose up to whip at old
wooden venetian blinds behind which astonished ladies commented variously on how unreliable the weather had been these
last few years. But the sun was out also, riding the wind and friend
of the cats, so there was nothing that would keep me from taking
a walk along the docks of the Seine and taking photos of the
Conservatoire and Sainte-Chapelle. It was hardly ten o'clock, and
I figured that by eleven the light would be good, the best you can
get in the fall; to kill some time I detoured around by the Isle
Saint-Louis and started to walk along the quai d'Anjou, I stared for
a bit at the hôtel de Lauzun, I recited bits from Apollinaire which
always get into my head whenever I pass in front of the hôtel de
Lauzun (and at that I ought to be remembering the other poet, but
Michel is an obstinate beggar), and when the wind stopped all at
once and the sun came out at least twice as hard (I mean warmer,
but really it's the same thing), I sat down on the parapet and felt
terribly happy in the Sunday morning.

One of the many ways of contesting level-zero, and one of the
best, is to take photographs, an activity in which one should start
becoming an adept very early in life, teach it to children since it
requires discipline, aesthetic education, a good eye and steady
fingers. I'm not talking about waylaying the lie like any old reporter,
snapping the stupid silhouette of the VIP leaving number 10
Downing Street, but in all ways when one is walking about with a
camera, one has almost a duty to be attentive, to not lose that
abrupt and happy rebound of sun's rays off an old stone, or the
pigtails-flying run of a small girl going home with a loaf of bread
or a bottle of milk. Michel knew that the photographer always
worked as a permutation of his personal way of seeing the world
as other than the camera insidiously imposed upon it (now a large
cloud is going by, almost black), but he lacked no confidence in
himself, knowing that he had only to go out without the Contax to
recover the keynote of distraction, the sight without a frame

around it, light without the diaphragm aperture or 1/250 sec. Right now (what a word, *now,* what a dumb lie) I was able to sit quietly on the railing overlooking the river watching the red and black motorboats passing below without it occurring to me to think photographically of the scenes, nothing more than letting myself go in the letting go of objects, running immobile in the stream of time. And then the wind was not blowing.

After, I wandered down the quai de Bourbon until getting to the end of the isle where the intimate square was (intimate because it was small, not that it was hidden, it offered its whole breast to the river and the sky), I enjoyed it, a lot. Nothing there but a couple and, of course, pigeons; maybe even some of those which are flying past now so that I'm seeing them. A leap up and I settled on the wall, and let myself turn about and be caught and fixed by the sun, giving it my face and ears and hands (I kept my gloves in my pocket). I had no desire to shoot pictures, and lit a cigarette to be doing something; I think it was that moment when the match was about to touch the tobacco that I saw the young boy for the first time.

What I'd thought was a couple seemed much more now a boy with his mother, although at the same time I realized that it was not a kid and his mother, and that it was a couple in the sense that we always allegate to couples when we see them leaning up against the parapets or embracing on the benches in the squares. As I had nothing else to do, I had more than enough time to wonder why the boy was so nervous, like a young colt or a hare, sticking his hands into his pockets, taking them out immediately, one after the other, running his fingers through his hair, changing his stance, and especially why was he afraid, well, you could guess that from every gesture, a fear suffocated by his shyness, an impulse to step backwards which he telegraphed, his body standing as if it were on the edge of flight, holding itself back in a final, pitiful decorum.

All this was so clear, ten feet away—and we were alone against the parapet at the tip of the island—that at the beginning the boy's fright didn't let me see the blond very well. Now, thinking back on it, I see her much better at that first second when I read her face (she'd turned around suddenly, swinging like a metal weather-

cock, and the eyes, the eyes were there), when I vaguely understood what might have been occurring to the boy and figured it
would be worth the trouble to stay and watch (the wind was
blowing their words away and they were speaking in a low murmur). I think that I know how to look, if it's something I know, and
also that every looking oozes with mendacity, because it's that
which expels us furthest outside ourselves, without the least guarantee, whereas to smell, or (but Michel rambles on to himself
easily enough, there's no need to let him harangue on this way).
In any case, if the likely inaccuracy can be seen beforehand, it
becomes possible again to look; perhaps it suffices to choose
between looking and the reality looked at, to strip things of all their
unnecessary clothing. And surely all that is difficult besides.

As for the boy I remember the image before his actual body (that
will clear itself up later), while now I am sure that I remember the
woman's body much better than the image. She was thin and
willowy, two unfair words to describe what she was, and was
wearing an almost-black fur coat, almost long, almost handsome.
All the morning's wind (now it was hardly a breeze and it wasn't
cold) had blown through her blond hair which pared away her
white, bleak face—two unfair words—and put the world at her feet
and horribly alone in front of her dark eyes, her eyes fell on things
like two eagles, two leaps into nothingness, two puffs of green
slime. I'm not describing anything, it's more a matter of trying to
understand it. And I said two puffs of green slime.

Let's be fair, the boy was well enough dressed and was sporting
yellow gloves which I would have sworn belonged to his older
brother, a student of law or sociology; it was pleasant to see the
fingers of the gloves sticking out of his jacket pocket. For a long
time I didn't see his face, barely a profile, not stupid—a terrified
bird, a Fra Filippo angel, rice pudding with milk—and the back of
an adolescent who wants to take up judo and has had a scuffle
or two in defense of an idea or his sister. Turning fourteen, perhaps fifteen, one would guess that he was dressed and fed by his
parents but without a nickel in his pocket, having to debate with
his buddies before making up his mind to buy a coffee, a cognac,
a pack of cigarettes. He'd walk through the streets thinking of the
girls in his class, about how good it would be to go to the movies

and see the latest film, or to buy novels or neckties or bottles of liquor with green and white labels on them. At home (it would be a respectable home, lunch at noon and romantic landscapes on the walls, with a dark entryway and a mahogany umbrella stand inside the door) there'd be the slow rain of time, for studying, for being mama's hope, for looking like dad, for writing to his aunt in Avignon. So that there was a lot of walking the streets, the whole of the river for him (but without a nickel) and the mysterious city of fifteen-year-olds with its signs in doorways, its terrifying cats, a paper of fried potatoes for thirty francs, the pornographic magazine folded four ways, a solitude like the emptiness of his pockets, the eagerness for so much that was incomprehensible but illumined by a total love, by the availability analogous to the wind and the streets.

This biography was of the boy and of any boy whatsoever, but this particular one now, you could see he was insular, surrounded solely by the blond's presence as she continued talking with him. (I'm tired of insisting, but two long ragged ones just went by. That morning I don't think I looked at the sky once, because what was happening with the boy and the woman appeared so soon I could do nothing but look at them and wait, look at them and . . .) To cut it short, the boy was agitated and one could guess without too much trouble what had just occurred a few minutes before, at most half-an-hour. The boy had come onto the tip of the island, seen the woman and thought her marvelous. The woman was waiting for that because she was there waiting for that, or maybe the boy arrived before her and she saw him from one of the balconies or from a car and got out to meet him, starting the conversation with whatever, from the beginning she was sure that he was going to be afraid and want to run off, and that, naturally, he'd stay, stiff and sullen, pretending experience and the pleasure of the adventure. The rest was easy because it was happening ten feet away from me, and anyone could have gauged the stages of the game, the derisive, competitive fencing; its major attraction was not that it was happening but in foreseeing its denouement. The boy would try to end it by pretending a date, an obligation, whatever, and would go stumbling off disconcerted, wishing he were walking with some assurance, but naked under the mocking glance which would follow him until he was out of sight. Or rather, he would stay there, fascinated or simply incapable of taking the initiative, and the woman would begin to touch his face gently, muss his hair, still talking to him voicelessly, and soon would take him by the arm to lead him off, unless he, with an uneasiness beginning to tinge the edge of desire, even his stake in the adventure, would rouse himself to put his arm around her waist and to kiss her. Any of this could have happened, though it did not, and perversely Michel waited, sitting on the railing, making the settings almost without looking at the camera, ready to take a picturesque shot of a corner of the island with an uncommon couple talking and looking at one another.

Strange how the scene (almost nothing: two figures there mismatched in their youth) was taking on a disquieting aura. I thought it was I imposing it, and that my photo, if I shot it, would reconstitute things in their true stupidity. I would have liked to know what he was thinking, a man in a grey hat sitting at the wheel of a car parked on the dock which led up to the footbridge, and whether he was reading the paper or asleep. I had just discovered him because people inside a parked car have a tendency to disappear, they get lost in that wretched, private cage stripped of the beauty that motion and danger give it. And nevertheless, the car had been there the whole time, forming part (or deforming that part) of the isle. A car: like saying a lighted streetlamp, a park bench. Never like saying wind, sunlight, those elements always new to the skin and the eyes, and also the boy and the woman, unique, put there to change the island, to show it to me in another way. Finally, it may have been that the man with the newspaper also became aware of what was happening and would, like me, feel that malicious sensation of waiting for everything to happen. Now the woman had swung around smoothly, putting the young boy between herself and the wall, I saw them almost in profile, and he was taller, though not much taller, and yet she dominated him, it seemed like she was hovering over him (her laugh, all at once, a whip of feathers), crushing him just by being there, smiling, one hand taking a stroll through the air. Why wait any longer? Aperture at sixteen, a sighting which would not include the horrible black car, but yes, that tree, necessary to break up too much grey space . . .

I raised the camera, pretended to study a focus which did not include them, and waited and watched closely, sure that I would finally catch the revealing expression, one that would sum it all up, life that is rhythmed by movement but which a stiff image destroys, taking time in cross section, if we do not choose the essential imperceptible fraction of it. I did not have to wait long. The woman was getting on with the job of handcuffing the boy smoothly, stripping from him what was left of his freedom a hair at a time, in an incredibly slow and delicious torture. I imagined the possible endings (now a small fluffy cloud appears, almost alone in the sky), I saw their arrival at the house (a basement apartment probably, which she would have filled with large cushions and cats) and conjectured the boy's terror and his desperate decision to play it cool and to be led off pretending there was nothing new in it for him. Closing my eyes, if I did in fact close my eyes, I set the scene: the teasing kisses, the woman mildly repelling the hands which were trying to undress her, like in novels, on a bed that would have a lilac-colored comforter, on the other hand she taking off his clothes, plainly mother and son under a milky yellow light, and everything would end up as usual, perhaps, but maybe everything would go otherwise, and the initiation of the adolescent would not happen, she would not let it happen, after a long prologue wherein the awkwardnesses, the exasperating caresses, the running of hands over bodies would be resolved in who knows what, in a separate and solitary pleasure, in a petulant denial mixed with the art of tiring and disconcerting so much poor innocence. It might go like that, it might very well go like that; that woman was not looking for the boy as a lover, and at the same time she was dominating him toward some end impossible to understand if you do not imagine it as a cruel game, the desire to desire without satisfaction, to excite herself for someone else, someone who in no way could be that kid.

Michel is guilty of making literature, of indulging in fabricated unrealities. Nothing pleases him more than to imagine exceptions to the rule, individuals outside the species, not-always-repugnant monsters. But that woman invited speculation, perhaps giving clues enough for the fantasy to hit the bullseye. Before she left, and now that she would fill my imaginings for several days, for I'm given to ruminating, I decided not to lose a moment more. I got it all into the view-finder (with the tree, the railing, the eleven-o'clock sun) and took the shot. In time to realize that they both had noticed and stood there looking at me, the boy surprised and as though questioning, but she was irritated, her face and body flat-footedly hostile, feeling robbed, ignominiously recorded on a small chemical image.

I might be able to tell it in much greater detail but it's not worth the trouble. The woman said that no one had the right to take a picture without permission, and demanded that I hand her over the film. All this in a dry, clear voice with a good Parisian accent, which rose in color and tone with every phrase. For my part, it hardly mattered whether she got the roll of film or not, but anyone who knows me will tell you, if you want anything from me, ask nicely. With the result that I restricted myself to formulating the opinion that not only was photography in public places not prohibited, but it was looked upon with decided favor, both private and official. And while that was getting said, I noticed on the sly how the boy was falling back, sort of actively backing up though without moving, and all at once (it seemed almost incredible) he turned and broke into a run, the poor kid, thinking that he was walking off and in fact in full flight, running past the side of the car, disappearing like a gossamer filament of angel-spit in the morning air.

But filaments of angel-spittle are also called devil-spit, and Michel had to endure rather particular curses, to hear himself called meddler and imbecile, taking great pains meanwhile to smile and to abate with simple movements of his head such a hard sell. As I was beginning to get tired, I heard the car door slam. The man in the grey hat was there, looking at us. It was only at that point that I realized he was playing a part in the comedy.

He began to walk toward us, carrying in his hand the paper he had been pretending to read. What I remember best is the grimace that twisted his mouth askew, it covered his face with wrinkles, changed somewhat both in location and shape because his lips trembled and the grimace went from one side of his mouth to the other as though it were on wheels, independent and involuntary. But the rest stayed fixed, a flour-powdered clown or bloodless man, dull dry skin, eyes deepset, the nostrils black and prominently visible, blacker than the eyebrows or hair or the black

necktie. Walking cautiously as though the pavement hurt his feet;
I saw patent-leather shoes with such thin soles that he must have
felt every roughness in the pavement. I don't know why I got down
off the railing, nor very well why I decided to not give them the
photo, to refuse that demand in which I guessed at their fear and
cowardice. The clown and the woman consulted one another in
silence: we made a perfect and unbearable triangle, something I
felt compelled to break with a crack of a whip. I laughed in their
faces and began to walk off, a little more slowly, I imagine, than
the boy. At the level of the first houses, beside the iron footbridge,
I turned around to look at them. They were not moving, but the
man had dropped his newspaper; it seemed to me that the
woman, her back to the parapet, ran her hands over the stone with
the classical and absurd gesture of someone pursued looking for
a way out.

What happened after that happened here, almost just now, in
a room on the fifth floor. Several days went by before Michel
developed the photos he'd taken on Sunday; his shots of the
Conservatoire and of Sainte-Chapelle were all they should be.
Then he found two or three proof-shots he'd forgotten, a poor
attempt to catch a cat perched astonishingly on the roof of a
rambling public urinal, and also the shot of the blond and the kid.
The negative was so good that he made an enlargement; the
enlargement was so good that he made one very much larger,
almost the size of a poster. It did not occur to him (now one
wonders and wonders) that only the shots of the Conservatoire
were worth so much work. Of the whole series, the snapshot of
the tip of the island was the only one which interested him; he
tacked up the enlargement on one wall of the room, and the first
day he spent some time looking at it and remembering, that
gloomy operation of comparing the memory with the gone reality;
a frozen memory, like any photo, where nothing is missing, not
even, and especially, nothingness, the true solidifier of the scene.
There was the woman, there was the boy, the tree rigid above their
heads, the sky as sharp as the stone of the parapet, clouds and
stones melded into a single substance and inseparable (now one
with sharp edges is going by, like a thunderhead). The first two
days I accepted what I had done, from the photo itself to the
enlargement on the wall, and didn't even question that every once

in a while I would interrupt my translation of José Norberto Allende's treatise to encounter once more the woman's face, the
dark splotches on the railing. I'm such a jerk; it had never occurred
to me that when we look at a photo from the front, the eyes
reproduce exactly the position and the vision of the lens; it's these
things that are taken for granted and it never occurs to anyone to
think about them. From my chair, with the typewriter directly in
front of me, I looked at the photo ten feet away, and then it
occurred to me that I had hung it exactly at the point of view of
the lens. It looked very good that way; no doubt, it was the best
way to appreciate a photo, though the angle from the diagonal
doubtless has its pleasures and might even divulge different aspects. Every few minutes, for example when I was unable to find
the way to say in good French what José Norberto Allende was
saying in very good Spanish, I raised my eyes and looked at the
photo; sometimes the woman would catch my eye, sometimes the
boy, sometimes the pavement where a dry leaf had fallen admira-
bly situated to heighten a lateral section. Then I rested a bit from
my labors, and I enclosed myself again happily in that morning in
which the photo was drenched, I recalled ironically the angry
picture of the woman demanding I give her the photograph, the
boy's pathetic and ridiculous flight, the entrance on the scene of
the man with the white face. Basically, I was satisfied with myself;
my part had not been too brilliant, and since the French have been
given the gift of the sharp response, I did not see very well why
I'd chosen to leave without a complete demonstration of the
rights, privileges and prerogatives of citizens. The important thing,
the really important thing was having helped the kid to escape in
time (this in case my theorizing was correct, which was not suffi-
ciently proven, but the running away itself seemed to show it so).
Out of plain meddling, I have given him the opportunity finally to
take advantage of his fright to do something useful; now he would
be regretting it, feeling his honor impaired, his manhood dimin-
ished. That was better than the attentions of a woman capable of
looking as she had looked at him on that island. Michel is something of a puritan at times, he believes that one should not seduce
someone from a position of strength. In the last analysis, taking
that photo had been a good act.

Well, it wasn't because of the good act that I looked at it between paragraphs while I was working. At that moment I didn't know the reason, the reason I had tacked the enlargement onto the wall; maybe all fatal acts happen that way, and that is the condition of their fulfillment. I don't think the almost-furtive trembling of the leaves on the tree alarmed me, I was working on a sentence and rounded it out successfully. Habits are like immense herbariums, in the end an enlargement of 32 × 28 looks like a movie screen, where, on the tip of the island, a woman is speaking with a boy and a tree is shaking its dry leaves over their heads.

But her hands were just too much. I had just translated: "In that case, the second key resides in the intrinsic nature of difficulties which societies . . ."—when I saw the woman's hand beginning to stir slowly, finger by finger. There was nothing left of me, a phrase in French which I would never have to finish, a typewriter on the floor, a chair that squeaked and shook, fog. The kid had ducked his head like boxers do when they've done all they can and are waiting for the final blow to fall; he had turned up the collar of his overcoat and seemed more a prisoner than ever, the perfect victim helping promote the catastrophe. Now the woman was talking into his ear, and her hand opened again to lay itself against his cheekbone, to caress and caress it, burning it, taking her time. The kid was less startled than he was suspicious, once or twice he poked his head over the woman's shoulder and she continued talking, saying something that made him look back every few minutes toward that area where Michel knew the car was parked and the man in the grey hat, carefully eliminated from the photo but present in the boy's eyes (how doubt that now), in the words of the woman, in the woman's hands, in the vicarious presence of the woman. When I saw the man come up, stop near them and look at them, his hands in his pockets and a stance somewhere between disgusted and demanding, the master who is about to whistle in his dog after a frolic in the square, I understood, if that was to understand, what had to happen now, what had to have happened then, what would have to happen at that moment, among these people, just where I had poked my nose in to upset an established order, interfering innocently in that which had not happened, but which was now going to happen, now was going to be fulfilled. And what I had imagined earlier was much less horrible than the reality, that woman, who was not there by herself, she was not caressing or propositioning or encouraging for her own pleasure, to lead the angel away with his tousled hair and play the tease with his terror and his eager grace. The real boss was waiting there, smiling petulantly, already certain of the business; he was not the first to send a woman in the vanguard, to bring him the prisoners manacled with flowers. The rest of it would be so simple, the car, some house or another, drinks, stimulating engravings, tardy tears, the awakening in hell. And there was nothing I could do, this time I could do absolutely nothing. My strength had been a photograph, that, there, where they were taking their revenge on me, demonstrating clearly what was going to happen. The photo had been taken, the time had run out, gone; we were so far from one another, the abusive act had certainly already taken place, the tears already shed, and the rest conjecture and sorrow. All at once the order was inverted, they were alive, moving, they were deciding and had decided, they were going to their future; and I on this side, prisoner of another time, in a room on the fifth floor, to not know who they were, that woman, that man, and that boy, to be only the lens of my camera, something fixed, rigid, incapable of intervention. It was horrible, their mocking me, deciding it before my impotent eye, mocking me, for the boy again was looking at the flour-faced clown and I had to accept the fact that he was going to say yes, that the proposition carried money with it or a gimmick, and I couldn't yell for him to run, or even open the road to him again with a new photo, a small and almost meek intervention which would ruin the framework of drool and perfume. Everything was going to resolve itself right there, at that moment; there was like an immense silence which had nothing to do with physical silence. It was stretching it out, setting itself up. I think I screamed, I screamed terribly, and that at that exact second I realized that I was beginning to move toward them, four inches, a step, another step, the tree swung its branches rhythmically in the foreground, a place where the railing was tarnished emerged from the frame, the woman's face turned toward me as though surprised, was enlarging, and then I turned a bit, I mean that the camera turned a little, and without losing sight of the woman, I began to close in on the man who was looking at me with the black holes he had in place of eyes, surprised and angered both, he looked, wanting to nail me onto the air, and at that instant I happened to see something like a large bird outside the focus that was flying in a single swoop in front of the picture, and I leaned up against the wall of my room and was happy because the boy had just managed to escape, I saw him running off, in focus again, sprinting with his hair flying in the wind, learning finally to fly across the island, to arrive at the footbridge, return to the city. For the second time he'd escaped them, for the second time I was helping him to escape, returning him to his precarious paradise. Out of breath, I stood in front of them; no need to step closer, the game was played out. Of the woman you could see just maybe a shoulder and a bit of the hair, brutally cut off by the frame of the picture; but the man was directly center, his mouth half open, you could see a shaking black tongue, and he lifted his hands slowly, bringing them into the foreground, an instant still in perfect focus, and then all of him a lump that blotted out the island, the tree, and I shut my eyes, I didn't want to see any more, and I covered my face and broke into tears like an idiot.

Now there's a big white cloud, as on all these days, all this untellable time. What remains to be said is always a cloud, two clouds, or long hours of a sky perfectly clear, a very clean, clear rectangle tacked up with pins on the wall of my room. That was what I saw when I opened my eyes and dried them with my fingers: the clear sky, and then a cloud that drifted in from the left, passed gracefully and slowly across and disappeared on the right. And then another, and for a change sometimes, everything gets grey, all one enormous cloud, and suddenly the splotches of rain cracking down, for a long spell you can see it raining over the picture, like a spell of weeping reversed, and little by little, the frame becomes clear, perhaps the sun comes out, and again the clouds begin to come, two at a time, three at a time. And the pigeons once in a while, and a sparrow or two.

The Sentinel
(2001: A Space Odyssey)

Arthur C. Clarke

Like Blow-Up, *Stanley Kubrick's* 2001: A Space Odyssey *(1968)* is an attempt to expand film, to exploit the primacy of its visual component. Through a stunning array of images, it expands the cinematic eye while understating many other of the traditional components of what we have learned to experience as a "movie." Only forty-three minutes of its one hundred and forty-one minutes contain dialogue. Human characters are deliberately under-sketched, and are subordinated in importance. The viewer is captivated instead by a series of symbols presented through some of the most striking special effects ever to appear on the screen.

Arthur C. Clarke's story "The Sentinel" does what a story does best: it inflames the imagination. Although graced by Clarke's authoritative narrative voice and controlled understatement, the story is essentially traditional. Its characters are ordinary people who find themselves in an extraordinary situation. The story's ending does not illuminate this situation as much as it states its inherent question.

Kubrick's film attempts to answer this question in a highly personal way; it is a visceral response to Clarke's story. His central character is not a person, or even a machine, but a stark black monolith that gives every indication of having had a controlling hand in mankind's destiny. In the film's opening section the slab, rising from a barren plain like reason irresolute amid chaos, bestows the gift of civilization, and of violence, on a group of humanoid apes. The film then jumps into the future, when a second monolith (or perhaps the same one) is discovered on the moon. Now, however, mankind is too sophisticated to simply accept; it must discover what menace this sentinel represents.

In the film's third section, machines have taken over primary roles. One is the graceful and intricately detailed spacecraft, the Discovery; *the other is Hal, a complex and omnipotent computer that has been programmed to possess the capability of humanlike response. Hal rapidly reveals himself to be the most human personality on board; although paranoid and treacherous, he is still less alien than the colorless astronauts against whom he plots.*

The visual impact of the film becomes increasingly awesome and mystical. The stark-white spacecraft, seen from some cosmically omniscient point of view, floats in a blue-black sea speckled with stars. The moons of Jupiter drift about the mother planet, itself alive with swirls of other worldly color. And among them, in sympathetic orbit, the monolith appears for the third time.

The transition from short story through filmic narrative to totally visual experience now becomes complete. The film reaches its conclusion through three images that stand entirely on their own, without narration, explanation, or resolution. A Star-gate opens, drawing the viewer through a distorted, swirling, rainbow-hued vortex into a deathly white room, furnished with Louis XVI trappings. A senile old man inhabits this room; amid the ancient elegance of a decadent past is imminent death, timeless and eternal. Finally, a climactic vision of Earth, suspended in the dark sky, and floating next to it, the gelatinous, translucent image of the Starchild, dwarfing the fragile planet.

Kubrick's theme is thus one of transcendance of vision; he is giving greater, more cosmic answers to the same questions Antonioni wrestles with. The basic concepts by which we regulate our lives—time and distance, individuality and self-awareness—are inadequate to the task of regulating the universe. Clarke's sentinel finally speaks, but its voice is complex and elevated. It is our responsibility to make the effort to understand.

It is revealing that many of the same critics who supported and praised Antonioni's experimental vision in Blow-Up criticized 2001 as repetitious, incoherent, and without character or conflict. The general audience felt otherwise. The children of the late 1960s adopted 2001 as their personal movie; the popular wisdom of the time that the film could be fully appreciated only by viewing it in a drug-induced state of altered consciousness was an attempt to *stake territorial claim on the film's vision. Perhaps those viewers saw themselves in the Starchild, parented by apes, astronauts, and technology, floating above the old world in a psychedelic vision of beauty and hope.*

THE SENTINEL

The next time you see the full moon high in the south, look carefully at its right-hand edge and let your eye travel upward along the curve of the disk. Round about two o'clock you will notice a small, dark oval: anyone with normal eyesight can find it quite easily. It is the great walled plain, one of the finest on the Moon, known as the Mare Crisium—the Sea of Crises. Three hundred miles in diameter, and almost completely surrounded by a ring of magnificent mountains, it had never been explored until we entered it in the late summer of 1996.

Our expedition was a large one. We had two heavy freighters which had flown our supplies and equipment from the main lunar base in the Mare Serenitatis, five hundred miles away. There were also three small rockets which were intended for short-range transport over regions which our surface vehicles couldn't cross. Luckily, most of the Mare Crisium is very flat. There are none of the great crevasses so common and so dangerous elsewhere, and very few craters or mountains of any size. As far as we could tell, our powerful caterpillar tractors would have no difficulty in taking us wherever we wished to go.

I was geologist—or selenologist, if you want to be pedantic—in charge of the group exploring the southern region of the Mare. We had crossed a hundred miles of it in a week, skirting the foothills of the mountains along the shore of what was once the ancient sea, some thousand million years before. When life was beginning on Earth, it was already dying here. The waters were retreating down the flanks of those stupendous cliffs, retreating into the empty heart of the Moon. Over the land which we were crossing, the tideless ocean had once been half a mile deep, and now the only trace of moisture was the hoarfrost one could sometimes find in caves which the searing sunlight never penetrated.

We had begun our journey early in the slow lunar dawn, and still had almost a week of Earth-time before nightfall. Half a dozen times a day we would leave our vehicle and go outside in the space suits to hunt for interesting minerals, or to place markers for the guidance of future travelers. It was an uneventful routine. There is nothing hazardous or even particularly exciting about lunar exploration. We could live comfortably for a month in our pressurized tractors, and if we ran into trouble, we could always radio for help and sit tight until one of the spaceships came to our rescue.

I said just now that there was nothing exciting about lunar exploration, but of course that isn't true. One could never grow tired of those incredible mountains, so much more rugged than the gentle hills of Earth. We never knew, as we rounded the capes and promontories of that vanished sea, what new splendors would be revealed to us. The whole southern curve of the Mare Crisium is a vast delta where a score of rivers once found their way into the ocean, fed perhaps by the torrential rains that must have lashed the mountains in the brief volcanic age when the Moon was young. Each of these ancient valleys was an invitation, challenging us to climb into the unknown uplands beyond. But we had a hundred miles still to cover, and could only look longingly at the heights which others must scale.

We kept Earth-time aboard the tractor, and precisely at 22:00 hours the final radio message would be sent out to Base and we would close down for the day. Outside, the rocks would still be burning beneath the almost vertical sun, but to us it would be night until we awoke again eight hours later. Then one of us would prepare breakfast, there would be a great buzzing of electric razors, and someone would switch on the shortwave radio from Earth. Indeed, when the smell of frying sausages began to fill the cabin, it was sometimes hard to believe that we were not back on our own world—everything was so normal and homely, apart from the feeling of decreased weight and the unnatural slowness with which objects fell.

It was my turn to prepare breakfast in the corner of the main cabin that served as a galley. I can remember that moment quite vividly after all these years, for the radio had just played one of my

favorite melodies, the old Welsh air "David of the White Rock."
Our driver was already outside in his space suit, inspecting our
caterpillar treads. My assistant, Louis Garnett, was up forward in
the control position, making some belated entries in yesterday's
log.

As I stood by the frying pan, waiting, like any terrestrial house-
wife, for the sausages to brown, I let my gaze wander idly over the
mountain walls which covered the whole of the southern horizon,
marching out of sight to east and west below the curve of the
Moon. They seemed only a mile or two from the tractor, but I knew
that the nearest was twenty miles away. On the Moon, of course,
there is no loss of detail with distance—none of that almost imperceptible haziness which softens and sometimes transfigures all
far-off things on Earth.

Those mountains were ten thousand feet high, and they
climbed steeply out of the plain as if ages ago some subterranean
eruption had smashed them skyward through the molten crust.
The base of even the nearest was hidden from sight by the steeply
curving surface of the plain, for the Moon is a very little world, and
from where I was standing the horizon was only two miles away.

I lifted my eyes toward the peaks which no man had ever
climbed, the peaks which, before the coming of terrestrial life, had
watched the retreating oceans sink sullenly into their graves, taking with them the hope and the morning promise of a world. The
sunlight was beating against those ramparts with a glare that hurt
the eyes, yet only a little way above them the stars were shining
steadily in a sky blacker than a winter midnight on Earth.

I was turning away when my eye caught a metallic glitter high
on the ridge of a great promontory thrusting out into the sea thirty
miles to the west. It was a dimensionless point of light, as if a star
had been clawed from the sky by one of those cruel peaks, and
I imagined that some smooth rock surface was catching the sunlight and heliographing it straight into my eyes. Such things were
not uncommon. When the Moon is in her second quarter, observ-
ers on Earth can sometimes see the great ranges in the Oceanus
Procellarum burning with a blue-white iridescence as the sunlight
flashes from their slopes and leaps again from world to world. But
I was curious to know what kind of rock could be shining so

brightly up there, and I climbed into the observation turret and swung our four-inch telescope round to the west.

I could see just enough to tantalize me. Clear and sharp in the field of vision, the mountain peaks seemed only half a mile away, but whatever was catching the sunlight was still too small to be resolved. Yet it seemed to have an elusive symmetry, and the summit upon which it rested was curiously flat. I stared for a long time at that glittering enigma, straining my eyes into space, until presently a smell of burning from the galley told me that our breakfast sausages had made their quarter-million-mile journey in vain.

All that morning we argued our way across the Mare Crisium while the western mountains reared higher in the sky. Even when we were out prospecting in the space suits, the discussion would continue over the radio. It was absolutely certain, my companions argued, that there had never been any form of intelligent life on the Moon. The only living things that had ever existed there were a few primitive plants and their slightly less degenerate ancestors. I knew that as well as anyone, but there are times when a scientist must not be afraid to make a fool of himself.

"Listen," I said at last, "I'm going up there, if only for my own peace of mind. That mountain's less than twelve thousand feet high—that's only two thousand under Earth gravity—and I can make the trip in twenty hours at the outside. I've always wanted to go up into those hills, anyway, and this gives me an excellent excuse."

"If you don't break your neck," said Garnett, "you'll be the laughingstock of the expedition when we get back to Base. That mountain will probably be called Wilson's Folly from now on."

"I won't break my neck," I said firmly. "Who was the first man to climb Pico and Helicon?"

"But weren't you rather younger in those days?" asked Louis gently.

"That," I said with great dignity, "is as good a reason as any for going."

We went to bed early that night, after driving the tractor to within half a mile of the promontory. Garnett was coming with me in the morning; he was a good climber, and had often been with me on such exploits before. Our driver was only too glad to be left in charge of the machine.

At first sight, those cliffs seemed completely unscalable, but to anyone with a good head for heights, climbing is easy on a world where all weights are only a sixth of their normal value. The real danger in lunar mountaineering lies in overconfidence; a six-hundred-foot drop on the Moon can kill you just as thoroughly as a hundred-foot fall on Earth.

We made our first halt on a wide ledge about four thousand feet above the plain. Climbing had not been very difficult, but my limbs were stiff with the unaccustomed effort, and I was glad of the rest. We could still see the tractor as a tiny metal insect far down at the foot of the cliff, and we reported our progress to the driver before starting on the next ascent.

Inside our suits it was comfortably cool, for the refrigeration units were fighting the fierce sun and carrying away the body heat of our exertions. We seldom spoke to each other, except to pass climbing instructions and to discuss our best plan of ascent. I do not know what Garnett was thinking, probably that this was the craziest goose chase he had ever embarked upon. I more than half agreed with him, but the joy of climbing, the knowledge that no man had ever gone this way before, and the exhilaration of the steadily widening landscape gave me all the reward I needed.

I don't think I was particularly excited when I saw in front of us the wall of rock I had first inspected through the telescope from thirty miles away. It would level off about fifty feet above our heads, and there on the plateau would be the thing that had lured me over these barren wastes. It would be, almost certainly, nothing more than a boulder splintered ages ago by a falling meteor, and with its cleavage planes still fresh and bright in this incorruptible, unchanging silence.

There were no handholds on the rock face, and we had to use a grapnel. My tired arms seemed to gain new strength as I swung the three-pronged metal anchor round my head and sent it sailing up toward the stars. The first time it broke loose and came falling slowly back when we pulled the rope. On the third attempt, the prongs gripped firmly and our combined weights could not shift it.

Garnett looked at me anxiously. I could tell that he wanted to go first, but I smiled back at him through the glass of my helmet and shook my head. Slowly, taking my time, I began the final ascent.

Even with my space suit, I weighed only forty pounds here, so I pulled myself up hand over hand without bothering to use my feet. At the rim I paused and waved to my companion, then I scrambled over the edge and stood upright, staring ahead of me.

You must understand that until this very moment I had been almost completely convinced that there could be nothing strange or unusual for me to find here. Almost, but not quite; it was that haunting doubt that had driven me forward. Well, it was a doubt no longer, but the haunting had scarcely begun.

I was standing on a plateau perhaps a hundred feet across. It had once been smooth—too smooth to be natural—but falling meteors had pitted and scored its surface through immeasurable eons. It had been leveled to support a glittering, roughly pyramidal structure, twice as high as a man, that was set in the rock like a gigantic, many faceted jewel.

Probably no emotion at all filled my mind in those first few seconds. Then I felt a great lifting of my heart, and a strange, inexpressible joy. For I loved the Moon, and now I knew that the creeping moss of Aristarchus and Eratosthenes was not the only life she had brought forth in her youth. The old, discredited dream of the first explorers was true. There had, after all, been a lunar civilization—and I was the first to find it. That I had come perhaps a hundred million years too late did not distress me; it was enough to have come at all.

My mind was beginning to function normally, to analyze and to ask questions. Was this a building, a shrine—or something for which my language had no name? If a building, then why was it erected in so uniquely inaccessible a spot? I wondered if it might be a temple, and I could picture the adepts of some strange priesthood calling on their gods to preserve them as the life of the Moon ebbed with the dying oceans, and calling on their gods in vain.

I took a dozen steps forward to examine the thing more closely, but some sense of caution kept me from going too near. I knew a little of archaeology, and tried to guess the cultural level of the civilization that must have smoothed this mountain and raised the glittering mirror surfaces that still dazzled my eyes.

The Egyptians could have done it, I thought, if their workmen had possessed whatever strange materials these far more ancient architects had used. Because of the thing's smallness, it did not occur to me that I might be looking at the handiwork of a race more advanced than my own. The idea that the Moon had possessed intelligence at all was still almost too tremendous to grasp, and my pride would not let me take the final, humiliating plunge.

And then I noticed something that set the scalp crawling at the back of my neck—something so trivial and so innocent that many would never have noticed it at all. I have said that the plateau was scarred by meteors; it was also coated inches deep with the cosmic dust that is always filtering down upon the surface of any world where there are no winds to disturb it. Yet the dust and the meteor scratches ended quite abruptly in a wide circle enclosing the little pyramid, as though an invisible wall was protecting it from the ravages of time and the slow but ceaseless bombardment from space.

There was someone shouting in my earphones, and I realized that Garnett had been calling me for some time. I walked unsteadily to the edge of the cliff and signaled him to join me, not trusting myself to speak. Then I went back toward that circle in the dust. I picked up a fragment of splintered rock and tossed it gently toward the shining enigma. If the pebble had vanished at that invisible barrier, I should not have been surprised, but it seemed to hit a smooth, hemispheric surface and slide gently to the ground.

I knew then that I was looking at nothing that could be matched in the antiquity of my own race. This was not a building, but a machine, protecting itself with forces that had challenged Eternity. Those forces, whatever they might be, were still operating, and perhaps I had already come too close. I thought of all the radiations man had trapped and tamed in the past century. For all I knew, I might be as irrevocably doomed as if I had stepped into the deadly, silent aura of an unshielded atomic pile.

I remember turning then toward Garnett, who had joined me and was now standing motionless at my side. He seemed quite oblivious to me, so I did not disturb him but walked to the edge of the cliff in an effort to marshal my thoughts. There below me lay the Mare Crisium—Sea of Crises, indeed—strange and weird to most men, but reassuringly familiar to me. I lifted my eyes toward the crescent Earth, lying in her cradle of stars, and I wondered what her clouds had covered when these unknown builders had finished their work. Was it the steaming jungle of the Carboniferous, the bleak shoreline over which the first amphibians must crawl to conquer the land—or, earlier still, the long loneliness before the coming of life?

Do not ask me why I did not guess the truth sooner—the truth that seems so obvious now. In the first excitement of my discovery, I had assumed without question that this crystalline apparition had been built by some race belonging to the Moon's remote past, but suddenly, and with overwhelming force, the belief came to me that it was as alien to the Moon as I myself.

In twenty years we had found no trace of life but a few degenerate plants. No lunar civilization, whatever its doom, could have left but a single token of its existence.

I looked at the shining pyramid again, and the more I looked, the more remote it seemed from anything that had to do with the Moon. And suddenly I felt myself shaking with a foolish, hysterical laughter, brought on by excitement and overexertion: For I had imagined that the little pyramid was speaking to me and was saying, "Sorry, I'm a stranger here myself."

It has taken us twenty years to crack that invisible shield and to reach the machine inside those crystal walls. What we could not understand, we broke at last with the savage might of atomic power and now I have seen the fragments of the lovely, glittering thing I found up there on the mountain.

They are meaningless. The mechanisms—if indeed they are mechanisms—of the pyramid belong to a technology that lies far beyond our horizon, perhaps to the technology of paraphysical forces.

The mystery haunts us all the more now that the other planets have been reached and we know that only Earth has ever been the home of intelligent life in our Universe. Nor could any lost civilization of our own world have built that machine, for the thickness of the meteoric dust on the plateau has enabled us to measure its age. It was set there upon its mountain before life had emerged from the seas of Earth.

When our world was half its present age, *something* from the stars swept through the Solar System, left this token of its passage, and went again upon its way. Until we destroyed it, that machine was still fulfilling the purpose of its builders; and as to that purpose, here is my guess.

Nearly a hundred thousand million stars are turning in the circle of the Milky Way, and long ago other races on the worlds of other suns must have scaled and passed the heights that we have reached. Think of such civilizations, far back in time against the fading afterglow of Creation, masters of a universe so young that life as yet had come only to a handful of worlds. Theirs would have been a loneliness we cannot imagine, the loneliness of gods looking out across infinity and finding none to share their thoughts.

They must have searched the star clusters as we have searched the planets. Everywhere there would be worlds, but they would be empty or peopled with crawling, mindless things. Such was our own Earth, the smoke of the great volcanoes still staining the skies, when that first ship of the peoples of the dawn came sliding in from the abyss beyond Pluto. It passed the frozen outer worlds, knowing that life could play no part in their destinies. It came to rest among the inner planets, warming themselves around the fire of the Sun and waiting for their stories to begin.

Those wanderers must have looked on Earth, circling safely in the narrow zone between fire and ice, and must have guessed that it was the favorite of the Sun's children. Here, in the distant future, would be intelligence; but there were countless stars before them still, and they might never come this way again.

So they left a sentinel, one of millions they scattered throughout the Universe, watching over all worlds with the promise of life. It was a beacon that down the ages patiently signaled the fact that no one had discovered it.

Perhaps you understand now why that crystal pyramid was set upon the Moon instead of on the Earth. Its builders were not concerned with races still struggling up from savagery. They would be interested in our civilization only if we proved our fitness to survive—by crossing space and so escaping from the Earth, our cradle. That is the challenge that all intelligent races must meet, sooner or later. It is a double challenge, for it depends in turn upon the conquest of atomic energy and the last choice between life and death.

Once we had passed that crisis, it was only a matter of time before we found the pyramid and forced it open. Now its signals have ceased, and those whose duty it is will be turning their minds upon Earth. Perhaps they wish to help our infant civilization. But they must be very, very old, and the old are often insanely jealous of the young.

I can never look now at the Milky Way without wondering from which of those banked clouds of stars the emissaries are coming. If you will pardon so commonplace a simile, we have set off the fire alarm and have nothing to do but to wait.

I do not think we will have to wait for long.

Two Bibliographies on Film
and Literature

The following bibliographies originally appeared in the Fall 1975 issue of Style, *a journal published by the University of Arkansas. Harris Ross recently received his doctorate in English literature from the University of Arkansas at Fayetteville; his dissertation is an expanded version of this bibliography. Norman DeMarco is professor emeritus of film and television in the Department of Speech and Drama at the University of Arkansas at Fayetteville. The bibliographies appear here through the kind permission of Dr. Ross and Dr. DeMarco, and the editors of* Style.

*A Selected Bibliography of Articles on the
Relationship of Film and Literature
by Harris Ross*

The purpose of this bibliography is to list articles appearing in journals and magazines, whose subject is the interaction that exists between literature and film. The articles vary widely in quality, as well as in approach. I have included informal reviews as well as more formal treatments in order to present a broad critical spectrum. But a few brief words about the approaches represented here might be pertinent. Most of the articles fall into these groups: (1) comparisons of film with the other arts (2) general discussions of adaptations from literature with attempts to explain why changes occur (3) discussions of specific adaptations with emphasis on what has been cut or added and how this relates to the film's theme vis-à-vis the novel's or drama's. Though the articles represent various opinions, they all follow a normative

233

approach, attempting to establish limits for what the various arts may or may not do and, in conjunction with this, attempting to break the arts down into essential parts (the word for the novel, the shot for the film). Recently, semiology has turned away from the normative approach to embrace a structural approach, attempting to see how various art forms use codes and whether there are codes unique to one art form.

Since my topic is a broad one, I have had to put three restrictions on the bibliography because of the limitations of space. Only articles appearing in English language journals and magazines are listed. Of the articles concerning adaptations of particular works, only those concerning works written in English appear. Articles appearing in books are omitted; they appear in the other bibliography. . . . I have also listed doctoral dissertations and M. A. theses, though I made no systematic search for them. I have listed only a few articles which appeared before 1930. Generally, articles written before this time are not especially useful. Those interested in the silents or early talkies should consult *The Film Index* (Vol. I: *The Film as Art*), which offers a lengthy listing of early articles on film theory and adaptation.

The bibliographies I consulted for this bibliography include *Film Literature Index, International Index of Film Periodicals, MLA Bibliography, Modern Humanities Research Association Annual Bibliography,* the bibliographies at the end of each issue of *Twentieth Century Literature,* and the bibliographies in various issues of *Modern Drama. The Critical Index: A Bibliography of Articles on Film in English, 1946–1973,* by John C. and Lana Gerlach, came out too late for me to use, but its very extensive listings of articles in film journals and helpful annotations should be valuable to researchers. *Guidebook to Film,* by Ronald Gottesman and Harry M. Geduld, contains a short bibliography of articles and books on adaptation and a list of dissertations on film. "A Researcher's Guide and Selected Checklist to Film as Literature and Language" by Wendell Daniel (*Journal of Modern Literature,* 3[1973], 323–50) contains both a list of bibliographies of articles on film and a bibliography of articles on film and literature.

Adams, Robert H. "Pictures and the Survival of Literature." *Western Humanities Review,* 25(1971), 79–85. The author sees film replacing certain literary forms.

Allyn, John. "Hawthorne on Film—Almost." *Literature/Film Quarterly,* 2(1974), 124–28. On Donald Foxe's adaptation of "Young Goodman Brown."

Alpert, Hollis. "Movies Are Better Than the Stage." *Saturday Review,* 23 July 1955, pp. 5–6, 31–32. Article explains why the author believes films are more vital than drama.

Appel, Alfred. "The Eyehold of Knowledge: Voyeuristic Games in Film and Literature." *Film Comment,* 9(May–June 1973), 20–27. The influence of various films on Nabokov's *Lolita.*

———. "Nabokov's Dark Cinema: a Diptych." *Tri-Quarterly,* 3(Spring 1973), 196–277. Filmic influence on Nabokov's fiction.

Arnheim, Rudolph. "Epic and the Dramatic Film." *Film Culture,* 3, No. 1 (1957), 9–10. Applies Goethe's theory of the epic to films.

Asheim, Lester. "From Book to Film: Mass Appeals." *Hollywood Quarterly,* 5(1951), 334–49.

———. "From Book to Film: Simplification." *Hollywood Quarterly,* 5(1951), 289–304.

———. "From Book to Film: The Note of Affirmation." *The Quarterly of Film, Radio, and Television,* 6(1952), 54–68.

———. "From Book to Film: Summary." *The Quarterly of Film, Radio, and Television,* 6(1952), 258–73. Using twenty-four samples of novels adapted to films, Asheim analyzes the deviations from the novels and finds that the adaptations stressed the conventions of mass arts (emphasis on love interest, happy endings, the rewarding of virtue, etc.).

Ashworth, John. "Olivier, Freud, and *Hamlet." Atlantic Monthly,* 183 (May 1949), 30–33.

Asquith, Anthony. "The Play's the Thing." *Films and Filming,* 5(Feb. 1959), 13. The director of *Pygmalion* discusses adaptation.

Atkins, Irene Lahn. "In Search of the Greatest Gatsby." *Literature/Film Quarterly,* 2(1974), 216–28. Evaluation of three adaptations of Fitzgerald's novel.

Atwell, Lee. "Two Studies in Space-Time." *Film Quarterly,* 26, No. 2 (1972–73), 2–9. Study of *Slaughterhouse-Five.*

Baird, James Lee. "The Movies in Our Heads: An Analysis of Three Versions of Dreiser's *An American Tragedy.*" *Dissertation Abstracts,* 28(1968), 557A (University of Washington). First examines the novel, then Eisenstein's proposed version, and Von Sternberg's and Stevens' versions.

Ball, Robert Hamilton. "The Beginnings of Shakespeare Sound Films." *Shakespeare Newsletter,* 23(1973), 48.

———. "The Shakespeare Film as Record: Sir Herbert Beerbohm Tree." *Shakespeare Quarterly,* 3(1952), 227–36. Chiefly a description of silent screen adaptations with a limited discussion of adaptation problems.

———. "Shakespeare in One Reel." *The Quarterly of Film, Radio, and Television,* 8(1953), 139–49. Descriptions of adaptations for the silent screen.

Barbarow, George. "Dreiser's Place on the Screen." *Hudson Review,* 5(1952), 290–95. Discussion of *A Place in the Sun,* Stevens' adaptation of *An American Tragedy.*

———. "*Hamlet* Through a Telescope." *Hudson Review,* 2(1949), 98–117. Evaluates Olivier's version.

Barron, Arthur. "The Intensification of Reality." *Film Comment,* 6(Spring 1970), 20–23. Discusses versions of *Babbitt, The Grapes of Wrath,* and *Moby Dick* with some general comments on adaptation problems.

Barrow, Craig W. "Montage in Joyce's *Ulysses.*" *Dissertation Abstracts International,* 33(1973), 1713A (Colorado). Using Eisenstein's theories as a basis, the author finds that Joyce conveys ideas and emotions by the juxtaposition of portions of narrative, frequently from varying points of view.

Barry, Iris. "A Comparison of Arts." *Spectator* (London), 3 May 1924, p. 707. A comparison of theater and film.

Barson, Alfred T. "Agee's Projected Screenplay for Chaplin: Scientists and Tramps." *Southern Humanities Review,* 7(1973), 357–64.

Battestin, Martin C. "Osborne's *Tom Jones:* Adapting a Classic." *Virginia Quarterly Review,* 42(1966), 378–93.

Becker, Henry, III. "The Rocking-Horse Winner: Film as Parable." *Literature/Film Quarterly,* 1(1973), 55–63.

Bedard, B. J. "Reunion in Havana." *Literature/Film Quarterly,* 2(1974), 352–58. Analysis of the adaptation of Greene's *Our Man in Havana.*

Benedik, Laslo. "Play into Picture." *Sight and Sound,* 22(Oct.–Dec. 1952), 82–84. Director of *Death of a Salesman* discusses the adaptation.

Bentley, Eric. "Monsieur Verdoux as 'Theater'." *Kenyon Review,* 10(1948), 705–16. Chaplin's film discussed in the light of Pirandello's theories and the traditions of Moliere and Jonson.

Berlin, Normand. *"Macbeth:* Polanski and Shakespeare." *Literature/Film Quarterly,* 1(1973), 291–98.

Blades, Joe. "The Evolution of *Cabaret." Literature/Film Quarterly,* 1(1973), 226–38. Adaptation of Isherwood.

Blossoms, Robert. "On Filmstage." *Tulane Drama Review,* 11(Fall 1966), 68–72. Dramatist discusses the influence of film on his work.

Bluestone, George. "Adaptation or Evasion: *Elmer Gantry." Film Quarterly,* 14(Spring 1961), 15–19.

———. "Time in Film and Fiction." *Journal of Aesthetics and Art Criticism,* 19(Spring 1961), 311–15. Finds both film and literature are time arts, but while the formative principle in novels is time, the formative principle in film is space. "The novel renders the illusion of space by going from point to point in time; the film renders time by going from point to point in space."

———. "Word to Image: The Problem of the Filmed Novel." *The Quarterly of Film, Radio, and Television,* 11(1956), 171–80. The difference in film and novels is the difference between visual and mental images. The two arts are "overtly compatible, secretly hostile." He finds the final standard for judging adaptations must be whether they stand up as autonomous works of art.

Blumenthal, J. *"Macbeth* into *Throne of Blood." Sight and Sound,* 34 (Autumn 1965), 190–95.

Bond, Kirk. "Film as Literature." *Bookman,* 84(July 1933), 188–89. General discussion of adaptation with emphasis on von Stroheim's *Greed.*

Boyers, Robert. "Kubrick's *A Clockwork Orange." Sight and Sound,* 42(Winter 1972–73), 44–46.

Brady, Alan. "The Gift of Realism: Hitchcock and Pinter." *Journal of Modern Literature,* 3(1973), 149–72. *Shadow of a Doubt* was "the realistic film at the height of its powers in the forties. *The Birthday Party* represents the theatre's reaction in the fifties."

Brakhage, Stan. "Metaphors on Vision." *Film Culture,* 30(Fall 1963), 64 unnumbered pages. Compares visual and written language; argues there is knowledge based on non-verbal communication.

Brinson, Peter. "The Real Interpreter." *Films and Filming,* 1(April 1955), 4–5. Olivier's versions of Shakespeare.

Bromwich, David. "Angst-pushers and Austenites." *Dissent,* 20, No. 2(1973), 219–23. Discusses the adaptation of Didion's *Play It as It Lays.*

Brown, Constance. *"Richard III:* A Re-evaluation." *Film Quarterly,* 20 (Summer 1967), 23–32.

Butcher, M. "Look First Upon This Picture: Books and Film." *Wiseman Review,* 238(Spring 1964), 55–64.

Camp, Gerald. "Shakespeare on Film." *Journal of Aesthetic Education,* 3(1969), 107–20. Finds several problems confronting adaptor: Shakespeare's reliance on off-stage action; the difference in verbal and visual images; making a film with mass appeal. Says there are two alternatives open to the adaptor: suppress the poetry and play against a realistic background or devise a stylized world from the poetry. The way to judge the adaptation is "the degree of cinematic form and unity which it shapes out of the language."

Carter, Huntly. "Cinema and the Theatre: The Diabolical Difference." *English Review,* 55(1932), 313–20.

Casty, Alan. "The New Style in Film and Drama." *Midwest Quarterly,* 11 (Winter 1970), 209–27. Discusses the common assumptions and conventions of film and drama.

Chandler, Raymond. "Writers in Hollywood." *Atlantic Monthly,* 176(Nov. 1945), 50–54.

Childs, James. "Penelope Gilliatt: An Interview." *Film Comment,* 8 (Summer 1972), 22–26. Includes a discussion on the development of *Sunday, Bloody Sunday* from her novel *A State of Change.*

————. "Interview with John Hancock." *Literature/Film Quarterly,* 3(1975), 109–16. Director of *Bang the Drum Slowly* discusses the adaptation of Mark Harris' novel.

Chittister, Joan. "The Perception of Prose and Filmic Fiction." *Dissertation Abstracts International,* 32(1972), 6580A (Penn. State). A group of students saw *An Occurrence at Owl Creek Bridge* while another group read the story. Through discussion with the students, the author found among other things that prose stimulated the imagination more than the film, the viewers talked more about the work, and viewers "made an overwhelming reference to textural details in their interpretation."

Clancy, Jack. "The Film and the Book: D. H. Lawrence and Joseph Heller on the Screen." *Meanjin Quarterly,* 3(Autumn 1971), 96–97, 99–101.

Clarke, T. E. B. "Every Word in Its Place." *Films and Filming,* 4(Feb. 1958), 10. Discussion of adaptation by the adaptor of *A Tale of Two Cities.*

Cobos, Juand, and Miguel Rubio. "Welles and Falstaff." *Sight and Sound,* 35(Autumn 1966), 158–62. Interview with Welles centering on his adaptation of Shakespeare *(Chimes at Midnight).*

Connor, Edward. "Sherlock Holmes on the Screen." *Films in Review,* 12(1961), 409–18. Chiefly filmography with some evaluative remarks.

Cook, Raymond. "The Man Behind *The Birth of a Nation." The North Carolina Historical Review,* 29(1962), 519–40. The career of Thomas Dixon, Jr., with emphasis on his relationship with Griffith.

Corbett, Thomas. "Film and the Book: A Case Study of *The Collector." English Journal,* 57(1968), 328–33.

Costello, Donald B. "G. B. S.: The Movie Critic." *Quarterly of Film, Radio, and Television,* 11(1957), 256–75. Shaw's view of film.

Coulthard, Ron. "From Manuscript to Movie Script: James Dickey's *Deliverance." Notes on Contemporary Literature,* 3, No. 5(1973), 11–12.

Crump, G. B. *"The Fox* on Film." *D. H. Lawrence Review,* 1(1968), 238–44.

———. "Gopher Prairie or Papplewick?: *The Virgin and the Gypsy* as Film." *D. H. Lawrence Review,* 4(1971), 142–53.

———. "Lawrence and *The Literature/Film Quarterly." D. H. Lawrence Review,* 6(1973), 326–32. Discussion of *Literature/Film Quarterly,* volume one, number one (Lawrence issue).

———. *"Women in Love:* Novel and Film." *D. H. Lawrence Review,* 4(1971), 28–41.

Daniels, Don. "A Clockwork Orange." *Sight and Sound,* 42(Winter 1972–73), 44–46.

Deane, Paul. "Motion Picture Techniques in James Joyce's 'The Dead'." *James Joyce Quarterly,* 6(1969), 231–36.

Debrix, Jean R. "The Movies and Poetry." Trans. Dorothy Milburn. *Films in Review,* 4(1951), 17–22.

Degenfelder, E. Pauline. "Essays on Faulkner: Style, Use of History, Film Adaptations of His Fiction." *Dissertation Abstracts International,* 33(1973), 35169A (Case Western Reserve). Discussion of *The Reiv-*

ers, The Story of Temple Drake, Sanctuary, The Long, Hot Summer, and *Today We Live* as a "transportation of novelistic techniques into cinematic equivalents."

————. "The Film Adaptation of Faulkner's *Intruder in the Dust.*" *Literature/Film Quarterly,* 1(1973), 138–48.

Deinum, Andries. "Film as Narrative: The Affinity of Film and Novel." Masters Theses U. C. L. A. 1951.

Delpino, Louis. "Transliteration: Joseph Strick's *Tropic of Cancer.*" *Film Heritage,* 6(Fall 1970), 27–29.

Dempsy, Michael. *"Deliverance:* Boorman, Dickey in the Woods." *Cinema* (US), 8, No. 1(1973), 10–17.

Devlin, Francis A. "A 'Cinematic' Approach to Tennyson's Descriptive Art." *Literary/Film Quarterly,* 3(1975), 132–44.

Dick, Bernard F. "Narrative and Infra-Narrative in Film." *Literature/Film Quarterly,* 3(1975), 124–31. An analysis of film's infra-narrative: "a visual plot unfolding concurrently with a verbal one."

Diether, Jack. *"Richard III.* The Preservation of a Film." *The Quarterly of Film, Radio, and Television,* 11(1957), 290–93. Discussion of Olivier's adaptation.

Dimeo, Steven. "Reconciliation: *Slaughterhouse Five*—the Film and the Novel." *Film Heritage,* 8(Winter 1972–73), 1–12.

————. "The Ticking of an Orange." *Riverside Quarterly,* 5(1973), 318–21. Discussion of *A Clockwork Orange.*

Durgnat, Raymond. "Images of the Mind—Part One; Throwaway Movies." *Films and Filming,* 14(July 1968), 4–10. Discusses film's relationship to the theater.

Eidsvik, Charles. "Demonstrating Film Influence." *Literature/Film Quarterly,* 1(1973), 113–21. Filmic influence on Dos Passos, Mudrock and the Imagists.

————. "Soft Edges: The Art of Literature, the Medium of Film." *Literature/Film Quarterly,* 2(1974), 16–21. Finds that there seems to be a relationship between the structures of verbal language and perception, though since our knowledge is limited, we should keep our distinctions "soft-edged." This limited language "makes distinctions between communication media highly suspect."

Estrin, Mark Walter. "Dramatizations of American Fiction: Hawthorne and Melville on Stage and Screen." *Dissertation Abstracts International,* 30 (1970), 3428A (N. Y. U.).

————. " 'Triumphant Ignominy': *The Scarlet Letter* on the Screen." *Literature/Film Quarterly,* 2(1974), 110–23.

Fadiman, William. "But Compared to the Original." *Films and Filming,* 11(Feb. 1965), 21–23. General view of adaptation problems.

Fagin, Steven. "Narrative Design in *Travels with My Aunt.*" *Literature/Film Quarterly,* 2(1974), 379–83.

Ferguson, Otis. "Screen Versions." *New Republic,* 12 Sept. 1934, pp. 131–32. *The Fountain* and *The Barretts of Wimpole Street.*

Field, Edward. "The Movies as American Mythology." *Concerning Poetry,* 2, No. 1(1969), 27–31. A poet's use of movie-derived myth.

Finlay, Ian F. "Dickens in the Cinema." *Dickensian,* 54(May 1968), 106–09.

Fisher, James E. "Olivier and the Realistic *Othello.*" *Literature/Film Quarterly,* 1(1973), 321–31.

Folsom, James K. " 'Shane' and 'Hud': Two Stories in Search of a Medium." *Western Humanities Review,* 24(1970), 359–72.

Freedman, Florence B. "A Motion Picture 'First' For Whitman: O'Connor's 'The Carpenter.' " *Walt Whitman Review,* 9(1963), 31–33.

Fuegi, John. "Exploration in No Man's Land: Shakespeare's Poetry as Theatrical Film." *Shakespeare Quarterly,* 23(1972), 37–49. General survey of Shakespearean adaptation.

Fuller, Stanley. "Melville on the Screen." *Films in Review,* 19(1968), 358–63. Filmography with some evaluative comments.

Fulton, A. R. "It's Exactly Like the Play." *Theatre Arts,* 37(March 1953), 79–83. Compares adaptations of novels and plays, noting what transformation must take place in adapting for the screen. Discusses *A Streetcar Named Desire* and *A Place in the Sun.*

Gaupp, Charles John. "A Comparative Study of the Changes in Fifteen Film Plays Adapted from Stage Plays." Diss. U. of Iowa 1950.

Geist, Kenneth. *"Carrie." Film Comment,* 6(Fall 1970), 25–27. On Wyler's adaptation of Dreiser.

Gerard, Lillian N. "Of Lawrence and Love." *Film Library Quarterly,* 3(Fall 1970), 6–12. Russell's *Women in Love.*

————. *"The Virgin and the Gypsy* and 'D. H. Lawrence in Taos.' " *Film Library Quarterly,* 4(Winter 1970–71), 36–42. Christopher Miles' adaptation.

Gerlach, John. *"Last Picture Show* and One More Adaptation." *Literature/Film Quarterly,* 1(1973), 161–66.

———. "Shakespeare, Kurosawa and *Macbeth:* A Response to J. Blumenthal." *Literature/Film Quarterly,* 1(1973), 352–59.

Gessner, Robert. "The Faces of Time: A New Aesthetic for Cinema." *Theatre Arts,* 46(July 1962), 13–17. The difference between drama and cinema is film's "seven faces": movement within frame, the frame, the cut for continuous action, cut for accelerated action, cut for simultaneous action, cut to previous action, cut for decelerated action.

Gianetti, Louis. "The Gatsby Flap." *Literature/Film Quarterly,* 3(1975), 13–22.

Giesler, Rodney. "Shakespeare on the Screen." *Films and Filming,* 2(July 1956), 6–7.

Gill, Brendan. "A Plague of Locusts." *Film Comment,* 11(May–June 1975), 43. On Schlesinger's *The Day of the Locust.*

Gilliatt, Penelope. "Courtly Love's Last Throw of the Dice." *The New Yorker,* 1 April 1974, pp. 93–98. Clayton's *Gatsby.*

Godfrey, Lionel. "The Private World of William Inge." *Films and Filming,* 13(Oct. 1966), 19–24. On *The Dark at the Top of the Stairs.*

———. "It Wasn't Like that in the Book." *Films and Filming,* 13(April 1967), 12–16.

———. "It Wasn't Like that in the Play." *Films and Filming,* 13(August 1967), 4–8. Both articles are general views of adaptations with discussions of *Death of a Salesman, Look Back in Anger,* and *Who's Afraid of Virginia Woolf?*

Gomez, Joseph A. *"The Entertainer:* From Play to Film." *Film Heritage,* 8(Spring 1973), 19–26.

———. "The Theme of the Double in *The Third Man." Film Heritage,* 6(Summer 1971), 7–12.

———. *"The Third Man:* Capturing the Visual Essence of Literary Conception." *Literature/Film Quarterly,* 2(1974), 332–40.

Gow, Gordon. "In Search of a Revolution: Peter Hall." *Films and Filming,* 15(Sept. 1969), 40–44. On *A Midsummer Night's Dream.*

Graham, John. " 'Damn Your A Priori Principles—Look!' W. R. Robinson Discusses Movies as Narrative Art." *The Film Journal,* 1(Summer 1971), 49–53.

———. "Fiction and Film: An Interview with George Garrett." *The Film Journal,* 1(Summer 1971), 22–25.

Greg, W. W. "Shakespeare through the Camera's Eye." *Shakespeare Quarterly*, 6(1955), 63–66. Primarily on television productions.

———. "Shakespeare through the Camera's Eye: III." *Shakespeare Quarterly*, 7(1956), 235–40. Olivier's *Richard III* and Welles' *Othello*.

Griffin, Alice Venezky. "Shakespeare through the Camera's Eye—*Julius Caesar* in Motion Pictures: *Hamlet* and *Othello* on Television." *Shakespeare Quarterly*, 4(1953), 331–36.

———. "Shakespeare through the Camera's Eye: IV." *Shakespeare Quarterly*, 17(1966), 383–87. Olivier's *Hamlet* and Kozintsev's *Hamlet*.

Griffith, D. W. "A Poet Who Writes on Motion Picture Film." *The Theatre*, 19(June 1914), 311–12, 314, 316. Some comparison of drama and film.

Griggs, Earl Leslie. "The Film Seen and Heard." *The Quarterly of Film, Radio, and Television*, 8(1953), 93–99. On Shull's adaptation of *The Ancient Mariner*.

Grossvogel, David I. "When the Stain Won't Wash: Polanski's *Macbeth*." *Diacritics: A Review of Contemporary Criticism*, 2, No. 2(1972), 46–51.

Gumenik, Arthur. *"A Clockwork Orange:* Novel into Film." *Film Heritage*, 7(Summer 1972), 7–18.

Guzzetti, Alfred. "Christian Metz and the Semiology of the Cinema." *Journal of Modern Literature*, 3(1973), 292–308. After briefly sketching Metz's theory, the author offers a counter theory of "deep structures" to explain how an audience understands a film. He questions Metz's reliance on the narrative film and criticizes Metz's scheme of "interference." He sums up by finding that Metz refuses to analyze art in terms of social, economic and political structure, and thus his theory "can be seen as not simply anti-normative but . . . anti-critical and anti-analytical as well."

———. "The Role of Theory in Films and Novels." *New Literary History*, 3(1972), 547–58. He finds that every novel is in form "the transcription of a voice in extended monologue." While the voice of the novel is language, the discourse of the film is visual. The novel rests upon language whose organization as narrative reference is given and so is not left to the writer. In film no comparable guarantee exists for the form of the image or sound. The "language" of film has "no body of speakers capable of generating utterances not within their experience and distinguishing the grammatical from the ungrammatical."

Halio, Jay L. "Three Filmed *Hamlets*." *Literature/Film Quarterly*, 1(1973), 316–20.

Hamilton, Harlan. "Using Literary Criticism to Understand Film." *Exercise Exchange*, 14(1966–7), 16–17.

Harcourt, Peter. "I'd Rather Be Like I Am: Some Comments on *The Loneliness of the Long-Distance Runner.*" *Sight and Sound,* 32(Winter 1962–63), 16–19.

Hartley, Dean Wilson. " 'How Do We Teach It?': A Primer for the Basic Literature/Film Course." *Literature/Film Quarterly,* 3(1975), 60–69.

Hartung, Phillip T. "Of the Same Name: Books-into-Movies." *Commonweal,* 29 Oct. 1943, pp. 36–38. *Jane Eyre.*

Haseloff, Cynthia. "Formative Elements of Film: A Structural Comparison of Three Novels and Their Adaptations by Irving Ravetch and Harriett Frank." *Dissertation Abstracts International,* 33(1973), 438A (U. of Missouri). Covers *Hud, The Sound and the Fury,* and *The Reivers.*

Hausen, Peter E. "From Novel to Film: A Study of Samuel Goldwyn, Jr.'s Production of *The Adventures of Huckleberry Finn.*" Masters Thesis U. of Southern Cal. 1962.

Heinz, Linda, and Roy Huss. *"A Separate Peace:* Filming the War Within." *Literature/Film Quarterly,* 3(1975), 160–71.

Henderson, Brian. "Metz Essais I and Film Theory." *Film Quarterly,* 28(Spring 1975), 18–23. After a discussion of Metz's theory, Henderson criticizes him on several points: Metz does not have an overall model of filmic signification; Metz has drawn a vaguely defined concept, the event, from several theories of narrativity; rather than historical materialism and psychoanalysis, he has founded his theory on phenomenology, which requires no break with ordinary experience in constructing its concept; he is too little concerned with narrativity, though he is exclusively concerned with the narrative film; he is unable to link segments with larger structures, and thus is no advance over the classical theories of Bazin and Eisenstein; finally, he cannot account for the patterns he has found existing nor why they are significant.

Hillway, Tyrus. "Hollywood Hunts the Whale." *Colorado Quarterly,* 5(1957), 298–305. Huston and Bradbury's adaptation of *Moby Dick.*

Hirsch, Foster. "Tennessee Williams." *Cinema* (US), 8, No. 1(1973), 2–7. Survey of Williams on film with a discussion of *Baby Doll* and briefer evaluations of the other films.

Hitchcock, Alfred M. "Relation of the Picture Play to Literature." *English Journal,* 4(May 1915), 292–98.

Hitchens, Gordon. " 'A Breathless Eagerness in the Audience'—Historical Notes on Dr. Frankenstein and His Monster." *Film Comment,* 6(Spring 1970), 49–51. Covers screen adaptations.

Houseman, John. "Filming *Julius Caesar." Films in Review,* 4(1953), 184–88.

———. "Filming *Julius Caesar." Sight and Sound,* 23(July-Sept. 1953), 24–27.

Houston, Penelope. "The Private Eye." *Sight and Sound,* 26(Summer 1956), 22–23. Contains information on Raymond Chandler.

———. "Room at the Top?" *Sight and Sound,* 28(Spring 1959), 56–59.

Hurtgen, Charles Livermore. "Film Adaptations of Shakespeare's Plays." Diss. U. of Cal. (Berkeley) 1962.

Huss, Roy, and Norman Silverstein. "Film Study: Shot Orientation for the Literary Minded." *College English,* 27(1966), 566–68. Compares film with drama and novels and finds "films are primarily a collection of shots rather than a story."

Huston, John. "African Queen." *Theatre Arts,* 6(Feb. 1952), 48–49.

Hutchins, Patricia. "James Joyce and the Cinema." *Sight and Sound,* 21(Aug.-Sept. 1951), 9–12. Historical study of Joyce's association with film and his relationship with Eisenstein. Contains part of a scenario for "Anna Livia Plurabelle."

Isaacs, Neil D. "Unstuck in Time: *A Clockwork Orange* and *Slaughterhouse-Five." Literature/Film Quarterly,* 1(1973), 122–31.

Jahiels, Edwin. "Literature and Film." *Books Abroad,* 45(1971), 259–61. Discusses Richardson's *Literature and Film,* Wollen's *Signs and Meaning in the Cinema,* and Huss and Silverstein's *The Film Experience.*

Jensen, Paul. "H. G. Wells on the Screen." *Films in Review,* 18(1967), 21–27. Filmography with some evaluative comments.

Johnson, Ian. "Merely Players: 400 Years of Shakespeare." *Films and Filming,* 10(April 1964), 41–48. Shakespeare on the screen.

Jones, Dorothy B. "William Faulkner: Novel into Film." *The Quarterly of Film, Radio, and Television,* 8(1953), 51–71. *Intruder in the Dust.*

Jones, Edward T. "Green Thoughts in a Technicolor Shade: Revaluation of *The Great Gatsby." Literature/Film Quarterly,* 2(1974), 229–36. Clayton's version.

———. "Summer of 1900: A la recherche of *The Go-Between." Literature/Film Quarterly,* 1(1973), 154–60.

Jorgensen, Paul A. "Castellani's *Romeo and Juliet:* Intention and Response." *The Quarterly of Film, Radio, and Television,* 19(1955), 1–10.

Kael, Pauline. "Anarchist's Laughter." *The New Yorker,* 11 Nov. 1972, pp. 155–58. Includes a discussion of *Play It as It Lays.*

———. "The Darned." *The New Yorker,* 12 May 1975, pp. 110–14. On Schlesinger's *The Day of the Locust.*

Kalker, Robert Phillip. "Oranges, Dogs and Ultra-Violence." *Journal of Popular Film,* 1(1972), 159–72.

Kallich, Martin, and Malcolm M. Marsdin. "Teaching Film Dramas as Literature." *The Quarterly of Film, Radio, and Television,* 11(1956), 39–48. Centers on *The Long Voyage Home* (O'Neill).

Kaplan, Abraham. "Realism in the Film: A Philosopher's Viewpoint." *The Quarterly of Film, Radio, and Television,* 7(1953), 370–84. Centers on *The Long Voyage Home.*

Kauffmann, Stanley. "End of an Inferiority Complex." *Theatre Arts,* 46 (Sept. 1962), 67–70. Author finds around 1958 a new maturity in films, a failing in power in the theater. Includes a brief discussion of the similarities and differences of the arts.

Kazan, Elia. "Writers and Motion Pictures." *Atlantic Monthly,* 199(April 1957), 67–70. Personal reminiscence and general discussion of writers' treatment by Hollywood.

Kestner, Joseph A. "Stevenson and Artaud: *The Master of Ballantrae.*" *Film Heritage,* 7(Summer 1972), 19–28. A planned adaptation by Artaud.

Keyser, Les. *"England Made Me." Literature/Film Quarterly,* 2(1974), 364–72. Adaptation of Graham Greene's *The Shipwrecked.*

Kirby, Michael. "The Uses of Film in the New Theater." *Tulane Drama Review,* 11(Fall 1966), 49–61.

Kirschner, Paul. "Conrad and the Film." *The Quarterly of Film, Radio, and Television,* 11(1957), 343–53. Demonstrates how techniques of Conrad parallel those of the cinema.

Kitchin, Laurence. "Shakespeare on the Screen." *Listener,* 14 May 1964, pp. 788–90. General thoughts on adaptations, centering on Olivier's three films.

———. "Shakespeare on the Screen." *Shakespeare Survey,* 18(1965), 70–74. Author feels that unless we feel movies can improve on the plays, its only function is to preserve individual performances.

Klein, Michael. "The Literary Sophistication of François Truffaut." *Film Comment,* 3(Summer 1965), 24–30. Brecht, Joyce, and Ionesco compared to Truffaut.

Klugman, Donald B. "A Discriminative Study of Adaptation from Theatre to Film with Emphasis on *The Country Girl* by Clifford Odets." Masters Thesis U. of Southern Cal. 1956.

Knoll, Robert F. "Women in Love." *Film Heritage,* 6(Summer 1971), 1–6.

Koch, Stephen. "Fiction and Film: A Search for New Sources." *Saturday Review,* 27 Dec. 1969, pp. 12–14. Compares modern films and novels.

Kramer, S. "Play and the Picture." *Theatre Arts,* 39(Aug. 1955), 20–21.

Lambert, Gavin. "Lawrence: The Script." *Films and Filming,* 6(May 1960), 9. Author wrote the script for *Sons and Lovers.*

Lane, John Francis. *"The Taming of the Shrew." Films and Filming,* 13 (Oct. 1966), 50–52.

Latham, Aaron. "The Motion Pictures of F. Scott Fitzgerald." *Dissertation Abstracts International,* 31(1971), 6617A (Princeton). Considers both the influence of film on his writing and his career in Hollywood as scenarist.

Laurence, Frank Michael. "Death in the Matinee: The Film Endings of Hemingway's Fiction." *Literature/Film Quarterly,* 2(1974), 44–51.

————. "The Film Adaptations of Hemingway: Hollywood and the Hemingway Myth." *Dissertation Abstracts International,* 31(1971), 5411A (U. of Penn.). Study of fourteen adaptations reveals that primary consideration in adaptations was to please a mass audience. Because of the audience's interest in Hemingway as a personality, autobiographical implications of his works were exaggerated.

Laurie, Edith. "Film—the Rival of Theater." *Film Comment,* 1(Fall 1963), 51–53. Discussion by Peter Brook, Kenneth Tynan, and Robbe-Grillet.

Lenfest, David S. *"Brighton Rock/Young Scarface." Literature/Film Quarterly,* 2(1974), 373–78.

Leonard, Neil. "Theodore Dreiser and the Film." *Film Heritage,* 2(Fall 1966), 7–17. Discusses Dreiser's ambiguous attitude toward the film and Hollywood and his attempts at writing screenplays.

Leyda, Jay. "The Evil that Men Do." *Film Culture,* 2, No. 1(1956), 21–23. Olivier's *Richard III.*

————. "Theatre on Film." *Theatre Arts Monthly,* 21(March 1937), 194–207. A history and appreciation of adaptations from film's beginning to 1930. Sees what started with Film d'Art as beneficial in that many legendary performances were preserved.

Lillich, Meredith. "Shakespeare on the Screen." *Films in Review,* 7(1956), 247–60. Filmography with some evaluative comments from the silents to Olivier's *Richard III.*

Lillich, Richard B. "Hemingway on the Screen." *Films in Review,* 10(1959), 208–18. Filmography with brief evaluative comments on films through *The Old Man and the Sea.*

Lodge, David. "Thomas Hardy and the Cinematographic Form." *Novel,* 7(1974), 246–54. Comparison of Hardy's techniques with the techniques of film.

Lokke, J. L. "A Side Glance at Medusa: Hollywood, the Literature Boys, and Nathanael West." *Southwest Review,* 46(1961), 35–45. West's career in Hollywood with emphasis on *The Day of the Locust.*

Long, Robert Emmet. "Adaptations of Henry James' Fiction for Drama, Opera and Films; With a Checklist of New York Theatre Critics' Reviews." *American Literary Realism, 1870–1910* (U. of Texas at Arlington), 4(1971), 268–78.

Luciano, Dale. *"Long Day's Journey into Night:* An Interview with Sidney Lumet." *Film Quarterly,* 25(Fall 1971), 20–29.

MacDonald, George B. "An Application of New Critical Methodology to the Study of the Narrative Film." *Dissertation Abstracts International,* 32(1972), 6435A (Lehigh U.). Film programs need a new film criticism and aesthetics. The author attempts to fill the gap by applying New Criticism to film study.

MacGowan, Kenneth. "O'Neill and a Mature Hollywood Outlook." *Theatre Arts,* 42(April 1958), 79–81. On *Desire Under the Elms.*

MacMullan, Hugh. "Translating *The Glass Menagerie* to Film." *Hollywood Quarterly,* 5(1950), 14–32. Author was the dialogue director of the film.

Madden, David. "James M. Cain and the Movies of the Thirties and Forties." *Film Heritage,* 2(Summer 1967), 9–25.

Madden, Roberta. " 'The Blue Hotel': An Examination of Story and Film Script." *Film Heritage,* 3(Fall 1967), 20–34. Study of Agee's adaptation.

Marcus, Fred H. "Film and Fiction: 'An Occurrence at Owl Creek Bridge.' " *California English Journal,* 7(Feb. 1971), 14–23.

Marcus, Mordecai. *"A Farewell to Arms:* Novel into Film." *Journal of the Central Mississippi Valley American Studies Association,* 2(1961), 69–71.

Marder, Louis. "The Shakespeare Film: Facts and Problems." *Shakespeare Newsletter,* 23(1973), 42, 49.

Margolies, Alan. "F. Scott Fitzgerald's Work in the Film Studios." *Princeton University Library Chronicle,* 32(Winter 1971), 81–110. Includes influence of film techniques on his fiction.

———. "The Impact of Theatre and Film on F. Scott Fitzgerald." *Dissertation Abstracts International,* 30(1970), 3467A(N.Y.U.). Examines his early theatre work and his novels, and finds in his scripts many of the techniques used in his novels and plays.

Mass, Roslyn. "A Linking of Legends: *The Great Gatsby* and *Citizen Kane." Literature/Film Quarterly,* 2(1974), 207–15.

———. "The Preservation of the Character of Sarah Miles in The Film Version of *The End of the Affair." Literature/Film Quarterly,* 2(1974), 347–51.

McBride, Joseph. "Welles' *Chimes at Midnight." Film Quarterly,* 23(Fall 1969), 11–20.

McCaffery, Donald W. "Adaptation Problems in the Two Unique Media: The Novel and the Film." *Dickinson Review,* 1(Spring 1967), 11–17. Finds that unlike the novel the film needs unity of action.

McConnell, Frank D. "Film and Writing: The Political Dimension." *Massachusetts Review,* 13(1972), 543–62. Film as a literary medium. Compares *Gold Diggers of 1933* and *In Dubious Battle.*

McCracken, Samuel. "Novel into Film, Novelist into Critic: *A Clockwork Orange* . . . Again." *Antioch Review,* 32(1973), 427–36.

McGlynn, Paul D. "Rhetoric in Fiction and Film: Notes Toward a Cultural Symbiosis." *English Record,* 21(1970), 15–22. Informal discussion of a rhetoric common to both media, rhetoric being "methods of achieving effects."

McGugan, Ruth E. *"The Heart of the Matter." Literature/Film Quarterly,* 2(1974), 359–63.

McManaway, James G. "The Laurence Olivier *Hamlet." Shakespeare Association Bulletin,* 24(Jan. 1949), 3–11.

McVay, Douglas. "Hamlet to Clown." *Films and Filming,* 8(Sept. 1962), 16–19.

Mellen, Joan. "Film and Style; The Fictional Documentary." *Antioch Review,* 32(1973), 403–25. The documentary novel translated into film.

———. "Outfoxing Lawrence: Novella into Film." *Literature/Film Quarterly,* 1(1973), 17–27. *The Fox.*

Metzger, Charles R. "The Film Version of Steinbeck's *'The Pearl.'* " *Steinbeck Quarterly,* 4(1971), 88–92.

Miller, Henry. "Scenario." *Cinemage,* Special Issue, No. 9(Aug. 1958), 39–56. Unfilmed scenario.

Mizener, Arthur. "The Elizabethan Art of Our Movies." *Kenyon Review,* 4(1942), 181–94. Critics' difficulty in dealing with a mass art, with film linked to Elizabethan theatre.

Moore, Harry T. "D.H. Lawrence and the Flicks." *Literature/Film Quarterly,* 1(1973), 2–11. Adaptations of Lawrence.

Morrissette, Bruce. "Aesthetic Response to Novel and Film: Parallels and Differences." *Symposium,* 27(1973), 137–51. Reviews pros and cons of the correspondences between the two art forms and finds that basically both produce sensorial images in the mind.

Morsberger, Robert E., and Katherine M. "Screenplay as Literature: Bibliography and Criticism." *Literature/Film Quarterly,* 3(1975), 45–59.

Mullin, Michael. *"Macbeth* on Film." *Literature/Film Quarterly,* 1(1973), 332–42.

Murray, Edward. *"In Cold Blood:* The Filmic Novel and the Problem of Adaptation." *Literature/Film Quarterly,* 1(1973), 132–37.

Mycroft, Walter. "Shaw—And the Devil to Pay." *Films and Filming,* 5 (Feb. 1959), 14–15. Shaw's views on film.

Naremore, James. "John Huston and *The Maltese Falcon." Literature/-Film Quarterly,* 1(1973), 239–49.

———. "The Walking Shadow: Welles' Expressionistic *Macbeth." Literature/Film Quarterly,* 1(1973), 360–66.

Nathan, George Jean. "Movies Versus the Stage." *American Mercury,* 58 (1944), 682–86. A tongue-in-cheek dialogue between the author and Rouben Mamoulian in which Nathan shows that the film has duplicated effects thought to be unique to stage.

Nathan, Robert. "A Novelist Looks at Hollywood." *Hollywood Quarterly,* 1(1946), 146–47. "A picture is not at all like a play . . . on the contrary it is like a novel to be seen, instead of told."

Nelson, Harland S. *"Othello." Film Heritage,* 2(Fall 1966), 18–22. Welles' version.

Nelson, Joyce. *"Slaughterhouse-Five:* Novel into Film." *Literature/Film Quarterly,* 1(1973), 149–53.

Nichols, Bill. "Style, Grammar, and the Movies." *Film Quarterly,* 28 (Spring 1975), 33–49. Says that digital communication must not be preferred to analog and that "we might advance toward a Marxist film theory (and practice) without becoming trapped in the hopeless either/ or opposition to neoromantic *auteurists* and pseudo-Marxist semio-structuralists.

Nicoll, Allardyce. "Literature and Film." *English Journal,* 26(1937), 1–9. Discussion of genres suitable for adaptation with discussion of *A Midsummer Night's Dream* (Reinhardt) and *Dodsworth.*

Nin, Anaïs. "House of Incest." *Cinemage,* Special Issue, No. 9, (1958), pp. 38–39. Unfilmed scenario.

Nolan, Jack Edmund. "Graham Greene's Movies." *Films in Review,* 15(1964), 23–25.

Noxon, Gerald. "The Anatomy of the Close-Up: Some Literary Origins in the Works of Flaubert, Huysmans, and Proust." *Journal of the Society of Cinematologists,* 6(1961), 1–24.

———. "Some Observations on the Anatomy of the Long Shot: An Extract from Some Literary Origins of Cinema Narrative." *Journal of the Society of Cinematologists,* 5(1965), 70–80.

Nulf, Frank. "Luigi Pirandello and the Cinema." *Film Quarterly,* 24(Winter 1970–71), 40–47. Pirandello's influence on film.

O'Grady, Gerald. "The Dance of *The Misfits." Journal of Aesthetic Education,* 5(Apr. 1971), 75–89.

Pasolini, Pier Paolo. "Cinematic and Literary Stylistic Figures." *Film Culture,* 24(Spring 1962), 42–43.

Petrie, Graham. "Dickens, Godard and the Film Today." *The Yale Review,* 64(1974), 185–201. After tracing the influence of theatre and pantomine on Dickens' art, the author suggests that the later novels have much to offer a director attempting to reconcile "realism" and "illusionism."

———. "The Films of Sidney Lumet: Adaptation as Art." *Film Quarterly,* 21(Winter 1967–68), 9–18.

Pflager, Godfrey H. "Play into Film: A Study in Transition of Tennessee Williams' *Night of the Iguana."* Masters Thesis Boston U. 1966.

Phillips, Gene. "Faulkner and the Film: Two Versions of *Sanctuary." Literature/Film Quarterly,* 1(1973), 263–73.

———. "Graham Greene: An Interview." *Catholic World,* 209(Aug. 1969), 218–221. Discusses his adaptations.

Phillips, James E. "Adapted from a Play by W. Shakespeare." *Hollywood Quarterly,* 2(1946), 82–90. Olivier's *Henry V.*

————. "By William Shakespeare—with Additional Dialogue." *Hollywood Quarterly,* 5(1951), 224–36. Welles's *Macbeth.*

————. *"Julius Caesar:* Shakespeare as a Screen Writer." *The Quarterly of Film, Radio, and Television,* 8(1953), 125–30.

————. "Some Glories and Some Discontents." *The Quarterly of Film, Radio, and Television,* 10(1956), 399–407. Olivier's *Richard III.*

Pichel, Irving. "Revivals, Reissues, Remakes and *A Place in the Sun." The Quarterly of Film, Radio, and Television,* 6(1952), 388–93. Stevens' adaptation of *An American Tragedy.*

Plotkin, Frederick. *"Othello* and Welles: A Fantastic Marriage." *Film Heritage,* 4(Summer 1969), 9–16.

Podeschi, John B. "The Writer in Hollywood." *Dissertation Abstracts International,* 32(1972), 4629A (U. of Ill.). Discusses Odets, Inge, A. Miller, Sturges, T. Williams, Fitzgerald, Chandler, Schulberg, Arch Oboler, Chayefsky, Dudley Nichols, and Robert Sherwood.

Probst, Robert E. "Visual to Verbal." *English Journal,* 61(1972), 71–75. Classroom use of adaptations.

Pryluck, Calvin. "The Film Metaphor Metaphor: The Use of Language-Based Models in Film Study." *Literature/Film Quarterly,* 3(1975), 117–23.

Purcell, James M. "Graham Greene and Others: The British Depression Film as an Art Form." *Antigonish Review,* 15(1973), 75–82.

Purdy, Strother B. "Can the Novel and the Film Disappear?" *Literature/-Film Quarterly,* 2(1974), 237–55. Conjectures on the future of film and novels.

Raynor, Henry. "Shakespeare Filmed." *Sight and Sound,* 22(July–Sept. 1952), 10–15. Welles's and Olivier's adaptations.

Reddington, John. "Film, Play and Idea." *Literature/Film Quarterly,* 1(1973), 367–71. Polanski's *Macbeth* and Brook's *King Lear.*

Reeves, Geoffrey. "Finding Shakespeare on Film: From an Interview with Peter Brook." *Tulane Drama Review,* 11(1966), 117–27.

————. "Shakespeare on Three Screens: Peter Brook Interviewed." *Sight and Sound,* 34(Spring 1965), 66–70.

Reynolds, Leslie M. "Film as a Poetic Art and Contemporary Fable." *South Atlantic Bulletin,* 38, No. 2(1973), 8–14. Film's purpose is the same as literature: the illusion of life. It is epic in its ability to convey vastness of time and space; its use of language shows a relationship to poetry.

Richardson, Dorothy. "Talkies, Plays and Books: Thoughts on the Approaching Battle Between the Spoken Pictures, Literature, the Stage." *Vanity Fair,* 32(Aug. 1929), 56.

Richardson, Robert D., Jr. "Visual Literacy: Literature and the Film." *Denver Quarterly,* 1(1966), 24–36. Became a portion of *Literature and Film.*

Riesman, Evelyn T. "Film and Fiction." *Antioch Review,* 17(1957), 353–63. The qualities that limit the two media are that film finds meaning in things and novels create things from thought. Internal states are natural to novels, external states to films.

Riley, Michael. "Gothic Melodrama and Spiritual Romance: Vision and Fidelity in Two Versions of *Jane Eyre." Literature/Film Quarterly,* 3(1975), 145–49.

Roberts, Meade. "Williams and Me." *Films and Filming,* 6(Aug. 1960), 7. Author, who collaborated on *The Fugitive Kind,* explains how Williams works on screenplays.

Robinson, David. *"Look Back in Anger." Sight and Sound,* 28(Summer-Autumn 1959), 122–25.

Roll-Hansen, Diderkik. "Shaw's *Pygmalion:* the Two Versions of 1916 and 1917." *Review of English Literature,* 8(July 1967), 81–90. Discusses the film adaptations.

Roman, Robert C. "G.B.S. on the Screen." *Films in Review,* 11(1960), 406–18.

———. "Mark Twain on the Screen." *Films in Review,* 12(1961), 20–33.

———. "O'Neill on the Screen." *Films in Review,* 9(1958), 296–305.

———. "Poe on the Screen." *Films in Review,* 12(1961), 462–73. The above are essentially filmographies with some evaluative comments.

Rosenbaum, Jonathan. "A Commentary on *The Heart of Darkness* Script." *Film Comment,* 8(Nov.-Dec. 1972), 27–33. Welles's unfinished film.

Rothwell, Kenneth S. "Hollywood and Some Versions of *Romeo and Juliet:* Toward a Substantial Pageant." *Literature/Film Quarterly,* 1(1973), 343–51.

———. "Roman Polanski's *Macbeth:* Golgotha Triumphant." *Literature/-Film Quarterly,* 1(1973), 71–75.

Roud, Richard. "The Empty Streets." *Sight and Sound,* 26(Spring 1957), 191–95. On *The Member of the Wedding.*

————. "Going Between." *Sight and Sound,* 40(Summer 1971), 158–59. Pinter's adaptation of Harley's *The Go-Between.*

————. "Novel, Novel; Fable, Fable?" *Sight and Sound,* 31(Spring 1962), 84–88. Both novels and film, which share a similar development, are returning to the fable and non-realistic plots which recognize the importance of the irrational and the gratuitous. To judge such films we must not use the standards developed from the nineteenth-century novel.

Rudman, Harry W. "Shaw's *St. Joan* and Motion Picture Censorship." *Shaw Bulletin,* 2(Sept. 1959), 1–14.

Ruhe, Edward. "Film: the 'Literary' Approach." *Literature/Film Quarterly,* 1(1973), 76–83. Analysis of Bluestone's *Novels into Film* and Richardson's *Literature and Film.*

Rutherford, Charles S. "A New Dog with an Old Trick: Archetypal Patterns in *Sounder.*" *Journal of Popular Film,* 2, No. 2(1973), 155–63.

Ryf, Robert S. "Joyce's Visual Imagination." *Texas Studies in Literature and Language,* 1(1959), 30–43. Joyce's use of cinematic techniques.

Samuels, Charles. "The Context of *A Clockwork Orange.*" *American Scholar,* 41(1972), 439–43.

Samuels, Charles Thomas. "How Not to Film a Novel." *American Scholar,* 42(1972–73), 148–54. *Deliverance* and *Fat City.*

Sargent, Seymour H. "*Julius Caesar* and the Historical Film." *English Journal,* 61(1972), 230–33, 245.

Savarese, Sister Paul C., C. S. J. "Cinematic Techniques in the Novels of William Faulkner." *Dissertation Abstracts International,* 33(1973), 1179A (St. Louis U.). Finds equivalents to such film techniques as flashback, slow motion, montage, editing devices such as straight cuts, dissolves and fades.

Schein, Harry. "A Magnificent Fiasco?" *The Quarterly of Film, Radio, and Television,* 10(1956), 407–15. Olivier's *Richard III.*

Schneider, Harold W. "Literature and Film: Marking Out Some Boundaries." *Literature/Film Quarterly,* 3(1975), 30–44.

Schultheiss, John. "The 'Eastern' Writer in Hollywood." *Cinema Journal,* 11(Fall 1971), 13–47.

Schupp, Patrick. "*King Lear.*" *Sequences,* No. 72(Apr. 1973), 38–39. Brook's version.

Scott, James F. "The Emasculation of *Lady Chatterly's Lover.*" *Literature/Film Quarterly,* 1(1973), 37–45.

Scott, Kenneth W. "Hawkeye in Hollywood." *Films in Review,* 9(1958), 575–79. Adaptations of Cooper.

Seaton, George. "A Comparison of Playwright and Screen Writer." *The Quarterly of Film, Radio, and Television,* 19(1956), 217–26. Examines what makes a good adaptation of drama.

See, Carolyn. "The Hollywood Novel: An Historical and Critical Survey." *Dissertation Abstracts,* 24(1964), 5418 (U. C. L. A.).

Seldes, Gilbert. "Vandals of Hollywood: Why a Good Movie Cannot Be Faithful to the Original Book or Play." *Saturday Review,* 17 (Oct. 1936), 3–4. The essence of film is movement; the essence of the novel is the word.

Sharples, Win. "The Art of Filmmaking: An Analysis of *Slaughterhouse-Five." Filmmakers Newsletter,* 6(Nov. 1972), 24–28. Concentrates on the editing.

Shaw, G. B., and Archibald Henderson. "The Drama, the Theatre, and the Films: A Dialogue Between Bernard Shaw and Archibald Henderson." *Harper's Magazine,* 149(Sept. 1924), 425–35.

Shull, William M. "Translating with Film." *The Quarterly of Film, Radio, and Television,* 8(1953), 88–92. Preparing a version of *The Rime of the Ancient Mariner.*

Sidney, George R. "Faulkner in Hollywood: A Study of His Career as a Scenarist." *Dissertation Abstracts,* 20(1969), 2810 (U. of New Mexico).

Silver, Allyn. "The Untranquil Light: David Lean's *Great Expectations." Literature/Film Quarterly,* 2(1974), 140–53.

Silverstein, Norman. "Film and Language, Film and Literature." *Journal of Modern Literature,* 11(1971), 154–60.

———. "Film Semiology." *Salmagundi,* 13(Summer 1970), 73–80. General introduction to semiology. "Semiology enables the filmgoer to speak the complex communication of film, particularly as a force of political and social change. . . ."

Simon, John. *"The Day of the Locust." Esquire,* 84(August 1975), 10, 12.

Sirkin, Elliott. "The Group." *Film Comment,* 8(Sept.-Oct. 1972), 66–70.

Skerrett, Joseph T., Jr. "Graham Greene at the Movies: A Novelist's Experience with the Film." *Literature/Film Quarterly,* 2(1974), 293–301.

Skoller, Donald S. "Problems of Transformation in the Adaptation of Shakespeare's Tragedies from Play-Script to Cinema." *Dissertation Abstracts,* 29(1968), 2830A (N. Y. U.). Sets out "to determine the nature of the transformational problems involved in creating film adaptations of Shakespeare's tragedies . . . and to evaluate the effectiveness of the adaptations. . . ."

Slout, William L. *"Uncle Tom's Cabin* in American Film History." *Journal of Popular Film,* 2(1973), 137–51.

Smith, John Harrington. "Oscar Wilde's *Earnest* in Film." *The Quarterly of Film, Radio, and Television,* 8(1953), 72–79.

Smith, Julian. "Hester, Sweet Hester Prynne—*The Scarlet Letter* in the Movie Market Place." *Literature/Film Quarterly,* 2(1974), 100–09.

———. "Orson Welles and The Great American Dummy—Or, the Rise and Fall of Benjamin Franklin's Modern American." *Literature/Film Quarterly,* 2(1974), 196–206. Pop fiction as a source for *Citizen Kane.*

———. "Short Fiction on Film: A Selected Filmography." *Studies in Short Fiction,* 10(1973), 397–409.

———. "Vision and Revision: *The Virgin and the Gypsy." Literature/Film Quarterly,* 1(1973), 28–36.

Sobchack, Thomas. *"The Fox:* The Film and the Novel." *Western Humanities Review,* 23(1969), 73–78.

Solecki, Sam. "D. H. Lawrence's View of Film." *Literature/Film Quarterly,* 1(1973), 12–16.

Sontag, Susan. "Film and Theatre." *Tulane Drama Review,* 11(1966), 24–37. Disagrees with the conventional distinctions made between the two. The distinction may be that theatre entails a continuous use of space while the film entails a discontinuous use.

Southern, Terry. "When Film Gets Good. . . ." *The Nation,* 16 Nov. 1962, 330–32. Best novels are those that exploit the potential of their own medium.

Spatz, Jonas. "Hollywood in Fiction: Some Versions of the American Myth." *Dissertation Abstracts,* 25(1965), 6637 (Indiana U.).

Spiegel, Alan. "Flaubert to Joyce: Evolution of a Cinematographic Form." *Novel,* 6(1973), 229–43. Cinematic techniques compared with literary techniques.

Sragow, Michael. *"The End of the Road." Film Society Review,* 5(Feb. 1970), 36–39.

Staples, Leslie C. "The New Film Version of *A Tale of Two Cities." Dickensian,* 54(1958), 119–20.

Steele, Robert. "The Two Faces of Drama." *Cinema Journal,* 6(1966–67), 16–32. Defining the boundaries of film and drama.

Stern, Milton R. "The Whale and the Minnow: *Moby Dick* and the Movies." *College English,* 17(1956), 470–73. Huston's version.

Stolnitz, Jerome. "Kracauer: Thing, Word and Inferiority in the Movies." *The British Journal of Aesthetics,* 14(1974), 351–67.

Stone, Edward. "Ahab Gets the Girl, or Herman Melville Goes to the Movies." *Literature/Film Quarterly,* 3(1975), 172–81.

Storrer, William. "A Comparison of Edward Albee's *Who's Afraid of Virginia Woolf?* as Drama and as Film." *Dissertation Abstracts,* 29(1969), 3544A (Ohio U.).

Tarratt, Margaret. "An Obscene Undertaking." *Films and Filming,* 17 (Nov. 1970), 26–30. Lawrence on the screen.

Taylor, Henry. "Poetry of the Movies." *Film Journal,* 1(Fall-Winter 1972), 36–49. Influence of film on contemporary American poetry.

Thegze, Chuck. " 'I See Everything Twice': An Examination of *Catch 22.*" *Film Quarterly,* 24(Fall 1970), 7–17.

Thomaier, William. "Conrad on the Screen." *Films in Review,* 21(1970), 611–21. Filmography with some evaluative comments.

Thorp, Margaret. "The Motion Picture and the Novel." *American Quarterly,* 3(Fall 1951), 195–203. Decries the film's ignoring point of view; shows that the movie shares with the novel a "command of space."

———. "Shakespeare and the Movies." *Shakespeare Quarterly,* 9(1958), 357–66. The poetry gives the movies trouble for it impedes motion; but the pentameter line, if read well, will give a sense of motion. The most important action is that in the actor's face.

Tiessen, Paul. "A Comparative Approach to the Form and Function of Novel and Film: Dorothy Richardson's Theory of Art." *Literature/Film Quarterly,* 3(1975), 83–90.

———. "Malcolm Lowry and the Cinema." *Canadian Literature,* 44(Spring 1970), 38–49. Film influence on his fiction.

Trimmer, Joseph F. *"The Virginian:* Novel and Films." *Illinois Quarterly,* 35(Dec. 1972), 5–18.

Tupper, Lucy. "Dickens on the Screen." *Films in Review,* 10(1959), 142–52. Brief reviews from the 1908 *A Christmas Carol* to J. Arthur Rank's *A Tale of Two Cities.*

Tyler, Parker. *"Hamlet* and Documentary." *Kenyon Review,* 11(1949), 527–32. Olivier's *Hamlet.*

Van Wert, William. "Film and Literature: Adaptations." Masters Thesis Indiana U.

————. "Narrative Structure in *The Third Man.*" *Literature/Film Quarterly,* 2(1974), 341–46.

Wald, Jerry. "Screen Adaptation." *Films in Review,* 5(1964), 62–67. Various problems of adaptation such as length of work, what to cut, "opening up" of plays, and rendering novels by compression.

Walker, Roy. "Bottle Spider." *Twentieth Century,* 159(Jan. 1956), 58–68. Olivier's *Richard III.*

Weales, Gerald. "Teaching Film Drama as Film Drama." *The Quarterly of Film, Radio, and Television,* 11(1957), 394–98. A refutation of Kallich and Marsdin's article.

Weightman, John. "Trifling with the Dead." *Encounter,* 34(Jan. 1970), 50–53. Russell's *Women in Love.*

Weinburg, Herman G. "An Introduction to *Greed.*" *Focus on Film,* No. 14 (Spring 1973), 51–53.

————. "Novel into Film." *Literature/Film Quarterly,* 1(1973), 98–102. Brief survey of adaptations.

Welsh, James M. "Shakespeare With-and-Without Words." *Literature/-Film Quarterly,* 1(1973), 84–88.

Wilder, Thornton. *"Our Town*—From Stage to Screen: A Correspondence Between Thornton Wilder and Sol Lesser." *Theatre Arts,* 24(1940), 815–24.

Williams, W. E. "Film and Literature." *Sight and Sound,* 4(Winter 1935–36), 163–65. Finds film unable to create character in depth and to use literature's verbal language. Analyzes Reinhardt's *A Midsummer Night's Dream.*

Wilmington, Michael. "The Fugitive." *Velvet Light Trap,* 5(Summer 1972), 33–35. Adaptation of *The Power and the Glory.*

Wilson, Robert. "Which is the Real *Last Picture Show?*" *Literature/Film Quarterly,* 1(1973), 167–69.

Wilson, Robert F. *"Deliverance* From Novel to Film: Where is our Hero?" *Literature/Film Quarterly,* 2(1974), 52–58.

Wolfe, Glenn J. "Vachel Lindsay: The Poet as Film Theorist." *Dissertation Abstracts,* 26(1966), 1222 (U. of Iowa).

Worth, Sol. "The Development of a Semiotic of Film." *Semiotica,* 1(1969), 282–321. Sees the need for a model of the whole experience of film and proposes one: Sender-Image Event-Receiver. He then discusses the elements of film and considers it as a language, discovering that, accepting Chomsky's definition of language, film is not a language. We need a methodology, Worth says, "that will enable us to say . . . how it is, and with what rules, that we make implications using film signs with some hope of similar inferences."

Yutkevitch, Sergei. "The Conscience of the King: Kozintsev's *King Lear.*" *Sight and Sound,* 40(Autumn 1971), 192–96.

Young, Vernon. "Fat Shakespeare and Fat City: Lean Wilderness." *Hudson Review,* 26(1973), 170–76. *Macbeth* and *Fat City.*

Zambrano, Ana Laura. *"Great Expectations:* Dickens and David Lean." *Literature/Film Quarterly,* 2(1974), 154–61.

———. *"Great Expectations:* Dickens' Style in Terms of Film." *Hartford Studies in Literature,* 4(1972), 104–13.

———. "Greene's Visions of Childhood: *The Basement Room* and *The Fallen Idol." Literature/Film Quarterly,* 2(1974), 324–31.

———. "The Style of Dickens and Griffith: *A Tale of Two Cities* and *Orphans of the Storm." Language and Style,* 7(1974), 53–61.

———. *"Throne of Blood:* Kurosawa's *Macbeth." Literature/Film Quarterly,* 2(1974), 262–74.

———. *"Women in Love:* Counterpoint on Film." *Literature/Film Quarterly,* 1(1973), 46–54.

Zlotnick, Joan. "Nathanael West and the Pictoral Imagination." *Western American Literature,* 9(1974), 177–85. Influence of comic strips, painting, and movies.

A BIBLIOGRAPHY OF BOOKS ON LITERATURE AND FILM
by Norman DeMarco

The relationship between literature and film cannot be complete without attention to the language and narrative devices of the two disciplines. Since a major portion of films derive from literary works, and since there has been a growing concern for courses that recognize an affinity between film and literature, the following source materials have been compiled as one step toward the expanding study of literature/film reciprocity.

The sources here listed, though not intended to be exhaustive, concern themselves with the following topics: (1) The language of film. (2) Analyses of film scripts adapted from novels, short stories and plays. (3) The interrelationships of film and literature. (4) Reviews of films derived from literary works.

Agee, James. *Agee On Film*. Vols. 1 and 2. New York: McDowell, Obolensky, Inc., 1958. Eminently readable reviews, essays, and film scripts by this most knowledgeable critic.

————. *Agee On Film: Reviews and Comments*. Boston: Beacon Press, 1964. These personal responses to film by one of the country's outstanding critics offer many illuminating comments on films derived from literature.

Alpert, Hollis. "Film and Theatre," in *The Dreams and the Dreamers*. New York: The MacMillan Company, 1962, pp. 233–51. Discusses differences and similarities between the two media, and concludes that film is "technically more facile than the stage" and more satisfying.

Appel, Alfred, Jr. *Nabokov's Dark Cinema*. New York: Oxford University Press, 1974. Some pertinent thoughts on relationships between film and theatre.

Arnheim, Rudolf. "A New Laocoön: Artistic Composites and the Talking Film," in *Film as Art*. Berkeley: University of California Press, 1957. The essay "discusses general aesthetic rules for the combination of different media-word, image, sound—and leads to an evaluation of the talking picture as a medium for artistic expression."

Balazs, Bela. *Theory of Film*. New York: Roy Publishers, Inc., 1953. The focus of attention is on differences between film and theatre. Theoretical observations on uses of sound, dialogue, space and time in both media. See Clair.

Ball, Robert Hamilton. *Shakespeare On Silent Film*. New York: Theatre Arts Books, 1968. This detailed discussion of Shakespeare's films in the "silent" era includes excerpts from scenarios as well as reviews and numerous photographs from the films. See Eckert.

Barrett, Gerald R., and Thomas L. Erskine, eds. "Silent Snow, Secret Snow," in *From Fiction to Film*. Belmont, Ca.: Dickenson Publishing Co., Inc., 1972. To facilitate the study of the problem of adaptation, the authors provide the following material: an introduction to the problem of transferring fiction to film, the short story, critical essays related to the history, a shot analysis of the film, essays relevant to the film, suggested discussion and theme topics.

————, eds. "An Occurrence at Owl Creek Bridge," in *From Fiction to Film*. Belmont, Ca.: Dickenson Publishing Co., Inc., 1973. Provides one with the original story, critical essays related to the story, a shot analysis of the film script (two film versions of the story are included), thoughts about the films, and suggested topics for discussions.

————, eds. "The Rocking-Horse Winner," in *From Fiction to Film.* Belmont, Ca.: Dickenson Publishing Co., Inc., 1974. This third book in the series *From Fiction to Film* includes the short story, criticisms of the story, the film script, criticisms of the film, and suggestions for reports.

Battestin, Martin C. "Osborne's 'Tom Jones': Adapting a Classic," in *Man and the Movies,* ed. W. R. Robinson. Baltimore: Penguin Books, 1967. A highly informative account that explores the process of transferring a novel into film.

Bazin, Andre. *What is Cinema?* Berkeley: University of California Press, 1967. A series of ten essays that explore the language and aesthetics of film theory as related to theatre and to literary adaptations.

Bergman, Ingmar. "Film Has Nothing to do with Literature," in *A Montage of Theories,* ed. Richard MacCann. New York: E. P. Dutton & Co., 1966. Bergman states that "we should avoid making films out of books . . . the character and substance of the two art forms are usually in conflict . . . the written word is read and assimilated by a conscious act of the will in alliance with the intellect. . . . When we experience a film, we consciously prime ourselves for illusion. Putting aside will and intellect, we make way for it in our imagination."

Bettetini, Gianfranco. *The Language and Technique of Film.* The Hague: Mouton Publishers, 1973. An analysis of "cinematographic codes" as a means of understanding film, and a consideration of "traditional technical problems from a linguistics point of view."

Blotner, Joseph. "Faulkner in Hollywood," in *Man and the Movies,* ed. W. B. Robinson. Baltimore: Penguin Books, 1967, pp. 261–303. An interesting account of Faulkner's years as screenwriter and "screen doctor" under the aegis of three major studios—MGM, Twentieth-Century Fox, and Warner Brothers.

Bluestone, George. *Novels Into Film.* Berkeley: Univ. of California Press, 1971. A penetrating insight to problems of adapting novels into film. Contains an extended analysis of "Wuthering Heights," "The Grapes of Wrath," "Madame Bovary," "Pride and Prejudice," "The Ox-Bow Incident," and "The Informer."

Brecht, Bertold. "The Film, the Novel, and Epic Theatre," in *Brecht on Theatre,* ed. John Willett. New York: Hill and Wang, 1964, pp. 47–50. Brecht discusses problems encountered in the production of the film version of "Threepenny Opera" and offers ideas concerning the potential of the film medium.

Burch, Noel. *Theory of Film Practice.* New York: Praeger Publishers, 1973. A scholarly presentation of key theories related to film studies. Essays are devoted to Renoir's adaptation of "Nana," and to the "written cinema" novels of Robbe-Grillet.

Ciment, Michel. *Kazan On Kazan.* New York: Viking Press, 1974. Since Kazan has adapted some of his own novels for film and since his career as a director extends into film and theatre, this extensive interview offers valuable and incisive comments about both media.

Clair, Rene. "Theatre and Cinema," in *Cinema Yesterday and Today,* ed. R. C. Dale, trans., Stanley Applebaum. New York: Dover Publications, 1972, pp. 159–69. Contains interesting comments of Clair's attitude toward the use of sound and dialogue in films. See Balazs.

Corliss, Richard. *Talking Pictures: Screenwriters in the American Cinema.* New York: The Overlook Press, 1973. (From book jacket) "Attempts to identify the screenwriter as the crucial missing link in the creation of the American film." See Froug.

Costello, Donald P. *The Serpent's Eye: Shaw and the Cinema.* South Bend: University of Notre Dame Press, 1965. The book presents interesting details of Shaw's encounters with the film world from the silent era through the sound period. Most valuable additions are scenes for a proposed film of "The Devil's Disciple," a complete script for an adaptation of "Arms and the Man," and an analysis of script changes for "Pygmalion."

Cross, Brenda, ed. *The Film Hamlet: A Record of Its Production.* London: Saturn Press, 1948. Essays related to the Olivier "Hamlet" written by persons responsible for some aspect of its production. See Dent.

Daisne, Johan. *Filmographic Dictionary of World Literature.* New York: Humanities Press, Inc., 1970. An extensive and scholarly collection of literary sources for fiction films. The entries are arranged alphabetically by book and film titles with cross references to authors.

Dent, Alan, ed. *Hamlet: The Film and the Play.* London: World Film Publishers, 1948. The screenplay of Olivier's "Hamlet" accompanied by three essays related to the film. See Cross.

DeVries, Daniel. *Kubrick: The Films of Stanley Kubrick.* Grand Rapids: Eerdmans Publishing Company, 1973. Analyses of seven Kubrick films adapted from literary works.

Eckert, Charles W., ed. *Focus On Shakespearean Films.* Englewood Cliffs: Prentice-Hall, Inc., 1972. A tasteful selection of essays that examine critical attitudes toward filmic adaptations of eight plays. Of exceptional merit are MacLiammoir's chronicled diary of Welles'

"Othello" and Agee's excellent analysis of Olivier's "Henry V." See Ball.

Eisenstein, Sergei. "Dickens, Griffith, and the Film Today," *Film Form,* ed. Jay Leyda. New York: Harcourt, Brace and World, 1949, pp. 195–255. Eisenstein's classic delineation of the link between the structural techniques in Griffith's narrative films and Dickens' structure in the novel.

———. "Lessons from Literature," in *Film Essays and a Lecture,* ed. Jay Leyda. New York: Praeger, 1970, pp. 77–83. Eisenstein suggests that although cinema has "no direct ancestors," the filmmaker can discover filmic potential through an examination of literary classics. He cites works of Balzac and Zola, among others, that offer particular features which can serve a director's filmmaking techniques.

———. "Through Theatre to Cinema," in *Film Form,* ed. Jay Leyda. New York: Harcourt, Brace and World, 1949, pp. 3–17. Explains how his theories of cinema evolved from experiences and observations of theatre productions.

———. "Word and Image," in *The Film Sense,* ed. Jay Leyda. New York: Harcourt, Brace and World, 1970, pp. 3–68. The essay projects the idea that while montage can bring dynamism and excitement to a film, it is incumbent on a filmmaker to study "play-writing and the actor's craft" if he hopes to master the subtleties of montage.

Enser, A. G. S. *Filmed Books and Plays, a List of Books and Plays from which Films Have Been Made, 1928–1967.* London: Deutsch, 1971. A useful list of American and British films derived from books and plays. The indexes are arranged alphabetically according to Film Title, Author, and Change of Original Title, thus simplifying the search for any particular item.

Evans, Robert O. *Graham Greene: Some Critical Considerations.* Lexington: Univ. of Kentucky Press, 1963. The chapter titled "The Curse of the Film" centers attention on the argument that "the most often praised films of Greene are those adapted from novels considered second-rate as literature." See Phillips.

Fell, John L. *Film and the Narrative Tradition.* Norman: University of Oklahoma Press, 1974. To substantiate his idea that the narrative tradition had been developing unsystematically for a hundred years, Fell cites examples from art, literature, the comics, slide shows—all of which utilized story-telling devices that have become commonplace in filmmaking.

Fiedler, Leslie. "What Shining Phantom: Writers and the Movies," in *Man and the Movies.* Baltimore: Penguin Books, 1967, pp. 304–23. Discusses writers' reasons for moving to Hollywood and the agonies and frustrations encountered. Attention is given to James M. Cain, Daniel Fuchs, Nathanael West, Scott Fitzgerald, and Norman Mailer.

French, Warren. *Filmguide to "The Grapes of Wrath."* Bloomington: Indiana Univ. Press, 1973. The first book of an innovative series idea whose objective is an analytical investigation of specific films. Other titles in the series include "A Space Odyssey," "Rules of the Game," and "Henry V." These volumes can be useful to anyone interested in the techniques of "descriptive analysis" as related to the narrative film.

Froug, William. *The Screenwriter Looks at the Screenwriter.* New York: Macmillan Company, 1972. Contains interviews with twelve professional screenwriters as well as excerpts from a number of screenplays. See Corliss.

Fulton, A. R. "From Play to Film," in *The Development of an Art from Silent Films to the Age of Television.* Norman: Univ. of Oklahoma Press, 1960. Attention is given to the process and the problems of adapting the play to its filmic counterpart.

Garbicz, Adam, and Jacek Klinowski. *Cinema, The Magic Vehicle: A Guide to Its Achievement.* Metuchen, N.J.: Scarecrow Press, 1975. Included in this "panoramic view of cinema achievement" is the "development of film technique and its influence on the language of the cinema."

Gassner, John. *Twenty Best Film Plays.* New York: Crown Publishers, 1943. Included among the screenplays adapted from literature are "The Grapes of Wrath," "Rebecca," and "Wuthering Heights."

Geduld, Carolyn. *Filmguide to 2001: A Space Odyssey.* Bloomington: Indiana University Press, 1973. (From book jacket) ". . . authoritative studies designed to introduce the student to the film, present guidelines for its viewing, examine its message and techniques, and provide a point of departure for further research and discussion."

Geduld, Harry M. *Authors On Film.* Bloomington: Indiana Univ. Press, 1972. Interviews with outstanding writers offer pertinent thoughts on adapting novels for the screen. The book "analyzes the film's resources for the poetic dramatist, and exposes many different aspects of the writer's interest in and involvement with film."

Gessner, Robert. "The Informer," in *The Moving Image.* New York: E. P. Dutton & Company, 1968, pp. 161–71. Analyzes to what "extent structure may develop character, rather than plot."

———. *The Moving Image.* New York: E. P. Dutton & Co., Inc., 1968. This knowledgeable discussion of classic and contemporary films explores a number of films adapted from literary works, including

"Hamlet," "Wuthering Heights," "Great Expectations," and "The Informer."

————. "Pygmalion," in *The Moving Image*. New York: E. P. Dutton & Company, 1968, pp. 362–66. Compares the dramatic dialogue of the original stage play with that of the 1938 film version.

Giannetti, Louis D. *Understanding Movies*. Englewood Cliffs: Prentice-Hall, Inc., 1972. Special attention is given to such film/literature concepts as metaphors, tropes, points of view, adaptations, symbols, and language, as these relate to meaning in film. An extensive glossary serves to clarify terminology.

Harrington, John. *The Rhetoric of Film*. New York: Holt, Rinehart and Winston, Inc., 1973. This brief volume offers information essential to an understanding of film terminology and its application to a serious discussion of films. See Huss.

Hurt, James, ed. *Focus On Film and Theatre*. Englewood Cliffs: Prentice-Hall, Inc., 1974. Essays written by critics, directors, and playwrights. Among the titles are the following: Nicoll's "Film Reality: The Cinema and Theatre," Kaufmann's "Notes on Theatre and Film," Handke's "Theatre and Film: The Misery of Comparison."

Huss, Roy, and Norman Silverstein. *The Film Experience: Elements of Motion Picture Art*. New York: Harper & Row, 1968. This book is especially useful for those film students and teachers desirous of becoming conversant with the language of film. See Harrington.

Jinks, William. *The Celluloid Literature*. Beverly Hills: Glencoe Press, 1971. Six chapters delineate interrelationships of film and literature. The book projects "an extended analogy between structural units of the novel and the elemental building blocks of the film."

Jones, Karen, ed. *International Index to Film Periodicals*. New York: R. R. Bowker, 1973. This annotated index is organized into the following areas: (1) General subjects. (2) Film reviews—cross referenced to foreign films from their English titles. (3) People. A valuable research source.

Kael, Pauline. *Deeper into Movies*. Boston: Little, Brown and Company, 1973. Among the many critical reviews, the following give attention to adaptations: "Kazan's Latest Arrangements: 'The Arrangement,'" "The Last Picture Show," and "Stanley Strangelove: 'A Clockwork Orange.'"

———— *Going Steady*. New York: Bantam Books, 1971. This fine collection of film reviews and critical comments includes "Making Lawrence More Lawrentian: 'The Fox,'" and "Filmed Theatre: 'The Seagull.'"

————. *I Lost it at the Movies.* New York: Bantam Books, 1966. Some pungent critical reviews include the following adaptations: "The Innocents," "A View from the Bridge," "Lolita," and "Billy Budd."

————. *Kiss Kiss Bang Bang.* New York: Bantam Books, 1969. Included among the reviews are a number of films adapted from novels and plays—Joyce's "Ulysses," Olivier's "Othello," Bradbury's "Fahrenheit 451," and Bolt's "A Man for All Seasons."

Katz, John S. *Perspectives on the Study of Film.* Boston: Little, Brown and Company, 1971. Among the many fine essays in this book, the following may have special interest for Literature/Film teachers: "Theatre and Film," "Style and Medium in the Motion Pictures," and "Time in Film and Fiction."

————, et al. *A Curriculum in Film.* Toronto: The Ontario Institute for Studies in Education, 1972. This brief volume presents an approach to "the teaching of film as it relates to literature, allowing students to see how each medium works and to explore similarities and differences between the two media."

Kauffmann, Stanley. *A World on Film.* New York: Dell Publishing Co., 1966. Reviews of films adapted from novels and plays include "Desire Under the Elms," "Cat On a Hot Tin Roof," "The Trial," "The Sound and the Fury," "Lolita," and "Long Day's Journey Into Night."

————. *Living Images: Film Comment and Criticism.* New York: Harper & Row, Publishers, 1970. In addition to numerous reviews of films adapted from literature, the author gives some interesting comments on the relationship of theatre and film.

Kawin, Bruce. *Telling It Again and Again: Repetition in Literature and Film.* New York: Cornell Univ. Press, 1972. Approaches the treatment of repetition "both as an aesthetic device in literature and film, and as a state of mind." Attention is given to plays, prose works, and films.

Kirby, E. T., ed. *Total Theatre: A Critical Anthology.* New York: E. P. Dutton & Co., Inc., 1969. A rich source of information with special emphasis on interrelationships between film and theatre.

Klein, Michael. "The Literary Sophistication of François Truffaut" in *The Emergence of Film Art,* ed. Lewis Jacobs. New York: Hopkinson and Blake, Publishers, 1969, pp. 303–12. Techniques of dislocation, found in the modern novel, and irony, a basic ingredient of all forms of literature, are applied to Truffaut's films.

Kracauer, Siegfried. "The Theatrical Story," and "Interlude: Film and Novel," in *Theory of Film.* London: Oxford Univ. Press, 1960, pp. 215–31, and 232–44. Argues that sufficient differences between the two media substantiate his point that film is a discrete art form unrelated to any other art.

Lambert, Gavin. *GWTW: The Making of "Gone With the Wind."* Boston: Little, Brown and Company, 1973. Based on recorded conversations, opinions, and recollections of persons closely associated with the production.

Langer, Suzanne. "A Note on the Film," in *Feeling and Form*. New York: Charles Scribner's Sons, 1953, pp. 411–15. The author reflects on the following ideas as suggested by some of her former students: "(1) that the structure of a motion picture is not that of drama and indeed lies closer to narrative than to drama; (2) that its artistic potentialities became evident only when the moving camera was introduced."

Lawson, John Howard. "Film and Novel," in *Film: The Creative Process*. New York: Hill and Wang, 1964, pp. 205–18. Compares scenes from the novel *Great Expectations* with director David Lean's film version as a means of showing the relationship of novel and film.

———. *Theory and Technique of Playwriting and Screenwriting*. New York: Putnam, 1949. Approaches to writing in both media are presented lucidly and with insight by a master craftsman.

Leech, Clifford, and J. M. R. Margeson, eds. *Shakespeare 1971*. Toronto: Univ. of Toronto Press, 1972. The chapter "Shakespeare in the 20th Century: Theatre and Film 1" focuses on the Russian director Grigori Kozintsev and his film versions of *Hamlet* and *King Lear*.

Linden, George W. *Reflections On The Screen*. Belmont, Ca.: Wadsworth Publishing Co., 1970. Teachers of literature will find the chapters on "The Staged World" and "The Storied World" of incalculable aid in drawing analogies to film, the novel, and drama.

Lindsay, Vachel. "Thirty Differences between the Photoplays and the Stage," in *The Art of the Moving Picture*. New York: Liveright Publishing Corporation, 1970, pp. 179–98. Although Lindsay's theories seem naive, film students will be interested in his argument that "in order to be real photoplays the stage dramas must be overhauled, indeed, turned inside out and upside down."

McBride, Joseph, ed. *Persistence of Vision: A Collection of Film Criticism*. Madison: The Wisconsin Film Society Press, 1968. Of particular significance in this collection of essays is a re-examination of Welles' "The Magnificent Ambersons."

———. *Orson Welles*. (Cinema One Series). New York: The Viking Press, 1974. A critical analysis of the films of Orson Welles. Makes an interesting comparison of the original script for "The Magnificent Ambersons" with the film as seen by audiences.

MacCann, Richard Dyer. *Film: A Montage of Theories*. New York: E. P. Dutton & Co., 1966. Included in this wide-ranging series of articles is the section titled "Film and the Other Arts" which focuses on "The Film is Modern Theatre," "Epic and Dramatic Film," "A Novelist Looks at Hollywood," and "Film Has Nothing to do with Literature."

MacDonald, Dwight. *On Movies*. Englewood Cliffs: Prentice-Hall, Inc., 1969. Reviews of many films adapted from literature, including "Hamlet," "Phaedra," "The Misfits," "Dr. Strangelove," and "The Loneliness of the Long-Distance Runner." The *Forenotes* offer useful guidelines for judging films.

Maddux, Rachel. *Fiction into Film; a Walk in the Spring Rain*. Knoxville: The Univ. of Tennessee Press, 1970. (From the cover) "This unique study of the making of a major Hollywood film is the first to assemble an original work of fiction, the screenplay adapted from that work, and full and lively commentary by an objective observer on the transformation of fiction to script to finished film."

Madsen, Roy Paul. "Adaptation: Novels and Stage Plays into Cinema-Television," in *The Impact of Film*. New York: Macmillan, 1973, pp. 244–64. "Intrinsic differences in the two media determine many of the changes required in any adaptation from one medium to another."

————. "Dramatic Structure in Cinema and Television," in *The Impact of Film*. New York: Macmillan, 1973, pp. 195–218. Some references to specific films help reinforce this discussion of basic necessities of dramatic structure.

Manvell, Roger. *Shakespeare and the Film*. New York: Praeger Publishers, 1971. Thirteen films adapted from Shakespeare are discussed. The author's purpose is "to show how the plays have been presented to make them effective as films, and how the technique of the film has to be modified to make it effective as a medium for Shakespeare."

————. *The Film and the Public*. Baltimore: Penguin Books, 1955. Chapter 2, "A Miscellany of Films," is devoted to a critical appraisal of films, a number of which are adaptations from literature—"The Italian Straw Hat," "The Oxbow Incident," "The Informer," "Beauty and the Beast."

Marcus, Fred H. *Film and Literature: Contrasts in Media*. New York: Chandler Publishing Co., 1971. In addition to nine essays devoted to film as an art form, the book offers an analysis of seven film adaptations including "The Grapes of Wrath," "Tom Jones," "Romeo and Juliet," "Catch-22," "Pygmalion," "Midnight Cowboy," and "An Occurrence at Owl Creek Bridge."

Mast, Gerald, and Marshall Cohen. *Film Theory and Criticism*. New York: Oxford Univ. Press, 1974. This series of essays gives special attention to syntax and structure in film, the relation of film to literary arts, and to the uniqueness of film as an art form.

Maynard, Richard A., ed. *Literature of the Screen*. Chicago: Scholastic Books, 1974. A 4-volume anthology of screenplays grouped according to theme. Included from literary sources are the following: "The Hustler," "The Candidate," "Splendor in the Grass," and "The Loneliness of the Long-Distance Runner."

Mendilow, A. A. *Time and the Novel*. New York: The Humanities Press, 1972. Most rewarding is Chapter 6 which explores the element of time in the film and the novel.

Metz, Christian. *Film Language*. New York: Oxford Univ. Press, 1974. The author argues the need for developing a language of cinema comparable to the language of grammar as a means of bringing clear understanding and incisiveness to film aesthetics. Comparisons are made showing relationships of film with art, literature, and poetry.

Morsberger, Robert E., ed. *Viva Zapata, by John Steinbeck*. New York: The Viking Press, 1975. (From Viking Press) "This edition contains the complete final shooting script of the screenplay and includes notations to show how the final film was changed. Two essays provide an analysis of the film and Steinbeck's involvement with it."

Murray, Edward. *The Cinematic Imagination*. New York: Frederick Ungar Publishing Co., 1972. A comprehensive exploration of problems related to film adaptations. Discussions center around such questions as: "Under what circumstances does cinematic imagination function legitimately in drama?" "What happens to the film adaptation of a play that reveals filmic techniques?"

Nabakov, Vladimir. *Lolita: A Screenplay*. New York: McGraw-Hill, 1961. This is Nabokov's version of the screenplay for "Lolita" as distinct from the version that finally appeared on the screen. The "Foreword" gives an interesting account of his wavering decision about undertaking the task of preparing the screenplay.

Nathan, Robert. "A Novelist Looks at Hollywood," in *A Montage of Theories*, ed. Richard MacCann. New York: E. P. Dutton & Co., 1966. While recognizing the screen play as a valid form and recognizing further that film and novel have many common characteristics, Nathan expresses the opinion that whereas a "written novel is the complete work of art," the film script is "only one step toward the final film product—a fact that discourages potential film writers."

Nichols, Dudley. "The Writer and the Film," in *A Montage of Theories*, ed. Richard MacCann. New York: E. P. Dutton & Co., 1966. Argues that "A screenplay is not and can never be a finished product." It is just one step in a collaborative process involving many skills and talents before it attains a final form ready for an audience. A large portion of the article is devoted to a comparison of the problems of writing an adaptation with those of writing an original script. See Rilla.

Nicoll, Allardyce. *Film and Theatre*. New York: Crowell Publishing Co., 1936. This classic book explores differences between theatre and film. Among the problems discussed are the illusion of reality, filming Shakespeare, and typecasting. See Pudovkin.

Phillips, Gene D. *Graham Greene: The Films of His Fiction*. New York: Teachers College Press, 1974. An excellent study and comparison of Greene's novels and film scripts. See Evans.

Pinter, Harold. *Five Screenplays*. New York: Grove Press, 1974. Contains scripts of "The Servant," "The Go-Between," "The Pumpkin Eater," "The Quiller Memorandum," and "Accident."

Pudovkin, V. I. "The Film and the Theatre," in *Film Technique and Film Acting,* trans. Ivor Montague. New York: Bonanza Books, 1949. Pudovkin's classic theoretical discussion of some differences and interrelationships of film and theatre. See Nicoll.

Richardson, Robert Dale. *Literature and Film*. Bloomington: Indiana Univ. Press, 1972. The volume contends that "the connections that exist between literature and film are worth concentrating upon because literature and film are near neighbors and because these forms of artistic expression appear to be increasingly dominant in the formation of modern aesthetic responses."

Rilla, Wolf. *The Writer and the Screen*. New York: William Morrow & Company, Inc., 1974. The book examines and explains the disciplines and techniques of writing for the screen. See Nichols.

Ross, Lillian. *Picture*. New York: Avon Books, 1969. Some acerbic comments accompany this interesting account of John Huston's film, "The Red Badge of Courage."

Ross, T.J. *Film and the Liberal Arts*. New York: Holt, Rinehart and Winston, 1970. A compilation of essays relating the film medium to literature, the visual arts, and to music. The complete script of Agee's "The Bride Comes to Yellow Sky" and a discussion of Kurosawa's "Throne of Blood" are included.

Rossen, Stephen, ed. *Three Screenplays, by Robert Rossen*. New York: Anchor Press, 1972. These screenplays, adapted from novels, were written, produced and directed by Robert Rossen—"All the King's Men," "The Hustler," and "Lilith." See Salem.

Rowland, Richard. "Miss Julie," in *Renaissance of the Film,* ed. Julius Bellone. New York: The Macmillan Company, 1970. Some interesting analogies between Strindberg's one-act play and its filmed version.

Salem, James M., ed. *A Guide to Critical Reviews: Part IV: The Screenplay from "The Jazz Singer" to "Dr. Strangelove."* Metuchen, N.J.: Scarecrow Press, 1971. This substantial sourcebook begins with the first sound feature of 1927 and carries through to 1963. See Rossen.

Simon, John. "Adaptations," in *Movies Into Film.* New York: Dell, 1971, pp. 25–65. These reviews of films adapted from literary works include "Marat/Sade," "Falstaff," "The Heart is a Lonely Hunter," "Tropic of Cancer," "The Seagull," "Justine," "Women in Love," "Far From the Madding Crowd," "Ulysses," and "War and Peace."

Solomon, Stanley J. "The Nature of Plot Structure: Dickens Versus Antonioni," in *The Film Idea.* New York: Harcourt, Brace, Jovanovich, 1972, pp. 363–70. A discussion of the Dickensian narrative mode and its application to film by D. W. Griffith and the unique characteristics of plot structure as seen in the contemporary films of Antonioni.

———. *The Film Idea.* New York: Harcourt, Brace, Jovanovich, Inc., 1972. The author states the purpose of the book as follows: ". . . to examine the nature of the narrative film in regard to those characteristics that distinguish this art form from the other narrative arts."

Sontag, Susan. "A Note on Novels and Films," in *Against Interpretation.* New York: Farrar, Straus and Giroux, 1961, pp. 242–45. Despite analogies that can be made with the novel, film has its own language and its own "methods and logic of representation."

———. "Theatre and Film," in *Styles of Radical Will.* New York: Farrar, Straus and Giroux, 1960, pp. 99–122. Incisive comments on contemporary aspects of film and theatre.

Spencer, T. J. B., ed. *Shakespeare: A Celebration 1564–1964.* Baltimore: Penguin Books, 1964. The author evaluates problems of adapting Shakespeare's plays to various media and also suggests that attention be given to filming Shakespeare as a stage production as an "unvarnished record" that will have permanent value for historians and research scholars.

Stewart, Lawrence P. "Fitzgerald's Film Scripts of 'Babylon Revisited,'" in *Fitzgerald/Hemingway Annual 1971,* Bruccoli, Matthew J., and C. E. Clark, Jr., eds. Washington, D. C.: Microcard Editions, 1971, pp. 81–104. A revealing account of Fitzgerald's problems and frustrations encountered in preparing drafts for his film scripts of "Babylon Revisited."

Taylor, John Russell. *Graham Greene On Film*. New York: Simon and Schuster, 1972. This collection of Greene's film criticism covers a period from 1935 to 1940. It includes a number of adaptations—"Anna Karenina," "The Petrified Forest," "Idiot's Delight," "A Midsummer Night's Dream," "The Informer," and others.

Tyler, Parker. "The Play is Not the Thing," in *The Hollywood Hallucination*. New York: Simon and Schuster, 1970, pp. 3–21. Some thoughts on comparisons between film and literature, and on the pressures that often accompany the writing of a film script.

Vardac, A. Nicholas. *From Stage to Screen*. Cambridge: Harvard University Press, 1949. This scholarly account of "Theatrical Method from Garrick to Griffith" explores the relationship of film to theatre of the nineteenth century.

Wake, Sandra, ed. *Modern Film Scripts*. New York: Simon and Schuster, 1971. The scripts are concerned with a detailed shot analysis and relationships of shots to the actual film product. Scripts include "The Trial," "The Third Man," and "Oedipus Rex." See Rossen.

Wald, Marvin, and Michael Werner. *Three Major Screenplays*. New York: Globe Book Company, Inc., 1972. A collection of filmscripts that includes "High Noon," "The Ox-Bow Incident," and "Lilies of the Field." Critical reviews about each screenplay and a section on film terminology round out the book. See Wake.

Weiss, Paul. *Cinematics*. Carbondale: Southern Illinois Univ. Press, 1975. Students of film writing will be interested in the chapter devoted to the script. The focus here is on the prime objective of the script in the process of filmmaking and its relationship to the novel.

White, William. *Nathanael West: A Comprehensive Bibliography*. Kent, Ohio: Kent State Univ. Press, 1975. A most useful reference to the scripts West created for films.

Wilbur, Richard. "A Poet and the Movies," in *Man and the Movies,* ed. W. R. Robinson. Baltimore: Penguin Books, 1967, pp. 223–26. The author expresses a feeling that some techniques characteristic of his poetry may have been influenced by what he has observed in films.

Williams, Raymond. "Shakespeare on the Screen," in *TV as Art,* ed. Patrick D. Hazard. Champaign, Illinois: National Council of Teachers of English, 1966. Contains an analysis of "Macbeth" filmed for television. The author believes "it is possible to conceive that the flexibility of place, the mobility of viewpoint, the variation of imagery, which cinema and television make possible, will take us farther into an understanding of Shakespeare than the static theatres of a past generation."

Wollen, Peter. *Signs and Meaning in the Cinema*. Bloomington: Indiana Univ. Press, 1969. The emphasis is on a semiology of film as a vital study area of film aesthetics. Wollen's discussion of meanings and thematic motifs is especially illuminating.

Youngblood, Gene. "Intermedia Theatre," in *Expanded Cinema*. New York: E. P. Dutton & Co., 1970, pp. 365–86. ". . . in intermedia theatre, the traditional distinctions between what is genuinely 'theatrical' as opposed to what is purely 'cinematic' are no longer of concern."

Filmography

FREAKS

Metro-Goldwyn-Mayer, 1932. Directed by Tod Browning. Screenplay: Willis Goldbeck and Leon Gordon. Dialogue: Edgar Allen Woolf and Al Boasberg. Photography: Merritt B. Gerstad. Editor: Basil Wrangell. Sound: Gavin Burns. Running time: 64 minutes.

Phroso	Wallace Ford
Venus	Leila Hyams
Cleopatra	Olga Baclanova
Roscoe	Roscoe Ates
Hercules	Henry Victor
Hans	Harry Earles
Frieda	Daisy Earles
Madame Tetrallini	Rose Dione
Siamese Twins	Daisy and Violet Hilton
Rollo Brothers	Edward Brophy, Matt McHugh
Bearded Lady	Olga Roderick
Boy with Half a Torso	Johnny Eck
Hindu Living Torso	Randian
White Pin Heads	Schlitzie, Elvira, and Jennie Lee Snow
Living Skeleton	Pete Robinson
Bird Girl	Koo Coo
Half-Woman Half-Man	Josephine-Joseph
Armless Wonder	Martha Morris
Turtle Girl	Frances O'Connor
Midget	Angelo Rossito

Specialties: Zip and Pip, Elizabeth Green. Landowner: Albert Conti. Jean, the Caretaker: Michael Visaroff. Sideshow Patron: Ernie S. Adams. Maid: Louise Beavers.

IT HAPPENED ONE NIGHT

Columbia, 1934. Directed by Frank Capra. Produced by Harry Cohn. Screenplay: Robert Riskin. Art Director: Stephen Goosson. Assistant Director: C. C. Coleman. Photography: Joseph Walker. Editor: Gene Havlick. Sound: E. E. Bernds. Costumes: Robert Kalloch. Music Director: Louis Silvers. Running time: 105 minutes.

Peter Warne	Clark Gable
Ellie Andrews	Claudette Colbert
Oscar Shapeley	Roscoe Karns
Alexander Andrews	Walter Connolly
Danker	Alan Hale
Bus Driver	Ward Bond
Bus Driver	Eddy Chandler
King Westley	Jameson Thomas
Lovington	Wallis Clark
Zeke	Arthur Hoyt
Zeke's Wife	Blanche Frederici
Joe Gordon	Charles C. Wilson
Reporter	Charles D. Brown
Henderson	Harry C. Bradley
Auto Camp Manager	Harry Holman
Manager's Wife	Maidel Turner
Station Attendant	Irving Bacon
Flag Man	Harry Todd
Tony	Frank Yaconelli

Drunken Boy: Henry Wadsworth. Mother: Claire McDowell. Detectives: Ky Robinson, Frank Holliday, James Burke, Joseph Crehan. Drunk: Milton Kibbee. Vender: Mickey Daniel. Dykes: Oliver Eckhardt. Boy: George Breakston. Secretary: Bess Flowers. Minister: Father Dodds. Best Man: Edmund Burns. Maid of Honor: Ethel Sykes. Old Man: Tom Ricketts. Radio Announcer: Eddie Kane. Reporter: Hal Price. Bus Passengers: Ernie Adams, Kit Guard,

Billy Engle, Allen Fox, Marvin Loback, Dave Wengren, Bert Starkey, Rita Ross.

ACADEMY AWARDS:

Best Picture
Best Actor: Clark Gable
Best Actress: Claudette Colbert
Directing: Frank Capra
Writing (Adaptation): Robert Riskin

It Happened One Night was remade twice: as *Eve Knew Her Apples* (1945), and in a musical version as *You Can't Run Away From It* (1956).

STAGECOACH

United Artists, 1939. Directed by John Ford. Produced by Walter Wanger. Screenplay: Dudley Nichols. Music Director: Boris Morros. Horsemen: Yakima Canutt, John Eckert, Jack Mohr. Photography: Bert Glennon, Ray Binger. Editors: Dorothy Spencer, Walter Reynolds. Music Adaptation: Richard Hageman, Franke Harling, Louis Gruenberg. Themes: "Bury Me Not on the Lone Prairie" and "I Dream of Jeannie." Locations: Kernville, Dry Lake, Fremont Pass, Victorville, Calabasas, Chatsworth (California); Kayenta, Mesa, Monument Valley (Arizona). Produced with the cooperation of the Navajo-Apache Indian agencies and the U.S. Department of the Interior. Running time: 96 minutes.

The Ringo Kid	John Wayne
Dallas	Claire Trevor
Dr. Josiah Boone	Thomas Mitchell
Curley Wilcox	George Bancroft
Buck	Andy Devine
Hatfield	John Carradine
Lucy Mallory	Louise Platt
Mr. Peacock	Donald Meek
Gatewood	Berton Churchill
Lieutenant Blanchard	Tim Holt
Chris	Chris-Pin Martin
Yakeema	Elvira Rios

Sergeant Billy Pickett	Francis Ford
Mrs. Pickett	Marga Ann Daighton
Nancy Whitney	Florence Lake
Captain Sickle	Walter McGrail
Express Agent	Paul McVey
Mrs. Gatewood	Brenda Fowler
Cheyenne Scout	Chief Big Tree
Cavalry Scout	Yakima Canutt
Indian Leader	Chief White Horse
Lordsburg Sheriff	Duke Lee
Luke Plummer	Tom Tyler
Ike Plummer	Joe Rickson
Hank Plummer	Vester Pegg

Captain Whitney: Cornelius Keefe. Telegrapher: Harry Tenbrook. Doc's Landlady: Nora Cecil. Jerry (Bartender): Jack Pennick. Sheriff: Lou Mason. Lucy's Baby (2½ days old): Mary Kathleen Walker. Billy, Jr.: Kent Odell. Cavalry Sergeant: William Hopper. Saloonkeeper: Ed Brady. Ranchers: Buddy Roosevelt, Bill Cody. Ed (Editor): Robert Homans. Bartender: Si Jenks. Jim (Expressman): Jim Mason. Deputy: Franklyn Farnum. Ogler: Merrill McCormick. Lordsburg Barfly: Artie Ortega. Lordsburg Express Agent: Theodore Lorch.

ACADEMY AWARDS:

Best Supporting Actor: Thomas Mitchell
Score: Richard Hageman, Franke Harling, John
    Leipold, Leo Shuken

ACADEMY AWARD NOMINATIONS:

Directing: John Ford
Cinematography (black-and-white): Bert Glennon
Interior Decoration: Alexander Tuloboff
Film Editing: Otho Lovering, Dorothy Spencer

Stagecoach was remade under the same title in 1966.

THE WILD ONE

Columbia, 1954. Directed by Laslo Benedek. Produced by Stanley Kramer. Screenplay: John Paxton. Art Director: Walter

Holscher. Cinematographer: Hal Mohr. Editor: Al Clark. Running time: 79 minutes.

Johnny	Marlon Brando
Kathie	Mary Murphy
Harry Bleeker	Robert Keith
Chino	Lee Marvin
Sheriff Singer	Jay C. Flippen
Mildred	Peggy Maley
Charlie Thomas	Hugh Sanders
Frank Bleeker	Ray Teal
Bill Hannegan	John Brown
Art Kleiner	Will Wright
Ben	Robert Osterloh
Wilson	Robert Bice
Simmy	William Vedder
Britches	Yvonne Doughty
Gringo	Keith Clarke
Mouse	Gil Stratton, Jr.
Dinky	Darren Dublin
Red	Johnny Tarangelo
Dextro	Jerry Paris
Crazy	Gene Peterson
Pigeon	Alvy Moore
Go Go	Harry Landers
Boxer	Jim Connell
Stinger	Don Anderson
Betty	Angela Stevens
Simmonds	Bruno VeSoto
Sawyer	Pat O'Malley
Dorothy	Eve March

Cyclist: Wally Albright. Chino Boy No. 1: Timothy Carey. Official: John Doucette.

REAR WINDOW

Paramount, 1954. Directed by Alfred Hitchcock. Screenplay: John Michael Hayes. Cinematographer: Robert Burks. Special Effects: John P. Fulton. Sets: Hal Pereira, Joseph McMillan Johnson, Sam Comer, Ray Mayer. Music: Franz Waxman. Editor: George Tomasini. Costumes: Edith Head. Assistant Director: Herbert Coleman. Sound Engineering: Harry Lindgren, John Cope. Technicolor. Running time: 112 minutes.

L. B. Jeffries	James Stewart
Lisa Fremont	Grace Kelly
Thomas J. Doyle	Wendell Corey
Stella	Thelma Ritter
Lars Thorwald	Raymond Burr
Miss Lonely Hearts	Judith Evelyn
Song Writer	Ross Bagdasarian
Miss Torso	Georgine Darcy
Woman on Fire Escape	Sara Berner
Fire Escape Man	Frank Cady
Miss Hearing Aid	Jesslyn Fax
Honeymooner	Rand Harper
Mrs. Thorwald	Irene Winston
Newlywed	Harris Davenport
Party Girl	Marla English
Party Girl	Kathryn Grandstaff
Landlord	Alan Lee
Detective	Anthony Ward
Miss Torso's Friend	Benny Bartlett

Stunt Detective: Fred Graham. Young Man: Harry Landers. Man: Dick Simmons. Bird Woman: Iphigenie Castiglioni. Carl (waiter): Ralph Smiley. Stunt Detective: Edwin Parker. Woman with Poodle: Bess Flowers. Dancer: Jerry Antes. Choreographer: Barbara Bailey. A Butler: Alfred Hitchcock.

ACADEMY AWARD NOMINATIONS:

Directing: Alfred Hitchcock
Screenplay: John Michael Hayes
Cinematography: Robert Burks
Sound Recording: Loren S. Ryder

THE HUSTLER

   Twentieth Century-Fox, 1961. Directed and produced by Robert Rossen. Screenplay: Robert Rossen, Sidney Carroll. Cinematographer: Eugen Shuftan. Camera Operator: Saul Midwall. Assistant Camera Operator: William Cronjager. Associate Art Director: Albert Brenner. Set Decorator: Gene Callahan. Production Designer: Harry Horner. Editor: Dede Allen. Assistant Editor: Richard Stone. Music: Kenyon Hopkins. Louisville Music: Dan Terry. Sound: Jim Shields, Richard Vorisek. Sound Editor: Edward Beyer. Music Editor: Angelo Ross. Assistant Directors: Charles Maguire, Don Kranze. Unit Production Manager: John Graham. Script Supervisor: Marguerite James. Costume Designer: Ruth Morley. Makeup: Robert Jiras. Hairstyles: Donoene. Optical Effects: Film Opticals. Technical Adviser: Willie Mosconi. Still Photographer: Muky. Chief Electrician: David Golden. Chief Grip: Martin Nallan, Jr. CinemaScope. Running time: 133 minutes.

Eddie Felson	Paul Newman
Minnesota Fats	Jackie Gleason
Sarah Packard	Piper Laurie
Bert Gordon	George C. Scott
Charlie Burns	Myron McCormick
James Findlay	Murray Hamilton
Big John	Michael Constantine
Preacher	Stefan Gierasch
Bartender	Jack LaMotta
Turk	Clifford Pellow
Bennington's Cashier	Gordon B. Clarke
Scorekeeper	Alexander Rose
Waitress	Carolyn Coates
Young Hustler	Carl York
Bartender	Vincent Gardenia
Willie	Willie Mosconi

Girl with Fur Coat: Gloria Curtis. Old Man Attendant: Art Smith. Bartender: Tom Ahearne. Waiter: Charles Andre. Old Doctor: William P. Adams. Reservation Clerk: Charles McDaniel. Hotel Proprietor: Jack Healy. Racetrack Ticket Clerk: Don Koll. Players and Hangers-on: Don De Leo, Charles Mosconi, Brendan Fay, Donald Crabtree, Charles Dierkop.

ACADEMY AWARDS:

Cinematography (black-and-white): Eugen Shuftan
Art Direction/Set Direction: Harry Horner, Gene Callahan

ACADEMY AWARD NOMINATIONS:

Best Picture
Best Actor: Paul Newman
Best Actress: Piper Laurie
Directing: Robert Rossen
Writing (best screenplay based on material from
    another medium): Sidney Carroll, Robert Rossen

THE MAN WHO SHOT LIBERTY VALANCE

Paramount, 1962. Directed by John Ford. Produced by Willis
Goldbeck. Screenplay: James Warner Bellah, Willis Goldbeck.
Cinematographer: William H. Clothier. Art Directors: Eddie Imazu,
Hal Periera. Set Designers: Sam Comer, Darrell Silvera. Editor:
Otho Lovering. Music: Cyril Mockridge. "Young Mr. Lincoln"
theme: Alfred Newman (originally written for *Young Mr. Lincoln,*
1939, directed by John Ford). Sound: Philip Mitchell. Assistant
Director: Wingate Smith. Unit Manager: Don Robb. Costumes:
Edith Head. Makeup: Wally Westmore. Running time: 122 min-
utes.

Ranse Stoddard	James Stewart
Tom Doniphon	John Wayne
Hallie	Vera Miles
Liberty Valance	Lee Marvin
Dutton Peabody	Edmond O'Brien
Link Appleyard	Andy Devine
Doc Willoughby	Ken Murray
Pompey	Woody Strode
Peter Ericson	John Qualen
Nora Erickson	Jeanette Nolan
Reese	Lee Van Cleef
Floyd	Strother Martin
Cassius Starbuckle	John Carradine
Jason Tully	Willis Bouchey
Maxwell Scott	Carleton Young
Amos Carruthers	Denver Pyle
Handy Strong	Robert F. Simon
Ben Carruthers	O. Z. Whitehead
Mayor Winder	Paul Birch

Hasbrouck . . . . Joseph Hoover
Bartender . . . . Jack Pennick

Stagecoach Passenger: Anna Lee. Election Council President: Charles Seel. Drunk: Shug Fisher. With Stuart Holmes, Dorothy Phillips, Buddy Roosevelt, Gertrude Astor, Bill Henry, Monty Montana, John B. Whiteford, Helen Gibson, Earl Hodgins, Eva Novak, and Slim Talbot.

BLOW-UP

Premier Productions (subsidiary of Metro-Goldwyn-Mayer), 1966. Directed and story by Michelangelo Antonioni. Produced by Carlo Ponti. Executive Producer: Pierre Rouve. Screenplay: Michelangelo Antonioni, Tonino Guerra. English Dialogue Collaborator: Edward Bond. Cinematographer: Carlo Di Palma. Camera Operator: Ray Parslow. Art Director: Asheton Gorton. Editor: Frank Clarke. Sound Recorder: Robin Gregory. Sound Editor: Mike Le Mare. Dubbing Mixer: J. B. Smith. Assistant Director: Claude Watson. Production Manager: Donald Toms. Continuity: Betty Harley. Location Manager: Bruce Sharman. Dress Designer: Jocelyn Richards. Wardrobe Supervisor: Jackie Breed. Makeup: Paul Rabiger. Hairdresser: Stephanie Kaye. Dialogue Assistant: Piers Haggard. Photographic Murals: John Cowan. Music composed by Herbie Hancock; "Stroll On" written and performed by The Yardbirds. Running time: 110 minutes.

Thomas . . . . David Hemmings
Jane . . . . Vanessa Redgrave
Patricia . . . . Sarah Miles
Patricia's Husband . . . . John Castle
Teenagers . . . . Jane Birkin, Gillian Hills
Ron . . . . Peter Bowles
Verushka . . . . Herself
Mimes . . . . Julian Chagrin, Claude Chagrin
Thomas' Assistant . . . . Reg Wilkins
Thomas' Receptionist . . . . Tsai Chin
Antique Shop Owner . . . . Susan Broderick
Shopkeeper . . . . Harry Hutchinson

Fashion Editor . . . . Mary Khal
The Yardbirds . . . . Themselves

Jane's Lover: Ronan O'Casey. Models: Jill Kennington, Peggy Moffitt, Rosaleen Murray, Ann Norman, Melanie Hampshire.

2001: A SPACE ODYSSEY

Metro-Goldwyn-Mayer, 1968. Directed and produced by Stanley Kubrick. Screenplay: Stanley Kubrick, Arthur C. Clarke. Associate Producer: Victor Lyndon. Cinematographer: Geoffrey Unsworth. Additional Photography: John Alcott. Camera Operator: Kelvin Pike. Art Director: John Hoesli. Production Designers: Tony Masters, Harry Lange, Ernest Archer. Editor: Ray Lovejoy. Assistant Editor: David De Wilde. Sound Supervisor: A. W. Watkins. Sound Mixer: H. L. Bird. Dubbing Mixer: J. B. Smith. Sound Editor: Winston Ryder. First Assistant Director: Derek Cracknell. Wardrobe: Hardy Amies. Makeup: Stuart Freeborn. Special Photographic Effects Designer and Director: Stanley Kubrick. Supervisors of Special Photographic Effects: Wally Veevers, Douglas Trumbull, Con Pederson, Tom Howard. Special Photographic Effects Unit: Colin J. Cantwell, Bryan Loftus, Frederick Martin, Bruce Logan, David Osborne, John Jack Malick. Scientific Consultant: Frederick I. Ordway III. "Gayane Ballet Suite," by Aram Ilich Khachaturyan, performed by the Leningrad Philharmonic Orchestra, conducted by Gennadiy Rozhdestvenskiy. "Atmospheres," "Lux Aeterna," "Requiem," by György Ligeti; "Atmospheres" performed by the South West German Radio Orchestra, conducted by Ernest Bour; "Lux Aeterna" performed by Schola Cantorum of Stuttgart, conducted by Clytus Gottwald; "Requiem" performed by the Bavarian Radio Orchestra, conducted by Francis Travis. "The Blue Danube," by Johann Strauss, performed by the Berlin Philharmonic Orchestra, conducted by Herbert von Karajan. "Thus Spake Zarathustra," by Richard Strauss, performed by the Berlin Philharmonic Orchestra, conducted by Karl Böhm. Running time: 160 minutes on original Washington, D.C., and New York release; cut to 141 minutes for general distribution.

David Bowman . . . . Keir Dullea
Frank Poole . . . . Gary Lockwood
Dr. Heywood Floyd . . . . William Sylvester
Voice of Hal 9000 . . . . Douglas Rain
Moonwatcher . . . . Daniel Richter
Smyslov . . . . Leonard Rossiter
Elena . . . . Margaret Tyzack
Halvorsen . . . . Robert Beatty
Michaels . . . . Sean Sullivan
Mission Controller . . . . Frank Miller
Poole's Father . . . . Alan Gifford
Stewardesses . . . . Penny Brahms, Edwina Carroll

"Squirt," Dr. Floyd's daughter: Vivian Kubrick. With Bill Weston, Mike Lovell, Edward Bishop, Ann Gillis, Heather Downham, John Ashley, Jimmy Bell, David Charkham, Simon Davis, Jonathan Daw, Peter Delmar, Terry Duggan, David Fleetwood, Danny Grover, Brian Hawley, David Hines, Tony Jackson, John Jordan, Scott Mackee, Laurence Marchant, Darryl Pacs, Joe Refalo, Andy Wallace, Bob Wilyman, Richard Wood, and Glenn Beck.

ACADEMY AWARD:

Special Visual Effects: Stanley Kubrick

ACADEMY AWARD NOMINATIONS:

Directing: Stanley Kubrick
Writing: Stanley Kubrick, Arthur C. Clarke
Art Direction/Set Direction: Tony Masters,
  Harry Lange, Ernest Archer

Sources for Film Rentals

The following agencies specialize in the rental of 16-millimeter prints of feature films for film society screenings and classroom use, and will supply current catalogs on request.

Audio Brandon Films
34 MacQuestion Parkway South, Mount Vernon, New York 10550 OR 1619 North Cherokee, Los Angeles, California 90028

Budget Films
4590 Santa Monica Boulevard, Los Angeles, California 90029

Cine Craft Company
1720 N.W. Marshall, P.O. Box 4126, Portland, Oregon 97208

Clem Williams Films, Inc.
2240 Noblestown Road, Pittsburgh, Pennsylvania 15205 OR 298 Lawrence Avenue, South San Francisco, California 94080

Em Gee Film Library
16024 Ventura Boulevard, Encino, California 91436

Films Incorporated
440 Park Avenue South, New York, New York 10016

Ideal Pictures
915 N.W. 19th Avenue, Portland, Oregon 97209

Institutional Cinema
915 Broadway, New York, New York 10010

Janus Films
745 Fifth Avenue, New York, New York 10022

Kit Parker Films
Carmel Valley, California 93924

McGraw-Hill Films/Contemporary
1221 Avenue of the Americas, New York, New York 10020

Modern Sound Pictures
1402 Howard Street, Omaha, Nebraska 68102

Select Film Library
115 W. 31st Street, New York, New York 10001

Swank Motion Pictures, Inc.
393 Front Street, Hempstead, New York 11550 OR
6767 Forest Lawn Drive, Hollywood, California 90068

Twyman Films Inc.
175 Fulton Ave, 306, Hempstead, New York 11550

United Artists/16
729 Seventh Avenue, New York, New York 10019

Universal/16
445 Park Avenue, New York, New York 10022

Warner Brothers Film Library
4000 Warner Boulevard, Burbank, California 91522

Welling Motion Pictures
800 Meacham Avenue, Elmont, New York 11003

Westcoast Films
25 Lusk Street, San Francisco, California 94107

Wholesome Film Center
20 Melrose Street, Boston, Massachusetts 02116

COPYRIGHT ACKNOWLEDGMENTS